SPARK

SPARK

rachael craw

WALKER BOOKS
AND SUBSIDIARIES
LONDON • BOSTON • SYDNEY • AUCKLAND

First published in 2014
by Walker Books Australia Pty Ltd
Locked Bag 22, Newtown
NSW 2042 Australia
www.walkerbooks.com.au

National Library of Australia Cataloguing-in-Publication entry:
Craw, Rachael, author.
Spark / Rachael Craw.
ISBN: 978 1 922179 62 3 (paperback)
For young adults.
Subjects: Genetic engineering – Juvenile fiction.
Science fiction.
NZ823.4

Cover image (woman) © Jeff Thrower/Shutterstock.com;
Cover image, p.464 (tree silhouette) © ksyproduktor/Shutterstock.com;
Cover image (lightning bolt) © Hubis/Shutterstock.com.

Typeset in Adobe Caslon Pro
Printed and bound in Australia by Griffin Press

The paper this book is printed on is certified against the Forest Stewardship Council® Standards. Griffin Press holds FSC chain of custody certification SGS-COC-005088. FSC promotes environmentally responsible, socially beneficial and economically viable management of the world's forests

To Ma and Mum & Dad,
for love and DNA

PROLOGUE

The dream is always the same. I'm running through a forest at night, air like warm water, lapping my skin, warming my lungs. Above me a canopy of branches filters the moonlight in black and white – a strobe effect exaggerating the feel of speed, the pumping of my arms and legs. I am strong. Powerful. Fearless.

I move instinctively through the unpredictable space, sure-footed and skimming the undergrowth, the darkness an envelope around me. To the right, the crash of the river echoes off carved banks of rock. Though I can't see the gorge through the trees, I know the tight bends and sheer faces that churn the water before it opens out wide and deep from the last jagged mouth at the foot of the mountain.

Then the urgency that drives me becomes panic and I remember why I'm running. Someone is out here in the dark and they're in terrible danger. The realisation coincides with a faint whimper on the wind, the cry of a woman or child, the sound of fear. A painful surge of adrenaline cramps my muscles, electrons explode in my spine, crushed glass through my bones. I have to reach her before – before something else, someone else.

SYMPTOMS

I jolt up from the floor, panting, half-strangled by my two-sizes-too-short pyjamas and a sweat-soaked sheet.

How did I get on the floor?

Where is the carpet?

It takes me a couple of desperate seconds to untangle and figure out I'm not in my bedroom back home, but in Aunt Miriam's spare room in New Hampshire. Grief, forgotten in sleep, returns heavy in my chest. I sink onto the side of the bed, leaning elbows on knees, willing away the nightmare-panic, trying to hear past the *thlack-thlack* of my pulse. I should be immune to it by now, waking terrified in the dark; it's been going on for months, even before it all went down with Mom. I knit my trembling fingers together, try to ignore the uncomfortable zip-zap of pins and needles in my spine. The zip-zap and the bad dreams go together – started at the same time – but unlike the bad dreams, the zip-zap lasts all day. Sometimes it's a tepid fizz, other times, like angry bees.

But pins and needles belong in the feet, or a leg that's been sat on, an arm that's been slept on – not the spine. If it were only the growth spurt and loss of appetite, I wouldn't worry, but all of it together ...

I sit there, staring at the boxes stacked in the corner of the room, concentrating on slowing my breaths. It usually helps calm the palpitations. I should have unpacked the boxes by now – it's not healthy. Miriam's gone to a lot of trouble to make me welcome: new paint on the walls, new quilt on the bed, the antique wrought-iron headboard polished to gleaming. The thoughtfulness in the details makes me ache, from the fringed lamp and the stack of books she's placed by the bed, to the box of tissues on top. No doubt she has visions of me sobbing myself to sleep every night. The desk and chair under the window, the ornate mirror above the dresser – all new. I'm grateful, but my boxes still sit untouched, and Miriam pretends not to notice.

She won't push me.

But I've been here for weeks, haven't I? Maybe even a month? A lot can happen in a month: a bad cough, medical tests, a diagnosis. Back when it mattered, I knew the number of days until Mom's lab results; the hours between doctor's rounds; the minutes that passed before her meds kicked in; how long I could hold my breath, waiting for the crease of pain to lift from her clammy brow. Then I kept time like a stingy accountant. Now I let it pour through my fingers, let it escape from my life like heat from a house with the door left carelessly open. Maybe that's what makes the urgency in my dream so alarming. It's nothing like my real life.

But I should care and I should make an effort. It's not like I've been forced to live with a stranger in an uncaring home in a town I don't know. Didn't I long for my holidays here every year? Moan every time we had to go back to Pennsylvania? It's selfish to act like I own the patent on grieving. What about Miriam? She's lost her twin and been landed with me. That's a crap deal.

Slowly, the pounding in my chest begins to settle and I realise the sound of rushing water isn't just in my head or a hangover from my dream. The faucet is running in the bathroom.

The clock reads 3 am.

Miriam's back?

I pad to the door, off kilter and shaky in the knees. Light streams from the bathroom onto the landing between my aunt's room and mine. The door hangs partway open and the copper faucets roar over the claw-foot tub. Miriam leans on the vanity, her black pants pooled on the hardwood floor. She holds something in her hand and bends over a gash on her thigh. The shock is enough to bypass the inward twinge I usually feel looking at Mom's spitting image. I nudge the door, squinting against the light. "Miriam?"

She jerks up and drops the thing she's been holding, a syringe. It clatters at her feet. She presses her hand to her chest and closes her eyes. "Good grief, Evie."

"What happened?"

Panting, she picks up the syringe, tosses it in the bin and sits heavily on the side of the tub, her long dark hair obscuring her face. "You gave me a fright."

"What did you do?"

She tucks her hair behind her ears, an unconscious yet bruising Mom gesture, and reaches for my hand. I grimace at her torn nails, the skin she's taken off her knuckles, and sit beside her. She feels icy. Sweat beads her lip and brow, she looks paler than normal and the freckles on her nose stand out.

"Clumsy is all. Sorry I woke you." She turns through the billowing steam and cranks the faucet until the raucous flow ceases. Not meeting my gaze, she picks up the damp gauze from the sink and dabs at the cut. "I fell out of the car trying to carry too much equipment. Caught myself on the door before I hit the gravel. Typical. First time with my new Canon. If I've broken any lenses–"

"Shouldn't I take you to the hospital?"

She shakes her head. "It'll be okay."

"Then what's with the needle?"

"Adrenaline suppressant." She downsizes it with a shrug. "I have an adrenal disorder. Occasionally, when I get hurt, my heart races and I can't get it to calm down."

Adrenal disorder. "Since when?"

"Since ages, I guess. Look, it's not that big a deal. I can usually manage it."

I think of my catalogue of symptoms: my palpitations, my crazy dreams, the weight I've lost and the strange growth spurt that means everything I wear is too loose and not long enough. I almost blurt, *maybe that's what I have,* but bite my lip instead. She worries about me as it is. When Mom got sick, Miriam watched me like I teetered on a precipice, and at times I didn't like the unsettling length of her stare.

I want normal. I crave normal.

She gestures at the open medicine cabinet. "Pass the tape, kiddo."

I reach for it, the moth-like flap of my thoughts careening around my skull.

Miriam frowns over her wound and rips three neat strips of tape. "Just so you know, it's not always about intravenous drugs." She dries the skin either side of the wound. "Diet and exercise usually take care of it. Running helps."

I keep my eyes on Miriam's oozing leg. The cut looks deep and angry to me. "You're sure it won't need stitching?"

She shakes her head. "I'll bandage it after I've had a bath. Need to warm up first." She gives me an inscrutable look, her brown eyes skating over me. "How are the pins and needles?"

"Fine." I wish I never told her. "I'm fine."

"Liar." She strokes my cheek. "I'm sorry I left you by yourself. I should have turned them down."

"Don't be silly, I didn't mind." I am a liar. I hated her being away. But she'd passed up so much work to look after me while Mom was in that fancy-schmancy clinic we'd put all our hope in. I couldn't be the reason she missed out on a whole editorial for a glamour magazine in New York. What started as a one day job evolved into a full week. "It was an awesome gig. You couldn't say no. Did they take you out for dinner?"

"I left early."

"So you could drive five hours in the dark?"

"It was too soon to leave you alone for so long."

"Alone? With Mrs Gallagher on the phone and at the door every five minutes?"

"*Barb*," Miriam corrects me. I'm not allowed to call her Mrs Gallagher; she says it makes her feel old. "Barb's gold."

I grin. "Yeah, she is."

She is. Once she gave up trying to convince me to stay at their estate, she brought meals, did laundry, baked and called me twice a day for the whole week. Barb, the heiress! Truthfully, it was almost too much. Barb had loved Mom like a sister and was big on talking about feelings, unafraid to laugh and cry over remember-when-April this and remember-when-April that. She probably thought I was a damn robot, nodding, silent, half-suffocated by the lump in my throat.

"She's excited about Kitty." The one thing I am happy to talk about.

Kitty would fly in from Heathrow in the morning. *I* feel excited, an emotion I haven't felt in months. In fact, I can't remember the last time I actually looked forward to anything. When I moved up here, the prospect of being Nigel no-friends in New Hampshire didn't worry me. Besides, grief is a social handicap. But when I heard Kitty was coming home early, for the last weeks of summer, I couldn't deny the sense of relief. Someone who knows me and knows my stuff. No awkward questions to field. No work required.

Miriam grins knowingly. "What about Jamie?"

I give her a disdainful look. "He's in Berlin."

"That's a shame."

I stand up. "You need a hand getting in the bath?"

With a chuckle, she rises next to me then does a double take. "How much have you grown?"

I shrug, but she counts it out on her fingers. "End of April, May, June, July." The length of time from diagnosis to funeral. "Must be at least three inches in three months."

"I'm not in charge of the DNA." I fold my arms around my hollow waist.

Nodding at the cotton flapping above my ankle she says, "We need to take you shopping, kid."

I produce a noncommittal grunt.

She looks at me for a moment and I look at the wall. I swallow, about to turn and go, when she touches my arm. "I'm glad you're here," she says. I bite the inside of my cheek and nod. She pulls me against her and locks her arms around my back. I let her hold me, squeezing my eyes tight shut. "I'm so sorry this has happened to you, Evie," she murmurs.

Then something flashes behind my eyes, a waking vision felt through someone else's skin, a memory that isn't my own. A sunlit room, a warm embrace. The same words but my mother's voice, "I'm so sorry this has happened to you." The brief moment disorientates me, vivid to the point of tangible and then gone. I'm back in the bathroom, in Miriam's arms.

Now I'm hallucinating?

I can't hold back my tears. I drop my face to her shoulder and sob.

"It's okay." She strokes my back. "You're okay. Everything will be okay."

It isn't. I'm not. Nothing will be.

SCARS

"Buffy!" I miss her collar, nearly ramming my head into the refrigerator. Black satanic fluff blurs between my bare feet, skidding before making the sharp turn to the laundry room. "Feathers." I groan, dabbing a single dun-coloured plume with the tip of my finger. "She's got a bird."

"A mouse and I would've thanked her." Miriam puts her spatula down, a mound of yellow eggs left to sizzle on the grill. "Now, I have to go. Breakfast is ready. Please, for the love of sanity, eat."

I look for the time on the microwave. "What about your leg?"

"I'm just going over proofs with clients. I'll be sitting all morning." She grabs her purse from the table and shrugs her coat on. She looks too good for someone on less than four hours sleep. Hair. Face. High heels? That seems reckless after the night before.

"And don't forget I'm shooting the Governor's Ball

tonight." She pats her pockets. "I wish you'd come. I could use help lugging equipment. Besides, it would be good for you to get out, meet some people. The Gallaghers will be there."

I give her my you-must-be-out-of-your-mind look.

She gives me her what-am-I-going-to-do-with-you look.

I turn to the laundry.

"You can't reason with a cat in that state," she says. "She may be one hundred and six but the little vampire slayer's still got her edge."

A reasonable person would leave it, but I go after the cat where she hides between the washer and dryer. I get down on my knees, peering through the fluff and darkness. Green eyes shine back at me. I imagine the frenetic heartbeat of the bird. "Buffy, come on, be good."

A guttural growl rumbles back at me.

"Haven't changed, have you?" Miriam sighs, jingling her keys. "You used to cry watching *Animal Planet*."

"Not helping." I love this stupid cat, and not just because it's Mom's, but the poor bird. I reach for the scruff of Buffy's neck. "Ouch!" I yank my hand back; a thin red trench gleams on my knuckle. Frustration sits in my chest like a hot brick. I stand up, sucking on the wound, wincing at the sting, and glare at my aunt. "Could you at least help me shift the washer? There's still time."

"Let it go, kiddo. It's too late. Cats eat birds. It's nature." She opens the back door and warm air swims in around my legs. "See you at one. We'll go find you some clothes that fit. Maybe a dress."

She slips out the door and I stand there like an idiot with my stinging hand and my stinging eyes, listening to her heels clip-clop down the steep back steps. "You are completely heartless!" But I can't make out her reply. Soon comes the *thunk* of the car door and the consumptive hacking of the Volkswagen.

A feeble tweet echoes up from the floor, then Buffy's feral hiss. "Nature sucks," I mutter, hating the constriction in my throat and the twist of deeper feelings I can't name. Suddenly furious, I grab the washing machine with a surge of energy and shove. There's a loud crack against the wall then a bone-rattling thump on the floorboards. The light bulb above me makes a tinkling noise – a small explosion. Tiny glass shards fall about my head and shoulders, and Buffy bolts through the flap to the backyard, the bird still in her mouth. My pulse skips. My spine zip-zaps. Everything appears painfully bright. I squint against the sharpness of the light, shaking glass out of my hair. "Oh, crap."

The hole in the wall, about a hand's breadth in diameter, gapes easily a foot higher than the washer stands. Dry mouthed, I stare at the chipped paint where the corner of the washer has broken the plasterboard. How the hell did I lift it like it was nothing more than a cardboard box? And what about the light bulb? I must have damaged wiring in the wall, creating some kind of power surge, but I can't spot any wires. I grab the jumbo tub of laundry detergent and position it to conceal the hole, wondering how I'll explain it to Miriam.

Dizzy and rubbing my eyes, I step back into the kitchen. Everything pulses in high definition: the panelled ceiling, the jars of last season's preserves, the cast-iron oven where it sits in the cavity of the old chimney, the wooden countertops, everything.

Am I having a stroke?

I go to the cupboard by the sink. The pewter knob snaps off in my trembling hand. I manage to work the cupboard open with my fingertips. I take a glass and turn the faucet. The glass cracks, collapsing inwards, grazing my thumb, clattering in the drain. I frown at the broken pieces, the cupboard, the laundry door. "What is this?"

I drink straight from the faucet and splash my face, trying to pull myself together. In the windowpane above the sink, I look paler than usual; the freckles on my nose stand out. My dark hair hangs lank past my shoulders. It desperately needs washing. I look gaunt and tired. All this is familiar, but my eyes, my messy eyes – blue, green, flecked with gold and black – aren't the eyes that look back at me. I lean closer, a prickling feeling at the nape of my neck.

They're even darker than Miriam's, as though the pupils have expanded, eclipsing the irises. Solid pools of black.

I close my eyes and rub my face. *Seizure, epilepsy, tumour, brain cancer?* The options grow wider and worse.

The phone rings and I shake myself. I blink once, twice, and the strange high definition effect recedes. I check my reflection in the window; my messy eyes are back. "You are losing your mind, Everton. Rein it in."

I exhale and go to find the phone. It sits in the hall on a cramped table beneath Nan's statue of the Virgin, one of the nostalgic fingerprints Miriam left untouched when she reclaimed her childhood home. I lift the handset. "Everton Images. Evangeline speaking."

"It's me. I'm home. Flight was a bloody nightmare. Six crying babies, I mean to say. Six!"

I lean my forehead on the bookcase and grin, gently wiping dust from the Virgin's robe with my finger. "Sounds nasty."

"It was." Kitty's accent, crisp and round from the first ten years of her life in England. "Honestly, I'm dead."

I chuckle.

She makes a strangled sound. "Evs. Hell. I'm sorry."

"Don't be." I turn and sit at the bottom of the stairs, let Kitty apologise a couple more times – get it out of her system – and throw myself in the first gap to ask about London. She's been doing time with her famously abrasive

Uncle Jeremy, getting a taste for the family textiles business, which Jeremy heads in the UK and Leonard heads in the States. It's expected of the Gallagher children, like some high-powered work experience thing – supposed to help them decide on their focus for senior year and their majors for college, with the prospect of finding their niche in the business after graduation. I struggle to imagine such a well-planned life.

"Uncle Jeremy's such a bloody schemer. He's got me pegged for legal, but Dad's always fancied me in trade."

"I love how you say that like I have a clue what it means."

She grumbles. "It means they'll both be pissed off because I don't want either."

My eyebrows spring up. "Have you told them that?"

"Don't be ridiculous. I actually want to enjoy my summer."

I snort and she launches into a wandering rant based on the trials of being a Gallagher heiress. I usually hear a version of it at least once a summer, or whatever holiday it is that we end up sharing. Kitty and I have been holiday buddies since she was eleven and I was ten. When they moved back to the States, Barb had been determined to throw us together. While Kitty's vacation spots ranged through European capitals, mine was always New Hampshire, with the occasional summer camp at this lake or that. I can't even imagine a summer that doesn't involve Nan and Pop's old house, the forest around it, the familiar mountains and the wild Border River that circles the small town of Burton. I can't imagine a summer that doesn't involve the Gallaghers, though I could happily erase one of them.

"Jamie's taking the heat off me, thankfully," Kitty says, as though she's sensed my thoughts have strayed to her brother. "He's told them outright he doesn't want a bar of textiles. Dad's on the warpath."

"Really?" I wish I wasn't interested.

"Says he wants to build boats and that doesn't require an MBA."

"Boats?"

"Yachts, specifically."

"Then what's he been doing in Berlin for the last year?" I can't keep up with the twins' complicated education. Barb, a New England WASP, insisted her children have some time at her alma mater here in New Hampshire – Gainsborough Collegiate, where she and Mom had become the best of friends – but Leonard's ties were in the UK, Eton, Oxford, land and titles. Apparently, Jamie's year boarding with his uncle hadn't gone well.

"Who knows? Uncle Jeremy sorted it out. Some uber-international school. Probably a bribe. Here are some mountains and lakes, lad. Ski. Sail. Get it out of your system, then when you're all safely graduated come and be a good boy at Oxford."

"You think he'll cave?"

Kitty sighs. "Don't know what his problem is. I guess he must have had a really miserable time at Eton for them to pull him out and pack him off to Germany. Bloody waste of time. He was perfectly happy at Gainsborough with me."

I can't imagine Jamie struggling anywhere. He's naturally popular, looking like he does, with his family as it is. Athletic, easy going, funny – if you liked bastards. Aces any subject he looks at. On what basis would Jamie Gallagher, heir to a multi-billion dollar textiles empire, ever find himself miserable?

"Boats, then," I say. "Guess it could be worse."

Kitty snorts. "Listen to you, all magnanimous and whatnot."

"Don't start."

"I thought you'd be spitting."

"What do I care if Jamie wants to build boats?"

"I meant about him coming home."

My stomach flips and I press a hand to my eyes. "Ah, crap."

"He gets in this afternoon. In time for the Governor's Ball thing. Didn't Barb say about Jamie?"

It always jars me to hear Kitty call her mother by her first name but it is Barb's rule. It jars me more to imagine facing Jamie.

She chuckles. "Well, I suppose she wouldn't want to put you off."

I groan. The phone feels too hot against my ear and I swap sides.

"You will come to the ball though, won't you?"

"No."

"Not even to see me?"

"No."

"You could meet my friends."

"Right," I choke. "Hey everybody, this is Evie. She has no money and has never been anywhere, but please be nice to her, her father doesn't know she exists and her mom's just died." Kitty always loved the lurid mythology of my conception: April on a college bender waking up with a foreign exchange student in her dorm-room bed. He shipped out after the one-night stand. She didn't even have a name to follow up when I appeared on the radar a few weeks later. All a bit hard to imagine, growing up with my pathologically sensible mother.

"Everybody loves a poor orphan."

"No."

She heaves a colossal sigh. "You suck."

"'Fraid so."

Eventually she gives up bullying me and starts in on school and subject options. I pretend to listen but my brain churns: *Jamie, Jamie, Jamie.* I finger the tiny scar in my hairline, the mark of our first encounter when he "slipped" and pushed me in the river. Head versus rock and the rock won – a blinding *thwack* then a watery blackout. He dragged me out – not that I remembered – but the sharp pain, coming round on the bank, the spitting up water, the abrupt end to our families' picnic and the stitches afterwards were clear as day. It's one of the only times I ever saw those grey eyes express fear, as he peered down at me, his dark gold hair dripping water into my eyes.

I let Kitty talk on, shaking my head. Was it really eight years ago? I had such sky-high expectations that summer with the Gallaghers moving from London; the prospect of ready-made holiday friends – glamorous, exotic friends, with accents and everything, whose family home may as well have been Disneyland. But I can't smile at the memory, not when there's a present-day threat. Jamie. Home. This afternoon. My chest feels all fluttery. I want to get back into bed and put my head under a pillow.

Kitty says something derogatory about Burton Central High School and I try to tune in.

"You should seriously consider it," she says. "You're the year-ahead-brainiac, you could easily get a scholarship."

"Scholarship? BC's a high school, Kit."

"No, you numpty, Gainsborough Collegiate."

Illustrious in name and notorious in price. Nan and Pop worked themselves to the bone to put Mom and

Miriam through the school, but it's well out of my price range. "As if. And I'm no brainiac. Being forced up a grade at seven was an optimistic failure by the state."

"But it's utterly ridiculous for us to be living in the same town, for once in our lives, and not be going to school together."

"If you're that worried about it, ditch Gainsborough and slum it with me."

She gags.

"Snob." I chuckle. "Our whole relationship is based on seeing each other during school holidays. It would all fall apart if we were in each other's pockets every day. We'd be sick to death of each other."

"I suppose that's true. We've only been on the phone half an hour and I'm already fed up."

KITTY

There are more hunting and fishing shops than fashion boutiques in Burton, but I keep my whining to a minimum and let Miriam lead me through the handful of clothing stores that dot Main Street. I'm not against shopping. I love to shop. I undoubtedly need new clothes. It just makes me uncomfortable to see Miriam hand over her credit card. When we come to the counter at a denim outlet, I cringe at the cash register's tally.

"Don't get all twitchy." She has her don't-mess-with-me lips on. "When your house sells in Penn you can do what you like, but for now I get to spoil you."

The saleslady laughs. "Most girls are thrilled to see their mom pull out the credit card."

My "I'm not–" collides with Miriam's and I choke on the rest.

We get out onto the street and neither of us says anything, though I can see Miriam glancing at me. I finally stop and face her. "Hey, listen. It's no big deal. Bound to happen, right?"

Miriam nods, scanning my face. "You look pale."

I feel faint and my pins and needles are going nuts. The day has become hot and I'm suddenly parched. Miriam takes the bags from my hands. "Did you eat this morning?"

I think of the eggs I left congealing on the skillet. "Um ..."

"Lunch?"

"Does the last of the chocolate milk count?"

She shakes her head and nudges me towards a cafe with empty tables out front; the lunch crowds have long gone. She pulls out a sticky chair and I sit without protest. "Pins and needles?"

I shrug. No point lying, she can tell I'm uncomfortable.

"Have you been sleeping?"

I shrug again. I haven't had a full night's sleep since Mom got sick. If I manage to slip consciousness, I dream and wake in sweating panic. "I'm thirsty."

"Wait here." She pats my head.

I close my eyes and take deep breaths, trying to ease the tension in my chest.

"Evie!"

My eyes pop open and there she is, Kitty Gallagher, grinning on the sidewalk with a bag in each hand.

"Hey!" I get to my feet, head spinning with the upwards

rush. She practically throws herself on me and my pins and needles amplify like I'm plugged in. Stars burst before my eyes and a roaring fills my ears.

"You're so tall!" She laughs and hugs me tight, her chin barely reaching my shoulder. "Why are you so tall?"

"I – I really need to sit."

"Sorry." She steps back, teary eyed. "It's so good to see you. Blimey, you do look a bit peaky."

I sit heavily and hold my head, dizzy and weirded out. "Just a little faint. Miriam's gone to get me something to eat."

Kitty takes in the array of shiny boutique bags. "You're coming tonight?"

"No," I say. "Replacing essentials. Everything's a bit short these days. It's great to see you, Kit." She's cropped her honey-blonde bob closer to her chin. Her dove-grey eyes sparkle and she looks pretty damn good for someone after a long-haul flight.

She takes the seat opposite and lays her hand on my wrist, sending a strange electric current shooting up my arm to meet the zip-zapping in my spine.

"Are you feeling sick?" Kitty looks genuinely worried.

But I can't concentrate to answer, too baffled by my body's reaction to her touch. At that moment Miriam appears. She carries a tray with a muffin, a soda and a chocolate bar. "Kitty! You're here!"

Kitty lets me go. My arm instantly stops tingling and the roaring in my ears dims, but the pressure in my chest increases. *It must mean something.* Kitty rises briefly to kiss Miriam's cheek. Miriam places the tray in front of me. "Eat." She takes a seat, darting furtive glances up and down the street. "Are you by yourself, Kit?"

I rip the wrapper off the chocolate bar and take a big bite. Sugar. Sugar will settle my system. Kitty grins and covers my hand again, producing the same alarming surge in electricity. The chocolate lodges in my throat and I cough to clear the obstruction, pounding my chest with my fist. "Don't worry," she laughs. "Jamie's not behind me. Barb and Dad are on their way to meet him at the airport."

Miriam gives me a guilty smile and sits back. She must have known he was coming home. I take a swig of soda. Content to sit and eat and let them do the talking, I concentrate on the competing sensations in my body. I don't feel so dizzy thanks to the sugar hit. My thirst has backed off with the soda. My pins and needles seem to respond to Kitty like she's a magnet. Yet, despite this, being with her comforts me. Maybe it's the whole familiarity thing, a friend on hand after weeks of moping around Miriam's place. I can't stop looking at Kitty, like I'm relieved somehow to see her happy and well. But why relieved? And why the tight feeling in my chest? Anxiety tight? How can I feel relieved and anxious at the same time? *That's easy. You're losing it.*

"You know you're going to have to see him sometime." Kitty's back on her brother. "If you come tonight it would be over and done with. Then we could get on with our last few weeks before school without things being all awkward. It's been three years. Can't you be grown-ups?"

"I'm not coming to the ball to prove something to your brother."

"Oh? But you are coming?" She sits up straight, eyebrows high. Seeing her so hopeful fills me with a strange unwillingness to disappoint her. I shake my head. Her shoulders slump and I feel bad.

The waitress comes out with the coffee pot and places cups on the table.

"I'm good with soda," I say.

"I'll have hers," Kitty says.

As the waitress fills two cups, an eerie feeling comes over me. A tingling awareness of the moment that magnifies small details: the silver rim of a passing bicycle winking in the sunlight, the shimmer of heat rising from the asphalt, the breeze lifting a child's bangs as she whines at her mother on the sidewalk. To my right a man counts change into his palm, the coins chinking.

My spine tightens.

The circumference of awareness narrows, the micro-details of the periphery diminish. The glint of light on Kitty's coffee becomes the riveting focal point. Steam pearls upwards, dewing the inside rim. The porous ceramic bears signs of wear and a hairline fracture on the handle catches my eye. Kitty says something and goes to pick up her coffee by the bowl. It's too hot. She takes the handle instead. Electricity crackles in my spine. I squint at the sharpening light and time stretches. Kitty raises her cup in slow motion. I observe the gradual trajectory of her hand, hear a small pop like the sound of chalk snapping and the handle of her cup breaks away. The bowl of hot coffee falls in a long elastic second.

The instinct to protect Kitty seems as natural as the solution. I simply reach out to catch the falling bowl. I don't even feel the burn on my wrist where it splashes, scalding my skin.

Time snaps back to its regular speed, my ears clear and I stare at the cup in my hand. Miriam's on her feet.

"Bloody hell." Kitty shoves her chair back. She drops the handle on the table and takes the still full cup from my hand. "How did you do that?" She rubs at a few stray drops on her jeans. "Look at your wrist." A blister rises in a red weal.

"No idea." I feel awake, like I've just come out of a long foggy dream and the world is back in technicolour. "Ha!"

Miriam frowns. "You need something for your hand." She turns away and goes back into the cafe.

I look at Kitty, who still gapes at me. I feel more alive

than I have in weeks and filled with certainty. My social phobia is irrelevant. Jamie is irrelevant.

Being with Kitty is important. Urgent. Inexplicably urgent. If she's going to this thing tonight, then so am I.

"All right," I say, as if she's asked me again. "I'll come."

PANIC

"You're going to look killer, Evs." Kitty leans to peer at me through the window of her shiny European car. "Everything, it all works."

"For the sake of Miriam's credit card, I hope so."

Kitty argued for a ball makeover, which apparently meant a total overhaul. Face, hair, dress, shoes, accessories. Miriam had been unsure about leaving me to shop, worried I wasn't well enough, but even with the electricity in my spine and the roar in my ears, being with Kitty made me feel better than I had in ages. I argued. Miriam conceded. Kitty had to promise to bring me home if I felt faint, and I had promised to use Miriam's credit card. Sort of a compromise, I guess.

"All for a good cause," Kitty says. "It's always the best revenge to turn up looking gorgeous when there's an ex around."

"Jamie's not my ex," I mutter, but I still feel buoyed

enough to laugh it off. In fact, I had followed Kitty around in a daze all afternoon from salon to boutique to shoe store, compliant, content, bolstered to the point where the prospect of meeting her snooty schoolfriends no longer seems to faze me. Seeing Jamie won't be such a big deal. He's eighteen, I'm seventeen. Like Kitty says, we can be grown-ups. I even picture us laughing off old misunderstandings.

The strange inner workings of my body reassure me. Zip-zap, Kitty's very important to me. Zip-zap, she's probably the best friend I've ever had. Zip-zap, it isn't such a hardship making her happy. Besides, zip-zap, saying yes to Kitty makes me feel good.

"Still," she says, "won't hurt him to feel a little regret."

I roll my eyes.

She waves. "See you tonight."

"Okay." The vague anxious feeling tugs at me. "Thanks again." I hold my breath as her car pulls away. It doesn't feel right. The not-right feeling peaks when she reaches the corner. I almost cry out. Then the car turns out of sight and the feeling evaporates.

POOF!

The tightness in my chest disappears. Even the zip-zap of pins and needles dies down to a barely perceptible hum. The certainty I felt that everything Kitty said was right evaporates.

Oh crap.

I stand beneath the thick leafy canopy of Columbia Avenue, paralysed by dawning horror, my rational self clawing its way painfully to the surface. Whatever spell I've been under has lost its hold and I look back on the afternoon like a hung-over partygoer whose flashes of memory fill them with cringing regret. What the hell have I done, saying yes to this ball? Why did I let Kitty talk me into it? Now I've bought all this ridiculous stuff with Miriam's money! Had I really believed I could get all dressed up and these rich kids wouldn't see right through me? What on earth did I expect to talk about all night? How will I dodge questions about my family, my non-existent dad, my dead mom? And Jamie! Jamie, my living nightmare, will be there, smirking, indifferent and gorgeous. I'll be the idiot trying to act like I don't remember that he humiliated me in front of his asshole friends, breaking my fourteen-year-old heart.

The memory of crowing boys bursting into the secluded hollow beneath the willow tree, while Jamie and I were mid-kiss, makes my ears burn whenever I'm dumb enough to let it resurface. I remember Jamie's face paling as his friends crowded in. While most of the boys cheered and money changed hands, one had said, "I knew we should have waited. I could have made another forty bucks."

The aftermath was a blur. I ran. Jamie yelled at his

friends and called after me. The boys' laughter faded as I tore out of the reserve, blind with shame and fury.

The trouble is, three years ago, before the moment when everything was ruined, it was the best summer of my life. Jamie had shot up – a staggering six-foot-two. His wiry frame had filled out and his square shoulders broadened. Basically, he got hot. For my part, I finally got boobs; changes to catch both our attentions.

Over the months of that holiday, we circled each other with uneasy awareness and the bickering stopped. I was painfully self-conscious and he was less smug than usual. For me it was a big-time crush.

It all came down to that day by the river. We'd wandered away, found the secluded hollow, he'd even called me Evie instead of Everton. Then heart-racing silence, spectacular prolonged eye contact and the softest, sweetest kiss of my life. The price of humiliation.

Thankfully, the summers that followed were Jamie-free. He left his sister and his friends at Gainsborough Collegiate and returned to London. I'm not vain enough to believe it has anything to do with me. I understand there are family expectations surrounding the twins' education. Though I noticed none of his holidays home coincided with my New Hampshire visits. Suited me. Once or twice I might have allowed myself to imagine a reconciliation, but the thought of having to actually face him tonight is a whole other matter.

* * *

"Grab the Nikon," Miriam calls. "Not the grey case, that's the Sony. The Nikon has the blue handle."

The front door clatters open and I watch her from the hall as she goes down the path, two tripods and a crate balanced before her, trying to keep marks off her black silk dress.

Move, you coward. Panicked, I shoulder my way back into the studio, off balance in my high heels. I place the lens case on the counter, carefully, then turn to the darkroom and recite the access code as I tap the keypad. The light comes on automatically when I slide the door back. I push through the old blackout curtain, hoping I won't get dust on my dress. Since Miriam has gone digital, the darkroom is simply a glorified storeroom. I scan the shelves, tempted to lock myself in and hide.

I should have blurted my change of mind when I had the chance, railed about Kitty's voodoo manipulation. Miriam even handed me the very get-out-of-jail-free card I needed, "You don't have to come tonight, not for my sake." But she spends so much time worrying and looking after me, sacrificing work and freedom to make room for me in her life, give me a home, even her credit card, for crying out loud! Can't I slap on a smile and make an effort for a change? So, here I am in high heels that make me feel like Gigantor, my strapless gown in charcoal silk and teardrop earrings, ready for a long night of dying on the inside.

I spot the grey Nikon case, the one she doesn't want, but where is the case with the blue handle? It isn't lying out in the open. I turn to the utility cupboard. When I was a kid, going anywhere near it had been a big no-no because of the developing chemicals she stored in it. It has a keypad too, but I don't know the code. I try the handle. Surprisingly, it gives. I open it with an uncomfortable sense of breaking taboo. The chemicals are gone. There are shelves of filed negatives, clients' names on the tabs. There's the case with the blue handle. I lift it down as Miriam comes in behind me.

"What do you think you're doing?" She pushes past me and the scene changes. It flashes with bright colour that stings my eyes and stops my heart. Again, I see a memory that isn't my own: a metal rail under my hand, a row of mirrors disorientating me with the reflection of my aunt moving in a circular blur across a blue floor.

Then, snap!

The vision disappears, plunging me back into the dimly lit room. Miriam doesn't notice my "episode". She shuts the cupboard door, a sharp clap of sound in the small room, and resets the lock on the keypad.

"I was looking for the–"

"There's a lot of expensive equipment in there and you can't go poking around."

I pass her the case. "I wasn't."

She sighs and shakes her head. "Sorry. I'm just – we should go. They want photos of the guests arriving."

ANTICIPATION

It's my third trip to the car. We parked around the back by the service entrance to unload, and my new shoes are killing me already. Carrying Miriam's last tripod and extension cord, I navigate the high-traffic corridors, dodging caterers and waiters who file back and forth with trays of canapés and bowls of flowers.

Governor Dean's mansion is big on marble: the steps out front, the colossal columns by the front doors, the gleaming floor in the grand foyer. From what I glimpse of the house and grounds, the Deans' fancy statuary, fountains and gilt frames, everything about the place seems self-conscious, as though it has to shout and bully to impress. I wonder how they came by their cash.

Afraid to slip, I take it slow across the foyer. Miriam's up on the second-floor landing, where there's room to set up for a wide shot of the scene below. At the bottom of the staircase two young men stand talking. They aren't staff. They wear tuxedos and look about my age. The one with his back to me leans on the banister with proprietary ease. He gesticulates and shakes his head, laughing like the other guy has said something stupid. His friend, if he is his friend, is a square-shouldered guy about my height with dark precision-combed hair. Not bad looking, in an understated way. Something about the freckles on his nose and Playstation tan draws my sympathy. As I come near I can tell he's annoyed by the guy leaning on the banister but controlling his expression. He meets my gaze with startling hazel eyes, gives me a polite nod then notices what I'm carrying. "Here," he says. "Can I give you a hand?"

"I'm fine," I begin, but he's already reaching for the tripod and it seems rude to pull away. I let him take it. "Oh, all right. Thanks."

The banister guy straightens up and regards me boldly. "You're the photographer?" He's a similar height to the helpful guy but narrower through the shoulders. Light brown hair. Slightly receding chin. An air of self-assurance.

"My aunt is." I nod up the stairs. "I'm helping her."

He follows my gaze and his eyebrows rise. "Excellent."

I'm not sure what's "excellent". I glance at the guy holding my aunt's tripod. He looks resigned to waiting.

"You're not at Gainsborough?" The confident young man cocks his head like he's trying to pick me from a memory.

Here we go. I shake my head.

"Didn't think so," he says, all blue eyes and white teeth. "I would definitely remember you."

"I'm from out of town." Why did I say it? It only invites more questions. "Um, I better–"

"I'm Richard Dean." He stretches out his hand, expecting to be known. I catch a whiff of stale breath.

"Oh, right." Dean. That fits. I heft the extension cord under my left arm and take his hand. The bees in my spine give an angry buzz. "Nice place."

He chuckles, narrowing his eyes, appraising me, head to toe and back again. "Well, thanks. I'd be very glad to show you around the place if you're not busy later. There are some nice quiet spots if you know where to look. What's your name?"

"Richard?" A gorgeous, caramel-skinned girl with sleek dark hair crosses the foyer. She eyes me with outright suspicion, and Richard makes a show of rolling his eyes like he's been caught out.

"I better keep moving." I turn up the stairs. The guy with Miriam's tripod steps beside me.

"Hey, nice move, buddy," Richard calls after him. "But don't be too long; the boss might have some files for you to organise."

The helpful guy's jaw tightens but he doesn't react.

I glance over my shoulder.

"I'm kidding." Richard smirks and lifts his palms. "He's so serious."

I turn back and nearly trip on my dress.

"Here," the helpful guy says, slipping the cable from my arm, the brush of his hand coinciding with a brief muting of the bees.

"Sorry." I hitch my dress a few inches to allow myself a proper stride.

"No problem." He looks like he's about to say something then presses his lips together.

Make an effort.

"So, you know Richard?"

"I work for his dad." He shrugs. "We're not friends."

"You have to see him much?"

He exhales wearily. "Every day."

The staircase narrows and curves near the top. I can't see Miriam though her case lies open on an ornate table. "Bummer, I mean, if you don't get on and you have to see him all the time."

"Suppose it could be worse." He props the tripod against the table and slips the cable underneath, straightening up with a rueful expression. "Could have no job. No Gainsborough scholarship and be stuck at BCH."

I bite my lips to keep from smiling. "I'll be at BC this year."

He cringes. "I hear they have a great, um, arts program."

We both chuckle.

"Sorry," he says. "I'm an ass."

He has nice eyes.

I look away.

Down at the bottom of the stairs, Richard watches us. He has his hand on the girl's waist but she looks sullen and annoyed. He gives me a knowing smile and winks even though she stands right there beside him. I can't help turning in disbelief to the helpful guy. Had he seen that?

"Yeah." He nods. "That's Richard."

"He's kind of a dick."

"Yep."

The view from the second-floor landing is dominated by the chandelier, beyond it the wide front doors stand open where the governor's wife greets her guests. Either side, triple-height windows look out on the drive, where a queue of limousines slowly deposits guests onto the marble steps. My stomach knots. The Gallaghers might be out there in one of those shiny black cars.

"Wish I could've stayed home." He pinches the bridge of his nose, squeezing his eyes shut.

I heave a sigh. "Same."

He opens his eyes and looks at me.

I shrug.

He grins. "Suppose I better go and see if the governor needs me."

"Hey, thanks for your help."

"Aiden." He reaches out, a self-conscious gesture.

"Evie." I take his hand. Again, the odd muting of the zip-zap in my spine. I need this guy to follow me around all night to keep the pins and needles away.

He releases my hand. The bees crackle back to life. "Evie, I wouldn't recommend a tour with Richard."

"Way ahead of you."

He smiles and nods before taking quick steps down the stairs.

Behind me the French doors open and Miriam steps in from the outside balcony, looking frazzled, camera around her neck. Music floats up from the band rotunda. She disconnects her lens with a practised flick of her wrist and deposits it in the case. "Where's my wide angle?" She finds the lens and attaches it. "How are you feeling? Pins and needles? How's your wrist?"

"I'm fine."

"Promise you'll tell me if you're not feeling right."

"Sure."

She glares. "I'm serious."

"I'll tell you."

"Make sure you eat."

I nod.

"And no alcohol."

I roll my eyes.

"Hold this." She gives me the camera and lifts the tripod, releasing the legs and clicking the locks. She then scans the foyer and moves to the right, waiting for the perfect spot to reveal itself. "Here." She plants the tripod and holds her hand out for the camera. "You want to take some atmosphere shots for me?" She nods at the case where her old Pentax sits. "Good practise and you won't have to talk to anyone."

I must have been about eight when Miriam bought me my first camera – a sweet instamatic point and shoot. Mom had disapproved, the extravagance, the responsibility. She relaxed when I was confirmed as having "a natural eye" and by seventeen I was on my third SLR, heir to Miriam's cast-offs. Tonight, a camera could give me something to hide behind. I could always fake a dead battery if I needed a quick getaway. "Yeah, okay."

"Great. Table settings, candles, flowers, whatever. Be creative." She attaches her camera to the tripod and adjusts the angle. "If it gets too much, you can hide in the library."

She leans down to peer through the viewfinder.

I pick up the Pentax and check the memory card.

"Gallaghers have just pulled up."

"Shit." I swing around. "Already?"

"Evangeline." Miriam purses her lips.

I scoot to the side and hide behind the edge of the

corridor, wondering if there's a back staircase I can nip down. "What are they doing?" Why am I whispering? I hug the camera to my chest, back pressed against the wall.

Miriam shakes her head. "They're getting out of the car. Barb's in salmon silk, off the shoulder, perfect. Leonard … that man is gorgeous. Here's our girl, Kitty, in baby blue … chiffon, I think. Some serious diamonds on that child's neck."

I brace for it.

"And here comes the enemy." She falls silent a moment then stands slowly upright to look at me with wide eyes. "Holy smoke."

I grimace. "Really?"

She nods and bends back over her camera, adjusting the zoom. "Jamie's eighteen, right?"

"Miriam!"

She chuckles. "You could go out through the balcony and hide in the garden? I want photos of the lanterns on the patio and the dance floor on the lawn."

"There's a dance floor on the lawn?"

"Parquet. They had it installed."

I slip across the landing to the French doors.

"Don't forget," Miriam says, suddenly serious. "If you're not feeling up to it–"

"I know." I raise my hand and nip out into the humid

air. My staccato pulse races the up-tempo number being played in the band rotunda below and I take the two-tiered stone staircase to the patio on wobbly legs. It's going to be a long night.

CONTACT

"Filigree." A petite almond-eyed girl fingers the black lace on the bodice of her dress, her black hair coiled high on her head. "I think that's what she called it. Filigree lace?"

"What's the difference between filigree lace and regular lace?" A tall girl hunches beside her. The bronze sheen of her dress matches the highlights in her hair and she keeps her freckled arms crossed around her waist.

The petite girl screws up her nose. "Seriously, no clue."

I try not to grin behind my camera, sizing up a row of champagne flutes on a patio table, bringing the first one into focus, letting the rest blur. I click a couple of shots and straighten up to examine the LCD screen. Not bad. I glance around, hyper-vigilant. I've dodged the Gallaghers for a good hour. Thankfully, most of the guests have arrived, a buffer of bodies to hide behind.

I've had two glimpses of Jamie so far. A back of the head and a profile. I snapped sneaky stalkerish shots.

Miriam was right. Holy smoke. My chest flutters and I breathe through my mouth for more air.

The two girls watch the doors like they are waiting for someone. "Imogen." The petite girl nudges her tall friend and nods at the patio steps leading up to the balcony.

The tall girl frowns.

There are Richard and his date. His date doesn't look happy. Her mouth shapes fierce words. Richard darts a nervous glance at the crowd and touches her arm. The girl flings her hand up. He strokes her shoulder, leans in and whispers. She shrugs. He brushes his knuckle under her chin and whatever he says seems to dampen her anger.

A waiter passes with a tray of champagne. Richard takes two glasses and I watch to see if the waiter will demand some ID. There's a hesitation. Richard says something, his expression scathing, and the waiter backs away. I bet he played the "do you know who I am?" card. None of the guests seem to notice. I shake my head, partly disgusted, partly impressed. Richard sips from one glass before passing it to his date. She drinks it down, a defiant look on her face. He smiles, sips from the second before handing it to her also, his expression goading. She doesn't hesitate, bringing it to her lips. He's trying to get her drunk? I abandon partly impressed for completely disgusted.

"She needs to be careful," the petite girl says, genuine

concern in her voice. "Honestly, what does Kaylee see in him?"

"Dollar signs?" Imogen says.

The petite girl purses her lips. "She should have held out. Could have tried her luck with Jamie."

I turn my back, not wanting my face to give me away as an eavesdropper.

"Wish someone would say that about me," Imogen says.

"Huh?"

"Imogen should try her luck with Jamie."

"Sweetie," the petite girl giggles. "You couldn't even look at him when he was talking to you in the foyer."

Imogen sighs. "Kaylee should have held out."

"Definitely," the petite girl says. "Where *is* Kitty?"

"In there," Imogen says. "The governor's got her."

I resist the urge to turn around and look. Jamie might be in the glossy reception room with her. I can't decide what would be worse, eye contact from a distance or being caught off guard by a shoulder tap. Though I can't deny there is a worse fear – no eye contact, no shoulder tap.

"I'm dying to talk to her about California," the petite girl says. "I want to start planning."

"She's only just off the plane, Lila," Imogen says.

"She'll be all over it," Lila says. "Last days of summer road trip, baby. The four of us – if Kaylee doesn't bail."

I feel a stab of jealousy. These are Kitty's friends, planning a road trip to California. So much for the rebirth of my social life.

"Noooo!" A booming male voice then uproarious laughter.

I turn by reflex, freeze for one brief second of recognition and snap back again. Four young men have crossed the threshold out onto the patio. Jamie is in the middle of them. The booming voice belongs to a bear-sized blond guy, with a buzz cut, mussing Jamie's hair. "You're killing me. You're actually killing me."

Short of throwing myself over the stone balustrade and trampling the governor's flowerbed, I'm hemmed in. In full-flight panic, I lift a glass of champagne from a tray left unattended on the table beside me, the waiter reaching for a box of glasses beneath the table. With a furtive glance for any frowning adult eyes, I chug it back then repeat the maneuver with a second glass. The sweet fume of alcohol burns the back of my nostrils, making my eyes water. I hoist my camera up to my chest, let my hair swing out to cover the side of my face and try for a casual sidle around the drinks table, so lightheaded I can't feel my feet.

I get about three steps round the table.

"Everton?"

I close my eyes, bite my lips and turn. Four hulking boys in black tuxedos framed against the full glamour of the governor's emblazoned reception room. A high-impact, imprinted-forever moment, that tableau. Big band music rising behind me. A thousand twinkling lights. The heady aroma of champagne and a garden full of roses. My blood can't absorb the alcohol fast enough.

Jamie takes a step towards me, squinting and looking like he's just finished on the set of a Ralph Lauren advertisement. "It *is* you."

I know I'm supposed to say something – social convention requires that someone say something – but for the life of me I can't think what, and now it's officially awkward. Heat burns my cheeks. "Hey." I sound breathless and grip the camera like it can hold me upright.

"Kitty said you would be here." His accent is the same but deeper in tone. The sound of it produces a swoop in my stomach. "She's been looking for you."

I can't remember my plan. Do I have a plan? Aloof? Indifferent? I can feel the boys and girls behind him watching me. "I've been helping Miriam." I lift the camera, grateful for a prop and an excuse. "Where is Kitty?"

"Is this really all the welcome I get?" He tilts his head, a grin plays at his lips and he opens his hands before him. "Everton, you're not still mad at me, are you?"

I stand immobilised, my mind at war.

When he finds no answering smile, his face falters and his hands fall.

"What? No. Of course not. You took me by surprise. It's good to see you, Gallagher."

He lowers his head with a brief flash of teeth. "I don't think you really mean that, but I'll take it anyway. Come here, you." In two strides he crosses the patio.

I barely manage to swing the camera out the way before he grabs me to him, lifting me off the ground. My bees have never felt so good, spine, sternum, arms and legs. Best buzz yet. And, wow, he smells like Christmas. But the sensory onslaught fills me with a deep unexpected ache.

Then a vision eclipses my sight, sudden, violent and shocking. The thwack of bone against bone. Strength in my arms, unfathomable speed as I move – a memory that isn't my own. A fight, formless, furious. And just like that it disappears.

Jamie laughs. "You got tall, Everton."

"Yeah." My head spins as he puts me back on my feet and I grip the edge of the table to avoid stumbling. Another hallucination? I steel myself to look up. He's taller too, broader, bigger, ridiculously handsome. I want to cry.

He holds me with his stare, grey eyes, darker and more dangerous than his sister's. He drops his voice. "I'm really sorry about your mother." Simple, direct, sincere. "She was brilliant."

There's no air in me to speak, but I nod.

He studies my face and puts his hand on my arm,

turning me away from his friends. “Sorry. I shouldn’t have brought it up.”

“It’s fine.”

“I saw Miriam inside.”

I nod.

“She looks great.”

I nod again. The giddy feeling hasn’t lifted. I reach for another glass of champagne but the waiter is standing up and the tray is back in his hands. He offers me orange juice, warning in his eyes. I smile shakily and take it. Lips pinched, he turns his back and walks away.

“So do you,” Jamie says. “Look great, I mean.”

There’s a chinking sound, a splash of juice, a sting in my palm, glass falling at my feet and a stain spreading on the front of my dress. “Oh, crap.”

“Whoa,” Jamie says. “Here, let me.” He grabs a napkin from the table, takes the broken stem of the glass and turns my hand palm up. A large shard has lodged in the base of my thumb. Roaring fills my ears and Jamie’s touch sends pins and needles zapping up my arm.

“Are you okay?” The petite girl, Lila, appears beside us.

“Ouch!” The big blond bear sticks his head in the gap. “Flesh wound.”

If I had any blood left in my face, I would burn red. Making a public display of myself is high on my list of things I would rather die than endure. Here I am with an audience of strangers, Team-Jamie strangers, witnessing my public humiliation.

I don't think. I pull the shard out.

A collective groan of horror goes up around the group. It was a full inch deep and the glass gleams red and drips from the tip. Blood bubbles from the hole in my hand and we all stand there staring as it wells. Jamie snaps to attention and clamps the napkin over it, cupping my hand in both of his, his eyebrows high. "You don't know your own strength."

"Triage!" the blond bear barks. He claps his ham-sized hand on another boy's shoulder. "Abe, the infirmary!"

But Abe squints at me, recognition dawning in his eyes. His chocolate-brown face dimples with a fiendish smile and he points from the elbow, waiting for Jamie to confirm. "Is that who I think it is?"

Immediately they are familiar to me and I quickly find the context. Under a willow by the Border River. I turn my glare on Jamie and find his rueful expression.

"You guys remember Evangeline Everton," Jamie says, squeezing my hand as he bites back his grin.

The big blond bear lets out a long, "Ooooh," and elbows the third boy, who joins him in theatrical chorus.

I nearly bite through my tongue.

Jamie clears his throat. "This is Abe Lincoln." Abe gives me a wide smile. I blink at his name but manage a nod. "Pete Tilson." The dark-haired boy next to the blond bear smirks and raises his hand. "And Gil Bishop." I remember well enough – Mr President, Pete and The Bishop.

"Shoulda cut the bastard with the shiv, Van," the Bishop says, surprising me with a shortening of my name I haven't heard since Pennsylvania. The rest of the group snort and laugh.

My ears ring and the dizziness reaches a peak.

"Let's find someplace to get you cleaned up," Jamie says.

"It's not that bad," I mutter.

With a doubtful look, he unfolds the napkin. The group winces at the oozing red hole. My head swoons.

"Easy." He staunches the flow and wraps a steadying arm around my waist. Phenomenal tingling sweeps through my side where I press against him. If he lets me go, I'll hit the dirt.

"We can cut through to the library," Abe says.

"Give us a little space, you lot," Jamie says.

They make way but trail behind us.

Never could I have imagined a worst-case scenario as elaborate as this: that the first time I face Jamie in three years is in a stained gown, at the Governor's Ball where I swoon at my own blood, humiliated again before the very same set of boys.

Worse yet, when we cross the threshold into the

brightly lit reception hall, my pins and needles amplify to a painful stabbing. I grip Jamie's arm and almost cry out.

"Are you okay?" he murmurs.

I nod, but the thunder in my chest and the ocean pounding in my ears alarms me. The light takes on the strange sharpened quality I remember from the cafe with Kitty. I search the crowd, looking for her, needing to see her, that strange anxiety tightening inside me. "Where's Kitty?"

Then I spot her across the room. Jamie leads me between guests. People turn, expressing concern when they see the blood-soaked napkin and how Jamie holds me up. But all I can focus on is Kitty surrounded by a crowd of people. I recognise Aiden, Richard, Kaylee. Leonard stands there with an older man who looks so much like Richard it has to be the governor. But my eyes are only for Kitty.

Someone jostles the group. Kitty jumps back. Others exclaim. Aiden steadies her with a hand on her arm, Richard with a hand on her back. Someone has dropped a glass. We draw closer. Aiden goes to find a cloth. Leonard puts his hand on Kitty's shoulder. Her dress is stained. Kaylee lurches unsteadily towards Kitty, commiserates, patting her back. Richard hooks his arm around Kaylee's waist and steers her away. Kitty looks up and spots Jamie leading me through the crowd.

She comes towards me, her left leg saturated, the baby blue chiffon dark where the drink has soaked through. "You cannot be serious. Not you too? Oh, crumbs, look at your hand!"

"Kit," I rasp, letting Jamie go, reaching for her. A sickening high-pitched whine pierces my eardrum.

"So unfair," she grumbles and laughs. "We were both looking so good!" She flings her arms around my neck and I jolt like I've been plugged into an electrical socket. A tray of glasses carried by a waiter explodes beside us. Electricity burns in my spine, down my legs, through my arms and chest. I bite hard on my lip to stifle a scream and blood fills my mouth. The clamour in my head reaches a crescendo as I fall backwards slowly, endlessly, through space. My eyes lock on Kitty; her mouth open in the shape of a perfect "o".

When will I hit the floor? I can't see. My pulse thrashes. I want to call out. Someone cries. Movement. Urgent voices. I must be on the floor already because the surface under me feels cold and hard. Someone touches me. A muffled grunt. I'm hoisted up, unable to resist or cooperate. Despite my inner riot, a wonderful smell reaches through the murk, erasing everything else. Warm skin against my face – an aroma that conjures the forest, the river, irresistible and intoxicating. I can't do anything but breathe, so I breathe hungrily.

A low voice vibrates against my cheek. Higher anxious voices demand. The low voice soothes. Soon, the strong arms lift me onto a cool, soft surface. The incredible-smelling skin is above me then moving away. I want to get up and follow it.

Warm hands touch my face and stroke my arm. Someone murmurs. The storm drowns it all.

INSTINCT

The electric current becomes a tepid fizz. Colours flicker behind my eyes. Blurred images. Faces. A scrolling catalogue of faces. My Pennsylvania friends, my math teacher from last year. Mom. I lock in on her face and feel bruised in my chest. They scroll again and this time there are others: Barb, Aiden, Lila, Jamie. His face draws me like a zoom lens, my body humming its own response.

The images flick again and this time I see Kitty. She absorbs my focus with unshakeable urgency and my heart drums. Urgency becomes anxiety. Anxiety lurches to fear. Fear swallows me whole.

A shadow looms, obscuring Kitty's face. I want to cry out, but something more powerful takes hold of me.

Rage.

I jerk up from the pillow, disorientated in the lamplight. I don't know where I am. Panic burns up all the oxygen in my system and I gasp for air.

"Evie?" Miriam stands, gripping the ornate footboard, her hand to her mouth like she's witnessed a calamity. I see a gilt mirror, brocade drapes, and hear the distant sound of big band music floating through the open window. We're still at the Governor's Ball. And only one thing matters.

Kitty.

"Where is she?" My throat scrapes, my lip throbs, my head spins. A strange tight feeling tugs behind my bellybutton. I don't wait for an answer but scramble to my feet, nearly careening into a gleaming chest of drawers with the dizzying rush of blood.

Miriam steadies me. "Evie, sit down."

I push past her and stagger across the room, banging my hip against the footboard. I reach the door and fumble with uncooperative hands to open it. It won't give.

"Stop. I need to talk to you."

I turn in circles, holding my head. "You don't understand. Where is ...? I have to find … she's not …" I can't say it and pull at the handle, too weak to wrench it.

She holds up a key then closes it in her fist.

I stare at her balled hand and almost growl. "Open the door."

"No." She doesn't move. "You need to listen–"

"Open the damn door, Miriam!" I thrust my hand out, horrified by the loss of time, static burning me up. I barely notice my wound has been bandaged or the faint ache in my thumb. "Give it to me. I don't have time to explain. You won't get it – just – I have to – I have to–"

"What? You have to what?" Miriam searches my face, her eyes fierce.

Pressure builds in my chest and the strange tightness in my stomach constricts. The urge to tear the key from her hand seizes me. Her mouth hardens and she puts her hand behind her back. Next, I want to push her to the ground and force the key from her grip. She steps towards me. "Try it, kid."

I catch my breath. Has the intent shown in my face? "Please," I groan. "You don't understand."

"You wanna bet?" She exhales. "There's no way I'm letting you out of this room until you tell me what you want to do to Kitty."

"Do?" I can't get a hold on the word, astounded by her knowledge that it's Kitty I want. "Do?"

"You heard me."

"She's – she's not safe."

"Not any more, no." Her eyes narrow. "Because why? Because she's dangerous?"

She couldn't surprise me more if she punched me. "Dangerous?"

"Answer me, Evangeline."

A breeze ruffles the drapes at the window. It brings

the sound of the band from the rotunda, the murmur of voices from the patio and beyond that a faint whimper on the wind, the cry of a woman or child, the sound of fear. It grips me like it has come straight from my nightmare.

"That's her!" I run to the window and shove back the voluminous curtains, knowing I sound crazy, sure I'm losing my mind. But I've never been more certain of anything than I am in this moment: something terrible is happening to Kitty.

I lean out the window. The room looks over the garages. I strain to hear more but there's nothing. "Miriam! I swear, that was her!"

"You don't want to hurt her?"

"What?" I spin around. "No!"

She closes her eyes, her head rocking back.

"I can't explain it. I just – feel it." I put my hand on my stomach. "She's in danger. Something bad is happening now! Please! Help me!"

Tires squeal below. I freeze. So does Miriam; she definitely heard that.

My desperation reaches its peak. Something tears. Curtains fall from my hands. "Miriam," I cry. "Give me the key."

The slam of a car door echoes. A man's shout follows.

"I'm begging you."

Resignation hollows her eyes. She steps aside, opens her hand and there's the key. I take it, stagger across the room and fumble at the keyhole then a sharp pain jars the back of my head. I hit the door, then the carpet and black out.

CHOSEN

"Evie." A cold hand touches my cheek. "Evie?"

I can tell I'm sitting up, but my head hangs forwards, too heavy to lift. An egg-sized lump throbs on the back of it. I try to swallow and unglue my eyes but both sting. I go to touch my parched mouth but can't lift my arms. Even my panic doesn't feel right, instinct bubble-wrapped and weighed down. I know I should shout and flail but can't quite get at it. I moan and the cold hands cover mine.

"Evie, it's me."

Miriam.

I crack my eyes open and find a blur of light and colour.

"Are you thirsty?" Her pale arms move. A plastic straw touches my lips. "Drink."

I sip at first, then gulp until I'm gasping.

"It's the Fretizine." She picks something up from the table. "It dries you out."

It's like peering through a tunnel of fuzz, but I make

out the syringe she's holding. It's empty. She puts it down. The details don't add up. We're home in Miriam's kitchen. Something binds my wrists to the arms of a dining chair. Dishcloths? Something else binds my legs, like I've woken in a movie where I'm the hostage and Miriam's the lunatic who's struck me, bound me, drugged me, dragged me back to her lair. "What are you doing?"

"Protecting you from yourself. Suppressing your adrenaline. Keeping you calm." She sits back, elbow on the table, head propped on her fingertips. "I won't untie you till you've heard me out, till I can be sure you're not going to do something stupid."

Protecting? Suppressing?

A thought balloons in the weirdness, big and red. "Kitty." I pull numbly at my bonds, making the chair creak. "Is she here? Where is she?"

"Kitty's in hospital. You were right."

My bubble-wrapped panic strains for release. I want to fight and scream but all I can do is groan and close my eyes, making the dizziness worse. "She's hurt? Someone hurt her?"

"She came and found me after you fainted." Miriam rubs her face. "She followed Jamie and me when he carried you upstairs. I convinced them to go back to the party, said you would be embarrassed, that it would be better if they went. She wouldn't leave unless I promised to text her as soon as you came around. Apparently, she couldn't find her phone and went to look for it in the car. She was attacked. The police think someone was after the necklace."

I sway in my seat.

"A service van pulled in. The driver saw the attacker drop Kitty, and vault the wall into the grounds. The necklace was in pieces beside her."

"How bad – how bad is she hurt?"

"Ligament damage to the neck. Dislocated elbow. Bruising to the face."

Dismay thickens my throat. "If you'd let me–"

"What?" She raises her eyebrows. "You could barely walk straight. Your hands were so weak you couldn't get the key in the lock."

Tears prick my eyes. "You don't understand."

"I wish I didn't." She draws a long breath. "I really wish we were all just losing our minds."

"Tell me they got the guy."

"I highly doubt it. I got you out of there as soon as the cry went up."

I twist weakly in my seat. "Untie me–"

"You'd only fall over and hurt yourself. Listen, I'm going to tell you some things now that aren't going to make sense. You won't want to believe me, but if you listen to your body, you'll know I'm telling the truth."

The words are too strange. "I don't–"

She touches the back of her neck and grimaces. "I will tell you as much as I can before they come. I have some time, I think."

"What?" I choke. "Who's coming?"

She ignores me and ploughs on, "You're worried about Kitty because she's in danger and you feel you need to protect her. Your body's been changing, preparing to," she pauses, touches the back of her neck again, and lowers her voice, "*Spark.*" She gives the word as little weight as possible as though stress or inflection might set it off like a landmine. "*Priming*," volume dips for this word, too, before she continues in her normal voice, "*Priming* is the technical term. That's what all the pins and needles have been about. The growth spurt, breaking things, I'm guessing the hole in the laundry wall and your reaction to Kitty at the cafe."

It's like watching a badly dubbed movie with the wrong audio track laid over the picture. I stare at her, confounded, but I can't deny the fear that floods me, the crash and roar of it in my head.

"Bursts of adrenaline, heart palpitations."

"I never said I had palpitations." Like it matters, like it proves something.

"*Priming* prepares your body to respond to a *Spark.*"

Aggravated by the soft landing of her first and last

words, I screw my lips up. "I don't know what you are talking about."

"Kitty is the *Spark* for the synthetic gene in your DNA. You've transitioned." Her brow furrows. "It's what you were made for – you're a *Shield*, Evangeline. *Shields* are defenders, protectors. Turns out you were made to protect Kitty." Shield gets the soft touch with the other landmine words, but I lock on the only thing that makes sense: protect. One true word in the jumble of crazy and I cling to it like it's solid rock. It names the tension in me. But the rest of it: synthetic gene, DNA? "You're making fun of me, all this whispering bullshit."

"Drugging you and tying you to a chair is a little extreme for a joke."

"Then, what? You're trying to teach me some insane lesson about post-traumatic stress? That I'm deluded? That what I'm feeling isn't – that Kitty's not my–"

"What you're feeling is real and Kitty is your responsibility. You're bound."

Bound.

I pant, floundering again for a secure hold, but she just sits there, watching, waiting for me to concede. Disdain makes my voice low and rough. "So? I'm a lunatic with a saviour complex?"

"Same as me."

A vivid scene flashes to the foreground of my mind, a

waking vision, like I've hit replay: Miriam in the bathroom, the faucets roaring over the tub, the gash on her thigh. I shake my heavy head and I'm back in the kitchen, disorientated.

"I saw that," Miriam gasps.

"Saw?" The word doesn't fit. "Saw what?"

"Your memory of me in the bathroom." Her eyelids flutter. "Like – like a movie clip. Even fully matured – I mean, not all of us can do that."

All of us?

I feel myself recoiling and tighten my grip on the arms of the chair, needing the sting in my cut thumb. "You think you *saw* what I was just thinking?"

"Kinetic Memory Transference. You recalled a memory and projected it." She waves her hand in front of her face. "Without even touching. Normally, KMT requires touch."

"Miriam." I shake my head. "You're not – that doesn't make any sense. You have to untie me–" She cuts me off, putting her hand on my shoulder and closing her eyes. Instantly, I see myself from Miriam's point of view, sitting across from Kitty at the cafe, my hand darting to catch the bottom of her coffee mug. I flinch and the vision ends.

She sits back. "You saw that."

"Hallucinations."

"You've had them before? But I've never Transferred

anything to you." Her mouth opens and closes. "You can Harvest?"

"What?"

"KMT is what you project for someone to see, but KMH is when you access someone's memory, whether they like it or not, and experience it as they experienced it. Like being in their movie clip as them. It should be impossible for you."

I want to deny all of it, but the evidence piles up against me: when she hugged me in the bathroom the night she got home; when she pushed past me in the darkroom to lock the utility cupboard; when Jamie lifted me in his arms on the patio before I cut my hand and passed out. Each time a vivid hallucination reliving a memory that wasn't my own. My eyes sting with tears. "This is crazy. I don't understand."

She leans towards me. "You're not listening to your body."

My fear for Kitty is a physical ache. "We're wasting time. I don't know what any of this means and right now I don't care. I just have to see her. Untie me."

She looks at her hands, clasping them together as though she's about to chair a meeting. "I can't do that. You're in no state–"

"Because you knocked me out and pumped me with drugs!" It's as close as I can get to a proper shout.

"You can scan for a threat."

"What the hell does that mean?"

"It's what it's all about, kid, what you have to protect her from. The *Stray*." Again the drop in volume. "Not a vague threat or a clumsy thief. Like you were made to keep Kitty safe, the *Stray* was made to kill her."

My head spins and I don't know what infuriates me more, the ridiculous whispered terminology or Miriam's determination to keep up her rambling. "You think," I finally say, "that someone actually wants to kill her?"

"That is what every cell in your body is telling you. But for now she's safe. He won't try again straight off. He'll need to recover from exposing himself. *Strays* are all about dark corners, lonely places and self-preservation. They would never attempt anything in a crowd."

"It was the Governor's Ball." I grasp at something to argue against. "Hundreds of people."

"She was well past the service area. It would only have taken a moment to subdue her and drag her off."

The idea makes me shake. Other bubble-wrapped feelings strain inside me, darker than anger. I want to run, screaming or throw up on my feet.

"She's in hospital," Miriam says. "There are people everywhere and more importantly her family is with her. But you can scan for a threat, right now, for the sake of peace of mind. We're not going to make any progress until you can relax."

"Relax?" I choke. "Is that a joke?"

"Close your eyes. Bring Kitty into focus."

At first, I scowl, but the need to do something makes me compliant. I close my eyes. Kitty arrives in vivid detail. I stop breathing.

"Can you feel anything?"

I can't express what I feel. My body vibrates as the panic comes loose of its bubble wrap and I groan.

"Let the fear pass. See if the shadow rises."

I grip the chair at the painful peak of emotion, then gradually the tide ebbs. The shadow doesn't come. I slump back and open my eyes. The drug fog has lifted. Though I can finally see clearly, it's as if I've been sucked through a wormhole and everything is upside down. "I don't understand. This isn't real. I'm going to wake up and this will–"

"Still be happening to you."

I close my eyes. "Please, untie me. I'm not going to do anything stupid. My cut hurts."

She frowns, lips parting to argue.

"Please, Miriam. I'll listen."

She hesitates then rises from her seat to unknot the dishcloths. "I'm sorry I hit you." Her hard mask falters. She looks devastated, as if her worst fears have been realised. "I had to get you home. I was afraid you'd hurt yourself trying to help her. You're not ready. You're too weak and there's so much to explain, so much you need to understand first."

One arm comes free and the rush of circulation makes me wince. I flex my fingers, swivel my hand. She releases the knot on the other and I rub at the red marks. Blood has begun to seep through the bandage. She bends to untie my ankles and I wonder distantly what she's done with my high heels. Miriam straightens up and hovers like she might throw herself on me if I make a false move.

"Tell me just one thing that makes sense."

Miriam sits and frowns at the table. Her face assumes that look people get when they're about to break terrible news. "I think I might be able to show you. If I can show you, it will make the explanation a lot easier to swallow."

"Show me what?"

"KMT. To show you how I got hurt and what it is we do. But it would be more powerful if you could Harvest. You'd feel what I felt and in this case the feeling is more important than anything else."

"I don't know how."

She reaches her hand out to me, palm up. "Concentrate. I'll do my best to remember, but you'll have to take hold of it and really look, okay?"

Goosebumps flash across the back of my neck and the hair on my arms prickles. "I'll see it?"

She nods, swallows, spreads her hands and closes her eyes.

I hold my breath and brace, but when I touch her I'm not ready for the immediate sensory plunge. "Oh. Oh God."

KMH

It's a night scene. A street scene. A park fenced by a low stone wall and pointed iron railings. Opposite, there are restaurants spliced with narrow alleys, black mouths open in the dark.

I sit in a parked car. It smells of air freshener and Armor All. The dash is pristine and raindrops bead on smudge-free windows. This isn't Miriam's old VW. When my head moves, I catch my aunt's reflection in the rearview, eyes black. My hands are her hands, gloved and gripping the steering wheel, waiting.

One restaurant draws my eye; its lacquered door, hooded by a blood-red canopy, reflected in the wet road, vivid and almost vibrating in its significance for me. The longer I look, the stronger the pull grows. From somewhere behind my bellybutton, an invisible bungee stretches like a tether to someone in that restaurant. Stress discharges adrenaline through my body.

The door opens and four men step out. Middle-aged men in suits. Two of them have bellies spilling over their belts as they pull on coats against the weather. One is thin and serious, hugging his jacket closed. The fourth is where the tether finds its connection. Squat, pug-faced and stumbling over his shoes. He turns to the thin man, mouth blistering with profanities. Though the window is up, I have no difficulty making out their voices.

Pug-face is out of control.

"You're such a momma's boy, Kelsy. Grow some balls," he says, spraying spittle.

The thin man draws his lips back. "You've had too much to drink, Phil."

Phil swears again. "Leave me alone, you weak son of a bitch."

The other two step between them. "That's enough." One puts his hand on Phil's shoulder and the tension in me – in Miriam – stretches like a bowstring. "I'll get you a cab and you can go home and sleep."

Phil shrugs him off and teeters towards the curb. The men try to catch him but Phil rights himself and ducks out of their reach, swaying as he stands to face them.

"Go to hell, Michael," he says. "You always side with that bastard."

The picture flickers, a lapse in time. I find myself

outside the car now; warm, moist air touches my face. I run behind the fence line of the park and bound over the iron spikes, a lazy scissor leap, landing noiselessly on the pavement. The incredible sense of confidence in what my body can do holds me only for a moment, then I blur across the street into the shadows.

Phil staggers a full block away and the static in my head grows. Fear for Phil evaporates. Certainty, like a compass alert, crackles in my head. He nears a yawning alley. I know the threat lurks there. I gain quickly and slip past him as he stumbles out of the streetlight into the dark. It's wet, black and dank with dumpsters and yesterday's food. Bent, heaving, Phil empties his stomach in an obscene splatter at the foot of the wall. I scan the lane and my eyes adjust in seconds; the details are as distinct as the danger pulsating from the shadows.

It feels shocking to step away from Phil even as he slumps in the mouth of the alley, oblivious as I ghost through the dark. The tether stretches behind me while all my senses focus forwards. Instinct prompts me to move into the middle of the path and make no pretence of my approach. After all, I could be a waitress on her way to a late shift. I pull my phone from my back pocket and let the screen light up, pretending to text.

Oily water oozes in rivulets across the lane and I let my feet fall harder, splashing and scraping my shoes on the ground. I kick a soggy box so that it slaps against a rusted dumpster.

The threat hides behind it. I can feel him. A chemical odour fills my nose. As I pass the edge, I stop, close my phone and turn.

He stands ramrod straight. Dressed like me in black pants and jacket. He's handsome. He's young. Maybe nineteen or twenty. Blond, pale, taller than me. His pupils are so dilated, his eyes are black. Regret squeezes my chest for an instant, but the tug towards Phil extinguishes the feeling and anger burns in its place.

"Don't try to run," I say, with Miriam's voice.

The night explodes in violence.

He swings at me, but I duck the blow like it's happening in slow motion. Before he throws himself forwards, I see it coming and stand up under him, flipping his legs towards the narrow stretch of night sky. I watch him spiral through the air, letting him land on his feet, amazed by my – Miriam's – sense of control.

He runs for it but I know I can take him. As I fly up behind the attacker, his intent flashes in my mind's eye and I know he'll reach for a battered metal canteen, jagged at the edge where it lies ripped open. He scoops it up and flings it at me and I arch to the side. It only scrapes my thigh; a lick of fire through the muscle. The flood of adrenaline propels me and I reach for him like it's an embrace. His body is hard and strong as I pull him out of his stride, jerking his neck with the sudden stop.

Time skips again.

I shake my head as though I can shake the horror off, then notice the tether is gone. I can't feel my feet moving across the ground, or my hands brushing against my legs. I bend over Phil, who squints up at me against the streetlight. Vomit pools on his wilted tie. A leer edges his lips. "Hello, beautiful."

"I'll call you a cab, Phil."

Then the brightness of Miriam's kitchen dazzles me. She sits back, looking pale, exhausted. Something like awe touches her expression as she stares at me. "You got all that?"

I hug my stinging hand. "That's what you were doing in New York?"

She nods.

I close my eyes and cry.

DNA

"I don't even know where to start with all this." Miriam rubs her face, fingers trembling. "I'm not sure how much time we have before they come – or if they'll come."

There's a hitch in my throat as I ask, "Who?"

"*Affinity*."

Affinity sounds like a cosmetic brand or dating website, or maybe a pretentious marketing company. Though I might be thinking of Eternity or Infinity. But here, now, in this context with Miriam giving it the whisper treatment, I've never heard anything more creepy. My ears pop and my vision gets swimmy. A weird sense of dislocation makes me feel like I'm not all in my body and some essential part of me has come loose.

"The *Affinity Project* is the organisation responsible for what we are and what we do. They created *Optimal*, the synthetic gene in our DNA that gives us our abilities and determines our path."

There's irony in that last word, and trauma in the others, but I need to get things straight. "These people are coming for *me*?"

"Not at first. But when they sense you've *Sparked*, yes. For now, they'll come if they've registered my breach in protocol." She touches the back of her neck. "My tracker is overdue for an upgrade, it's almost completely dissolved. They didn't respond after the alley so there's a chance they might not register the breach."

Tiny white stars pop in my peripheral vision and I'm picturing a futuristic laboratory, bodies on slabs, scientists in white masks with lethal hypodermic needles. An alarm going off and heads turning to flashing red computer screens. A breach! Men in black with laser guns leaping into hover cars. Behind Miriam's head the cupboard doors begin to pulsate.

"The tracker relays my signal to their database. It tells them where I am, if I've bonded with a *Spark*, deactivated a *Stray*, or if I'm injured and in need of medical attention. It also picks up on illegal terminology. Red flags. You hit enough demerits you'll get a call from your *Watcher*. Hence the whispering, not that volume probably makes much difference. If my tracker were at full strength, I could scramble the speech receptor with a magnet." She makes an impatient noise in her throat and rubs her face again. "Screw it. There's too much to explain. If they call, I'll say I was deliberately using illegal terms to get their attention."

I barely notice Miriam's sudden resolve. My head feels cavernous, vaulted ceilings of echoing space. You'd think with all that ballooning room the important questions could form a civilised line, biggest to smallest, from *Why God, why?* to *Do we get uniforms?* Instead, I blurt, "It's in your neck?"

"Base of my skull. When it's at full strength it feels like a small pea-sized lump beneath the skin."

I feel squeamish and she says something about nano-tech and dissolving amino-acids and the stars turn supernova around me.

"Put your head between your knees." She catches me by the shoulders. I was slumping sideways? Next I'm bent double, drooling on my charcoal silk, eyes watering at grooves in the floorboards and the scarlet enamel on my naked toes. Blood rushes in my ears. "I'm sorry."

She rubs gentle maternal circles on my back. "I know. It's a lot to take in."

The clatter of the cat door, paws padding the floor, then the nudge of a soft furry skull. Buffy purrs in my ear, rubbing her whiskers against me. I want to bury my face in her fur and sob. Pressure swells my lips and face. I mumble, "Who are they, though? What do they want?"

"They were a paramilitary operation that specialised in biotechnology, genetic engineering, private security. Things got messy and then there was a change in management. Now they want to right their experimental wrongs."

I leap at the hint of blame. "So, it's *their* fault I'm like this and Kitty's in danger? Affinity *made* the Stray?"

"They weren't always the Stray. They were Strikers. Optimal amplifies the natural affinity of those with Active Frequency Sensitivity for defence or attack. The Stray are a result of a mutation in those with the attack affinity."

I groan, no better for asking. Probably worse. Overwhelmed, my mind goes blank again. I flap my hand, bonelessly weak. "I'm bleeding." The stain has seeped right through the bandage across my palm.

"Damn. Hold on." She rises from the table and I tilt my head a little, catching a blur of staggering speed as she disappears up the hall, scaring Buffy who darts away to hide in the living room. Goosebumps prickle my arms and legs. A cupboard hinge squeaks through the ceiling, heavy things shift and shush over the wood floor, a pause then the whisper of movement in the hall. She's back in the kitchen with a brown leather case and I've had no time to gather a coherent thought. "Keep your head down."

"You're so fast," I whisper.

"Yes." She moves above me, unzipping the case on the table. The rustle of plastic packaging, the clink of glass and metal. "We have speed, heightened senses, reflexes, strength, precognition, increased pain threshold; there's a bunch of stuff. Oh, and your fingerprints will fade, helps make us untraceable."

"Miriam," I whimper, unable to take it all in. "I don't understand. How can this be happening to me?"

The rummaging stops. "Fate? Natural selection? No *good* reason, kid. You inherited the Optimal gene from your grandmother, Kitty inherited the trigger gene from someone in her family, the two of you came together and bam."

I jerk up, nearly cross-eyed with the rush. "Nan was like this? Not Mom, too?"

"Careful," she steadies me. "No, Nan wasn't genetically engineered, just a carrier like your mom."

"Mom was normal?"

"Completely."

The relief is intense but momentary. "What on earth was Nan into?"

"Nothing. She took pregnancy supplements. She had no clue they were laced with Optimal." She releases my shoulders, watching to see if I'll keel over. "That was the second generation trial."

"They put it in pregnancy vitamins?" Stunned, I prop myself against the table, leaning heavily on my elbow like a drunk. "This is too huge."

"Let me look at your wound." Gently, she untucks the sopping bandage and begins to unloop it while I stare blankly into middle distance.

My brain is so murky, my thoughts break the surface half-seen. Trance-like, I begin, "How can you be sure I'm one of these protectors? A Shield? I can't move like you or fight or anything. How can you be sure it wasn't just a guy after Kitty's necklace?"

She pauses mid-loop. "If he were a civ – sorry, a civilian – you wouldn't have reacted the way you did. As to your abilities, they'll come quickly and you'll be trained. But it's the tether that's your proof, that tug behind your bellybutton. You had your hand over your stomach when you came round at the governor's."

I knew what she meant. It was what frightened me the most, in Miriam's alley memory, that primal tug, more than the impossible feats of speed and strength. "I don't feel it now."

"You will, as soon as you get near her again. It's the true sign of your bond."

"It doesn't make sense. Why would anyone want to hurt her? What did Phil do to that guy in the alley?"

"Phil didn't do anything and neither did Kitty." The bandage comes loose, Miriam sets it aside and we stare at the deep cut in the base of my thumb. She angles my wrist to examine it in the light. The cut glistens like a faceted ruby, glinting and hypnotic. "It's called the Fixation Effect." It's what you experience when you think of Kitty, when you see her, what you feel, that sense of being drawn to her. For a Shield, it's what compels us to protect our Spark. But for the Stray, you take everything you feel about Kitty and twist it so she no longer looks like the victim who needs your help but the virus destroying your sanity and threatening your life."

"That's impossible."

She lowers my hand to the table and turns to her case. "Things are blurred for you because you already have a relationship with your Spark. You already care about her. Phil," she rocks her head back to indicate the memory I've seen, "is a total bastard, who beats his wife and cheats at cards. You saw him. He's not much different sober. Beyond a basic human decency, I have no reason to care about what happens to him, but you saw how I was, felt what I felt. I *had* to protect him."

"You didn't even know him?"

She arranges supplies on the table, scissors and gauze and tape. "I shook his hand at the office where I dropped off proofs after the shoot. That was it."

I feel like I'm being pulled backwards, dragged by an undertow into rough waters. "Your whole Phil situation happened in the space of a week? A week!" My mouth snaps open and closed with the impossibility of it all. Me, facing off with some genetically engineered psychopath? I have never been in a fight in my life. If someone hit me, I'd probably burst into tears. "I can't learn karate or whatever that was in week! How on earth will I protect her?"

"Your guy's an amateur. If he were experienced, Kitty'd be dead. I'd say he's only been active a few months, at most. I've seen this before. I've been here before. Trust me."

The casual use of "dead" and "Kitty" in the same sentence stirs something darkly territorial inside me. I remember what it felt like in Miriam's alley memory, what I felt at the governor's when I knew Kitty was in trouble and I couldn't get to her. Perhaps I could fight.

"You'll learn what you need to know. It's different for all of us, but the ability is in your DNA. The fact that you can Transfer and Harvest is a sign that you'll be a fast learner. They're usually the last of our gifts to develop." She nods at my hand. "This is going to need stitching."

"Hospital?" The thought of having to leave the house and function around normal people renews my panic.

Miriam lifts latex gloves from her case and a packet of blue sutures. "I'll do it."

"You will?"

But she's already pulling the gloves on, snapping them over her wrists. "Don't worry, I've done this a lot – though that might not be so comforting. At least you'll heal quickly."

"What? Why?"

"Rapid regeneration is one of the perks of the synthetic gene. Here, lift my hem."

I frown.

"My thigh. There's barely a mark."

Hesitant, I take the hem and slide the black silk up to her hip, expecting a sturdy bandage to unwind. There is no bandage. Just clear skin with nothing more than a faint pink line where the gash used to be. I drop the hem and slump back, my breath coming quick and shallow.

Miriam nods. "I know, right?" She splashes a cotton swab with antiseptic and sits to dab carefully at the mess on my thumb. "You won't heal that fast. Your frequency sensitivity will need to mature, but it'll come."

"What sensitivity?"

"When Optimal bonds with our DNA, when it's activated, it creates Electro-Telepathic Radiation. We generate a signal and develop a sensitivity to the ETR of others. It's called AFS, Active Frequency Sensitivity. It's what enables us to recognise our Spark and sense the threat of the Stray. It also creates telepathic receptors that trigger precognition. KMT and KMH were simply side effects, not intentional design elements, but they provide a pretty good indication of the strength of our signal and sensitivity." She wads the blood-soaked cotton swab into a ball and tosses it into the sink.

"Telepathy?" I choke. An uncontrollable urge to laugh

rises inside me and quickly drops away with a memory. "I could see what he was going to do, the blond guy in the alley. Is that telepathy?"

"Precognition." Miriam opens another packet with her teeth and removes a syringe. Inserting the needle through the rubber head of the vial, she draws the plunger and gives me an assessing look, like she's wondering how much more I can take. "Kind of hard to explain. Shields, with mature AFS, can read an opponent's intent as they project it. But in the alley memory you experienced my precognition. I doubt you'd be able to do that yet yourself." She holds the syringe to the light, taps the barrel, compresses the plunger and discharges a teardrop of anaesthetic, speaking almost to herself. "But then you shouldn't be able to Transfer or Harvest at all – you don't exactly fit the mould. You didn't throw up when you transitioned and it wasn't even like you had a seizure. You simply fainted."

It had felt like an apocalyptic storm to me. "Throw up?"

"It's a fairly common reaction to all the upheaval."

I can imagine.

"Relax."

I can't.

She takes my hand and inserts the needle beneath the wound. The icy sting makes me wince, but Miriam is careful as she discharges the anaesthetic and withdraws the shaft, pressing a cotton ball in its place. "Hold that."

Numbness spreads like cold water through my palm. "What about making things explode?"

Frowning, she rips another packet open to reveal a tiny curved needle, like a cat claw. She lifts it with a pair of tweezers, the blue suture uncurling. "What do you mean?"

"Wineglasses. Light bulbs."

"You can do that?"

"Not on purpose. Just seems to happen when I'm worked up."

She taps the end of my thumb. "How does it feel?"

I tremble with cowardice or horror. Probably both but I can't feel anything. I nod and grit my teeth as she bends over the wound and inserts the needle in a deft dig.

"I've never heard of it." She catches the tip and draws it through, glancing up as she tugs my senseless flesh. "Maybe it's a third-generation anomaly. I don't know a lot about third-generation distinctions." She knots the thread and snips at the base.

"Third generation? You said second generation before." I feel suddenly present, no longer hovering outside myself, and the questions I haven't been able to form in my dazed state all press forwards. "What's the point of all this? Affinity? What on earth were they hoping to achieve?"

Bending back over the wound, she stabs the skin, making me wince though I feel nothing, explaining as she works. "Imagine the perfect soldier. One who doesn't fear death, or pain, who never quits, never gets sick. A soldier stronger than ten men, fast as a horse and able to sense the approach of danger. Imagine a soldier untroubled by heat or cold, able to heal in a day from a bullet wound and who, in hand-to-hand combat, could anticipate the enemy's every move and counter it."

"We're supposed to be soldiers?" I'm so breathless it comes out like a whisper.

"I guess that was the goal back then, in the early seventies. A human weapon, or whatever."

"For what, an army?" Instead of a lab, I visualise a high-tech bunker with zombie-eyed rows of men and women dressed in black body armour, waiting to be deployed.

"For hire. Corporate, private, political or military application. Short- and long-term assignments. Defence, acquisition and protection were the services on offer."

"Hired assassins?"

"Who can say where they would have drawn the line? Now it's all about damage control."

"Because of the Strays? Explain that again. They were a mutation?"

The crease in her brow sharpens as she cuts the thread. Her cell phone starts up on the counter and she swears. "It's them."

I clamp my good hand to my mouth as though afraid I might scream.

She peels her gloves off, crosses to the counter and answers the call. "Carolyn?" She uses her business voice, assertive but polite, though she looks pale and presses her hand to her forehead. "I've been trying to get hold of you. Yes, I know, the alert didn't seem to go through. I've been clocking up demerits in the hope you'd call … Last night. New York … It was clean. Ready for disposal."

Disposal? I shudder at the implications, picturing the blond boy and his wild black eyes, the feel of his breaking bones still fresh in my mind.

Carolyn talks. Miriam listens. Her eyes flick to me. "Of course. I'll be expecting you." There are no parting words. She turns her phone off. "You have to go upstairs."

"What? Why? Shouldn't I meet her?" The idea is terrifying but if it will help me save Kitty–

"No." She makes a choking sound. "She may not be a Warden, but still, I don't want her anywhere near you."

"Why?" My voice flies high. "What's a Warden?"

Coming to the table, she starts throwing medical supplies back into the leather case, jams the lid closed and holds it out to me. "She'll be here any minute."

Bewildered, I take it with my good arm. "You're scaring me."

"Go upstairs. Hide this. Get into bed and pretend to sleep." She turns me around and unzips my dress.

I have to pin my elbows to my sides to keep it from

falling to my feet. "Miriam! What the hell?"

"You wouldn't be able to get it off one-handed. Now go and do as you're told. Put your pyjamas on, just in case. Actually–" She opens the lid of the medical kit, pulls out a bandage and tucks it under my chin. "Bind your hand once you're in bed. Lie facing away from the door. Breathe long and slow. Do not come out for any reason."

"I don't understand!" I feel myself skidding towards hysteria.

She flips the lid of the case again and digs out a preloaded syringe. She removes the sheath from the needle and jams the point in my shoulder.

I grunt, trying to jerk away but she grabs my elbow.

"I'm sorry. This will calm you down and dampen your signal. Carolyn is coming to debrief *me*. When she gets here, she'll take a reading of my signal, but I have no idea if she will be able to detect yours. Pray she can't, for Kitty's sake."

FRETIZINE

Fretizine. Without it my heart would gallop right out my chest and I would be found out. Not that I'm exactly sure how my pulse impacts the mysterious signal I apparently now emit.

As instructed, I lie on my side, away from the door, taking slow fake-sleep breaths. The only thing I grasp in the panicked minutes before Carolyn knocks on the door is the certainty that being found out would somehow be dangerous for Kitty. It's all the threat I need to comply. Paralysed by fear and Fretizine, I strain to hear anything below.

I left the door ajar a couple of inches but all I catch after the initial knock and greeting in the hall is the scrape of chairs in the kitchen. It's nearly one in the morning. Clearly, the Affinity Project isn't concerned with business hours, or maybe that's part of their MO, conducting affairs under cover of darkness. I wonder if Miriam has any intention of reporting what's gone down at the Governor's Ball. Perhaps they already know. They must monitor police bandwidths for signs of their clients. I shiver. It's too easy to let my mind wander into dark places. Somewhere, out in the night, a lunatic twists inside with regret over a missed opportunity. He'd had Kitty right in his hands, had her by the neck. How easy would it have been for someone with the kind of strength and speed Miriam had described to snap her spinal cord? Rage makes me cold and I forget my measured breathing. Even through the drug fog I can feel my heart stamp.

Stop it.

I can't jeopardise things by losing control. Where are my heightened senses? My Superman hearing? I strain to hear. Buffy pads through the door, jumps on the bed, kneads the quilt and purrs loudly. "*Go away!*" I hiss, dislodging her. She drops to the floor and stalks out, her tail flicking in agitation.

I try again to hear, my ears pop, roar then clear. The tap drips in the bathroom, wind keens beyond the window, boughs creak, and beyond that is the faint song of the river. I force myself to focus on the kitchen below, amazed to note a rising inflection, a foreign cadence, a pause, a question …

"… coordinates for the car? … very good … you make my job easy, Miriam …"

"… Recovery Team will find him in the trunk."

"Excellent."

"He was young," Miriam says. "I hate it when they're young."

"You can't look at it like that …" Carolyn, brisk and school teacher-ish. "… mercy … kept him from a nightmare life … a monster. Think of the lives you've saved, the families you've kept from heartbreak."

"I don't know that Phil's wife would thank me for saving him."

"The next Spark might have been a good man, a good woman. Don't regret your gift, Miriam. You save lives."

"A hair's breadth of a chromosome and you'd have needed someone to save the world from me."

Sick realisation dawns on me. I recall Miriam's fierce eyes when I came round in the bedroom at the governor's, the way she questioned me. She'd been afraid I was a Stray.

"These are common feelings post-assignment," Carolyn says. "They'll pass."

A chair creaks, fabric brushes, a plastic clipping sound.

"I'm overdue," Miriam says, like she's answered a question. "I can barely feel it."

"Hence the delay in your signal registering. I should've checked on you sooner, Miriam, updated your tracker. I'm sorry to have put you at risk. If you wish to make a negligence complaint, that would be fair."

"No. Of course not."

"If you're certain. Tip your head." An electronic beep follows. "Something's not right."

I dig my nails into the back of my hand. My ears pop and I lose the conversation as fear floods in. She's sensed me. She will be up the stairs any minute. I can't hear past the static in my head. She has some kind of signal scanner and the reading is wrong because I'm up here confusing reception. Frozen, I wait for threatening footsteps on the stairs. They come into the hall. The jingle of keys. Miriam's voice. A response. The front door opens then closes. Silence.

I sit up in bed, heavy in head and limb.

Car doors open and close.

Two slams.

The engine revs and the car pulls away.

Two slams?

Heaving the blankets off, I rise shakily to my feet and shuffle past my waiting-to-be-unpacked boxes. I pause at the door. "Miriam?" I take cautious steps out onto the landing and lean on the rail. "Miriam?" No reply. Afraid to fall, I strangle the banister, forcing my lead-heavy legs downstairs, but I can tell she's gone. The house is empty. I'm alone.

At a total loss I stand in the hall, staring into space. I turn to the front door as though I expect it might open again and Miriam will appear and start explaining things. There on the wooden crossbeams hangs a yellow sticky note. She's written only one word, "WAIT!" The capital letters and exclamation mark, full of promise and warning. She'll return soon and I mustn't do anything stupid.

I pull the piece of paper off the door and shuffle into the living room, flicking the lamp on, slumping in the old wingback. Buffy looks up from the couch, ready to forgive me for the sake of a warm lap. I let her come and jump onto my knee, stroking her with my good hand. I stare at the sticky note and Miriam's familiar hand writing. I can do as I am told, can't I?

* * *

But after a couple of hours, I'm not so sure.

My thumb aches. I run my tongue over a bite inside my lip, raw, coppery. The lump on the back of my head is tender when it bumps against the headrest. The clock on the mantelpiece reads half-past three and the undertow of bone-deep fatigue pulls at me, but I can't let myself fall asleep. I finger the sticky note, waiting with my stitches and my horror and a mouthful of unasked questions. I relive the Governor's Ball detail by detail, linger over Jamie's smile, his embrace and my humiliation. If I close my eyes and really concentrate, can I remember the smell of his skin? I shake myself. As if anything like that matters any more. Miriam's singleness now makes total sense. Mom had blamed her pickiness, her crazy schedule, but really, what hope is there for romance when your life is ruled by mutant DNA?

It's like manning a valve, allowing my mind to trace back on the night without letting emotion overwhelm me. Kitty's face blazes, interspersed with flashes of Miriam's alley memory and the stitching of my skin. I catalogue every male face I can remember from the party, casting them in the role of lurking psychopath. It doesn't help. I mistrust every one of them, from obnoxious Richard to helpful Aiden. How many people touched her, hugged her, or shook her hand in one day?

Behind all this surges the enormity of my new life, the genetic mistake that runs in my blood, the wrongness of me in skin, muscle and bone. I wait for Miriam. I need Miriam but I want Mom. The longing and the pointlessness of it wring me out. Tears escape the valve and I quake in my seat.

I let it take me for a while, let the pain pull me along, slam me up against the "why me?" over and over until I think I might start screaming and tear the place apart. Eventually, sheer exhaustion closes the valve. I sniff and swipe the back of my hand across my face, my swollen eyes, disgusted with the waste of time and tears. I lift Buffy to the floor; she growls and sits disconsolately as I push up from the chair. I can be grateful at least that the Fretizine has worn off and I have full use of my muscles again. Miriam wants me to wait? Well, she has until I'm showered and dressed to get back and tell me whatever else I need to know. Then I'm going to the hospital to find Kitty.

Upstairs, I lean towards my reflection above the bathroom vanity, looking for a sign that I'm still in there, that the shell of skin is still mine. I lick the edge of my finger, wipe the last smear of mascara and frown. Yesterday's makeover has washed away in the flood, but there's no shadow beneath my eyes. They're a little puffy and red but there should be shadows. Trenches.

I drop my gaze and stall.

My boobs.

"Holy–" I turn side on and run out of exclamation. It's not the lighting, the tank top or the mirror – my boobs are bigger. I reach for the hem of my top, pulling it over my head, careful of my bandaged hand, feeling immediately the weight of my breasts without the support of Lycra. I slouch, straighten and turn, checking my reflection from every angle.

My small Bs are gone.

These are definitely a step up the alphabet.

I tug my pyjama pants from my hips and peer back over my shoulder to see if there are any other changes. My butt looks the same.

Just the chest.

"Miriam." I close my eyes and I'm crying again at

yet more evidence that my body is no longer my own. Helpless tears, messy, unhinged sobbing, tapping wells of grief old and new. I weep for Mom and leaving home and feeling utterly lost and alone. I weep for Kitty and the Miriam I never knew and even the boy in the alley. I weep because I am so afraid, so hopelessly, agonisingly afraid of what I have to do. Worse is my fear that I won't be able to do it.

WARD

The moment the elevator doors open, it hits me – I can almost visualise the tether reaching from my bellybutton like a magnetic cord to the thing that matters most, where she lies in the private room at the end of the ward. Just like the feeling from Miriam's alley memory. I grip the handrail, afraid to step into the corridor as my spine zip-zaps and my heart claps its valves. That my aunt had felt this for a total stranger blows my mind. The elevator chimes, its doors about to close. I nip through the gap and freeze in the T-junction. A janitor guides a boxy polisher, buffing the linoleum to a high sheen.

I have to batten down my suspicion as instantly as it rears. The man is well into his sixties and almost as wide as he is short, straining the seams of his coveralls. I don't need to see his ID to know he isn't Kitty's stalker disguising himself for a sneak attack.

Calm down.

Hadn't Miriam told me the hospital was a safe place? Too busy and unpredictable for a Stray to make an attempt? But as I draw near the nurses' station, the desk sits empty. I don't know whether to be outraged no one is on watch or relieved that it will be so easy to slip by unquestioned. Where are the medical personnel I pictured patrolling the corridors, filling it with their Stray-deterring presence?

I scan the whiteboard with its list of room numbers and patient names and see "Kitty Gallagher" written in green marker, but I could find her room with my eyes closed.

My pulse sprints as I make my way up the corridor, soundless in my sneakers, sweatpants and hoodie. It had seemed more responsible to dress for ease of movement, plus my sports bra is the only one that fits, but really, what do I think I can do? I'm not ready for anything. In the ten seconds it takes me to reach her door, a thousand insane thoughts shoot through my brain. What if someone threatens her right here? Can I protect her? Am I fast enough? Strong enough? I curse Miriam for leaving me so unprepared.

It's barely seven in the morning. I had waited in Miriam's car in the visitor's parking lot for almost two hours, debating what to do, afraid they would turn me away. I'm not family. It's not visiting hours. Who do I think I am, expecting to barge into a hospital ward in the early hours of the morning? Now, here I stand outside Kitty's room, the tether vibrating, too afraid to knock.

The door opens fast and wide, the gap filled by Jamie, glowering and disheveled in last night's suit. His expression makes the quicksilver adjustment to surprise. "Everton?"

"Evangeline?" Leonard stands at Jamie's shoulder. The similarities between father and son have grown more startling in the three years since I last saw them side by side. I glimpse Barb sitting beside the bed, pale with fatigue, Leonard's suit jacket over her gown. Clearly none of them have been home.

"I'm sorry," I say, keenly aware of violating a private situation. "They wouldn't tell me anything over the phone."

Jamie stares. Leonard pushes his glasses up the ridge of his nose, glancing past me, looking for someone. Barb rises from the bedside, frowning.

"Where's Keith?" Leonard's low aristocratic voice almost sounds menacing. "They let you come up here?"

I have no idea who Keith is but I gather he's in trouble. "There was no one on the desk. I'm sorry. I was worried. I couldn't sleep. I thought if I came up …"

Leonard's expression softens. He steps out and squeezes my shoulder. "Forgive me, Evie, and excuse me a moment. There's supposed to be a security guard." He marches up the corridor to the nurses' station.

I catch a brief glimpse of Kitty asleep in the bed, her

neck braced, bruises on her face, her right arm held in a sling. Rage twists my insides and tears prick my eyes. I want to kill someone. "Kitty," I squeeze her name out. Jamie still stands there, staring at me. Barb draws close beside him, petite and blonde like her daughter. She's unpinned her hair. I've never seen Barb without makeup and I wonder if hers also washed away with tears.

"She's asleep," Barb says. "We don't want to wake her."

"No." I drop my voice to a whisper. "Of course not. I – I wanted to see her, make sure she's okay. I mean, obviously she's not okay, but if there's anything I can do." I wish Jamie would say something.

"Is Miriam here?" Barb looks out the door.

"No." I tuck my hands into the pockets of my sweatshirt, wincing as I bump my thumb. Jamie's eyes finally move from my face, flicking to where my bandaged wound hides. "She doesn't know I'm here. She wanted me to wait." Neither statement is a lie, but I feel the heat in my face, pressure in my chest, and an unwelcome tear slips the corner of my eye. I lower my head. "I'm sorry. This was a bad idea. I should have waited."

Jamie's wide warm hand grips my shoulder, producing the distinct charge in electricity I felt in his arms the night before.

"Everton," he says. "It's all right."

I look up and he slides his hand behind my neck,

squeezing briefly at the base of my skull before letting go. He turns his face away as though suppressing his own wave of emotion.

"It's been a long night." Barb brushes her hand up and down my arm. "She'll recover but she's had a terrible fright. You can come and see her. We just need to keep our voices down."

The room is big enough for three chairs and even has a window. Kitty's blue chiffon gown lies folded neatly on the table at the end of the bed. There are no flowers or get well cards yet, but I know the room will be full of them by the afternoon. Everybody loves Kitty. Seeing her lying there makes my insides twist. "She's so small." I blink through my tears, realising too late I'd said it aloud. I blush and wipe my eyes. "I mean …"

"I know what you mean, sweetie." Barb moves to let me draw closer to Kitty's side. Jamie stands opposite, staring at me again, his face impossible to read.

Kitty groans and we all freeze. Her head moves but the brace holds her still. She winces, opens her eyes; the left one is so swollen it makes her look like she's mid-wink. She spots me. "Hey," she rasps, lifting her good hand, searching.

I bite the inside of my cheek – *please don't let me pass out* – and clasp her hand between both of mine. Magically, nothing happens even though my heart thunders like it will lift out of my chest. "Hey. I'm sorry. Did I wake you?"

She tries to shake her head and grimaces. "This thing blows."

"That thing's keeping your brainstem attached to your spinal cord." Jamie leans over her. "Lie still."

She grumbles and squeezes my hand, brushing the bandage. "Oh, how are you?"

I give her an incredulous look. "Don't worry about me, Kit. I'm fine."

"You hit the floor pretty hard. I was worried you'd cracked your skull."

I shrug.

"You remember Everton fainting?" Jamie says, fully alert.

Kitty makes a face. "Don't get excited. I told you, everything after I left the party's a blank."

"You don't remember anything?" Disappointment winds me. What had I expected, a name and address for the sick bastard who'd hurt her?

"A shadow." She closes her eyes. "But I guess that's a bit stupid. It was dark."

A shadow. I shiver.

"You don't have to go over it now, darling," Barb says. "The police will review your statement later this morning. For now you need to rest."

Kitty screws her nose up. "There goes summer."

"Jamie, why don't you see Evie out?" Barb says.

"Come back, though. I'm stuck here at least a week," Kitty says. "Barb, will you tell the desk that Evs can come whenever she wants? None of this family only bollocks."

Barb purses her lips.

Jamie frowns.

I feel the pressure to say I'll stay away and let her rest, but my need to keep close overrides social rules. "I'll be here every day, Kit."

She grins. Jamie and Barb exchange looks. I feel awkward and a little hurt. I can understand Barb, the over-protective mother, but what's Jamie's problem?

"I'm sure short visits won't hurt. I'll tell Keith." Barb opens the door.

Jamie waits for me to step out into the corridor ahead of him.

Down at the nurses' station Leonard is speaking with the security guard. Judging by the guy's face, he's getting the message. I feel the same immediate suspicion towards him as I felt towards the janitor. Paranoia? My pins and needles burn and static crackles in my head like a badly tuned radio, but I sense no threatening shadow. I conclude Keith isn't a murderous lunatic, but I also decide he's too weedy and unfit for the job of security guard – though I doubt an entire SWAT team built like Jamie would satisfy my idea of protection.

"You got a sec?" Jamie nods towards a small sitting area by the stairwell exit, and I walk beside him, distracted by the pull of the tether stretching behind me.

Thinly upholstered chairs sit around a coffee table littered with out-of-date magazines. We take seats at right angles and I cross my legs to keep from bumping his knee. Jamie leans on his elbows, one hand covering the other, his mouth pressed to his knuckles. Stubble shades his jaw, and I can't help but notice the strong angle of the bone where it curves beneath his ear. I recall the warm scent of his skin. *Quit it, you pervert.* Am I really checking Jamie out in the middle of the greatest crisis of my life – his sister's life? *Besides, he doesn't want you here.*

"Look," he squints up from beneath his furrowed brow, "I don't know that it's a good idea for you to come up here every day." He reads my face and drops his gaze. "It's nothing personal, but things are complicated and Kitty needs–"

"Complicated how?"

"Until there's someone in custody for this." He opens his palms, choosing his words with care, "We need to keep the environment ... contained."

I can't agree more, but there's no way I'm giving up my free pass. "Kitty's one of my best friends, Jamie. If she wants me here, I'm here."

"It's not that simple."

"I can sit in the corridor. I won't get in anyone's way."

"It might not be safe."

I swallow. "You think the attack was personal?"

Jamie chews the inside of his lip. "Where were you?"

I stall at the sudden change of course.

"After the police came, I went upstairs to find you and Miriam but you were gone."

My mind races. I have no idea how Miriam got me out of the governor's mansion in the middle of all the hubbub. Did she sling me over her shoulder? "Um, Miriam took me home. I don't really remember. She said she messaged Kitty."

He searches my face, his expression so intent I can't look away. Flecks of charcoal, smoke and shadow, eyes to get lost in. "She never got to her phone."

I groan. "If I hadn't fainted–"

"It's not your fault. I didn't mean to imply that."

"I should've stayed home. I'd been dizzy all day. I haven't been sleeping well since Mom–"

"You've been through hell, Everton. It's completely understandable." He leans forwards and digs his fingers into his scalp. "I just thought you might have seen something. Or maybe Miriam might have seen something?"

"I'll ask her." I watch him with his head bowed, exhaustion and worry heavy about his shoulders. It's difficult to remember the old Jamie in the face of the new.

It's not only the trauma of what happened to his sister. I felt it when we met on the patio, a new air of sincerity, compassion, maturity? Something.

"The police want to make out it was attempted robbery." He looks up, his expression etched in disgust. "That's the governor in damage control, trying to keep his son out of the papers."

I stare, a prickling sensation at the back of my neck. "Richard?"

"You know him?"

"I met him at the party."

Jamie glowers. "He's a complete bastard."

"Do you think Richard had something to do with the attack on Kitty?" The prospect of a suspect almost makes me giddy.

"I don't know. We've got DNA, at least, skin under Kitty's nails."

I fight to hide the trembling that rocks through me at the thought of her fighting the Stray.

"We'll get a look at the security footage this afternoon, but I don't know what to think about Richard." He links his fingers and his knuckles whiten. "He hurt Kaylee last night."

I draw a blank. "Who? What happened?"

"She's a friend of Kitty's – of ours. She's been dating Richard – why, I'll never know. 'Someone' sexually assaulted her out in the grounds. It all seems to have gone down around the same time as the attack on Kitty. Apparently, Kaylee was pretty wasted."

I feel like I've just walked into a door. The beautiful girl with the sleek hair. "I saw them at the party, before I saw you. She was upset. Drinking. Richard was handing her champagne."

"She's not talking." Jamie's lips contract. "You don't want to know the rumours about Richard. Girls being paid to keep their mouths shut."

My skin crawls. "How did you find out?"

"Lila and Imogen, the girls from the patio, they were with Kaylee afterwards. She was a bit of mess. They told me what had happened. I spoke to the bloke who stopped the assault and carried her back to the house. Aiden someone. Says the guy got away."

Smack. Another door. I can't keep up with the sudden turns, and speak almost to myself. "Aiden doesn't like Richard."

"Doesn't mean he wouldn't lie to protect his boss," Jamie mutters, pauses and looks at me. "You know him?"

"He helped me shift Miriam's gear."

Jamie nods and frowns. "Apparently he's a stand-up guy. I'd like to believe it, but he's on Charles Dean's payroll and he won the governor's scholarship for Gainsborough. He's hardly going to bite the hand that feeds him, yeah?"

"And if Richard hurt Kaylee, you think he might have hurt Kitty?"

He growls. "I don't know, but it's all a bit of a bloody coincidence, isn't it?"

Jamie's suspicion slips seamlessly into mine. He's right. As innocuous as Aiden seemed on first impression he's now tainted by association, and the things Jamie said about Richard … I take the effortless step from imagining him as a regular son of a bitch to picturing him as a genetically modified one.

"Let me visit. Let me be here for her. I promise I won't get in the way."

He gives me a hard, searching look.

I put my hand on his, surprising myself with my boldness, impressed again by the immediate increase in electricity. I hold his gaze and project all my longing into the universe, willing him to relent. "Jamie, please."

Doubt troubles his eyes, worry and behind that … fear? I brace for "no", but then he swallows and sighs. "Fine."

I squeeze his hand once, let go and sit back. He frowns, flexing his fingers where I touched him, looking much older than his eighteen years. I chew my thumbnail, consumed by the new puzzle pieces, determined to form a suspect list.

Jamie looks at me. "Have you really forgiven me, then?"

Heat creeps up my face. "I'm sorry?"

"Everton." He draws my name out and arches his

eyebrow. "The unmentionable incident? Mistakes were made?"

I didn't have the energy to fake it. Instead, I roll my eyes and shrug. "I guess you were young and needed the money."

A weary smile tugs at his lips. "I won't offend your intelligence going back over the details of my part as the innocent pawn, however accurate and truthful that may be." He sits back, resting his head on the wall and closes his eyes. "No excuses."

I definitely don't recognise *this* Jamie; it's like being in a body-snatcher movie. "Terrible apology."

He smirks, cracks one eye open. "That's three years of rehearsal for you."

In a small compartment of my brain – the compartment in denial about the nightmare of my new life – the urge to laugh is almost irresistible. "Who are you?"

"People change, yeah?" He keeps his eyes closed. "You've changed, Everton. So have I."

I cringe inwardly at the thought of my new boobs and I'm glad he can't hear the frenetic thump of my pulse. I wonder how different I seem. He's right though. I'm not the girl I was at fourteen. Without question the last six months have altered me at a foundational level. The last twelve hours have apparently altered me at a DNA level, which seems to alter every damn thing altogether. I stare at the clock on the wall. It's only seven-thirty and I want to lie down.

At the end of the corridor the elevator chimes, the doors open and Miriam steps out in her running gear, hair pulled back in a ponytail, face flush with colour and war in her eyes.

HISTORY

I lean my face into my hands. I'm only dimly aware of the traffic backing up on the road, too consumed by the physiological shock of walking out of the hospital. After no sleep and the trauma of the night, feeling the tether thin and finally evaporate has unhinged me. In the car, Miriam's reprimands for not waiting at home set me swearing and ranting that she was *deliberately keeping me from Kitty!* I have calmed down a little since then, though I still tremble and pant through my nose.

"I'm sorry I was away so long." Her tone is careful, not wanting to set off another avalanche, and I look up. One hand on the steering wheel, she digs in her pocket, retrieving a small roll of electrical tape and a smooth round disc. A magnet. "Here, rip some tape. Stick the magnet in the middle."

Initially blindsided, I remember something she said about scrambling receptors. I take the tape and the disc, my heart racing, like the Affinity Project is watching me break protocol. I fumble through it with shaking hands then pass her a small loaded strip. It's creepily fascinating to watch as she fastens it at the base of her skull, securing the edges along her hairline. "They upgraded my tracker. This will let me talk freely for short intervals."

I just stare.

"Carolyn was concerned about my signal being so high. There's normally a cool-down period to regenerate before you become susceptible to a new Spark. It's protocol to run tests when they find anomalies. I guess she picked up on the influence of your signal."

"She didn't suspect me?"

"I told her you had shown no signs of priming, but I think we have to accept that sooner or later they'll send a Warden to confirm that."

I'm relieved she's not whispering, but the jargon still makes me impatient. "I thought Carolyn was the Warden?"

"She's my Watcher, like a handler dealing with a field agent. I report to her. She uses a device called a grader to read my signal. Wardens monitor territories for … 'disturbances in the force' and they don't need a grader, they sense you because their own signals are amplified and their sensitivity is highly developed."

I know she's referring to the acronyms my head can't hold, ETR, Electro-telepathic something-or-other and

AFS, the Frequency Sensitivity thing. I visualise blank-eyed psychics with glowing temporal lobes lurking at the city limits, poised to move in. I shudder. "What are they, though – Shields, like us?"

"Mostly they're the surviving operatives of the first generation trial."

Goosebumps prickle my skin. "Survivors?"

The morning commuter traffic inches forwards and she keeps her eyes on the road. "In the first generation trial, adult soldiers – who thought they were being 'screened' for special ops training – were given a 'vaccine'. Well that's what they told them, but it was Optimal. Only one in a hundred responded to the treatment. Those that didn't were sent back to the ranks, thinking they'd missed a career opportunity. Those that showed signs of sensitivity became the first generation of agents. Seventy or eighty of them, I think. Not like now. The number has increased exponentially with each successive generation."

Increased exponentially. In my mind the world is suddenly swollen with genetically engineered psychos. I wonder how many I have shared a bus with, waited in line next to, browsed beside in a bookshop, supermarket, clothing store …

"They kept the first generation of agents in observation clinics, waiting for the optimised 'strengths and tendencies' to arise. Two affinities emerged in the process: the defender/

protectors and the attacker/pursuers. Shields and Strikers."

I bite back the urge to say something snide about Affinity's obsession with alliteration. I don't want to interrupt.

"It was a bumpy start. Only a few matured. It wasn't good enough for the suits – with their calculators and megalomania. They wanted a reliable trigger that would spur a stronger immediate response. The lab coats developed a catalyst enzyme, gathered control subjects and injected them with it."

My mouth is dry, but I force myself to say it, "Sparks?"

She nods, changing gear as the traffic begins to gain speed. "No side effects. For the Sparks, I mean. None of the extraordinary frequency benefits found in Shields or Strikers. Those with the enzyme were only meant to emit a signal that draws those primed to trigger. They took the soldiers exhibiting signs of priming – groups of ten – and brought them into observation clinics with the Sparks."

Repulsed by the wrongness of it all, I mutter, "Sparks were just what, walking lighter fluid?"

"Pretty much. During the clinics, Affinity learned that: physical touch was necessary to activate the primed; Sparks can only create a bonded triplicate – one Striker and one Shield per Spark at a time; Strikers always trigger first; and of course they discovered the Fixation Effect. Aggression levels went through the roof. Sparks died. Strikers became known as the Stray."

"I'm not sure they needed a name change. Striker's disturbing enough." I want to scrub my brain out but I need to understand. "How do we get from soldiers killing each other in a secret compound to lunatics roaming the streets? Was it the pregnancy drugs?"

"Supplements, actually, designed for multiple-birth pregnancies – that was the second generation trial. It was supposed to be the cure-all. Breed out the Fixation Effect by starting inside the womb. Clueless doctors prescribed the vitamins to civilian women pregnant with twins. Each tablet laced with Optimal two-point-o and the newly purified Spark enzyme. They believed they could circumvent the Stray mutation, like a quasi-natural selection process where unborn babies, or 'malleable untainted pre-forms', would bond to the element that best complimented their DNA."

"So the planet is crawling with mutant killers?"

"Not crawling, no. It was a limited production in select locations here and the UK, and like the adult test subjects, those that responded were rare."

It's not much of a relief and I stare at the busy road. "This is nuts."

"Clearly. But they had a vision for high-profit private security. Strikers available for short-term contracts to retrieve, acquire and eliminate. Shields available for protection, containment and secure delivery of sensitive property and or persons. They had enough interest from their investors to finance it and they believed they had the right technology and the ability to monitor it. This second generation – my generation – wouldn't surface until late adolescence. They spent a decade or so setting up compounds in strategic places for monitoring and orientation and appointed Wardens over districts to identify Sparks and those with AFS."

"They expected you guys to just agree to work for them?"

"I never had to deal with that particular problem, but I believe they had a whole system of persuasion, coercion and rewards. Psychological and physical."

It's like a glimpse into an alternate version of my life, an unthinkably horrible version that arbitrary chance has kept me from. Like avoiding a car crash by leaving a minute too late or too soon. Of course the current reality is dire enough. I briefly fantasise about throwing the car door open and pitching myself headlong into the advancing traffic. The fantasy is immediately quashed by a confronting sense of violation. How could I abandon Kitty to her fate? The idea is unthinkable.

"Unfortunately, the Fixation Effect was worse and the Stray mutation made their signals undetectable. Only the Shield who completed the triplicate could sense the specific threat to their Spark. That's when Affinity had a change in management."

"So the whole thing – *the whole thing* – was a complete and utter waste of time that results in lives being destroyed for absolutely nothing?"

"About sums it up."

There's a moment of time in which no amount of swearing will express my profound disgust. Finally, I mutter, "I'm not a twin." It's a little late for grasping at loopholes, but I can't help it.

"No, but your mom and I were. Once Optimal is in the system it gets passed down the gene pool like blue eyes or curly hair. Sure, there are more twins in the game than most but it's not a prerequisite. You're a third-generation Shield which is more complicated and unpredictable than the generations before because you aren't a drug baby, you're the next step on the evolutionary ladder."

I squeeze my temples and close my eyes but it's better to have them open because my imagination isn't a fun place to be.

"Each time, down the line, there's no guarantee how a pre-form will respond. It's rare to get any reaction at all. Usually, it's just a normal kid that carries the gene like a time bomb for the next generation."

"And what if I hadn't come along?"

Her knuckles tighten briefly on the steering wheel and

her shoulders sag with her sigh. "Many Sparks die without a Shield. Probably more than we know."

I groan and shake my head like I can throw the thought off. "And what if you had responded to Kitty before me? Would you be her Shield?"

"There's no guarantee I would have been a match. I wasn't even drawn to her. If a Warden had come through and read Kitty's signal, they would've sent contract agents to make contact in the hopes that one of them would respond to her, but she's bonded to you now and you're the only one who'll be able to sense the threat."

Again the enormity of it floods over me, a cold wash. *The only one.*

LAIR

"Lock the door."

I slide the darkroom door closed behind me, set the latch and follow Miriam in, brushing through the gap in the rough blackout curtain. On the far wall, she taps the key code for the utility cupboard and opens it. She moves an old box of negatives and reaches in to the back of the shelf. At the muffled clunking sound of shifting metallic cogs, my stomach lurches and I grip the counter.

"Hence the out of bounds," Miriam says. She pulls the shelf and it swings forwards, revealing a recess with a staircase leading not right to the basement but left beneath the front of the house where, as far as I know, there should be nothing. She steps down and a light flicks on. It shocks me to see the stairs go much lower than the basement. I follow after her, almost holding my breath on the steep metal stairs.

The room opens out into a wide, clinical space. The polished concrete floor has a large blue gym mat in the middle and a bank of mirrors lines the wall in front of it. It's just as I saw in Miriam's memory, when she growled at me for opening her darkroom cupboard. Four climbing ropes hang in a square formation from the high ceiling, their knots hooked against the wall. In one corner there's a treadmill, rowing machine, weight lifting equipment and even a suspended punching bag. Beside the innocuous gym gear sits a wooden sparing dummy and objects that look like they've been lifted from the set of a martial arts movie. I glance at Miriam. Her brief smile is self-conscious.

"How long has this been here?"

"When I took the place I had it built. Home gym."

My eyebrows lift. "Batcave, more like."

A long desk sits against the far wall with a computer and LCD screen. Filing cabinets crowd underneath. A mobile corkboard backs the red brick wall, covered with newspaper clippings and photographs. But directly beneath the metal staircase lodges a glass-fronted cabinet. Guns and ammo. I clutch the cold stair rail. "I have to completely rethink my opinion of you." The weirdness of having known Miriam my whole life and yet never really *knowing* her unnerves me. I can't take my eyes off the artillery. "What are you doing with this stuff?"

"Come on, half of America has a gun cabinet." She sees my scowl. "Don't worry, they don't get out much, but a good girl scout is always prepared."

"How many girl scouts are packing heat?" I wrap my arms around my waist and walk slowly onto the mat. "Ninja zone?"

"Something like." She watches my face in the mirror. "You'll start with reflex training. Formal martial arts comes later."

I can't imagine it and I try not to look at our twin reflections; we're too alike. It's disturbing seeing my future watching me with worried eyes. "So?" I want everything, all the answers to my questions, even after the brain-clogging history lesson on the ride from the hospital.

Miriam crosses to the treadmill, flicks the power on at the wall and nods me over. "We need to get you moving first. The more we stimulate your adrenaline, increase your metabolism, the better. Your strength and stamina will have skyrocketed already and if you don't get moving, the pins and needles will start driving you nuts."

I can't deny the zip-zapping has become uncomfortable and the prospect of action makes it hard to sulk. I pull my hoodie off, tingling with anticipation. Do I really have more strength and stamina? I want to test it.

"Jump on. You can warm up with a jog." Miriam taps the arrow keys and the motor whirs. I hop on the conveyor and hold on to the handrail until I find my pace. Moving feels good, really good.

She nods, knowingly.

"This is why you always go running?"

"Therapy for body and soul, trust me," she lifts her voice above the whir of the treadmill.

"So where did Carolyn take you?"

"I don't actually know. They always put you to sleep before transportation. You wake up in the facility, somewhere underground."

"Underground?" I grip the handrail so I can look at her as I jog.

"I was only there a few hours. I'm guessing the rest of the time is spent travelling, maybe by air. I really don't know."

"It's big?"

"Pretty big. Bigger than an airplane hangar. There are different levels. Departments. A hospital. Training rooms. Sleeping quarters. It's where you'll go when they take you in."

I blow through my lips. "What did the tests show?"

"Just that my signal's taking longer to cool than usual."

"Because of me?"

"Fluctuations in signal strength aren't unheard of, especially during periods of high stress. April's only been gone a month or so and I've been settling you in. I let them believe it's post-traumatic stress."

I ignore the pang in my chest.

She touches the back of her neck, checking the magnet and tape are still in place.

"The tracker thing – they can find you but you don't want them to find me?"

"Not yet. For Kitty's sake it's best if they don't know about you." She waves at the treadmill for me to get moving. Distracted, I nearly trip again and she taps the arrow key, increasing the speed to a proper run, forcing me to concentrate or risk wiping out. She waits for me to find my rhythm. She really has to raise her voice now, to compete with the motor and my pounding feet. "It's hard to explain. For them, we're the assets. Sparks are collateral damage, useful only because they bring the Shields to light. I mean they want you to succeed, for sure, but the survival of a Spark is not a primary objective."

She presses on before I can voice outrage. "There are two primary objectives. Acquisition of assets is the first. Shields are the assets. They monitor, train, protect and utilise the assets for the second primary objective. Deactivating Strays. Saving innocent lives is gravy."

I duck the migraine material with another question, struggling with the idea of the Affinity Project requiring anything from me. "They'll expect to utilise *me*?"

"I suppose it's waste not, want not. Mop up the mess and make the most of the assets. Only fully matured Shields," she gestures to herself, "are used for contract assignments." She leans in to check the readout on the panel and nods in approval. "You're not even puffing."

I hadn't noticed, too busy taking it all in. I remember what she said about Wardens sending contract agents when they sensed an active Spark and it dawns on me. "That's what you do. They send you to a town to shake hands with some poor bastard with an invisible target on his head and hope you'll bond to his signal?"

"Yep."

"That was Phil?"

She nods.

I shake my head. "Did you actually do a photo shoot?"

"I did. Vocational matching's a bonus."

"But they don't do it for the sake of the Spark?"

"For the Affinity Project, saving Phil would be counted as the indirect benefit of fulfilling a primary objective, eliminating the Stray."

I want to punch something.

"It is what it is, kiddo. I don't get involved with the politics. Besides, there's no democracy in Affinity. There's protocol and that's that."

"You mean rules."

"Big rules." She taps the arrow key, forcing me into top speed. I let out a cry, nearly losing my balance. Righting myself, I lengthen my stride. The motor rumbles. I've never felt so energised. Miriam smiles. "Feels pretty great, huh?"

It does. After months of inactivity, I'm surprised my muscles haven't atrophied. I thought for sure my thighs and calves would burn in minutes and I'd have to hit the stop button to collapse on the console red-faced and gasping. But the burn doesn't come. My lungs fill and empty with ease. I realise my body is simply cruising and if I wasn't limited by the capacity of the motor, I could, in fact, go faster. Much faster.

"One of the most important rules we live by is never allowing our Spark to know they're in danger."

The rightness of it seizes me. Imagining the fear Kitty would experience if she knew what threatened her life is completely intolerable. "Good. That's good."

"I wish I could tell you it's for the benefit of the Spark. I suppose in an indirect way it is, but for Affinity it's just part of protecting the organisation."

I scowl at the mercenary truth, but another thought demands my attention. "How do you protect someone without letting them know they're in danger?"

She gives me a sad smile. "It's an art form, kiddo. You'll learn. You have a major advantage. Kitty's your friend. You have an excuse to be near her."

It doesn't feel like a sufficient answer but my questions are backing up. "Aren't you breaking the rules – not telling them I'm active? I don't understand how that helps Kitty."

"Most newly triggered Shields don't have the benefit of a live-in mentor," she almost has to shout. "Most of us think we're losing our minds and some of us actually do.

When your DNA Sparks there's a period of time before the Wardens pick up on the signal, track you down and take you in. Usually after your first Spark."

I listen keenly, pumping my arms and legs.

"It takes time. In the beginning your frequency sensitivity is weak. The more exposure you have to your Spark the stronger your signal and sensitivity become. If I told them you'd triggered, they would take you in now and put you through orientation."

"Like training and stuff?" I call over the motor, beginning to breathe more deeply. "Wouldn't that be a good thing?"

"Orientation takes a month, minimum. You wouldn't be allowed to leave the compound."

I put one hand on the rail to steady myself. "But surely if they knew Kitty was–"

"No. They wouldn't let you leave, for any reason."

I punch the stop button. The motor groans and I jump off the back of the conveyor. "They'd leave her unprotected?"

"You're the only one tuned to her signal. If they took you, I could watch her but I'd have no way of knowing when the threat was coming."

Momentarily speechless, I shake my head, unable to think of any curse foul enough for the situation. "That can't happen. They can't find out."

She holds my gaze, pity in her eyes. "Come over here."

She crosses to the sparring dummy, pulling it out into the middle of the floor. "Watch me closely and concentrate." She shoves one of the protruding handles. The dummy whirs on its base. She brings her hand up to stop the spinning; a thwack of wood against bone. Then she lifts her knee, tapping one of the sticks with her foot so that it spins in the other direction. An arm whips towards her face and she stops it with a deft block. "It's only a matter of time, Evie. They know you're living with me now and they keep a close eye on families who've produced AFS. They will have been monitoring you since you were fourteen or fifteen."

"They've been watching me?" I shiver. "What am I going to do?"

"Pay attention." She repeats the maneuver with the dummy, creating a rhythmic muted smack with each turn. "It's not like the countryside is crawling with agents. Until now, I was the only registered Shield in the district. Carolyn's been my Watcher for years. I've never given her reason to doubt me and I've been in for a debrief. That will buy us a little time before they sweep the area again."

"I don't understand."

"I know." She stops the spinning dummy and leans her head on it. "They don't send out a timetable to let you know, hey, we'll be coming your way March, August and December, but they're regular and mostly they'll track homicides. New Hampshire isn't what you'd call a hotspot.

Plus, I've just completed an assignment. So for now they won't be looking for a high frequency here."

"Timing? Luck?" I throw my hands up. "That's all that's to keep them from coming for me?"

"Our location works in your favour." She starts up again, striking, blocking, grunting with each thwack as the dummy spins back and forth. "Water blocks our signals. Large bodies of water. Rivers, oceans, lakes, springs, that sort of thing. But even rain or a running tap can distort your senses, make it hard to pick up small sounds. A Warden would need to cross the Border River into town to feel your signal."

"That makes no sense."

"It's the facts, kiddo. When I'm active, I can feel a Warden's approach. Not sure about in between times."

In between times. Life ruled by mutant DNA.

Miriam steps up her speed and what looks at first like solid form quickly becomes fierce intensity, ducking, twisting, her arms blurring. She spins and thrusts her foot against the thick mid-section. The dummy careens towards me. With no time to cry out or even think, I jump back and stop it with my foot. The impact shoves me and I land in a partial squat, bug-eyed at my involuntary response.

"See you got the boobs, then."

I straighten up, adrenaline thrumming in my arms and legs. "They're because of this?"

"It's like you're on fast forward." She frowns. "Most newbies develop gradually."

Indignation makes me hot and I spin, in an echo of my aunt's maneuver, collecting the dummy with a loud smack, sending it spiralling back towards her. The ease and accuracy of the move shocks me.

She stops it with one hand. "*See.* Rapid Kinetic Learning. Let's see if you can do it with something else." But she doesn't explain. "And I meant your frequency sensitivity, not your boobs."

I purse my lips in disgust.

"You're not going to like this, but your magical new C-cup is an intentional design element, like a propagation of the species thing." She swallows. "The gene modifier always finds the strongest candidates. Inevitably they're smart, good-looking, physical people. Once the modification happens, these things are enhanced. As your frequency sensitivity matures you get smarter, stronger and better looking."

I splutter, unable to find words.

"Not very PC, huh?"

"But – but I'm not – I mean, I'm just me." My cheeks flame in the mirror.

"While you're choking, you should know about one of the side effects of our condition." She can't look at me; instead she pulls the sparring dummy back into the corner with the other equipment. "Your body's in overdrive on every level. Part of the design plan. Your reproductive potential quadruples." Her head pops up from behind the dummy and her cheeks redden. "Your body will basically start chucking multiple eggs at your uterus every cycle, which becomes weekly instead of monthly."

My mouth opens. "Tell me you're joking."

She grimaces. "You'll bleed for only an hour one day a week. It's a nightmare, the cramps are a bitch but at least they're solid warning the wave's about to hit." She turns her back, browsing a display of throwing knives. "Then there are the pheromones."

"Pheromones?" I say numbly, too grossed out by the thought of a weekly power-period to have the stamina for any more horrible surprises.

She removes a couple of knives with slim, leather-wrapped handles and gleaming four-inch blades and passes them to me. Their weight in my hands gives me a strange distracting thrill. Taking another pair for herself, she turns me to face the target by the stairs. On a wooden backboard she has attached a black paper silhouette of a man's upper body, already scarred with multiple entry wounds. "Watch me closely."

Left foot forwards, she extends both arms, left hand flat against the blade as she aims. Bringing the knife back by her ear, she points at the target, leans her weight on her back foot and launches the knife like she's fired a bullet. A blur and it lodges in the centre of the target's chest with a loud *pock*.

My spine zip-zaps with anticipation. "Again. Show me again."

"Evie, listen." She draws a deep breath. "When I say, pheromones, what I'm trying to say is from now on your scent is going to attract more attention than you're used to. From men – boys, guys generally."

I forget the knives and gape at her. "I'm in *heat*? Like a *dog*?"

"No! That's disgusting."

"Yeah?" I want to cover myself and hide. "Will they come up and *sniff* me?"

"You won't necessarily smell any different. Just ... more appealing."

I turn my back, yank my collar open and inhale deeply through my nose. I can't smell anything different about my skin. I'm about to ignite with more swearing and ranting when a startling memory arrests me. Jamie. The heady aroma when he carried me upstairs. I gasp, bringing my fists either side of my head, knives and all. "Jamie – Jamie, he's got this incredible scent – his skin – you think he's ...?"

Miriam gives me a hard look but the suggestion doesn't faze her. "Clearly the gene's in the family. It's a possibility.

Jamie's certainly," she clears her throat, "symmetrical." She assumes her stance before the target, aiming and throwing with ease. "But there's no way of knowing. Just because Kitty's a Spark, it's no guarantee that Jamie's anything."

It is too late; the wild idea has hold of me. I rake back over our meeting at the hospital; the intense appraisal as he questioned me. A memory springs up. "He touched my neck! At the hospital, he – he gripped me here and squeezed. You think he might have been checking?"

"It's not like you could ask him, kiddo." She comes behind me and takes me by the shoulders, positioning me before the target. "Recall what you saw and let your body replicate the moves."

She steps back and I adjust my stance, preoccupied by thoughts of Jamie.

"There are rules. If Jamie's an Affinity agent, then he knows the rules too. Anonymity is the big one and they police it. It's the first tenet they drum into you at orientation and trust me, Affinity will not tolerate indiscretion and won't hesitate to discipline you if you break the rules. Come on, aim."

I have to set Miriam's warning aside to concentrate on the throw. I draw my arm back and instinct provides an easy supply of instruction for my muscles, like my brain simply lifts it from a database. An irrational sense of confidence grips me and I shift my weight, pivot and release the knife.

It soars along the same trajectory, landing only an inch beneath Miriam's. *Pock.* An electric charge burns through me. "Whoa."

"Ha!" Miriam claps. "Excellent. Again."

I don't throw. I turn and look her right in the eyes. "You're breaking the rules. What will they do to you if they find out?"

She looks back to the target. "Don't worry about me, Evangeline."

"I don't want you to get in trouble."

"I know what I'm doing. Now, aim."

I'm not reassured but I resume my stance, replicating the exact same steps as before, landing my throw directly between my first and hers above it. The buzz is undeniable but fleeting. "There's no out, is there?"

She doesn't answer.

I spread my arms. "This is my life."

Her lips part but close again.

The injustice is crippling. I shake my head. "And Kitty's life."

"No," her voice lifts. "No. That's one good thing. The Spark only has one ignition in them. You deactivate the Stray and that's it. Kitty will never go through it again."

Fierce hope rises in me then fades almost instantly. So what if I can run faster, block a sparing dummy or throw a damn knife? All fluky beginner stuff. I felt the brutal reality and sheer violence of Miriam's alley memory, the total certainty it requires to respond the way she responded. I sit on the padded bench of the weights machine. "I have to kill him?"

She bites her lips. "You can't reason with the Stray, Evie. They don't stop."

"I'm not concerned for his wellbeing, Miriam." Feelings churn inside me that, pre-Spark, would have made me recoil. "I'm worried I'll be too useless to do it."

She nods brusquely, no judgement in her eyes – she knows what I feel. "You need to be aware that until this is over, you're going to be super paranoid. Anyone who looks at Kitty twice is going to seem like a threat, but you can't make assumptions. You have no idea who she's had contact with." She goes and removes the knives one by one. "It's a mistake to rely on anything other than the signals you sense. Think of it as a bandwidth you're scanning, interpreting what comes through. Unfortunately, when you're new, your sensitivity isn't strong or reliable – you'll pick up a lot of static. That's why you have to train hard and stimulate your frequency sensitivity."

After my visit to the hospital, I know paranoia is a factor. I can't imagine ever feeling normal again and hate the absence of the tether. I miss its reassuring pulse.

Miriam returns the knives to the display and goes over to the corkboard. She points to a photograph of a teenage boy. I draw close and stare at him. He grins through his messy brown hair. Scribbled in the corner, his name, Callum Greene. He doesn't look much older than thirteen. A black line of marker pen crosses through his picture. Next to this, a sticky note with a question mark. "He was my first Spark."

I hug my waist for something to hold on to. "He's so young."

"He was fifteen. I was twenty. He sold me coffee in a cafe in New York." Her mouth presses tight. "I couldn't save him. I didn't know what was happening to me. He was stabbed in the neck on his way home from work on a Saturday night."

It's like having a bucket of ice poured down my back. If she failed, what hope is there for me? For Kitty?

The next Spark, a woman in her mid-twenties. Lauren Sutton. Beside this, a photocopy of a driver's licence. Jason Lyle. His image, crossed out with a red marker.

"This guy was her Stray?"

She barely nods.

"And you got him?"

"I did."

There has to be nearly thirty, maybe thirty-five photographs of Sparks. Eight have black lines through them – the ones who didn't make it. They're closer to the top. Beside them are sticky notes with question marks.

The rest are shots of survivors and the Strays who've been crossed out with red marker.

Something fierce rises in my chest and I reach for Miriam's hand, staring at the board, the evidence of her DNA. "Show me how to save Kitty."

She turns to look at me, her brown eyes warm and deep. "We'll train during the day and run in the evening."

"In the dark?"

"Don't you want to check out your night vision?"

DELAY

"But Mr Gallagher, I – I explained to Jamie that I would stay out of the way." I stand rigid in the hall, trying not to crush the telephone in my hand. My heart pounds like it might break loose from its valves. I cannot be having this conversation. The thought of prolonged separation from Kitty is unacceptable.

Leonard Gallagher has the gift of immovability. Even if I let go of social restraint and flew into a full panic-induced rage, he'd still respond in the same polite unwavering tone. "Things have changed, Evangeline. Jamie didn't know the doctors would place restrictions. It's enough that detectives will be coming in and out over the next couple of days."

"I can wait in the corridor. I could–"

"No." The line crackles. "She needs rest, Evie. I'm asking you to respect my decision."

Arguing would only make me sound unreasonable and offensive, but holding back feels like swallowing a stone.

"Of course. I'm sorry, Mr Gallagher. I don't want to upset anyone."

Leonard sighs, a soul-deep sound. "Kitty's lucky to have friends who care as much as you do and we appreciate it."

My throat constricts. "Jamie said you were going to review the CCTV footage from the ball. Did it show anything?"

"It – it was very difficult to make out; the police are having it analysed."

"What about the DNA test?"

"It's too soon for results. Evie, I promise we'll keep you posted, but you might not hear from us until Kitty's been discharged and is settled in at home."

I close my eyes. "A week?"

"At the least."

There are parting words but the white noise in my head devours everything.

I hang up the phone and lean against the bookcase, closing my eyes to reach for Kitty; waiting for the peak in fear, the looming shadow. Nothing comes, nothing but static. It doesn't comfort me. I hate the feeling I'm missing something.

Miriam's head appears out the glass door of her studio. "Who was that?"

"Leonard. Doctors say no visits."

"Oh."

We look at each other in silence.

I straighten up. "Can I take the car? I can sit in the parking lot."

"That's ridiculous. She's safe there." Miriam steps into the hall and closes the studio door with a clap. "How many times do we have to go over this? You need to concentrate on training, stimulating your frequency so that you can read the bandwidth. It's the only thing you can trust. There's a difference between run-of-the-mill anxiety and the kind of signal that will build when Kitty's in danger."

Familiar anger flares inside me, the combination of frustration and fear. "Waiting across town for blind panic to hit me while some psycho guts her in her bed doesn't strike me as an efficient use of time!"

She closes her eyes as though searching for strength. "This is not the only time in your life you will feel this way. You still have to live, be a functioning human being, not some crazy vigilante."

"I want to go back over the photos again."

"You've been over them and over them. It's pointless, a dangerous distraction that only feeds your paranoia." She looks at her watch. "I have a bus load of models arriving in half an hour. I suggest you go downstairs and work out, and when I'm finished we'll do some reflex training."

She disappears inside the studio and I stand staring in the hall.

A week. Maybe more.

Twelve hours apart from Kitty has almost driven me mad. I can't imagine seven days of that kind of torture. I need the tether, that pulse that tells me she lives and breathes.

The Virgin sits beside me on her shelf, mournful eyes downcast, her blue robe filmed in dust already, lint at her feet. I wipe her carefully, my fingers trembling, wishing I'd prayed when I had the chance.

DINNER

The Gallaghers' rambling estate merges with the forest but the huge stone house sits on a rise near the south-east boundary, surrounded by gardens and manicured lawns. It has deep-set panelled windows, French doors opening onto sweeping porches, an elegant balcony running the length of the top floor and a slate roof. Less ostentatious than the governor's mansion and all the more impressive for its restraint – grand not grandiose.

The sun has nearly set but we're early on account of my seismic reaction to Miriam's dawdling. We sit silent and sullen in the idling car, waiting for the gates to open. I grit my teeth. The gates take too long, like everything that has placed itself between Kitty and me in the past *fourteen* days: drip-fed information, the Gallaghers' responses to calls and messages, endless days and sleepless nights and even time itself. Molasses slow. Then, finally, an invitation to dinner. I picture jumping out of the passenger seat, forcing my way through the increasing gap, charging up the long curving drive and launching myself through the dining room windows …

"Please don't break the armrest," Miriam mutters.

I release the groaning plastic and fold my hands in my lap, bouncing my knee in time with my pins and needles, zip-zap-zip-zap-zip-zap. I grip my knuckles and wince at the sting beneath my bandaids. I'd taken skin off each joint and the calluses inside my palms were just as bad – combination of rope burn and reflex training. At least my thumb has healed from the kitchen surgery.

I fidget with the hem of my dress, counting in my head until the gates are wide enough for Miriam's car. "Finally!" I lean forwards in my seat.

"Play it cool," Miriam says. "Remember what we talked about."

I doubt she can drive any slower, making me too irritated to enjoy the splendour of the Gallagher's estate. We pull in by the front steps and I'm out of the car before Miriam has turned off the engine. I have so much adrenaline in my body I don't notice the aches and pains from training. Miriam fishes in her purse and fusses with the collar of her shirt, seeming to invent new means of stalling. I grind my teeth, choking my purse between my hands until she gets out of the car and joins me on the drive, holding a pack with a selection of photos from the ball.

Halfway up the steps, it hits me, a magnetic pulse that hooks behind my bellybutton. The tether. I grab Miriam's arm. Tears spring in my eyes with the rush of irrational relief. I already know Kitty survived her stay in the hospital and returned home safely, but I still shake, overwhelmed by the proof of life. Immediately, my consciousness of the bandwidth heightens, like someone has turned the volume up. I don't even mind the static.

"Even from here?" Miriam says.

The door opens and there stands Barb, fastening a pearl earring, a faltering smile on her lips. Behind her carefully applied make-up she looks drawn. I dab at my eyes, trying not to smudge my own make-up. I have shadows to hide too.

"Goodness," she says. "Come in, come in. We're all running a bit behind, I'm afraid."

"Sorry, Evie's been itching to get here." Miriam mounts the porch, embracing Barb, kissing her cheek.

Barb looks teary eyed and shakes her head. "Sorry. Seeing you both – it makes me …"

"It's all right," Miriam says. "We all miss April."

I'm so wired I don't even feel the pang of grief. I follow Miriam into the vast foyer, gleaming, white-panelled woodwork, pale walls, sweeping central staircase, and a triple-height ceiling with a crystal chandelier. There are two sets of double doors to the left and right of the staircase. The first on the left lead to a formal dining room and out of sight beyond that, the kitchen. Second is the ballroom but its huge glass-panelled sliders are closed. A drawing room, living room and conservatory are through the first set of doors on the right, and Leonard pops his head out of the last set of doors, a phone pressed to his ear. He waves, makes an apologetic face and disappears again into his study.

"He's on the line to his brother." Barb's mouth thins. "Knowing Jeremy, it might take awhile. Why don't you come into the living room while we wait for the others. Jamie only just got in. He's been running on Allesford Ridge."

I couldn't sit and wait if she paid me. "Can I go up and see Kitty?"

"Oh, um."

I move towards the stairs before I register Barb's hesitation and Miriam's warning look.

"I'm sure she won't be long," Barb says.

"I'll let her know we're here." I bound up the stairs as though the tether reels me in like a fishing line.

"Well, I suppose," Barb's voice peters out before I make the landing. Miriam murmurs something apologetic and I head left to the family wing. I haven't been up here in three years but I know Kitty's room is the first on the left and Jamie's is at the end. Their parents have an apartment-sized suite on the right, running the length of the wing.

One of Kitty's double doors stands partly open. I have to stop in the hall, close my eyes and exhale before knocking.

I tap and call, "Hey, it's me," then nudge the door.

Kitty is at her desk in a casual blue dress with a high collar that disappears inside her foam neck support. She sits up, startled and closes her pen inside the cover of a brown journal. "Evie?" She glances at her clock and rises from her seat, pulling open the top drawer of her desk and sliding the journal in. "You're here early." She locks the drawer then slips the key into her pocket.

I stand on the threshold, taking in the stiffness and self-consciousness of her movements, trying to keep myself from running and squeezing the life out of her.

"Like my new foam?" She still sounds husky and though she makes a face as if it's a joke, her eyes water.

"Better than the full brace."

"Not by much."

The airy room hasn't changed from how I remembered it. A polished floor with a Gallagher textiles rug. The decor, white on white with raspberry hints in the exquisite drapes and quilt from their soft furnishings division. Big French doors, the balcony beyond. Hardbacks line an orderly bookcase and an old Audrey Hepburn movie poster hangs framed on the wall. I grin, close the door behind me and cross the floor, intending to hug her. She moves to the other side of the bed, tucks her hair behind her ears and brushes her hands down her dress, her eyes focusing on the pile of sweaters on her quilt. "Sorry about the run-around." she says, as though trying to come across offhand rather than embarrassed. "We're all a bit crap at returning calls."

I stop by her desk and shake my head, trying to come across easy-going rather than agonised, knowing full well I made a nuisance of myself, texting, leaving messages at the hospital and on their home line. I stare at the bruising that has yellowed around her eye. "Sorry, I guess I was worried."

"Good grief, don't be sorry. It's lovely." She picks through the pile and fishes out a light sweater and makes awkward work of trying to get it over her head. "It's been a bit mad with the police and so many bloody interviews and the doctors banging on about resting and whatnot."

"Can I help you?" I take a couple of steps around the bed, anxious she might strain herself.

"No!" She backs away with the sweater only halfway on.

I stop, surprised by her tone.

"Sorry." She gives a tremulous laugh. "But I have to learn to do these things by myself. I'm never going to come right if I let everybody treat me like an invalid, am I?"

"I guess not." I move back, feeling awkward and unsure. "And they're happy with your progress then? The doctors, I mean."

Kitty tugs the sweater into place, hair mussed, pink in the face and red-eyed. "Well, they let me leave."

The bedroom door opens, producing a gust of air. Jamie walks in, pulling a blue shirt on over a white T-shirt. I catch a glimpse of black ink circling his left bicep. Tattoos? His eyes are cautious, shifting from me to Kitty and back again. "I heard the car," he says. "I was going to tell Kitty to get a move on but here you are."

My consciousness of Jamie almost surprises me. With the potency of Kitty's signal, I expected to find it difficult to concentrate on anything else, but Jamie seems to fill the room. He steps past me, heat radiating from his skin – that faint aroma matching the one from my memory – to stand beside Kitty and put his arm around her shoulders. His size only reinforces to me how small and vulnerable she is and my chest constricts.

Is it me, or does everything seem off? I wonder if my emotional vertigo is infecting everyone around me.

"You ready?" Jamie asks.

"Just need to fix my hair." Kitty squeezes her brother's waist. Even the physical affection strikes me as weird. The twins have never been particularly huggy with each other. "Why don't you take Evie down and get her a soda or something. I won't be long and then I'll check on the dinner."

"She's gone all Master Chef." Jamie raises his eyebrows.

"Fills the hours of my solitary confinement," Kitty says, again attempting, and failing, to sound offhand.

He releases her and crosses to the door, holding it for me. I get the distinct impression I'm being ushered out. My pins and needles burn and my mouth feels dry. "I could use a drink."

* * *

"Miriam says she's got you running, Evangeline." Barb sits at the end of the table, shifting her cutlery with her finger, as though measuring for perfect alignment. "Jamie runs, don't you, dear?"

Jamie sits with his back to the French doors that overlook the garden. Miriam and I sit opposite the twins. I imagine the seating arrangement has been designed to give us the best view, but it's dark outside now and even if the sun were blazing, my eyes wouldn't be on Barb's garden. Kitty and, for different reasons, Jamie are too distracting. He looks up at the sound of his name. "You tried the ridge?"

I shake my head, turning to my aunt. "You'll have to show me."

"We mostly do the reserve," Miriam says, "since we can get to it through the backyard. It's not as steep but the terrain is nice and rough. Keeps you on your toes."

"Hard to really get your stride though," Jamie says.

Miriam shrugs. "We manage."

This, like each topic raised, fails to launch and ends in

silence. Miriam has talked about her work. Leonard has said something about the state of the business in Europe. Jamie only speaks when directly addressed and Kitty says nothing at all. I listen but find it hard to concentrate, what with the static in my head so loud it surprises me the others can't hear it. Every time I look at Kitty – and I try hard not to stare – she almost seems to vibrate on high frequency.

"When do you go back to Berlin?" Miriam asks.

Jamie presses his lips together and shakes his head. "No set date."

"He will go back," Barb says. "When – when everything settles down."

Jamie glances at his mother then away.

"Kitty, this looks delicious." Leonard leans forwards from the head of the table, reaching for the tureen of minestrone.

I sit there, impatient with the small talk, desperate to know what the police have come up with – DNA test results, anything – but sense the topic is taboo. Wouldn't they bring it up themselves if it's open for discussion? Things are definitely off. Maybe their family really is connected to the Affinity Project, and all this jumpy behavior is hyper-vigilance, and inviting us to come tonight is purely to get us off their case? I have to swallow the urge to blurt my secret right then and there. How crazy would it sound? I bite the inside of my cheek for self-control.

"Smells fantastic," Miriam says, tapping my ankle with her foot and breaking my trance. She passes me her bowl and I give it to Leonard who mans the ladle. Like a discordant background note, I can't pick why that also seems so strange and then it hits me. Where is the household staff?

"Tell us about Burton Central, Evie," Leonard says, after another awkward silence. "Will you know any of the Seniors there?"

I don't want to talk about it. With school only a week away and the future so uncertain, I have no intention of even starting the year until Kitty is safe. Miriam and I have argued about that too. Bitterly. Burton Central and Gainsborough Collegiate are on opposite sides of town. As far as I'm concerned it's completely out of the question. "I doubt it," I say. "Maybe I should look into those scholarships you were telling me about, Kit. Mom always raved about Gainsborough."

Kitty rises awkwardly from the table, eyes darting from side to side. "I forgot the other rolls. I – I made wholemeal rolls, and I better check the lamb. I'll just be a few minutes, sorry."

I hate to see her so fragile.

"You need a hand?" Jamie rises from his seat.

She shakes her head and steps away. We all watch her slip through the kitchen door. Her parents exchange worried looks. Conversation stalls completely and I become aware of an uncomfortable churning in my stomach. Miriam compensates for the silence by spooning soup into her mouth and *mmm*-ing repeated compliments, saying she'll have to get the recipe and Barb says something about it being handed down and then I lose the thread because the churning feeling quickly sharpens to a point. My lower abdomen contracts so fiercely, I nearly groan aloud and a horrible realisation hits me. The cramps. Miriam's warnings about my body, my monthly period becoming a weekly ordeal and the cramps that will signal its arrival. I have been living in dread of it for the last two weeks. *Not now. Please, not now.* Heat creeps up my neck and my ears feel hot. I lift my napkin and dab at my lips, about to excuse myself.

Jamie frowns across the table. "What did you do to your fingers?"

The heat in my ears fills my cheeks, my gut gripes and my mind blanks.

"Overzealous with the cheese grater," Miriam supplies the alibi, affecting a wry tone as if to say, poor, clumsy Evangeline.

My laugh sounds weak and I push my chair back. "Just need the powder room." I have to force myself not to run, feeling every eye on my back. But once I make the foyer, I snatch my purse from the console table and hurry up the corridor to the guest bathroom, thanking God for the emergency supplies I always keep zipped in the side pocket. I barely make it before the flood hits and I buckle over on the toilet seat, cursing but desperately relieved I left the table when I did. I can't bear to imagine the humiliation if I'd waited any longer.

It takes me a minute or two to pull it together and organise myself. Only an hour, Miriam said. I hope she's right. I wash my trembling hands, dry them and lean on the vanity, checking that my mascara hasn't bled down my cheeks. The tightness in my stomach contracts with the tether, stabbing behind my bellybutton. The static in my head crackles loudly, something changes and I became very still. An electric current expands from my spine to the tips of my fingers and the soles of my feet. Seconds, milliseconds, hours and years, I stand paralysed, lost in an internal storm. I blink once in an endless slow sweep, my pupils expanding in the mirror – black pools that make everything around me razor-edged and painful to look at.

I reach for Kitty in the bandwidth then a looming shadow fills my mind.

It's happening.

Energy flames to the center of my body, burning fear like oxygen, releasing an emission of black rage. Time fractures. I say her name, ramming the door and stumble out of the bathroom.

I bolt down the hall to the back entrance of the kitchen. Kitty's unearthly scream comes just before I burst through the door, wrenching the hinges. Instantly, I register a dark figure beyond the kitchen window and Kitty by the counter recoiling from it, teetering, falling, her basket of rolls flying up towards the ceiling. I launch myself across the floor, light bulbs popping above me, and catch Kitty before her head smacks against the black and white Italian tiles, unconscious of her weight or strain in my muscles.

In the same second, the door to the dining room bangs open. Jamie sees me crouched over Kitty and his features contort. He shouts and lunges towards us. Instinct and inspiration propel me away, a high-pitched ringing in my ears. I run at the counter, scoop up a knife and jump, levering off the side of the sink, curling my knees up to my chin, shoulder first. The sheet of glass explodes before I touch it. I cannonball through the window, uncurling in a shower of splinters, landing in the flowerbed, a faint burning at the top of my head, a chemical smell in my nostrils.

Jamie cries out, but I'm already halfway down the path beside the pool house, driven by the offending signal in the bandwidth. The deepening shadow of the garden wall cuts short and I skid into the stable yard where the rising moon silvers the shutters of the unused stalls. Disorientated, I close my eyes. The chemical scent lingers here too. A sound directs me to the north east and I sprint between the stable wall and utility sheds, out onto the vast stretch of lawn that dips down to the forest. There, near the edge of the trees, a dark figure slips into the shadows. I tighten my grip on the knife and lengthen my stride, spurred by a terrifying sound – the distant call of the river.

Water.

Water blocks the signal.

If he crosses over – I can't let that happen. I run. I fly, barely sliding on dew-damp grass, pumping my arms and legs. The forest seems to grow quickly up and up and up until I dart beneath the first outstretched arms of elm and birch that hem the firs beyond. It feels like stepping through a wall of ink but the black on black shifts and clarifies, my senses compensating in an instant.

The surprising sound of pounding feet echoes both before me and behind me. Why would Miriam leave Kitty unguarded? I shake it off, zeroing in on the sound ahead and the faint chemical waft as we head for the slender arm of the Border River where it winds onto the estate.

Thick brush rips the cardigan from my shoulders and branches slap at my arms, neck and face. I've entered the world of my recurring nightmare, moving by instinct through the unpredictable space, sure-footed as I skim the undergrowth. Just as I begin to feel that I'm gaining on the Stray, I become aware of those pounding feet behind me coming up on the right, hammering through the trees. Miriam pacing me?

A shot rings out; a painful clap of sound by my ear.

I skid, confused.

"Stop!"

The voice is all wrong.

Distracted for half a second, I slam into an outcropping branch. Like a baseball bat to my left side, it forces air from my lungs and jars the knife from my hand and the blade spirals away in the darkness. The impact spins me anticlockwise and I hit the dirt in a shower of muddy leaves. Skin tears from my knees and elbows. I scramble to get back on my feet, almost blind with pain, only to be flipped and flattened on the root-tangled earth. A knee in my stomach, a pan-like hand in the middle of my chest, Jamie pins me.

I can't think.

I can't breathe.

Jamie presses the hot mouth of his gun to my forehead and I struggle against him and imminent blackout.

"It was you." His black eyes are wild. "I didn't want it to be you."

Beyond the sound of our combined panting, I can hear the Stray getting away. I want to scream and throw Jamie off but can't move or cry out. Jamie presses harder then freezes, suddenly aware of the distant sound. The lock of his gaze lifts and he stares, horrified, into the darkness.

I hear the faint splash of water. The bandwidth goes blank, like going blind. I groan, limp in defeat, crushed by Jamie's weight. I flap at his arm. "He's gone."

He looks down like he forgot I was lying beneath him. He drops the gun and climbs off me. I roll to the side, gasping for air, feeling all the bones in my body. None of them are happy.

"Everton." Jamie grips his head and shakes where he sits. "I nearly killed you."

ALLIES

I push up against the rough base of a tree, my scraped and battered legs splayed in the dirt. It takes shallow breaths to stay conscious, holding myself to ease the white-hot pain in my side. I am filthy. My dress is torn in alarming places. I can't think. Jamie still pants grey-faced where he sits. His ripped shirt gapes from shoulder to elbow and his stare burns through me.

"Affinity?" I say.

He frowns and brings a finger to his lips but gives the barest nod.

I shut my eyes like I've been sucked through a black hole and wish Miriam would appear through the trees and take charge of things. Neither of us speak. We're on the same side of an impossible line, where we both imagined ourselves alone.

Frustration at a lost opportunity eats me up and I aim it at Jamie. "Why on earth would you let me in the house if you thought I was the Stray?"

"I didn't know what to think. I didn't want to believe it was possible. It was only after you left the table I really started freaking out. I could tell you were feeling something."

I don't react. No way will I explain that little episode.

He holds his head. "On the one hand you passed out at the ball, on the other, no seizure, no vomiting. But then you'd disappeared after the attack and it didn't seem to add up. When you arrived so early at the hospital …"

"I could have just been a worried friend."

"At seven in the morning?" He shakes his head. "I definitely worried when I couldn't feel your tracker."

I need to get back on my feet and I turn, grunting with effort, onto my knees. "I don't have a tracker."

He scrambles up to help me, taking me by the arm. "You should tell your *Watcher*," he whispers the word. "If it's dissolved. It's pretty bloody slack if she's let it reach that point."

Even with Jamie's support, hauling myself up sends blinding pain through my ribs. An involuntary groan shudders out of me and I shove Jamie aside, bringing up Kitty's minestrone in a kaleidoscopic splatter. Still functioning enough to wish Jamie hadn't seen, I wipe my mouth and step away. My throat rasps in the afterburn. "I don't have a Watcher."

"What?" He picks up his gun and tucks it into the back of his pants. "You must have."

"I think I'd know." The forest spins. Jamie catches me against his chest and his scent makes me even dizzier.

"Have you broken something?"

I right myself. "*You* broke something."

"Sorry." He grimaces. "You're not making sense. How can you not have one?"

"Can we please get back to the house? I need to know she's okay."

He takes my arm and directs our path, turning me to the left where the trees thin. "She's fine. They would've taken her straight to the panic room."

They have a room? "What? Your folks know?"

"I told them."

"What?" I exclaim, completely rattled. "You didn't tell Kitty? Tell me you didn't tell her."

"I had to."

"Oh shit, Jamie!" I try to yank my arm out of his, but he keeps hold of me.

"I couldn't take any chances. I only arrived the day before it happened, I had no way of knowing if a *Warden* had been through, if agents had been dispatched. You know the odds of a spontaneous response to a *Spark* aren't traditionally that great," he says, careful over the illegal terms.

"No wonder she's acting so weird," I groan.

Jamie keeps me moving and I am too upset to speak. We come out of the trees and onto the lawn. On the rise, the windows of the house shine in the darkness and we take it slowly up the gradual slope, each step jarring my side. Even through the fog of pain, the idea of the Gallaghers knowing anything about the Affinity Project does my head in. Finally, I say, "I guess that's why your mom's staff aren't around?"

He nods. "Easier for everyone."

It makes sense – one of the few things that does.

"Is it your dad who's active?" I ask.

"He's just a gene carrier. Uncle Jeremy's with the Project. He's pissed with me for breaking his cover."

It's too huge to comprehend.

"You?" he asks.

"Miriam."

Jamie's eyes widen. "Bloody hell."

"I can't believe we're having this conversation." My frustration diminishes with hope rising to take its place. Jamie is a Shield. He's strong. Capable. He'll be with Kitty when I'm not – not that I can imagine letting myself be separated from her now. "What made you realise it wasn't a mugging?"

"Something the driver of the van said about the speed of the attacker vaulting the estate wall. It frightened him like he'd seen a ghost."

"That wall's got to be twelve feet."

Jamie nods. "Once the DNA came back unreadable, I knew for sure we were dealing with a *Stray*."

"How?"

"The synthetic gene has very different markers. But we have a doctor of our own, thanks to Uncle Jeremy, someone familiar with our genetic anomaly who's running tests for us privately."

"That's fantastic."

"If we have time to draw any conclusions. We can only be grateful the *Stray*'s a beginner. Buys us a little time." He sighs. "What are you on? Your third or fourth?"

I stop on the lawn and turn to look up at Jamie. "Kitty's my first."

He scoffs. "That's not even funny."

I don't move.

His eyes widen. "No tracker. No *Watcher*. Illegal terms."

I sense bad news and my hope deflates like an old balloon.

"But – but you registered the – *guy* from a distance. First timers can't do that."

"Jamie," I struggle to produce volume. "Kitty's my first."

"That's impossible!"

"Why, exactly?"

"Because your frequency sensitivity is only in its early stages with your first. There's no way you can detect a threat unless you can feel your bond with the *Spark* and that requires close physical proximity when you're new. Surely, Miriam explained all this?"

I feel faint and hot. It doesn't make sense. Miriam assured me I would feel the threat. No mention of "close physical proximity".

"Kitty's your first and Miriam didn't tell you?"

"She told me I'd know when."

He rakes his hand through his hair. "I see."

"I don't get it."

He falls silent and stares at the house. Finally, he says, "I guess I can't really blame her."

"Why wouldn't she tell me?"

He meets my gaze briefly. "To save you from feeling bad."

The bitter resignation in his voice frightens me and my eyelids flicker like a strobe. "Obviously, it won't be easy. I've got a lot to learn but–"

"No one saves their first. Few even save their second. Maybe by your third or fourth you might expect a save, but by then your sensitivity would be more mature and you'd have had professional training. A newbie doesn't stand a chance."

No one saves their first.

His words are worse than a physical assault. Ringing fills my ears.

BLAME

The soft glow of lamplight washes the recessed cornices of the ceiling.

We don't have recessed cornices.

"Mom?" I have plastic lips and a matchstick throat.

"She's awake." Jamie's low urgent voice.

Nightmare reality rushes in.

I try to lift my head but it's rock heavy and stings at the scalp.

Miriam bends over me, pale with worry. "Just stay still."

Anger eclipses the pain and I groan.

"Evie?" Kitty's voice brings everything into focus. I know exactly where I am and what's going on. The confusing pressure in my stomach is the tether. Guilt, relief and shame war in my chest as she comes into view; her eyes are huge and swimming with tears. Barb holds her tight.

"Kitty." My tongue is too thick. "Are you hurt?"

She disengages from her mother, forcing Miriam aside and jostling me painfully, wrapping her arms around my neck. She sobs into my hair.

"Kitty," Jamie says. "Let her go. She might have a broken rib."

She sits back, wringing her hands. "Evie, it's all my fault."

"No," I say, choked by her obvious terror. "No, it isn't."

"I'm so, so sorry. I can't believe this is happening. I can't believe you're the one, and that this is happening."

"It's okay," Miriam says.

Where does she get the gall to soothe her? To be in the same room? No desire to protect me can make up for the lie that risked Kitty's safety! It makes me sick to look at Miriam, but turning my head hurts my scalp. I reach up and find a stinging graze beneath a patch of damp, sticky hair. I lower my hand and there's blood on my fingertips. I try to sit up but cry out at the stab in my side.

Jamie catches me. "What are you doing?"

I struggle, turtle-like, on my back. "I'm bleeding on your mom's couch."

"I don't care about the damn couch," Barb says. "Lie down."

Surprised by her sharp tone, I let Jamie lower me.

"Perhaps we should give Evangeline some space." Leonard's cool voice makes me want to curl up. Jamie must have told them the terrible news. I squeeze my eyes, wishing I could disappear. "I'll call the doctor," he says and my eyes spring open. "Don't worry. He's very discreet." He moves like he carries a heavy invisible load and pauses at the door. "Jamie."

His son watches me over the back of the couch, frowning, lost in thought.

"Jamie," Leonard says again.

"I'll be right back," Jamie says.

"Wait." I wince in the attempt to reach him and whisper, "Will she be safe now?"

Jamie freezes, his eyes fixing where I touch him. His brow creases and he pulls away. "You're the best chance we have to know that."

I shiver as he withdraws. The saviour they'd been hoping for is just useless, inexperienced me.

"I'll fetch you a damp cloth," Barb says, her voice and posture stiff. "Kitty, come and help me get a blanket and some clothes for Evangeline."

I don't want Kitty out of my sight, but I don't feel I have the right to ask for anything. So I lie like a leper as they draw away, the tether stretching, thinning until it blends with the atmosphere of dread.

Miriam kneels close, her face awash with emotion. She reaches to stroke my forehead and tries to hold my hand, but I turn away, balling my fists. "Why didn't you tell me the truth? Days she's been unprotected!"

She sighs. "You don't understand."

"You let me believe she was safe, that'd I'd feel it if she were in danger!"

"Listen to me." She leans forwards, her dark hair falling across her face, reminding me of my mother, a hot poker to the heart. "The odds are–"

"All the more reason you should *never* have kept me from her." Thinking about the failure rate of first timers burns me up.

"She was safe. She had her brother. He may not be tuned into her signal but still–"

"You didn't know that Jamie was with Affinity!"

"I wanted to protect you. I wanted–"

"That's bullshit!"

"Damn it, Evie, I could have given you up to *Affinity*," she mouths the word. "And then you'd have been right out of it, but I didn't – I didn't! So don't make out Kitty means nothing to me."

"I should be grateful?" Disgust twists my mouth. "Grateful you let me think there was a chance while she was across town and I was at your place, twiddling my damn thumbs, waiting for a signal I would *never* feel?"

She lowers her voice. "You're only seventeen."

I almost hiss. "What's that got to do with anything?"

"It's too soon. You're a kid for crying out loud.

Someone else might respond to her signal, you never know. Someone experienced."

"You're out of your mind! You know what this feels like! I can't walk away!"

"That's just the *Fixation Effect.*" The whisper is almost a hiss. "It would be hard, but you could do it."

"Can you hear yourself?"

She grabs my shoulders. "You'll die. Do you understand? *He* will kill you if you get in the way!"

I struggle under her grasp, furious with her and the weakness in my body. "Don't touch me!" She flinches and lets go. My ribs are on fire and black spots pop in front of my eyes. There is no decision. No choice. She knows that. "I'm not leaving and you can't make me."

"The doctor is on his way."

I freeze. Miriam wipes her eyes and stands up. Pale and fraught, she turns to Leonard who's stopped in the doorway, his expression so hard it alters his face. He heard us. I brace for a lash of words. They don't come. His eyes soften with despair and weariness that age him. "Evie, Jamie explained to me that this is your first."

Miriam stands rigid and I blink at Leonard, feeling young and useless. He sits on the ottoman, clasping his hands in an effort to conceal their trembling. "You understand this is a blow for us."

"It's not her fault," Miriam says.

"It's not." He inclines his head to me. "Forgive me. It was not my intention to imply blame. We just need to consider now what our options are."

"I don't know what your options are, Leonard. But I'm taking Evie home."

Jamie's "What?" and my "No!" converge as he appears through the door. I struggle up on my elbow, a cold sweat breaking out on my forehead. Jamie stalks towards us. He's removed his ripped shirt, leaving him in his plain white T-shirt and mud-streaked pants, his expression a mirror of Leonard's.

"Evie is my responsibility." Miriam won't be cowed. "Let's be realistic, Jamie. You know how this works. Without an experienced agent–" Leonard rises to face her and she doesn't finish. Instead she says, "Is it fair to put Evie through it?"

"I am not leaving!" I try to sound forceful but the effort to hold myself up is taking it out of me.

"Lie down." Jamie maneuvers me back, and I clutch his arm.

"I'm not leaving. Okay? No matter what she says." But the fog is closing in and I have to shut my eyes and breathe through my nose.

"It's okay," he says.

"It's not okay!" Miriam says. "There's only one outcome here. One. And I'm sorry for it. But it doesn't have to mean Evie's life. She's not ready. It's too soon."

Kitty materialises with her mother at this point, having come into the room so quietly no one's noticed. Absorbed in the argument, I don't register the compression in my stomach that I'm beginning to associate with our bond, not until she stands right in front of me.

"Only one outcome?" She stares around the circle, silencing us all. "So, I'm a goner?"

"Kitty." Miriam loses her wind. "I'm sorry. But you have to understand."

Barb steps between them. "How dare you?"

"Please, Barb." Miriam grows red in the face. "Evie has no one here but me."

I struggle on my back. "I don't want you!"

Every face turns towards me.

Miriam looks like I've slapped her. "If you had caught up with that guy, he would have killed you."

Kitty covers her mouth, drops the blanket and runs from the room.

"I think you should leave," Barb says to my aunt. "Now."

Miriam looks back at me, her eyes glistening. "Not without my niece."

"I'm-not-going-anywhere-with-you!" I say through gritted teeth.

Jamie picks up the fallen blanket and lays it over my torn dress. "Your aunt should stay." He looks from me to his mother. “Miriam can help–”

“You can’t trust her!” I say. “She lied!”

“To protect you,” he says.

“I don’t need protection!” Can’t he understand? Miriam is a liability. She’ll jeopardise everything. I would never be able to trust that she has Kitty’s best interests at heart. She’d just be fretting over me all the time and getting in the way. “This is your sister’s life!”

“And yours, Everton. I’m not okay with Miriam’s lie but I can understand it. You can’t because of the Fixation Effect.”

Am I the only one in my right mind? Barb alone seems to share my level of disgust. “Mrs Gallagher,” I begin, but Leonard steps in.

“Evangeline,” he says. “If you are willing to stay, then we are grateful.”

I nod at Leonard and glare at my aunt.

“Miriam,” he turns to her. “Evangeline doesn’t wish to leave and I won’t make her. For the sake of moving on from our stalemate would you consider staying, even if only to watch over your niece?”

Barb and I both open our mouths to argue, but Jamie presses my shoulder, his eyes on his mother. “Barb,” he says. “We need her.”

Barb hands the wet cloth to her son and speaks to her husband. “I’ll be with my daughter.” She walks stiff-backed from the room, refusing to acknowledge Miriam.

Leonard sighs and looks to my aunt. Miriam's dark gaze moves from father to son then rests on me. "I'll stay."

MORPHINE

"I'm a geneticist, you know. Haven't been a needle and thread man for quite some years, but needs must." Doctor Sullivan sets out his medical kit with a quick, light touch, nodding as he speaks as though in constant agreement with his own thoughts. "I've made quite a bit of progress with the sample, simply fascinating stuff. I'd seen a bit of it before, working with Leonard's brother, but it's dreadfully difficult to get your hands on Stray DNA, the markers are very unusual." He turns to me and nods with gusto. "You are in quite a state."

My skinned elbows, knees and shins are the least of my pain. I've cut my right shoulder and my scalp burns from the shattering glass of the kitchen window. My whole left side aches where I collided with the tree; I can barely lift that arm, and something is definitely broken – my ribs are on fire.

"You should lie down," Jamie says.

"I'm not ruining any more furniture." I can't look at him glowering beside me; I don't want to see the disappointment in his eyes. I still tremble in the aftermath of being carried upstairs in his arms – agony for more than one reason.

"We'll put some towels down." Doctor Sullivan swabs my arm and sticks me with the needle. "This will take the edge off. Jamie, fetch your mother. The young lady needs this dress off and a sponge bath."

Jamie disappears in a blur, obviously desperate to escape. I close my eyes against the slow-spinning room and lean back on the wall. "You work for Jeremy? You're with Affinity?"

"Ah-ah-ah," the doctor shakes his head. "We don't mention the A-word. Jeremy's fiercely strict about adhering to protocol and no, I don't. They know nothing about me." There's almost glee in that last bit, like a big kid breaking school rules. I want to ask more but struggle to form a coherent thought.

The doctor busies about the room, keeping up a constant flow of talk. "The real joy is having two samples to compare. Jamie was kind enough to supply me with some of his own blood. Layering the samples clarifies so very much, and then comparing it to unmodified DNA." He chatters on as he pulls the quilt off the guest bed, folds back the sheets and spreads towels from the en suite. "I hope you will allow me a sample of your own? I shall ask your aunt also. It's really too good an opportunity to pass up."

"Help yourself, seems I've left samples all over the house."

"Ha, well, indeed, never mind that, dear."

"How long until you have an ID?"

"It's an awfully long process, I'm afraid. The skin we collected from Kitty's nails has taken me two weeks to process and it will require thorough analysis. Even then, it will only be of use to us if the assailant has a criminal record and I can match it with a sample in the database. Otherwise, it won't tell us anything."

The magic of morphine may have eased my trembling, but it doesn't keep me from feeling depressed at the doctor's news. I focus on the tether. It comforts me more than pain relief.

The doctor takes my arm to lead me to the bed when Jamie reappears, new worry creasing his brow. "I'm afraid Kitty's a bit of a mess. Barb won't leave her and Dad's got the glazier arriving any minute. I could get Miriam?"

"No!" The force of my response makes me wobble and both of them reach to steady me. "Not her."

"Take it easy." He raises his hands. "I suppose you're stuck with me then."

I scowl.

Jamie shrugs. "Me or Miriam?"

I glare, embarrassed, but have to concede. "Fine."

"Good, good." The doctor picks up his medical case and pats my arm. "I better go and see what I can do for Kitty. I won't be long."

Jamie studies me a moment, his expression impenetrable, then runs his hand up the back of his hair with a long-suffering sigh. "I'll be right back. Don't fall over."

He leaves and panic sweeps in.

What the hell just happened?

But something besides panic slips past the sedative dulling my senses: a thrill at the thought of Jamie's electric touch.

No. Don't do that. He didn't want you three years ago, he won't want you now.

But I can't help it. Despite the fact that I shouldn't be thinking about anything like it at all with a genetically enhanced killer on the loose and Kitty falling apart down the hall, I want my new DNA to make him notice me.

That's sick.

I shuffle into the bathroom and stop short. My reflection extinguishes the thrill. I look like I've walked off the set of a horror movie. I should have let him fetch Miriam to save myself the shame. I turn away, shut the bathroom door and lock it, seizing the opportunity to check everything is okay post period cramps. I can't bend without excruciating pain and the effort nearly wipes me out, but thankfully it's all cleared up.

Sweat beads on my lip and I lean against the cold tiles. I can't wait to lie down. If I can only get out of my dress and under a sheet without humiliation, it will be something. I barely manage to kick my shoes into the corner when I hear Jamie return. "How is it?" he calls.

"It's not that bad." I open the bathroom door, trying not to pant. Jamie stands there, holding a round plastic tub and some folded face cloths. I pretend not to notice. "Is Kitty okay?"

"Doctor Sullivan's trying to give her a sedative. It's not going well." He steps past me to the bath and opens the faucet, filling the plastic tub, dipping his fingers, testing the temperature.

"Did she say – did she get a look at him?"

"His face was covered."

"Have you asked her about the people she met at the ball?"

"Guys who vomited and had seizures when they touched her?" He looks at me over his shoulder. "We've been over it. Nothing stands out."

"Who have the police interviewed?"

"Mainly the waitstaff, but they're making general inquiries of the guests."

"You think we could get a list?"

He shuts off the faucet and stands up frowning. "You can't think of it like that. Frequency sensitivity is what matters, your ability to read signals." He sounds like Miriam, and I deflate. He sighs. "Suppose we better get you out of that then."

"I might be able to manage." I turn my back, fumbling with the buttons of my dress, desperately trying to remember if I'm wearing matching underwear. When I try to pull at my sleeve even that slight movement hurts so much my head spins, I lose balance and stumble against the bathroom door.

Jamie grabs me. "Stop being ridiculous, Everton. Let me help."

There is no way around it – I need help. But I can't ignore the contrast between his golden perfection and my Halloween body reflected in the unforgiving glare of the bathroom mirror. Any scenario involving Jamie removing my clothes, as I may have imagined it in moments of weakness, looked nothing like this one.

He keeps his expression earnest and softens his tone. "It's just me, yeah?"

"Which is kind of the point." Morphine is no friend of dignity.

His chest expands inches from mine and his brow contracts. "Come on."

He leads me back to the bedroom where I'm grateful for sedate lamplight. He opens the wardrobe and digs out a folded sheet, unfurling it over his shoulder. "Here's the game plan." Brisk and businesslike. "The dress is on its last legs."

I bite my lip, having lost the power of speech somewhere back in the bathroom.

"No point arsing about."

He tears the dress from neck to waist, the fabric tugging around me. Air on my skin. A white flourish and Jamie swathes me with the sheet. He moves behind me and reaches through the back to slide the dress off my shoulders. Warm electric fingers. The shreds of material pool at my feet. He frees my arms, tucks the sheet tight, then slips the hair tie from my wrist and gathers the length of my hair up into a loose ponytail. I hold my breath, glad he can't see my face.

"Hang about." He fetches the tub of water and places it on the nightstand. "Tip your head." With hypnotic strokes, he wipes away the blood that has trickled from my scalp. The searing heat feels blissful on the back of my neck and between my shoulder blades. My eyes roll up and I stifle a moan.

"I-I think I'd better lie down."

In an instant he has me in his arms and on the bed with only a brief stab of pain.

I pant on the pillow. "You do this a lot?"

The shadow of a smile touches his serious mouth. He takes my left hand and keeps his expression purposeful, cleaning away the blood and dirt from the length of my arm, shoulder, neck and collarbone, careful over the grazes and cuts. He leaves a trail of goosebumps with each pass and my heart crashes like a lunatic on padded walls.

The combination of worry, morphine, pain and Jamie makes it hard to think. To find an anchor, I close my eyes, think about Kitty, focus on the tether and reach through the static, scanning for a threatening signal. Other than my amplified anxiety, there is nothing, but then I see flashes, vivid details of the forest, trees blurring, the weight of metal in my hand, the shock of gunfire vibrating up my arm.

I jerk on the pillow and open my eyes. Jamie has frozen where he leans over me with the blood-soaked cloth. "You can *Harvest*," he whispers.

My head swims. "I thought it was KMT?"

"You shouldn't be able to do either."

I rest my hand against the hard swell of his bicep and bring my memory forward. I don't even need to close my eyes, it's all there: the moment after the gunshot, the violent impact of the tree branch, the stinging skid on mud-packed earth, the crushing weight of Jamie's landing.

His sharp breath draws me out of the vision and he sits back, his hand on his forehead. "And you can do both."

"I guess."

"You did something to the glass too."

I cringe. "I was going through the window one way or other."

"I've never seen that before."

"I can't control it. Usually it's glasses or light bulbs and only when I get upset."

His frown kills me and I can't help myself. "I'm sorry, Jamie. I wish it wasn't me. I mean, I wish it was someone good, you know, someone who knew what the hell they were doing, for Kitty's sake."

"Evie."

A tear escapes and I bite inside my cheek for control. "I get that you're disappointed. You must be devastated."

His frown softens and he wipes the single track of my tear with the slow graze of his knuckle. "It's not you. It's everything. The whole thing's a bloody nightmare. But it's not your fault. We don't even know what it means – you being so far along."

"No one saves their first."

"Not that I've ever heard of. But you're nothing like a first timer."

"Because of some stupid party trick?"

"It's much more than that, Everton. It's a sign of your development." He wads the soiled cloth on the side table and picks up a fresh one, dipping it and wringing it out.

"There's no way you should have picked up on Kitty's guy, and you're way faster than you should be. These are good signs."

"Miriam knew I could do all this stuff."

His expression clouds. "I suppose it's one thing to go through it, another to watch someone you love go through it."

"I don't think I can forgive her."

He looks up. "That's the *Fixation Effect*." He gives it the soft touch. "She knows excuses mean squat if we think someone's a threat to our *Spark*. It's a primal bond. Stronger than anything. Except Synergist Coding." He keeps his eyes on the job and mutters, "I wonder if that's an illegal term."

As he leans over the mess of my right arm, I become distracted by the strong line of his neck and the hollow just beneath the corner of his jaw. He smells so good, I can almost imagine the warmth of his skin. "Synergist what?"

"It doesn't matter. What does matter is you'll have to work hard to forgive Miriam. We'll need her help if we're going to get you up to speed."

I shake my head, making myself dizzy. "I have you." Even through the sedative it sounds too intimate but I don't care.

"I don't have her experience."

"I trust you more."

His eyebrows lift. "That is saying something."

As he bends again over my wounds, I watch him with morphine's freedom from inhibition. Storm-grey eyes. Bronze arms ringed in a language I don't recognise. Latin? He really has the kind of skin that inspires touch and I ball my hands in the sheet, about to ask what the tattoos mean.

"Do you need me to stop?" He pauses, leaning over me.

"Excuse me?"

He touches his chest, frowning at mine. "Your heart is racing."

I cover the faithless muscle. "You can hear it?"

"Can't you?"

"Well, yeah. But it's my heart. In my chest."

"You haven't noticed how your senses heighten … when you're in the zone?"

I give him a narrow look. "Are you in the zone?"

He smirks but then his eyes move to my forehead and the humour evaporates. Almost tentative, he brushes his fingers across my brow. I don't need KMH to tell me he's remembering holding a gun to my head. His frown deepens as though listening for something and he strokes my cheek like it's an experiment.

Whether by morphine or wishful thinking, the gesture doesn't seem outrageous. My inhibitions are disabled to the point that I close my eyes for a moment and lean into his cupped palm, enjoying the electric pleasure of his touch. "Mmm."

His face splits with a slow grin. "You're stoned."

Relieved he doesn't pull away, I hold his gaze far longer than I would have dared drug free. I could look at him all night, if I could just keep my eyes open. "You are so …"

"Hmm?"

I hear the smile in his voice, my eyes closing in a long languid sweep. There's no coming up. Sleep presses me down into warm, dark, oblivion.

ARROW

Forty-eight hours ago I nearly ruined everything. Seeing her through the kitchen window, alone, weak, with the brace on her neck, it drove me crazy, made me reckless. I should never have gone so close to the house.

Now, I keep to the forest, watching, waiting, fixated on the light shining behind her curtain on the second floor. I count the windows to the end of the balcony, where lamplight cuts through the crack. I bare my teeth; the other has moved in there.

I press my hands into the dead bark of a rotting tree, needing the distraction of every rough edge against my skin, something to drown out the noise in my head and the sick pull in my stomach. Tired. So tired. Closing my eyes brings no relief, only an increase in volume and bloody dreams.

Pine sap, damp earth, night air; the inhale is everything, one sense that tells me I am real. I can't trust my eyes, I don't recognise them – black holes in a pale moon. My ears ring with static. My skin is a lie. Something has taken up residence in me:

a foreign voice and everything is wrong. I grip the trunk, the invisible umbilical twisting through the night, drawing poison from a well that won't leave me. I grind my forehead against the tree and clench my stomach, wishing I could dig my nails through my flesh and gouge it out.

The spike of electricity slices up my spine and I shove away from the tree with a hiss. There will be no peace–

"Kitty!"

I thrash and sit up on the bed, fully dressed, disorientated by the warm room that isn't mine, the slick of my shirt and the acrid smell of my own sweat. My feet feel choked in my shoes. I stand and stagger against the wardrobe, pressing my hand over the ache in my ribs. The alarm clock glows – two in the morning, but pain anchors me, giving me my place in time and space. "Kitty."

I stumble out into the hall, trailing the wall for balance and make my way down to her room. The house is quiet. I wipe sweat from my palm and turn the handle, too afraid to trust the feel of the tether.

Careful, soundless, holding my breath, I slip through the door and shut it behind me. Thanks to Doctor Sullivan's heavy-duty sleeping tablets, Kitty lies spread-eagled, her head almost off the mattress, one leg right out of the blankets, an arm flung over her face. I clamp my hand over my mouth at the rush of tenderness I feel. The tangible contrast to the sick hate of my nightmare gives me goosebumps and I shake, taking in the proof of life. She's safe. The tether is strong. It was only a dream, a nightmare, as though I slipped into the skin of the Stray, the same dream I've had for the last two nights, since the chase through the forest.

A stirring of blankets, a whimper and Kitty wakes with a start. I bump back against the wall, she gasps at the noise and I dart across the room to clamp my hand across her mouth, afraid she'll scream and wake the house. "It's me – it's just me, Kit."

Her face strains with terror and she grapples to take hold of me, jerking up in her bed. Muffled cries break beneath my palm. "He's here! He's coming!"

"No," I whisper. "No, Kit. You're safe. I'm sorry I frightened you. I couldn't sleep. I was checking to see you were okay. He's not here. You're safe." It's like I'm rushing to reassure myself, trying to wash away the nightmare taint.

I'm surprised by the strength of her grip considering the sedatives in her system. It's almost painful, her nails digging into the flesh of my upper arm but it's her tear-stained eyes that cut me. Fear, split open, an arterial gush of it, *the end, the end.*

I hold her until she believes me and her tension gives out, a slump of faith. She leans her face heavily into my shoulder, the neck foam impeding a proper embrace, and

I despise myself for her weeping. She'll never sleep again because of me.

"This is what it's going to be like, isn't it?" Her speech comes muffled and slurred from my shoulder. "Me freaking out every five minutes and losing the plot."

"I don't want you to be afraid." Achingly true but pointlessly stupid, said aloud.

There's a hysterical hitch in her sobbing, not quite a laugh. "A little less skulking in the dark might help."

I groan. "I'm so sorry, Kit. I can't describe what it's like. I feel better when I can see you, you know?"

She sits back, sniffing and wiping her eyes, her pupils so dilated she could pass for a Shield. "Jamie warned me you might get a bit mother bearish."

It's not a bad description for the feral protectiveness that's overtaken me since Sparking. I shrug. "You will have had enough of me by the end of the week."

She takes my hand in her cold, tear-dampened one. "Probably. Still, I'm glad it's you." She frowns. "Hang on, I mean, I absolutely wish it wasn't you – for your sake, but for my sake I'm glad it's you."

Her words sound familiar but all wrong. She should be shaking her fist at the sky, wailing at the injustice of it all like she had the other night. Imagine being stuck with someone as cosmically useless as me. If I were in her place, I would probably throw myself off the roof to save time.

But thinking this is treason, and I want her to believe that I can save her. I need her to believe it so I can believe it too. "Thanks."

* * *

The treadmill rumbles beneath me in the Gallaghers' gym – a room purpose-built beside the six-car garage, as a dance studio for Kitty when she was twelve years old. It has been overrun by workout equipment since then. I thump away at top speed, ignoring the ghost of pain in my side. That I can move so freely in less than a week blows my mind. Even the stitches in my scalp and arm are ready to come out.

Kitty sits on the weights bench with her journal and pen. It always seems to be in her hands, and I hate to think what her entries are about. *Dear diary, some sicko wants to murder me ...*

As tired as I am from nightmares, training and the waking reality of my new life, Kitty gives me strength. Her meltdown after hearing there is "only one outcome" ended far sooner than it should have and then she pulled it together – probably for the sake of her parents. I can't imagine where she finds her courage, but I let it fan my hope for a happy ending.

Seeing Kitty rally gave the whole household a sense of focused determination. Leonard upgraded the security system, installed guns in safes around the house, gave me codes to access them and taught me how to operate the panic room door. Its tomb-like walls of concrete and steel, built into the wine cellar beneath the kitchen, scare the crap out of me. Barb pours her emotion into creating vast quantities of food, which I can't consume fast enough. Jamie collaborates with Miriam on training techniques to help rebuild my strength, bridging the gap created by my hostility like a proper diplomat.

I glance up at movement in the courtyard. Leonard comes from the house, carrying a metal briefcase, Miriam beside him. I hit the stop button, the motor groans and I hop off the treadmill, taking a moment to recover my land legs. "Kit, you wanna find Jamie and tell him I'm done if he's ready to run drills?"

"Tell him yourself." She screws her nose up. "I'm stopping here."

She won't be kept out of the loop. I sigh.

Leonard pushes through the door and smiles a fleeting, weighed-down smile. "This arrived from Jeremy." He swings the briefcase onto the workout bench and unclips the latches. Miriam stands at Leonard's shoulder with the same even mask she's been wearing since I found out she's a liar.

"I thought he was against all this." I can't hide my disgust. Jeremy Gallagher didn't believe in breaking protocol. When he'd found out Jamie had not only told his parents about the Affinity Project, but broken his uncle's cover, things had got ugly. There had been more shouting in the study the night before as Leonard argued with his brother during yet another long-distance call.

"Jeremy's pragmatic enough to accept the damage is done. He supplied us with an expert doctor and he thought these might be of use." Leonard opens the lid on a set of six watches and phones. "They're all linked. Satellite communications. You two will be able to send an alert at any sign of trouble."

I slip the cold metal watch over my wrist and shiver. "Have you heard from Doctor Sullivan?"

Leonard purses his lips. "That was my next bit of news, or non-news."

"No ID," Kitty mutters.

"He managed to map past the synthetic gene to find the pre-modified markers, but there's no match in police records."

My stomach sinks.

"It was never fail-safe," Miriam says. "Only the signal matters and you're doing everything you can to strengthen your frequency sensitivity."

I grit my teeth. I don't need a pep talk from her.

"In the meantime," Miriam says, "school starts in three days and you're all going to Gainsborough."

Kitty pales. "School?"

I sit winded on the bench. In the future I picture, we stay holed up on the estate like survivalists, amassing arms, awaiting Armageddon. The idea of letting Kitty loose in an uncontained environment spins me out.

"A *Stray* won't touch you there," Miriam says. Her gentle assurance grates my nerves more than the whispering.

"And too bad if he's sitting next to her in math?" I mutter. Kitty frowns and I instantly regret not holding my tongue.

"It's the safest place you can be," Miriam says to Kitty as though she had voiced the concern. "A *Stray*'s instinct for self-preservation is our greatest advantage. Evie will be in all your classes and it will be better than hanging around home."

Kitty knots her fingers. "Boot camp is looking a bit tedious."

"And what about training?" I say, thinking of the wasted hours in a classroom.

"There's plenty of time before and after school," Miriam says. "It's really what's best for Kitty."

She may as well have poked me with a stick. "You don't get to tell me what's best for Kitty. If it had been up to you, I'd still be across town, waiting for–"

"Evie." Kitty gives me a scolding look. Even Leonard frowns, but Miriam keeps her hurt behind her mask.

I drop my gaze. "I can't afford Gainsborough."

"I can," Leonard says. I start to argue but he squeezes my shoulder, all final and brooking no disagreement so I shut my mouth. He closes the case and turns to the door, Miriam behind him.

"School together. It's what we always wanted." Kitty drops onto the bench next to me and bumps my shoulder. "When are you going to make up with her?"

I sigh. She had reached out to Miriam and can't understand why anyone else wouldn't. Her generosity makes me feel like a miser.

"You're so rude to her all the time and she never fights back."

"Give it a rest, Kit."

"Barb made up with her."

I snap my head towards her. "Since when?"

"Since this morning. They were hugging it out in the kitchen."

My one ally gone. "Great."

She taps her pen on the soft moleskin covered journal. "Miriam loves you."

Logically, I know it. Logically, I know I love her too. Being at odds with Miriam makes me uncomfortable and I don't take pleasure in my power to hurt her. But her violation of trust has formed a block in my mind that I can't get past. "School, huh?"

She narrows her eyes at the change in subject. "I missed

out on Lila's road trip, school might actually be fun."

The thought of trying to function in a social setting while playing bodyguard sounds exhausting.

"Well," she continues, "it's got to be better than sitting around all day watching you and Jamie circling each other."

I sit up straight, heat in my face. "Circling?"

"You heard me. Circling."

As though summoned, Jamie appears in the courtyard. I stand up, my back to the door, tucking my hair behind my ears. Kitty clicks her tongue. I scowl but when the door opens I adjust my expression and turn. Jamie strolls in looking too good in long shorts and loose shirt, buoyed and ready for action. His mood has lightened with each day's evidence of my swift healing – a sign of my "promising" development. I know he draws hope from it the way I draw hope from Kitty's optimism. But it makes me nervous that the whole house of cards will give out, and I swallow the urge to confess my horrible dreams. They've become worse each night, like I've tapped directly into the head of the Stray.

"School, then?" Jamie raises his eyebrows, that disarming up and down bounce.

"Apparently." I will Kitty not to say anything that'll embarrass me.

She rises beside me, rubbing her hands. "What's on this afternoon?"

"Actually," Jamie inclines his head, "I figured Everton deserves to see me on the receiving end of some target practice." Yesterday's "training sessions" involved paintball guns and me getting shot in the ass.

"Oooo!" Kitty brightens. "Jamie showed me this when I got home from the hospital. It's brilliant, Evs, you'll love it. I'll get the crossbow." She drops her journal on the bench and scoots out back to the storage room, the invisible tether stretching with her. I make the automatic reach into the bandwidth like I always do whenever she leaves my side. Now I can do it with my eyes open, though I tend to grow still and stare into the distance. But with nothing more than static in the signal I give my attention back to Jamie, who watches me with approval.

I fold my arms, self-conscious that he knows what I'm doing. "No dice with Sullivan then?"

He shakes his head, his expression resigned. "Would have made things a lot simpler."

We both sigh.

I frown. "Did she say crossbow?"

"Just some fun." He grins. "A good bit of Rapid Kinetic Learning for you."

I don't like the sound of it and when Kitty appears with the crossbow and a quiver of arrows, I definitely don't like the look of it.

"We should probably go outside," Jamie says. "Kitty's

aim can be a little off and Barb won't like it if she breaks another mirror."

Kitty levels the crossbow at his head. "You should have done this as one of your coming out tricks – would have convinced us you weren't completely barking."

I shiver, imagining the conversation Jamie has had with his parents. It makes me grateful to be an only child. The thought of a brother or sister in the mix is more stomach-churning than the threat of what Affinity will do about the break in protocol. Who would sit back and do nothing, let their sibling wander around unprotected with no promise of an emerging Shield and no way to tap into their signal to scan for a threat? Screw discretion. I would have done the same thing if I were Jamie; though, for his sake, I worry about what Affinity Project discipline looks like.

"He told us everything, after I was discharged. We thought he was raving, till he took us out on the lawn and we saw him move. Course, I still refused to believe it." Kitty hugs the crossbow. "Then he showed me his back–"

Jamie brings his hands together in a sudden loud clap. "Come on. You can shoot me, that'll cheer you up."

* * *

Out on the front lawn, Kitty strides away from us, swinging the crossbow. Jamie stops by the stone wall and nods me to the side, but I stand there looking back and forth between them. He really means for her to shoot him. Something clicks inside me and I stretch my hands out with a fierce rush of feeling. "This is not remotely funny."

Kitty ignores me and loads an arrow into the shaft. She holds it between her feet and pulls back the line with a grunt. I don't like it. I could hiss with how much I don't like it but it's the direction of my concern that baffles me. Why would I be anxious for Jamie? "Kitty. Stop."

They're actually going to do it.

She balances the weapon before her.

"Jamie. Stop her!"

He just winks. "You might want to step aside, love."

That last word gets my attention; casual, English, familiar. I'd worry at it for meaning but the let-down of adrenaline demands all of my attention. "I don't want to see this! Seriously!"

At the sound of the safety latch, instinct takes over. I swing around and fly across the grass before she can pull the trigger. Her eyes flash wide before I ram her and we fall through the air in slow-motion catastrophe.

Several things strike me in the vacuum of time. The sharp smell of panic sweat. The pounding of Jamie's feet. His shout. Kitty's escalating squeal. Two distinct heartbeats, one a frenetic metronome, the other a startled skip. The slow hurtling crossbow, turning over and over, glinting in the light. With an infusion of exquisite dread, precognition comes, midair. The crossbow will make three full rotations before it hits the ground, releasing the trigger, launching an arrow directly at Kitty's head – if I let her take the impact of our fall. I grip her tight around the waist and turn her above me, extending my arm over my head, palm down, ready to catch the missile.

Kitty lands with a mighty "Ooof!", forcing air from my lungs. There's a metallic click and a burning sensation in my right hand, Jamie above us, panting, swearing. Kitty struggles to get up but I hold her vice-like against me. I can't take my eyes off my hand. I hold an arrow as if I've just picked it up off the ground. It's hot in my palm like rope burn.

"Evie." Jamie kneels by my head and turns my face, his expression terrifying. The full horror of my mistake hits me. I gasp and release Kitty. She pulls back, sheet white. I sit bolt upright and drop the arrow like a stick of dynamite, and we all sit staring at it.

"Kitty, I'm sorry," I choke. I put her in danger – me and no one else. Nausea churns my stomach. I press my hands into the grass to still my trembling. "You could have been killed. I don't know why – I didn't want–" I shut my mouth. What can I say? That I was afraid for Jamie? The idea scrambles my brain.

Kitty lets loose a wild whoop, frightening me as she

bounces on her knees. "Did you see that? Bloody hell, Jamie!" But his face is impossible to read.

"I'm so sorry. I'm such an idiot. I – I was afraid."

He puts a hand on my shoulder and nods at his sister. "Look, she's fine."

Kitty jumps up. "I'm going to tell Dad!"

"No!" I shoot to my feet. "Leonard will freak." But she's already racing back towards the house. "This is terrible. Why would she tell him?"

"I expect because it's very good news. You don't get it. It took me a month to develop reflexes like that. I mean, serious practice." He rises up and moves towards me. "May I?" He takes my hand, his expression curious like he's listening for something. My trembling eases and he turns my palm over and blows on the red mark, rubbing it gently with his thumb. "Smarts, yeah?"

My whole body tingles. I swallow. "How did I do that?" I don't mean catching the arrow. I mean jeopardising Kitty's safety to protect him.

"No idea." He keeps up the circular pressure on my palm. "Incredible you could override your instinct like that. I didn't think it was possible."

But that's the thing, another instinct had taken over. It makes no sense. I squeeze my eyes closed, wishing I could undo it. "It was a mistake."

"I hope not."

My eyes pop open to find his gaze locked on mine.

"Unless of course it was an insult." He arches his eyebrow. "I might be offended if you thought I wasn't up to catching an arrow." His grin stretches out. "Works better for me if you couldn't help yourself."

I'm too upset to laugh. "But it's not good, is it?"

"I would say it was exceptional – that you're exceptional." He shakes his head. "Wait till they get a load of you."

Before I can ask what he means he looks past me at the house. I follow his gaze. Barb watches us from the newly glazed kitchen window, her face like stone. I pull away. "She didn't see that, did she?" I'm not sure if I mean the crossbow incident or the hand holding.

"Judging by her expression, yeah, she did."

PROMISE

I wake to the sound of quiet movement – Barb coming in with a tray of food.

"This is how you sleep?"

I'm so used to sleeping on top of the bed in sweatpants and sneakers that it takes me a moment to figure out what she means. "Is everything okay? What time is it?" I rub my eyes to erase the image of my nightmare, as though she might catch the shadow of it behind my eyes.

"Early. Everything's fine." She sets the tray on a stool then turns to open the curtains on a pale morning. "I know you'll be busy today, training and all." She fusses with the tie backs. "Thought you might need something to get you going."

"Um, thanks. You didn't need to do that." I tuck my hair back and sit up, resetting my compass, reaching for Kitty. The reassuring tug in my stomach warms me, cleansing powers against the twisted night.

"Dig in." She lifts the tray onto the bed.

I sip my juice, feeling awkward.

"I wish you could make peace with your aunt."

An ambush. Guilt twists inside me. "I'm sorry, Mrs Gallagher."

"Barb, sweetheart."

"Sorry, Barb." It still feels weird to say it. "I don't mean to make things difficult. I'm trying to let it go but it's almost like a – a stop sign I can't get past."

"I'm not much of an example, am I? I reacted very badly. But the truth is, if I were Miriam, I would have lied too." She gives me a sad smile. "You know I was jealous of Miriam when we were at school? I might have been April's best friend but I could never compete with her identical twin. April would have done anything to keep you safe, Evangeline, and Miriam's the same. She loves you like you were her own."

A lump forms in my throat. "I know. I'll try."

She pauses. "One other thing. I realise this is probably not my business and it's not my intention to pry, but I gather something's going on between you and Jamie?"

"Oh." Heat blooms in my face. "I – uh, I mean, no."

"Evie, I'm not blind or stupid."

I don't know what to say.

"Jamie has a girlfriend." Her eyes widen, embarrassed to have blurted it out. She fumbles in her pocket for a photo and places it on the bed. The image shows Jamie and a beautiful young woman with sandy hair and smiling blue eyes. They're wrapped up in ski gear, their faces pressed side by side.

A cold hand reaches through my ribcage and squeezes my heart. "Right."

I want to end the conversation this second. "You don't have to explain."

"You must understand, Jamie would never intend to deceive you. He's a good boy. But as I'm sure you are coming to realise – with the pressure he's under …"

I will her to stop.

"Complications could be distracting and dangerous."

"Mrs Gallagher – Barb, seriously, there is nothing going on."

She raises her hand to stop me, her eyes over bright. "Evie, my children–" Her voice breaks. "You can't possibly imagine what it's like to know that at any moment your children could be taken from you." Her voice rises. "And now here you are, my daughter's life in your hands. And my son, his own burden to bear, not knowing when the next crisis will come for him." She shakes and my insides knot. "I see the way he is with you, Evie. That's why I can't talk to him about this. He'd be furious with me for interfering." Tears slip down her face, her jewelled hand at her mouth. "Promise you won't let yourself be distracted. For his sake, for Kitty's, for your own."

"Of course." There is no other answer I can give.

* * *

After breakfast, I want to drown in endorphins so I march out to the lawn, hoping Miriam has planned something gruelling, something that will wear me out so I have no energy left to think.

Of course Jamie has a girlfriend, but if that doesn't surprise me, why do I feel so depressed? It's not like I have to give anything up – nothing exists between us. Besides which, I agree with Barb. I have enough going on and Kitty needs to be my sole focus. But still, I can't deny the bitter aftertaste of loss.

The muggy day has turned to rain but Jamie and Miriam seem unconcerned, waiting between the twin oaks that dominate the main lawn. Kitty waves me over and welcomes me under her umbrella. No evidence of a journal. For some reason that makes me feel better.

"Right," Miriam says, in the neutral voice she's taken to using since things have gone sour. "We've worked a lot on your reflexes but it's time to go hand-to-hand. You need to feel what it's like to be in a fight – but don't worry, we won't let you get hurt."

"I don't care about getting hurt," I snap. What worries

me is whether I'll be good enough or fast enough. What if I'm too slow to pick it up? I've been itching to learn something that makes me feel useful. Reflex training is all well and good, but I need to know how to break a man's neck, how to wrench a hip bone or drive someone's nose cartilage into their brain. "Let's do it."

"We still need to take it one step at a time. It's about building on your strengths."

I sigh.

"I'm talking about kinesthetic memory, or neuromuscular facilitation, as it's known in the trade – like we've been practising at home with the sparring dummy and knife throwing. You see it, store it," she taps her temple, "then do it." She rubs her hands together then turns to Jamie. "Shall we?"

A grin tugs at the corners of his mouth. He takes a few steps back and positions himself, knees bent, arms loose at his sides.

I hold my breath.

Jamie nods.

Miriam launches herself at him with ferocious speed.

My eyes struggle to keep up.

"Blimey," Kitty whispers.

Blimey about covers it.

They look like they're trying to kill each other. Miriam spirals over Jamie in a cartwheel blur. He counters with a low sweep of his leg to collect her ankle in landing. She flips back into a squat then they're both in the air, twisting in a collision I expect to end in a heap of limbs. They land light and without interruption to their sparring. Transfixed, I will my greedy brain to absorb the details, feeling the tension in my arms and legs as my muscles twitch in response. Jamie laughs and dodges out of Miriam's reach, pelting away from her. With Miriam hard on his heels, bellowing good-natured abuse, they disappear into the trees.

Kitty and I wait for them to reappear, scanning the tree line for a sighting. I glance at her. She chews her lip.

"If you want to go inside, I'd still sense you from here."

"I'd rather see. Imagining is worse."

I know from Miriam's alley memory that she's wrong. Not that I'll point that out. Instead, I take her hand and stare at the trees, wondering how far Jamie and Miriam have gone, trying to ignore the strange stirring of jealousy about what they might be doing and why it's taking so long.

You're sick.

Jamie appears first, powerful body, phenomenal stride. I realise I'm staring in a way that's unhelpful after Barb's warning but he makes it impossible not to. Miriam follows and I hope I look as good as she does at full speed. They skid to a standstill before us, the fabric of their clothes darkening with the damp. They laugh and clap each other on the back; everybody's friends with Miriam except me.

"Not bad." Miriam wipes the drizzle from her face. "You've been active what? Two years?"

"Two and a half."

"You're good."

"I was being a gentleman."

Miriam laughs but drops the smile when she turns to me. "Okay. Your turn."

"You think I'll be able to do that?"

"We'll start with a some cat and mouse. Get some speed on. Try some blocking." Her eyes move over my face in an awkward moment of indecision – will I spar with her or Jamie? She steps aside. "See if you can catch him."

Kitty gives me a bracing thumbs up and backs away with her umbrella, leaving me in the rain. "You'll be right, Evs."

Jamie darts past, nudging me with his elbow.

"Don't go too easy on her," Miriam says. "Make her work a little. Maybe try some obstacles."

"Come on, cat." He jogs backwards, beckoning, taunting. I leap forwards, my feet sliding in the damp. He laughs and takes off across the lawn. The twinge of embarrassment spurs my speed, but as I lean into the wind, gaining momentum, adrenaline charges through me. I almost close the gap as we near the forest, but part of me holds back, afraid of what might happen if I catch him:

us grappling in the damp grass, the urgent thrashing of limbs. *Stop it.* He slips through the trees, dodging quickly out of sight, and I skid to a halt, disoriented by the haze of grey and green. No sign of him. I turn on my heel, searching, feeling the cooler air chill my lungs and the clamour of my pulse.

Wind rushes at the back of my neck. I spin and find myself nose to neck with Jamie. I gasp. The branches overhead still shiver from his sudden drop. Not even puffed, he stands relaxed, hands in his pockets, an electric four or five inches between us. Neither of us moves.

"Want to try something?" His voice a low, warm vibration.

I can barely nod.

"All right. Concentrate. Forget about everything but me."

Well, I was already doing that.

"Good." He grins. "Try to block me when I move."

I stiffen.

"I'm not going to hurt you. I'm going to take hold of you. But you can stop me. Relax. You'll anticipate my move."

It feels like an exam I'm sure I will fail.

"Concentrate."

I would need to close my eyes and stop breathing altogether to do that. Instead, I inhale and exhale slowly through my mouth and wait. Something blurs in my peripheral vision then Jamie's wrist appears in my right hand before I hear the slap of our skin or feel the jarring impact in my shoulder.

"Wow." Adrenaline surges through me like soda water. I stare at my pale hand around his bronzed wrist. I have to give my fingers a direct command to unclench, leaving white indentations. He winces. "Sorry," I say.

But his face transforms with a brief, brain-scrambling smile. "Again?"

I nod.

Jamie assumes his relaxed stance. "Watch me now."

This time I see it happen as my hand connects with his right forearm, hear the echoing smack, feel my body swing back and the twinge in my ribs. "Jamie!"

A predatory glint narrows his gaze. The engine in my chest guns, the warning to flee flashes in my mind and I release his arm as though it burns my hand. An electric pause elapses.

"You have three seconds."

I debate passing out.

"Run, mouse."

In the first second, I can't deny a major part of me wants to be caught. The next, I run. Crashing through the brush on the left, I map out a path through the undergrowth that will lead me to the splintering arm of the Border River, in the vague hope I can cross over and he'll lose my signal. The third second hits and the sound of Jamie's pursuit fills my ears.

I hammer forwards, branches slapping my arms and legs. The ground, uneven with vines, broken logs and unexpected hollows, jars my steps. I vault a fallen tree trunk, landing untidily, my feet sliding on mud-slicked leaves. I resist the compulsion to squeal, right myself and almost trip again with the sound of Jamie closing in. But I find my footing and, as the roar of the river grows louder ahead, I mow through the last hundred yards like a locomotive. Even if Jamie can't see me, he can't help but hear me.

The river's edge arrives abruptly and I make a wild leap, the bandwidth going momentarily blank. I don't quite clear it. Freezing water swallows my leg up to the knee and I gasp, swinging my arms in a chaotic windmill up the opposite bank. The bandwidth comes back to life.

Jamie lands beyond a thorn break that runs parallel to the river and I veer left again to follow the bank. His low chuckle echoes through the undergrowth and I realise he could probably take me without breaking a sweat. It whips my pride and I force myself to lengthen my stride. Ahead, rocks and trees obscure the path and I have a choice to cross back over the river, or turn right where the wall of thorns parts. At the last second, I lunge through a gap in the bracken but falter when Jamie's hurtling body cuts through the trees far sooner than I expect. He collects me midair, a lung-crushing collision, turning us to take the force of the fall on his back. While we fly, the moment gives me the full feast of his expression and it isn't the landing that takes my breath away.

We skid a few yards, coming to a heavy stop at the base of a pine where we lie panting. "Are you okay?" he says.

"I think so." Conscious of lying on top of him, I sound strangled. "You?"

His chest vibrates, a low laugh bubbling up inside him. "I'm good."

I push back onto my knees, too awkward and exposed, blood thundering in my ears. "How did I do?"

"Very well." He smirks, leaning on his elbows, streaked in mud. "You make a hell of a lot of noise. Great reflexes though. I should do all my training with you as bait."

"Nice." I wrinkle my nose and try to find my feet. Jamie gets up, chuckling, and takes my hand, hauling me the rest of the way. My shirt clings to my skin, my ponytail has come loose and my hair hangs tangled and heavy. I regret my wet sneakers and self-consciousness.

"No, I actually think you make me faster." He pauses, frowning like he can hear something. "I've been wondering ..." His hand feels hot around my cold fingers. I notice because he still holds them, tingling in his grasp.

I wait for him to let go, to complete his thought, to look away.

He doesn't.

With total clarity I see he will kiss me. It flashes in my mind like a brightly lit billboard and the want of it drowns the warning bells. I can almost anticipate the taste of him and the infinitesimal sway of my body, like something magnetic, draws me in. He moves slowly, unblinking, his thumb sweeping over my knuckles. His gaze moves to my mouth, his body closing the gap between us, his lips almost touching mine. I waver on the brink. It comes to me, late but loud – the cause for alarm – Barb. With painful resolve I push away. "I'm sorry."

"Wait a minute–"

"We should get back." How far are we from the house? When did I lose sense of the tether? My recklessness appalls me. Barb was right, distractions are dangerous.

"You don't understand–" He steps towards me, palm out.

"I'm not comfortable being away from Kitty so long." Convenient and true.

His hand falls at his side and he looks troubled. "Of course, but, Everton–"

"Let's run."

He sighs. "After you."

I take off, running for my life.

GIRLFRIEND

It's getting late and I'm wiped out, thanks to another whole day of Miriam's sadistic training regime, but I don't want to go to sleep and open the door of horrors. As if the almost-kiss had invoked bad juju, last night I dreamed I was the Stray, choking Kitty, power in my arms, fragile bones beneath my hands. It can't be normal, these sorts of dreams. It terrifies me that I might be some kind of danger to her. But who can I ask? Not Jamie, he'd be appalled. Not Miriam, it would mean talking to her in private and I'm not ready for that. The memory prickles beneath my skin. I lean back on the kitchen counter, waiting for it to pass and my stomach growls a ferocious, gurgling reminder of my hopped up metabolism. I can't keep up with my appetite this side of Sparking.

I turn to the refrigerator. Jamie strolls in, and I duck behind the refrigerator door, swearing silently at the leftover chicken. After keeping my distance all day, avoiding eye contact through dinner and conversation afterwards (by going upstairs to "get my books ready" for school, which really meant getting Kitty to help me pick my outfit), now my luck has dried up.

He sets the kettle on the stove while I grab what I need and work hastily at the counter, throwing my sandwich together.

"Would you like some hot chocolate?"

I almost slice through my finger, unable to scramble a gracious no. "Um, sure. You want some of this?" Why did I feel compelled to reciprocate? Thankfully, he shakes his head, but it takes me by surprise. I pause over the squeezable cheese and blurt, "Why don't you eat like a horse?"

"I do."

"Not like this glutton-fest."

"Still more than most."

"So I'm not just a pig?"

"It's very normal. Part of early development, the high-octane metabolism." He digs out mugs and waits for the kettle. In his khaki pants and black T-shirt he balances one bare foot on top of the other, leaning by the stove. While his back is turned, I torture myself with looking. When he brings the steaming mugs to the counter it seems rude to march off, and that would only provoke a reaction which might lead to a conversation, one I can't face. I grit my teeth and pull up a stool.

"School tomorrow," he says.

I nod as though the idea doesn't completely terrify me.

"I think you'll enjoy Gainsborough. The setting's very picturesque."

I chew, keeping my eyes on my plate, not even tasting the food. I will him to let me eat in peace and for a moment or two it looks like I might get my wish.

"How are you coping?"

My head snaps up. There ought to be a law against eyes like his. It isn't fair. Barb's warning flashes in my mind and I look down. "I dunno. It's like one long panic attack." *Please, let Kitty come downstairs.* She's probably at her desk scribbling in that damn journal. "You think Kitty's okay?"

Jamie's expression grows weary. "Okay as she can be, I suppose."

"She writes a lot. You think that's healthy?"

"Probably better than keeping everything in her head."

"I don't like it." I take a massive bite so it's obvious I have nothing more to say.

"Training's coming along," Jamie says.

He's not going to let up. I shrug and chew.

"Scrapes are healing well. You look … good."

I look up and he looks down, blowing over the lip of his mug.

Careful. I pick up the hot chocolate. "Might finish this

upstairs." I almost make it to the door, resisting the urge to bolt, when he speaks again.

"Evie?"

Deflector shields up, I turn.

Elbows on the counter, he leans, head tilted, lips pursed. "So, we're not going to talk about it then?"

I mimic his head tilting and lip pursing. "Ah, nope." I push the door open with my foot and march through the dining room, aggravated by the thump in my chest. I make it halfway up the stairs when Jamie appears beside me, hands in his pockets. I ignore him. On the landing, I veer right, but he catches me gently by the elbow.

"*What?*"

He blinks at the snap in my voice and removes his hand. "Come on, Everton."

So we're back to last names. "Come on what? *Gallagher.*"

He smirks. "I actually quite like it when you use my last name."

"What do you want then, *Jamie*?"

It only inspires a long slow smile that reminds me of his smug former self. "I like it better when you say my first name."

Infuriated, I step past him.

He cuts me off. "You really want to act like nothing happened?"

"Keep your voice down." I dart a look back at the family

wing then nod towards my room. Unfazed, he follows me in. I put my mug on the dresser and close the door, crackling in my skin. *"Do you mind?"*

Jamie sits on the couch, elbows on his knees, hands in a loose clasp as he watches me. Aware of being alone with him in the bedroom, I have painful visions of Barb walking in and a cold sweat needles the back of my neck.

"Why so twitchy?" he says.

I picture flinging my mug at his head.

"I'm not sorry." He leans back, stretching his long legs out, crossing his feet. "I wanted to kiss you."

My pulse may have stopped for a second, hearing that, but I steel myself, determined to stay cool. I talk to the floor with my hands on my hips because I don't know what else to do with them. "You have a girlfriend, which means you're kind of an asshole. Worse still, I knew and nearly let it happen anyway, which makes me a traitor to the sisterhood."

He sits up, all traces of humour gone. "I see." He frowns at the floorboards and I fold my arms around my waist. "Helena and I–"

The blue-eyed girl's name is Helena. I don't want to hear "Helena and I." It opens the prison to my heart so the cold hand can reattach itself.

"We're not together in the way that you think."

I shift my weight from one leg to the other, squeezing

myself. "You know what, it doesn't really matter, does it?"

Jamie hangs his head, running his hands up into his hair. "*Affinity* matched us for … a research assignment about a year ago. We lived together a few months while I was in Berlin. Look, it's complicated and I can't really explain the ins and outs of it all, but we're not 'together'. Well, we are together, but not *together*, together."

I do not want to know. It's hard to believe that Barb and Leonard would have approved of their then seventeen-year-old son shacking up with a girl in Berlin. "What exactly are you saying?"

"Helena and I are not attached but I still have an obligation to *Affinity* and Helena is part of that obligation."

"So, you and me, it's extracurricular."

"No!" He gets to his feet. "It isn't." He steps towards me. I step back and he frowns. "Everton, I'm not trying to mess you around."

"Whatever." I shrug. "It doesn't matter."

"It matters to me." He balls his fists. "So, it's not an uncomplicated scenario, but I'm not being 'unfaithful' and I'm certainly not trying to take advantage of you on my 'downtime'." He relaxes his hands onto his hips, casting about for the right way forwards.

"Affinity would be okay with you and me?" I don't even blush.

He looks down. "Technically, no."

At least he's being honest. "Right."

"It's not easy losing the freedom to choose in certain situations." His eyes fix on mine. "Especially when you want something in particular."

My heart leaves the building, soaring up in the stratosphere like a little red comet. I rein it in and draw a shaky breath. "And what would Helena say?"

He doesn't hesitate. "She would understand."

"Would she?"

He doesn't falter. "She would."

"What exactly have you got in mind, Jamie? Any scenario where we were … involved–" it's hard to speak, "there's an inevitable ending where you're called up to render your services for the Affinity Project and you're back with Helena."

"That's not quite the sales pitch I would have offered." He runs his hands over his face. "Since you've been going through all this, I'm sure you've become aware that the issue of fairness, and the total lack of it, is part and parcel. Nothing about what we are, what we are compelled to do, is fair. I can let that eat me up, or I can live in the present the best way I know how."

It's too hard to look at him. I turn to the dresser and run my finger along the fringe of the lamp. "So, this is your like it or lump it speech?"

"Couldn't we just try to be normal?"

I would laugh except that it might verge on hysteria. Could we be normal? An ache of longing grips me for my old life, its predictable dynamics. I have no energy to play games. The reality is that if he had any clue about what went through my mind when I slept, he'd hate me. I swallow my grief and take the easy way out. "Your mom gave me the hard word to steer clear."

He jerks his head back. "She what?"

I feel the need to defend Barb. "Well, she doesn't want me off my game. I should be focusing on Kitty."

"That woman," he mutters and moves closer. "Take my hand."

I back away. "I will not."

"It's important." His expression remains serious and his tone businesslike. "Please, Everton, take my hand."

The emotional whiplash makes it hard to keep up. I give him a warning look before slipping my hand into his open palm. The immediate tingling spreads from my fingers, through my arm, to meet the hum in my spine.

He raises his eyebrow. "Can you feel that?"

"I always feel like that." It sounds less desperate than the whole truth. Only Jamie can produce that type of tingling.

"I don't." He rubs his thumb across the back of my hand. "Only with you."

I have no idea how to respond. Dumbly, I stare at our

linked hands, feeling my pulse in my head.

"You remember what I said about you making me faster? At first I thought it was just having something to pursue. That generally produces better results. But then I thought about what it feels like when I'm close to you, the pins and needles ..."

"Is it supposed to mean something?"

"I think we may be Syngerists. It's extremely rare. Synergist coding occurs only when complimentary signals meet and resonate at a particular frequency. The signals sync and form a bond which intensifies frequency sensitivity and increases the production of adrenaline, accelerating the development of the synthetic gene. Basically, if we were together, we'd become faster, stronger and more sensitive to the bandwidth."

I look at my hand in his then up into his eyes. "You're serious?"

He nods and knits his fingers through mine, sending a hypnotising surge of tingling up my arm. The incident with the crossbow – the instinct to protect Jamie – it wasn't bad wiring. Relief pours through me, raising hope for Kitty and hope for an antidote to the thing that lurks in my nights. Behind all of it stirs my Jamie-specific longing, and I can't help myself, the technicolour memory of our almost-kiss replays in my mind. His expression glazes for a couple of seconds and he draws a sharp breath at my involuntary KMT. I blush. "Sorry. I didn't mean–"

He steps closer. "Yeah, you did."

"Your mom–"

"I'll deal with her." He takes my waist and draws me against him. Heat, electricity, the intimacy of shared space, the strangeness and the wonder of it. *Do something.* I swallow, then slide my hands over his arms, something I have imagined doing so many times. Anticipation closes my eyes, lifts my chin and parts my lips. The kiss. Warm, sweet, restrained and full of ruin. What hope do I have of keeping my promise to Barb after this?

He pulls back, dazed and short of breath. "I mean, that's definitely something."

I can't even pretend I want to stop and push up on my toes to reach him.

I'm no expert. Aside from Jamie, I've kissed only one other boy in my life, on summer camp when I was fifteen, and mostly because I was determined to eradicate the memory of the first kiss beneath the willow – which had taken on mythic proportions in my mind. The awkward camp kiss featured clashing teeth, too much slobber and a pimply chinned boy with spaghetti hands. Now, back in Jamie's arms, it's effortless and I am unhesitating. Perfect non-verbal communication. Not even fear and uncertainty, wringing their hands in the wings, can ruin it.

Dizziness, on the other hand, might.

Pressed close, the scent of his skin, the thrill in mine – the whole sensory overload – makes my pulse race, not just in a swoony, soundtrack-and-fireworks way, but actual palpitations, like "oh crap, I think I'm having a cardiac arrest".

"Jamie," I gasp against him, trying to clear my head, but he only holds me tighter, knotting his fingers in my hair. My eyes roll back and the grey fog rolls in.

DOUBTS

For Kitty's sake, I ride in the back of Jamie's car, hunched low with my knees jammed to the side. She still has her neck brace to contend with and it's a forty-minute drive to Gainsborough. I don't want her to arrive sore and achy on her first day. She sits in the front passenger seat, eerily still, her breathing too fast and shallow. I doubt she's slept any better than I have.

Much to my disappointment, not even the after-glow of Jamie's kisses has kept the horror from my dreams. By four in the morning, I had turned the lamp on just to keep the shadows away. Lying awake had been another form of torment, raking over my suspect list – all the boys from the Governor's Ball – wondering how many of them shared classes with Kitty. I close my eyes and exhale slowly, wishing I could shake the sick stage fright that liquefies my limbs.

When I look up, I find Jamie watching me in the rearview mirror. His steady gaze makes me weak for other reasons. I fainted in his arms last night and woke on my bed with him sitting, grinning, beside me. A second and third attempt to settle into a solid make out session ended with the same humiliating results, though he claimed it did wonders for his ego. "You'll be fine," he said. But it's embarrassing and scary, the sort of thing that I desperately want (and want not) to talk to Miriam about. She'd hit the roof. Jamie thinks my body needs time to adjust to new adrenaline levels, like I'm too advanced for my own nervous system. He had a whole speech about the potency of Optimal and how it messes with our chemistry, but I was too busy swooning to take it all in.

Kitty swivels, awkward in her foam neck support, to look at me.

I press my lips into a smile I don't feel. "I am fine."

But I have no clue how I'll pull off "fine" at Gainsborough. My days revolve around preparing for an inevitable conflict where someone will end up dead. Over the last few weeks, I've tried to decide what taking someone's life means to me. I know what it should mean, that I should be repulsed, that the idea should seem horrific, but the memory of the pursuit into the forest and the grim resolve that overtook me is still fresh. Now I'll have to sit next to kids who *are* normal and pretend I'm not a genetically engineered freak who spends her time contemplating murder.

"Really?" she mutters. "You two have been acting weird all morning."

My ears get hot. Damn it. I knew we'd been too obvious at breakfast. Jamie's eyes on me were like a caress on bare skin, and sitting across from him over my uneaten bowl of Cap'n Crunch had been exquisite torture. He'd rested the side of his knee against mine under the kitchen table, leaned against my shoulder at the sink to rinse his bowl, brushed his knuckles across the back of my neck reaching for an apple from the fruit basket.

"Everton and I are together," Jamie says, point blank and unapologetic.

My eyes widen and I hunch lower. We haven't talked about going public. He'd promised to deal with his mother, but in my mind the whole "coming out" scenario was further down a fairly indistinct time line. Hearing it aloud makes me feel careless and selfish in the extreme. Breaking the news to Kitty should've been my job.

"Seriously, Jamie?" Outrage hardens her voice. "You couldn't bloody help yourself!"

Jamie stiffens. "Excuse me?"

"You're completely and utterly predictable!"

"What is that supposed to mean?"

"You do know he has a girlfriend?" Kitty struggles to turn sufficiently and do justice to her baleful glare.

My insides twist. "It's not – they're not–"

Kitty turns to her brother. "You just had to have Evie too!"

Jamie sighs, an aggravated, impatient burst of air. "Helena and I are not together in that way."

Helena. I drop my face into my hand.

"Right," Kitty says. "Does Helena know that?"

"Helena-has-a-boyfriend," Jamie growls through his teeth.

I look up. "She does?"

He reddens. "I meant to explain."

"Ugh!" Kitty says, disgusted with us both.

I have rarely seen Jamie so ruffled, and Kitty's response does not give me hope for how it will go down with the rest of the family, let alone Miriam. I squirm, claustrophobic in the back seat with no available door to throw myself from.

"This is completely bloody typical. Evie is my Shield-thing."

"I am, Kit–"

"She is," Jamie says. "Nothing has–"

"She's supposed to be looking out for me!"

"I am! I will!"

"Kitty–" Jamie says.

"She's hardly going to be able to concentrate with your tongue down her throat!"

My face flames and I splutter.

Jamie shakes his head. "Be reasonable."

"Reasonable? Reasonable!" Kitty makes a half-strangled noise and her face flushes pink to the tip of her nose. "You patronising shit! You have no idea. No idea what it's like waiting for some psychopath to … to–"

I want to cry. "Kit, you don't understand."

Kitty swipes the back of her hand across her eyes. "I understand just fine. It's exactly the way it always is. Even when we were kids. As soon as Jamie steps in the bloody room, I might as well be invisible."

Stung, I gape at her. "That is completely not true!"

"Everton always ignored me when we were kids!" Jamie exclaims.

"It's not just you, Evie," she says. "It's everyone."

Jamie runs his hand up into his hair and slaps it back on the steering wheel. "That's not true, Kitty."

"It is. Evie's *my* best friend, *my* Shield. She's supposed to pick me."

"I do pick you!" Hot tears spill onto my cheeks; she called me her best friend. "I do."

Jamie growls and slams his foot on the brake and we all lurch forwards. Kitty cries out, clutching the foam at her neck as her head smacks back against the seat.

"Jamie!" I strain against my belt, furious and terrified Kitty's been hurt.

"Oh, shit." He reaches for his sister. "Kitty. I'm sorry. I didn't mean to do that."

She hits his hands away. "I'm fine, you idiot."

Frantic, I spring my belt clip and lunge between them, shoving Jamie back into his seat, tears blurring my vision. "Kitty. I do. I choose you, okay? Forget about Jamie and me. It's nothing. It's over."

"It is not," Jamie mutters.

I glare at him over my shoulder. "Yes, it is. I should never have listened to you." I turn back to Kitty and touch her cheek like I can brush the hurt from her face. "I choose you, Kit. I'm sorry. I didn't mean to upset you. I won't let you down. Last night was a mistake."

"No, it wasn't," Jamie says.

"*Shut up.*"

"Last night?" Kitty looks repulsed. "You mean, you–"

"No!" I say. "He kissed me. That's all. It didn't mean anything."

"Yes, it did," Jamie says. "And you kissed me, plenty."

"Don't listen to him, Kit." I wipe her tears with my shaking fingers. "He doesn't know what he's talking about. He's delusional. I would never choose him over you."

Jamie makes a choking sound that verges annoyingly on a chuckle, and I twist around to give him the filthiest look I can muster.

"It's only because I understand the Fixation Effect that I'm not deeply insulted right now, Everton."

"It's over, Jamie."

"No, it isn't," he says. "I hate to break it to you, love, but when this is done and you've saved my sister, the Fixation Effect will be over but we'll still be Synergists."

"You'll be what?" Kitty says.

I stall. The way he said it like that – when I've saved his sister – like he believes I can, like he believes in me. A new feeling pushes through the block wall of the Fixation Effect. I swivel again to look into his eyes and find certainty burning back at me. "Say it again."

"We'll still be Synergists."

"Not that." I frown. "The other bit."

He gives an exasperated sigh. "When you've saved my sister."

I close my eyes and whisper, "You really believe I can, Jamie?"

"And you *don't*?" Kitty jerks in her seat. "Bloody hell, Evie!"

"I want to." I cover my face. "I just never thought anyone else believed I could."

"I hoped you could," Jamie says. "Before last night – before I was sure about what it was between us – when we kissed–"

Kitty groans but I drop my hands.

"Then I knew for sure, we're Synergists."

"Is anyone going to bother explaining what that means?" Kitty says.

"It means your odds, little sister, of surviving senior year are vastly improved." His eyes hold mine, his mouth curving. "I believe in you, Everton."

"I don't get it," Kitty says.

I can't take my eyes off Jamie's face. "It means, I choose you, Kit. But I choose Jamie too." His eyes startle, but I crush my lips against his, forcing him back into the seat, a grunt of surprise escaping from him before his arms come around me, pulling me closer still.

"Ew!" Kitty says. "I'm sorry, but how is this an explanation? Oh, please, is that really necessary?"

GAINSBOROUGH

Twin willow trees mark the entrance to Gainsborough Collegiate. We cross a bridge and cruise along the limestone drive that winds like a lazy snake in lush green lawn. The great structure of the school – three stories of beautiful stonework – unveils itself in increments as we pass beneath towering oak and elm, like something off the BBC.

Jamie veers right, taking the long way round the back to the student parking lot where the children of the privileged park their European cars. Students mill on the lawns and paths, faculty stroll to classes with their briefcases and folders.

"Nervous?" Jamie asks Kitty.

"A little."

For myself, not passing out feels like an achievement. My brief peak in confidence, fueled by Jamie's declarations, flatlined the moment we pulled off the road. Now, as we circle the lot, the scene looks like a line-up of potential killers, and I hear nothing but my own pulse. I scan the scattered groups of students as though I might lock on a threat there and then.

Kitty draws a shaky breath. "But this is a safe place, right?"

"Absolutely." Jamie pulls in between a sparkling SUV and a fluorescent convertible. "No one is going to hurt you. Even if the *Stray*," he dodges the word, "were a student, it's highly unlikely he would come to school. He'd be afraid of his own anxiety showing him up."

"Okay." She nods, a decisive up and down clip of her chin. "And for the record, two minutes difference doesn't qualify you for big brother status."

He clicks his tongue. "So bitter."

I admire Kitty's attempt at banter and struggle for the same easy tone. "Is it likely to be a problem if I punch one of your friends or start choking the person who sits next to you in math?"

"Start out as you mean to go on, I say." Kitty gives me a stiff-necked glance, her eyes dry, her nose back to its usual colour. "Will this whole test-tube romance increase the likelihood of random violence?"

Jamie grins. "Probably."

Kitty had listened to Jamie's explanation about Synergist coding, her eyes growing larger with the implications. When she finally conceded that it gave us an advantage,

I'd felt relieved, but her test-tube romance jokes make me uncomfortable. I don't want to think about what it means – did genetically engineered attraction count as the real thing? Hadn't I been drawn to Jamie since we were kids, long before the synthetic gene kicked in?

Lost in our thoughts, we sit there, the three of us, staring out the windshield until finally Jamie switches the ignition off. His eyes flick up to find me in the rearview. "Come on, then."

Kitty climbs out and waits by her door, brushing her skirt, hugging a folder to her chest. Even in her foam neck support she still looks pretty and put together. Jamie pulls his seat forwards and offers me his hand. I step out feeling conspicuous, releasing his hold. His eyebrow rises in question.

"Sorry," I whisper. Kissing him in front of Kitty was a total anomaly, an involuntary response to exceptional circumstances. As far as I'm concerned, public displays of affection go with public displays of anything – a no-no. Being the new girl will be more than enough spectacle to be getting on with. I cringe. "I can't do PDA. I'm sorry. People will stare."

A mystified grin curves his lips. "People will stare?"

"I'm new. That's bad enough. And you're, well, you."

He tucks his chin back. "What does that mean?"

"You're … you look … the way you do. You draw

attention." Heat creeps up my neck as Jamie frowns. Kitty watches us, her expression says we're taking too long. I rush to explain. "It's not your fault. I'm not saying you do it deliberately. You can't help it. People look at you."

He purses his lips. "People look at you."

Flustered, I shake my head. "What? No they don't."

He sighs and turns his eyes skyward. "You don't want anyone to know that I'm your boyfriend?"

Your boyfriend. It makes me breathless. The possession in that pronoun, the weight and significance of it next to the noun and, more dizzyingly, his willingness to bear the title. My voice gets small. "I – I didn't say that."

"But I'm not allowed to touch you in public?"

When he puts it like that, it makes me sound like a nut job. "Can't we play it cool? I like you. You like me. We don't have to be all over each other."

His mouth twitches. "Are you worried I'll make you pass out in the cafeteria?"

I scowl. "Look, I'm trying–"

"Everton." He tips his head forwards. "I can keep my hands to myself."

"Are we going in or what?" Kitty calls.

Jamie stands aside to let me pass, his eyes glinting with suppressed amusement. I join Kitty, irritated and embarrassed. She looks at me but I shake my head. "I'm fine." I tug at my clothes, regretting having let her pick my outfit the night before. The shoes are uncomfortable, the dress restricting. Now we're here it seems reckless and I miss my sneakers.

Jamie swings his pack over his shoulder and leads the way, looking too good in his military green shirt, epaulets on his broad shoulders – which was exactly my point. Surely he can see heads turning already? But that's the thing with Jamie – he pays no attention to the attention focused on him. I know few people as comfortable in their own skin and I envy his ease. Thanks to my priming growth spurt, I near six feet, even in flats, and the malnourished look I've sported since Mom died has been replaced with new boobs and muscle. My skin glows with good health that has nothing to do with my diet, and I realise the eyes flicking towards us aren't only landing on Jamie and Kitty. It takes all my inner resolve not to hunch my shoulders and duck my head.

A large group of boys – or a small group of large boys – spot us from the back entrance to the main foyer. They pelt across the lot and I grip Kitty's arm, about to wrench her behind me. She turns to growl in my ear, "It's just the guys. Cool it."

I let her go, balling my fists. The boys run, bellowing down the steps of the main pathway. They grab Jamie and lift him high, making so much noise people turn to watch. Pete, Mr President and the Bishop. A case study in male bonding.

"Kit! You all recovered, huh? Missed you in California." Gil Bishop releases Jamie and scoops his sister up in a bear hug that has me ready to either pass out or perform one of the random acts of violence Kitty mentioned in the car. "Love the foam. Dead sexy."

Jamie steps beside me and murmurs, "Relax, love."

Gil releases Kitty a little dented but happy.

Pete, the smallest of them at six foot, his dark hair tucked behind his ears, rests his hand on Kitty's shoulder. Dilated pupils, expanding chest, parted lips – he likes her. I hate him. Suspicion and over-protectiveness set it in stone. *Damn it.* I hadn't factored in "boys". Will I be playing chaperone as well as bodyguard?

Abe raises his hand to wave at me, interrupting my suspicious appraisal of Pete. "How's your hand?"

"My what?" I can't concentrate with the unpredictable movement around us.

"The broken glass, the blood, the swooning in our buddy's arms?" His grin widens.

"Oh, I um …"

"Swooning?" The Bishop leans in, his bushy blond eyebrows lifting as he makes the connections. "She's blocked it out? No wonder. Jamie has no technique. Now, when The Bishop …" A crowd of ponytailed cheerleaders shimmy past, giggling, calling out greetings. Several of them notice Jamie and flirtatious smiles part glossy lips.

Gil trails off like a child distracted by shiny things.

"I thought you were headed for Burton Central," Abe says, still focusing on me.

I hitch my pack higher, struggling to remember the story we'd rehearsed, torn between keeping my eyes on Pete or on the cheerleaders ogling Jamie. "Um … just a change of plans, I guess."

The Bishop swings back as the last of the short skirts flit away and he thunks his fist into Jamie's bicep. "Crew tryouts next week, Skipper?"

I haven't heard Jamie's nickname in years.

Jamie shrugs. "I'm too out of shape."

"Not likely." The Bishop hooks his arm around Jamie's neck, tugging up the hem of Jamie's shirt revealing an eyeful of pale gold muscle. "Look at you, you gorgeous, rippling specimen."

Jamie rams his elbow into Gil's stomach. Gil buckles and chokes but comes up laughing. "Seriously," Jamie says. "I haven't been on the water for months. I wasn't planning on …" he trails off at the blatant horror of his friends.

Even Pete looks up. "The sudden return to Gainsborough better not be a tease."

"Joining crew would make up for missing California," Gil says. "It could have been summer with the boys, like old times."

Kitty groans.

Jamie shakes his head.

Gil reaches over to muss the crop of his hair. "Don't be ashamed of your legendary past, brother."

I'm not sure what all that means, but before I can decide that I don't like it, Kitty scoops me out from between them. I have a brief parting glimpse of Jamie's face and it warms me inside despite my anxiety. Kitty hauls me towards the main building and the guys rumble along behind us.

"Still no leads on Kitty's guy?" Pete. I can tell by the edge of worry and impatience in his voice. The drop in volume indicates it isn't for Kitty's ears but I can hear clearly enough and it makes my skin prickle. He sounds too pushy for my liking.

"Nope," Jamie says.

"Damn. That's not right." A deeper voice this time, more resonant. I attribute it to Abe. His concern doesn't grate on me as much as Pete's. "Is the governor still dicking you around?"

"He let us look at the security footage, not that it was any use."

I can picture Jamie's careful expression.

"What a psycho." Definitely Gil, that time. I don't know if he means the governor or Kitty's attacker, but he produces a low growl that I can't help but approve of.

"Not around Kitty," Jamie says, cutting them off.

The subject changes, distracting me from measuring

Jamie's old friends for my list of suspects. I hear my name and some sniggering.

"She's living in Burton?" Maybe Pete.

Jamie's answer comes too low for me to hear.

"With you?" Gil hisses. "Hot damn! Well played, my friend. She is seriously ..."

I can't make out what I "seriously" am with my pulse pounding in my ears. Jamie mutters something corrective.

"But still," Gil says, "under the same roof."

There are whistles and guffaws. Hot with embarrassment, I consider blacklisting the lot of them. Kitty, however, rolls her eyes in a manner that implies the word "boys", and I worry about how much she has heard. Re-looping my arm, she pulls me up the wide stone steps.

We cross beneath the lintel of the huge stone arch. There are crowds of students in the foyer and we attract some whispered attention; most of it centres on the twins and Kitty's notoriety as assault victim. My hearing dims as I scan the faces in the crowd, noting any eyes that fix on Kitty. Someone jostles my arm and Jamie steps in front of me, arresting my focus. He puts his hand on my elbow and I tense, afraid he'll kiss me in front of everyone.

He smirks and leans down to whisper in my ear, "Relax. Kitty's safe. You can do this." His breath warms my neck and over his shoulder I see people watching us. "You look very beautiful, by the way."

"You're embarrassing me."

"I'm building up your tolerance." He strokes the side of my arm, a quick light brush of his knuckle before stepping back. "See you at recess." He winks and walks away, leaving me dizzy.

Kitty sighs. "Come on, heartbreaker."

I follow her past a group of gawking girls, none of them looked too pleased with me. I ignore my burning ears and keep my face impassive. I'm not there to make friends – which should make me sad. But it doesn't.

***

My school in Pennsylvania had yellowed linoleum, battered grey lockers and fluorescent strip lighting attached to watermarked ceiling panels. At Gainsborough there are highly polished hardwood floors, the lockers are burnished oak and pendant lights hang from bronze chains affixed to ornate plaster rosettes. High windows let in the sun and everything seems gilded. Kitty leads us to where the locker numbers match those on her list. She stops and hands me my code. Dazed by the atmosphere, the clamour of students and the static in my head, my fingers move numbly over the keypad. Kitty loads textbooks into her locker and I catch a flash of her journal.

I frown. "You brought that here?"

She lifts her chin. "Where I go, it goes."

"Kitty!" Three high-pitched voices break in and I swivel so fast I nearly give myself whiplash. Lila, the petite round-faced girl with almond eyes and jet black hair, leads the eager group. I grip the locker behind my back and gulp as they swamp Kitty. They talk over each other, equal parts admiring how good she looks (even in a neck brace), bemoaning that she missed the road trip, berating the police for failing to identify her assailant and wondering what on earth has she done in New Hampshire without them.

Imogen, the tall girl, stands at the back, rail thin with soft auburn curls and freckled complexion. She smiles at me, a shy, toe-in-the-water test of a smile, but my response comes too slowly and she falters. The third girl I recognise as Richard Dean's date, Kaylee.

It surprises me to see her at school, but what had I expected? She'd refused to lay charges. Only the attack on Kitty had received any press. Maybe no one at school, beyond Kaylee's close circle of friends, had any clue what Richard did to her. Her brown eyes run over me in open suspicion, as if she senses the vein of my thoughts. I try to smile, but she looks away, her lips compressing like she tastes something sour.

I know I'm giving off a misfit vibe, but I don't have the energy to be on point and play nicey-nicey at the same time, especially with someone so overtly hostile.

Kitty turns to include me in the huddle with a look that says, *please* try. "Told you about Evie boarding with us this year." She keeps to the script she laboured in her text messages and emails. "Kept me sane, stuck at home without you lot."

I nod mechanically and try to smile. None of them seem convinced.

"You know Lila and Imogen, but I don't think you've met Kaylee." She places her hand on the gorgeous, caramel-skinned girl. Kaylee swings her hair over her shoulder, nods brusquely and I nod back.

Lila, however, gives me a genuine smile. "You into debating, Evie?"

My brain blanks.

"Crumbs." Kitty laughs. "Give the newbie five minutes to acclimate herself."

Lila grins. "I already signed you up, Kit."

"Typical," Kitty says.

I hadn't given any thought to Kitty's compulsive need to join clubs, committees and teams. "Are you sure you want to be making commitments?"

Kitty glares at me. Lila frowns. Kaylee scowls and Imogen stares.

"I think my commitments will be just fine," Kitty says, her smile as stiff as wood.

SUSPECTS

We make our way up to a laboratory on the third storey of the north wing, the home of advanced placement chemistry. I hitch my book bag up my shoulder, wrinkling my nose at the faint whiff of ammonia. My pins and needles zap at the chemical scent and I scan the room, ready to pin guilt on anyone who looks at Kitty twice.

"Come on." Kitty nudges me, and I realise too late she's heading for the first row. Kaylee takes the stool by the window and diplomatic Kitty sits in the middle. It leaves me with the aisle seat. Not good. I would have much preferred the back row for the best vantage point.

"Do we have to sit here?"

The desks further back are already filling. It will be awkward swapping now, but I hate the idea of people sitting behind us, out of my line of sight.

"Oh." Kitty swivels, trying to find a compromise.

Kaylee flares her nostrils like I've fouled the air.

I look her square in the face. "Can I sit there?" I know it came out more like, "move it, now" but I don't care.

When she realises I'm not about to explain, she purses her lips, tucks her chin back and gets to her feet, edging past me like I have leprosy.

Kitty makes a meal of pulling out her textbooks, letting her hair swing past to hide her furious pink face. I catch her eye, mouth "sorry", and take the empty stool. I know I've just blown it with Kaylee, but with my back to the window I can see everybody and still take notes. Though I hate causing even a low-scale scene, the vantage point makes it worth it. I can live without popularity.

As we wait for the teacher, several more students come to lean on the desk and chat with Kitty or worse still, hug her. They ask if she remembers anything from the attack and whether the police have made any progress and Kitty supplies the same generic answers, no and not really. I sit strung like a bow, prickling with static while Kitty makes a point of not introducing me. I pretend not to notice, flipping blindly through my textbook, ignoring the whispered speculation about who I am and how I know her.

Chemistry depresses me almost as much as social suicide. By nature, I gravitate more towards the arts but my new subject list, advanced placement everything – all Kitty's classes – has only two redeeming features: English and phys. ed. Even the brief introduction given by the charming old chemistry teacher has me breaking out in a cold sweat. When class finishes, I trail behind Kitty and Kaylee, feeling seasick.

"Miss Everton."

I stop in front of the whiteboard. "Mr Thomas?"

Kitty says something I don't catch as she heads to the door and Mr Thomas shuffles out from behind his desk. The top of his head barely reaches my shoulder and I try not to look at the long wisps of his eyebrows. "I just wanted to welcome you properly." His smile congests the grooves of his face. "You must belong to either April or Miriam Everton."

It's like tripping into a freezing pool. "Um, April, yeah."

He chuckles. "Of course, of course. April and Kitty's mother … Barbara what was she then? Dearbourne! That's right. What a twosome."

I pray he doesn't know about Mom's illness, and that he won't ask how she is.

"Forgive me," he says, "but the likeness is quite something. You have her eyes."

I don't know what to say, pressure building in my chest.

"Well, my dear. If you're anything like your mother, I expect we'll enjoy an excellent year together."

My stomach sinks, knowing I'll disappoint him. I doubt that being a year ahead at a middle-of-the-road high school will help me be a high achiever at Gainsborough

Collegiate. I wish my mutant DNA would fast track the "getting smarter" part that Miriam mentioned.

Mr Thomas returns to his desk. "Come and see me if you need help with anything."

"Um, thanks, sir." Eyes stinging, I stumble out into the corridor and freeze in the flow of traffic. I can't see her. More terrifying than that, I can't feel her. I've lost the tether. A chill grips me and my hearing dims.

Please don't let this be happening now.

How can I possibly lose her already? I'm useless – worse than useless. I clutch my watch. Should I push the alert? I imagine the terror I'd cause and move through the crowd, pins and needles spiking with every bump and brush of elbow or shoulder. The end of the corridor opens onto another identical corridor. Almost hyperventilating, I stand at the T-section, scanning each direction, lost without the tether to anchor me.

"Evie, right?" The voice comes from around knee level. A dark-haired boy crouches on the floor, looking harried as he gathers books and folders, rescuing them from passing feet. The helpful guy from the Governor's Ball. He squints up at me with his startling hazel eyes. "You lost?"

"Oh, hey." *His name? Andrew? Adam?* "Aiden! Yeah – no – can't find Kitty. She's supposed to be showing me round." I search the crowd, digging my nails into the strap of my shoulder bag, the muscles in my legs pinching.

Delayed social cues kick in and I realise I should help and I get down beside him to grab a sheaf of notes before they're crushed.

"Thanks." He adds them to the stack and stands up, shuffling the chaotic heap, then nods past my shoulder. "She went into the girls' restroom with Kaylee. You okay?"

The pull of the tether returns as soon as I know where she is, a painful reminder of how unreliable my sensitivity is and how desperately I want it to be strong and sure. The bandwidth crackles and I feel almost dizzy with relief. "Sure. Just … you know … it's all pretty overwhelming."

"I remember." He balances the load in one arm and smothers a yawn with his free hand. "I only came here in my junior year; took me the whole first semester to find my way around."

He seems like a nice guy but he's on my list. He knew exactly where Kitty was and the shadows under his eyes pique my suspicion. Maybe bloody nightmares and plotting Kitty's murder keeps him awake at night. "You look exhausted."

He shrugs. "What happened to Burton Central?"

I watch him and form my response as a litmus test for guilt. "Kitty's my best friend. She's had a tough time and I wanted to be here for her."

He doesn't say anything but glowers down the hall.

I stop breathing. Have I pushed a button?

"Great," he mutters.

I follow his gaze to an approaching mob of boys in tan khakis and sweater vests.

"Look, could you do me a favour?" He touches my elbow, blanking the buzz in my spine as he leans and whispers, "You know Kaylee, right?"

"I – I just met her."

He lowers his voice and speaks rapidly, "This is going to sound insane but could you go in the restroom and stall her–" He cuts off, releasing my arm as the boys stop beside us, a wall of testosterone. A couple of them dart smirking glances at one another as though anticipating entertainment. The buzz in my spine zaps back to life. I recognise the boy in front, Richard Dean, with his brown hair, blue eyes and brimming self-confidence.

"Hey, buddy." Richard sidles in beside Aiden. "Batting outside your league?" He winks to include me in his joke.

I keep my expression blank, ignoring the sniggers of his friends.

"Richard." Aiden manages to control his face, but I get the feeling he'd like to punch someone.

Richard waits, frowns then nudges Aiden. "This is where you introduce me." But Aiden looks like he is having an unpleasant out-of-body experience. Richard shakes his head. "And yet he's so high-functioning at the office."

"Isn't he though?" A blond boy calls, clasping his hands

together in pantomime. "Why, yes, governor. No, governor. Anything you say, governor."

Richard ignores him. Aiden's knuckles whiten around his stack of books and papers.

"We've already met." I resist the feral impulse to snarl. What I know condemns him and makes it too easy to suspect him of worse crimes.

"We have?" Richard acts as though he struggles to access the memory and I feel the collective leer of his friends. In a remote part of my brain, I know how intimidating this scenario should feel – how it would have felt in my pre-Spark incarnation – a cocky governor's son and an audience of predatory males, their eyes roving aggressively over my body.

"Of course." Richard spreads his hands in a display of realisation. "The photographer's helper." He looks at me expectantly. When it becomes obvious I have nothing to say, Richard fills the pause with a smile. "You said you weren't at Gainsborough."

"I wasn't." I catch the chemical whiff of his breath and stiffen. "Now, I am."

"How mysterious." Richard reveals his white teeth. "I still don't know your name. Is it a secret?"

"Evangeline," Aiden says, catching my eye and flicking his gaze towards the restroom. "Her name is Evangeline Everton."

How does he know my full name?

"Ev-an-ge-line." Richard makes it sound like he's rolling candy on his tongue.

I shift to face Aiden, blocking Richard out. "Thanks for your help, Aiden. I'll see you around."

"Aw, don't be like that," Richard says. "We're just having fun."

I stalk away to the sound of groans and laughter. My sympathy for Aiden notches up; humiliation seems a high price to pay for a Gainsborough education and I hope for his sake it is worth it. I try not to slam open the girls' restroom door in case I take it off its hinges. I need to stall Kaylee. A long partition blocks the bathroom from view and I stop at the sound of her voice.

"Honestly, she's like an Addams Family freakshow, Kit." She could only be talking about me. "The whole seating fiasco?"

"She's new. It's an intimidating place."

"She can't afford to crack a smile?"

"It's been a rough year, all right. Cut her some slack."

"Like what kind of rough?"

I freeze.

Don't do it, Kitty.

Don't tell her about my mom.

"It doesn't matter." The sound of water running, hands being washed. "Give her a break."

I exhale.

Kaylee grumbles. "At least your brother's back."

Fine hairs rise on my forearms and my jaw juts forwards.

Kitty mutters something I can't make out over the faucet.

Kaylee swears. "He's taken?"

"Fairly definitely."

"Damn, that's all wrong. Who?"

More silent communication.

"No. Not Morticia!"

"Don't call her that."

"I'm officially depressed."

She sounds depressed. It lifts my spirits.

"And she's living with you? You think they're ...?"

"They've only just got together." But the lack of conviction in Kitty's voice makes my ears burn. Kaylee scoffs and Kitty clicks her tongue. "Besides, Dad would murder Jamie. Get your mind out of the gutter."

"Lucky Morticia."

I can't take it. I want to break something. Instead, I slink back out into the corridor and stop short. Richard stands there, alone, palms up, his expression wryly pleading. "I got rid of the zoo animals." Sparkling blue eyes, mischievous smile – no doubt practised weapons in his arsenal. "I feel like we've gotten off on the wrong foot."

I say nothing, let my stare chill down to sub zero.

At that point the restroom door opens and Kitty steps out, Kaylee behind her.

Inwardly, I cringe, glancing about for Aiden but I can't see him anywhere. I try to sound breezy, "There you are, Kit. Thought I'd lost you."

Kitty doesn't answer, eyeing Richard like she's stumbled on roadkill.

Richard purses his lips.

Kaylee loses her colour and looks at the floor.

"I won't hold you up," he says. "How's the neck, Kitty-Cat?"

Kitty scowls. "Piss off, Richard."

"Charming." He shakes his head. "Kaylee, you look lovely, as always."

She doesn't meet his gaze.

He reaches and touches her hair where it lies over her shoulder, casual, intimate, skin-crawling. "I've missed you."

She shifts away.

He shrugs and arches an eyebrow at me. "See you round, Evangeline."

VOLLEYBALL

I trudge upstairs behind Kitty, too much on my mind, not even sure what class we're going to. The episode with Richard has shaken me, seeing him touch Kaylee, watching her recoil. The wrongness of it – knowing the truth and yet saying nothing, doing nothing – that's what really gets me. I could have stopped him from touching her, grabbed him and slammed him against the lockers … something.

The deeper fear that eats me up is wondering if I've just encountered Kitty's Stray and yet felt no clear threatening signal. That's the problem when everything and everyone looks sinister. The static, the pins and needles, the paranoia: Jamie and Miriam's warning didn't do it justice. Until Richard arrived in the corridor, I had been working my way towards condemning Aiden. I'd been willing to read his clumsiness, distraction and nervous tension as symptoms of Stray guilt. Yet, the moment Richard appeared, I had effortlessly transferred all my suspicion onto him.

Proof of my fickle judgement puts me in a black mood.

"Oh, good, there you are!" Lila's head appears over the banister above us. "Calculus starts in five, come on." Her black ponytail whips out of sight.

Kitty turns to me on the landing. "Back row?"

I hug my folder and grimace. "Sorry about that." She looks pensive and wrung out. I touch her shoulder. "I'll do better. I promise."

"I'm not bothered about that." She lowers her voice. "Did you feel something? Before, with Richard, I mean?"

Familiar dread rolls in my stomach, eel-like, cold and heavy; I can't bear to see her afraid. I shake my head more emphatically than I feel; it doesn't seem the time to admit to uncertainty. "No. Nothing."

Shuddering, she exhales and closes her eyes. I stroke her arm, when really I wish I could cradle her like a child and croon promises that everything will be all right, that I'll never let anything hurt her.

"I – I wondered, you know, with what happened to Kaylee … If he could do that, then–"

"I know."

She bites her lips, dark thoughts lining up behind her eyes. "And the others?"

It takes me a moment to figure out what she means. "The guys?"

She nods, unwilling to speak her fear.

"No, Kit." I lean down, forcing her to meet my gaze. "Hell no. I felt nothing." Which also isn't entirely true, but relief transforms her face and posture, and I realise, again, how much she holds inside. I try for a rueful smile. "Other than Pete."

She jerks her head. "Pete?"

"He likes you."

"He does?" A surprised smile softens her lips and suddenly Pete doesn't seem so bad to me. Kitty needs a distraction. But her expression clouds again. "I should have gone after Kaylee." Kaylee had blown off Kitty's concern and stalked away to her Spanish class. "Lila and Imogen said she refused to talk about it at all in California."

I chew the inside of my cheek and we stand there lost in our thoughts. Lila appears at the top of the stairs, waving at us to hurry up. When we reach her, Imogen joins us and both of them fix me with meaningful looks. Lila grins, folding her arms. "Well?"

"Well what?" I say.

She leans towards me. "You and Jamie!"

Kitty groans.

Imogen looks faintly mournful.

My internal temperature rises even as my shoulders rise and I shrink into them. "It's no big deal."

Lila and Imogen produce identical scoffing sounds.

"Trust me," Lila says. "It's a big deal. Kitty, I can't believe you didn't tell us."

"I'm not that fussed about my brother's love life, to be honest."

Lila hooks her arm through mine and turns me towards the classroom. "Gil says Jamie's totally into you."

* * *

Mrs Jenner blows her whistle and we assemble, gym shoes squeaking on the polished floor. Kitty follows my lead, letting the others crowd forwards, keeping us safely on the outer edge. A blond boy with sparkling green eyes grins at me. Confused, I look away. I try not to think about Jamie who stands with Gil and Abe, try not to notice the ponytail flicks and mascara glances of girls looking at him, try to ignore the strange territorial tightening in my muscles. Can't he hear them giggling, their whispers as they ogle the bands of ink ringing his biceps? It's hard enough to concentrate as it is, static crackling in my spine, as I glare at the back of Richard's head, cursing the schedule gods for putting us all together.

I sniff the air but don't detect the chemical scent that I associate with the Stray, just school gym smells: liniment, industrial floor wax, feet and a pervading musty damp. It doesn't ease my mind. Kitty seems too conspicuous in her foam neck support. I hate the idea of her being sized up as an easy target. But she's been cleared for moderate exercise, and I have no intention of talking her into sitting the class out. I'd spend the whole time worrying about her waiting on the bleachers without me.

"You must work out a lot, huh?" Imogen whispers next to me, crossing soft arms over her concave chest.

I blush. "Um, I guess."

"I guess?" Lila says. "You're cut. What do you do, circuit training?"

I shrug, pretending to listen to Mrs Jenner explain volleyball rules.

"You and Jamie work out together?" Lila nods, a slow insinuating up and down swing of her head. "All sweaty and intense."

"Please stop," Kitty mutters. "I'll have to scrub my brain out with steel wool."

Mrs Jenner blows her whistle again and we begin orbiting the gym floor in jogging pairs. My body responds greedily to the physical activity, but I hate the feeling of people running behind us.

"Hello again." Richard. He bumps his way between Kitty and me to a chorus of encouragement from his friends. I tense, pins and needles zip-zapping at the unwanted physical contact and the way he separates Kitty from me. I scowl, but Richard acts like he doesn't notice. "Isn't this nice? Gym together."

Kitty keeps her eyes forward, not altering her pace.

"We'll have to compare schedules," he says.

"Good idea," Kitty says. "Then I'll know what class changes I need to submit at the office."

"I was talking to Evangeline."

"She has a boyfriend," Kitty says, giving him a disdainful look.

"She does." Jamie jogs up beside me, cutting Richard off.

Richard rolls his eyes. "Trust the Skipper to hit the ground running."

I flush with embarrassment, but can't decide what makes me so uncomfortable. Is it the public outing of my relationship status? The idea is ridiculous; I'm not ashamed to be Jamie's girlfriend. It's just the Richard factor and the feeling that something private has been handed over for public scorn.

When Mrs Jenner calls us to order again she divides us into teams and we spread out around the courts. Jamie, Abe and Gil are next to us with three giddy-looking girls. Kitty, Lila, Imogen and I have the grinning blond boy and his friend.

"Angelo." He flicks his hair back from his green eyes as introduction. "You're new, right?"

"Yeah." My attention shifts to the team gathering on the opposite side of our net. "Ugh."

Angelo looks over his shoulder at Richard and his entourage. "Not a fan?"

"No."

Angelo chuckles then ducks suddenly as his friend throws the ball and he just manages to catch it. Kitty, Lila and Imogen gather beside me.

"Could we file a complaint?" Lila whispers. "If Kaylee won't."

Kitty filled them in on the morning's drama with expertly timed whispers during math. She crosses her arms. "She's made it clear she doesn't want the police involved."

"He shouldn't be allowed to get away with it," I growl, but I need to cool the mercury on my injustice meter before I end up doing something stupid. Truth is, I can't separate my disgust from my fear that he might be worse than a rapist, or attempted rapist, or whatever, the details are unclear. But as far as sickos are concerned, at least a Stray has no choice – a victim of random selection (not that it makes any difference to me; God willing, I plan to put him down like a rabid dog) – but Richard with all that dissipated free will …

Angelo leans beside me with the ball. "Wanna serve?"

I shake my head. "I'll take the net."

The others spread out into position. Richard meets me at the center line, hooking his fingers in the crisscrossed nylon. "Destiny keeps throwing us together."

I'm at zero tolerance for bullshit. "Is there a name for your problem?"

"Don't be like that, Ev-an-ge-line. If you got to know me, you'd like me."

"Not what I heard."

He keeps his expression even but withdraws his fingers. "There are sad, deluded people in the world who'll say all kinds of things to pull a guy down. Don't believe everything you hear."

Laughter comes from the court next to us. We both look. Abe and Gil are showing off in front of the girls on their team. Jamie has crouched down to tighten a shoelace, his T-shirt lifting a few inches above the line of his shorts. I freeze. The whole band of revealed skin is covered in coloured ink and, just as shocking, there are three ragged scars disappearing up under his shirt, like someone has attacked him with a pitchfork.

"Wow." Richard turns to face me at the net, open mouthed and gleeful. "How long are your nails?"

I glare, hoping to hide how shaken I feel.

Why hadn't Jamie told me?

The student ref blows her whistle.

You only got together last night.

Richard's team wins the toss.

Why should Jamie tell you anything?

They serve.

But ... scars?

The ball flies back and forth, but my mind still reels and I barely engage until Kitty calls for the ball. I tune in to watch as Angelo sets an easy spike for her. She leaps, lifting her arm to hammer it home when Richard shoots up in front of her, barging her back from the net.

Electricity erupts in my spine.

I dart forwards, almost too quickly, to steady her landing. "She has a neck injury, you asshole!"

"Yeah, asshole!" Lila chimes in.

Kitty shakes it off, blushing. "Let it go, you guys."

Richard pouts. "Sorry, Kitty-Cat."

Break his nose.

Thunder crashes in my ears.

Break his nose.

Everything becomes razor sharp and painful to look at.

Break his nose.

Richard comes close to the net and taps his finger to his lips as the rally resumes, his eyes moving over me. "Just thinking about those scars. Should you ever find the Skipper isn't cutting it, I like it rough." He winks and blows me a kiss, a waft of sour breath.

Break his nose. Now.

"Sorry, Dick. Not without a mint." I spring upwards, intercepting the ball in its trajectory to drive it, full force, into Richard's upturned face. A delectable crunch, the punch of burst rubber, a shock of red spatters my shirt.

I land euphoric.

Kitty's eyes bug out.

Richard howls, hands to his face, writhing, swearing, blood everywhere.

His friends crowd in, and I adjust my expression.

"Whoa! You killed it." Angelo picks up the split ball that has rebounded onto our side and laughs. "Please marry me."

"Jeez, Evie." Lila grins. "I'd marry you after that."

Kitty squeezes my arm. "Here comes the law."

"What on earth?" Mrs Jenner rounds on us.

There's an upsurge in noise as Richard's friends hurl accusations and my team responds in loud defence.

Jamie appears beside me, brow corrugated. "What happened?"

"Um, he wasn't ready," I stutter. "The ball hit him in the face."

Jamie glances at the split ball in Angelo's hands but doesn't say anything, and I look away.

After several minutes of pointless debate, Mrs Jenner rules it was an accident, and instructs Richard's friends to take him to the nurse. He shuffles to the exit, cupping his nose, his parting scowl a black promise.

CONFESSION

Barb waits on the front steps, hugging her waist, a petite figure, stock still. Probably, she's been counting the seconds until we appeared. She lifts her arm, waving as we pull up the long curve of the driveway then darts back into the house, no doubt to alert Leonard and Miriam – we're home and Kitty lives.

"Brace yourselves," Kitty mutters from the front seat.

We drove home with only the radio filling the silence; the three of us lost in our thoughts. What would Miriam say about my gym exploits? The story spread like an airborne virus through the school, racing ahead of me from class to common room to cafeteria: mutating, expanding, accomplishing the total inverse of my hopes for the day. Now I could look forward to nothing but stares, whispers, or worse – high fives and congratulations for the rest of the semester and only myself to thank for the infamy.

Barb and Leonard rush out into the courtyard, where Jamie parks the car, crossing to meet us as we get out. Barb wraps her arms around Kitty, their honey blonde heads the same height. "I'm so glad you're home," she says, a tremble in her voice. Even Leonard looks uncommonly pale. He hugs his wife and daughter together, staring over them at me, searching my face for signs that I may have identified the Stray.

I wipe the worry from my face and shake my head. He closes his eyes, probably as relieved and frustrated as I feel.

"I'm not sure this is very good for my neck," Kitty says.

Leonard chuckles and they go inside, a happy tangle of limbs.

Miriam waits on the back step. I can tell she wants to hug me, but she restrains herself. I'm grateful for her restraint and ashamed of feeling grateful. Of course I want everything to go back to normal. I miss her; I miss the mom-replacement comfort only Miriam can give me, but the block in my mind still holds her accountable. Jamie nudges me with his elbow, and I force myself to move towards her.

"Hey," she says. "Survived the day?"

I lift my shoulders, a noncommittal shrug, and we trail down the back hall, joining the rest of the Gallaghers in the kitchen. The warm sugary smell of freshly baked cookies fills the air. Jamie and I groan in unison, dump our bags and go straight for the buttery stack cooling on the stove top. We both take cookies in each hand and stuff our mouths, slumping back against the counter, moaning. Barb smiles and sniffs, still teary in her relief. "Thought you two might be hungry," she says.

Kitty extracts herself from her mother to join us at the cookie pile.

"How did you go, Evie?" Leonard pours mugs of coffee. "First day in a new school can be overwhelming, let alone Gainsborough."

"She was great." Kitty's a generous liar.

I swallow the last of my oat and raisin; it goes down like a jagged plug. "I was awful."

"You were fine," Jamie says.

Miriam cringes. "You break something?"

My tally on crushed door handles at the Gallaghers' place was up around seven or eight.

"Just a guy's nose."

She and Leonard draw air through their teeth and Barb's hand goes to her mouth. Their worried eyes all flick to Kitty.

"I was fine." Kitty sits on the table, her feet on the seat in front of her. "It was only Richard Dean. Now everybody loves her – except Dick."

Jamie remains diplomatically silent, going to the fridge, emerging with three sodas. He tosses a can to me and his sister, and hitches himself up on the counter.

"Dean?" Leonard's eyebrows shoot up behind his glasses. "As in, Governor Dean's son?" He turns to Jamie. Jamie nods and I feel his silence.

"It was brilliant," Kitty says.

Miriam sits and rubs her forehead. "How and how bad?"

"Gym," Kitty says. "Split the volleyball on impact."

More gasps from Miriam and Leonard.

"Evie's not in trouble though," Kitty says.

Leonard scoffs. "You've met Richard's father?"

"What's the governor going to do?" She throws her hands up. "It was an accident."

"No, it wasn't," I mutter. Everyone stalls, coffee mugs halfway to mouths, cookies crumbling in the silence. "I'm going to lie down." I pick up my pack and slouch towards the door, setting my unopened soda on the counter beside Jamie, not looking at him, not looking at anyone.

***

I must have dozed off because when the bed shifts under me, I open my eyes on dim lamplight. Jamie lies on his stomach next to me, arms crossed beneath his head.

"Hey," I croak. A half second later, I jerk my head up. We're on my bed, alone. I look to the closed door, my ears straining for footsteps in the hall. "Where's Miriam?"

"She's about to leave to do some work in the studio and

feed the cat. Said she'll be here tonight. She wanted to see you, but I talked her down."

"Thanks." Again, the relief and the guilt. "Your folks know you're in here?"

He curbs his grin. "I told them I would check on you."

I reach into the bandwidth for Kitty's signal. Reflex.

"She's in the study."

I could have picked her location without Jamie telling me, simply by the quality of the pulse, and I wonder how much being near him improves my sensitivity.

"You've got bed face." Jamie brushes his fingers over the imprint on my cheek.

My whole body tingles. "Aren't you going to tell me off?"

He rises up on his elbows. "For?"

"Didn't I break the superhero code?"

"Which code might that be?"

I bury my face. "The one about using your powers for good and not evil."

The bed moves. His breath warms my ear. "The majority would say you were using your powers for good."

I look up. "Then why the thin lip all afternoon?"

He turns onto his side, exhaling. "I don't trust Richard. And not only as a suspect. I mean, at all, as a human being. He's a pig. I don't like the idea of him anywhere near you. Not because I don't think you can take care of yourself – obviously, you could snap him like a twig – but you're my girlfriend and he's a ..." He brings his teeth together. "And now you're in his head, and I don't like the idea of what he might be doing to you in there."

Wow.

"That's quite nice. Except the bit about what Richard might be doing to me in his head."

His expression darkens. "Was there something in the bandwidth that made you read him as a threat?"

"I'm not sure. There was a lot of static. He's high on my suspect list, but I couldn't tell if I was reacting to a real threat or if he just pissed me off." I shake my head. "I lost it pretty bad."

"It's hard at the beginning. You're paranoid. You've got all this adrenaline in your body. You're wired to protect. He did barge Kitty. It's an accomplishment you left him able to walk." Jamie touches his finger to my brow and traces my frown until it smoothes away, thrilling me again with the novelty of his touch.

I tease my lip and toy with courage. "Why didn't you tell me about your back?"

He sighs. "It never came up. What would I say, 'want to see something horrible?'"

"It's not horrible." I shoot up on my elbow. "I mean, it's horrible that you were hurt, of course–" I wish I had kept my mouth shut. "Sorry. You don't have to tell me anything."

He looks up at me from beneath long dark lashes, making me ache with his symmetry and shadows. "It's from my first. I fought the *Stray* in Uncle Jeremy's stables." He mouths the illegal term. "He threw me into a stall. The horse spooked, kicked me and a pitchfork did the rest. My *Spark* died."

My heart thuds like it's descending steep, erratically placed steps. "Jamie. I'm so sorry." I want to touch him but initiating contact still feels … audacious.

"I didn't want you to know. I didn't want it to mess with your head."

"I need to be prepared."

"Hearing my horror stories won't help."

"Couldn't be worse than my imagination."

"When this is over, I'll tell you everything you want to know. But right now your mindset is just as important as your physical training."

"It's never been done."

"I believe in you, Everton." And there's the same conviction in his voice as this morning. "And I'm only too willing to play my part." He leans over and brushes his lips on my cheekbone, sending blissful currents down through my neck, my chest. "Get that frequency nice and strong."

I have so many questions, but Jamie makes it impossible to concentrate: looking at me, reaching for me, scooping me effortlessly against his body, grazing his lips over mine.

He kisses like the gifted and talented, like someone light years ahead of the class, advanced placement lip science, up-skilling me with each undulating swivel of his head.

I can only hope his flair comes from natural sensitivity because if it comes from screes of experience, my new jealousy might burn the world down. I draw back to find some air. "I was right, you know? You draw attention. People look at you. Girls look at you. A lot of girls."

He frowns. "People probably don't know who I am. I've been away."

"That has nothing to do with it. You can't really be oblivious."

"Can we not talk about this?" Then his whole face changes and he narrows his eyes. "Unless of course it made you jealous?"

"No. That's not – I noticed, is all."

He snorts and rests his forehead against mine. "Jealousy is a Synergist thing."

I try to look at him without going cross-eyed. "I am *not* a jealous person."

He steals a kiss and dazes me with his leonine grin. "Synergist coding intensifies everything. I hate to break it to you, but any emotion you experience, as it relates to me, will be significantly magnified."

I groan.

"Don't worry, love. Only a room full of witnesses kept

me from murdering every one of those blokes who tailed you round that gym."

What blokes?

"And that blond boy who wants to marry you."

"Angelo?" I jerk in surprise. "He's not a bad guy."

"I saw the way he was looking at you."

"What? No, he wasn't."

"You think I'm oblivious?" He crushes my lips with his, rolling over me so that our legs scissor together, his arms forming a cage around me. My head spins and I grip the hard swell of his biceps like it can keep the waves from pulling me under but sort of wanting to drown in the pleasure of it too. *Don't faint. Don't faint.* The give and take of our mouths. Heat. Awareness of everywhere our bodies touch. Fog pearling at the periphery of my consciousness.

"Mmm," I mumble. "Feel faint." Lights pop behind my eyelids and I pant beneath him, still gripping his arms for dear life. He makes to roll off me, but I tighten my hold, unwilling to lose the press of his weight. "Give me a second," I try to catch my breath, peering at my fingers on his skin and the black ink beneath them. "You never told me what these say."

He looses a sigh and lifts his right arm. "*Quid est iniuria fieri non posse jus.* What is wrong cannot be made right." He nods at his left. "*Illud quod deperditur non posse eruit.*

What is lost cannot be recovered. It's from Ecclesiastes."

"What, like the Bible?"

"Yeah."

I frown as I piece it together. "But the words are so sad."

"I don't find them sad. They've helped me accept what I am, what my life is, my lot. I can't undo what's done, can't go back, can't fix it. Just have to get on with life."

I try to imagine Jamie at sixteen wrestling with a destiny determined by DNA. "Very stiff upper lip." But I want to cry for him, for me, for the loss of innocence that comes with the blood in our veins. Killers by design. "You think God has a loophole for people who don't have a choice?"

"Hope so, otherwise we're screwed."

We lie there, holding each other's gaze. "Will you let me look at your back?"

I see his uncertainty, but then he rolls away and sits up, his expression rueful. "I suppose if I have to get my kit off for anyone, you're preferable to the twelve sweaty guys in gym who've all examined it. But you have to promise me something."

I push myself up on weak arms, my head still swimming. "Promise?"

"No *KMH*," he whispers.

"Of course not. I mean, I wouldn't."

He turns, crosses his arms, takes hold of the hem of his

shirt and pulls it up and over his head, bending forwards, creating a long arc.

It's beautiful. He's beautiful. The bronze stretch of hard muscle. An angel, a Renaissance masterpiece in armoured breastplate. Scarlet, gold, cobalt, tremendous saturation of colour, shade, depth, movement and shape. The sword, gripped in its right hand. Its fierce face, turned to the side. Powerful wings spread over Jamie's shoulderblades, tips matching perfectly where the tattoos on his arms begin. "I've seen this. Who is it?"

"Michael. The Archangel, patron saint of warriors."

"Closet Catholic?"

He chuckles. "Someone to watch my back."

I can't not touch him, and it *is* audacious, reaching out, fingertips, thumb, palm, the warm press of flesh. He doesn't move. I fan my fingers over the angel, hesitating over the ridges of his scars.

"They don't hurt," he says.

I trace the diagonal lines from his right shoulder down to the left of his spine, just above the waist of his jeans. I press my cheek to his back, savouring the incredible scent of his skin, grieving over the pain he must have gone through, the blood he must have–

I snap upright. "Blood!"

"What?" He pulls his shirt back over his head and swings around, but I'm already across the room, ransacking my backpack with shaking hands. I pull my gym shirt out and hold it up. Several red raindrop splatters stain the fabric.

"Richard's blood! Doctor Sullivan can test it and see if it's a match!"

Jamie stares, understanding dawning on his face.

"Ha!" I launch myself, flattening Jamie on the bed, driving my lips into his, kisses fierce and hot. He wraps his arms around me, receiving everything and responding with more.

A sound of groaning metal brings us to attention. Miriam stands there glowering, purse and keys in one hand, door handle crushed in the other. "What the hell is going on?"

CHOICES

I sit like stone on the plush leather couch in Leonard's study, digging my nails into the groove of the cushion stitching, trying to channel my boiling sense of injustice and humiliation into the stuffing of the seat. All the joy and triumph of my realisation about Richard's blood has been overthrown by Miriam's tirade. It galls me to waste time, and judging by the look of Miriam, she's settling in for a major lecture.

Jamie sits next to me, his hands clasped loosely in his lap, his body relaxed. I envy his ease. His parents sit opposite while Miriam strides up and down the rug between us; a distraction from having to look directly at Barb whose hurt and disappointment almost undo me. Leonard seems the least agitated of the adults, his expression more resigned exasperation than anything else.

Kitty hovers by the door, looking uncomfortable. "I don't really need to be here for this, do I?"

I shoot her a desperate glance.

"I don't know, Kitty." Miriam uses the clipped tone that marched us all the way downstairs from my bedroom. "It doesn't bother you that while your life's been hanging in the balance, these two have been up to goodness knows what behind closed doors?"

"That-is-not-how-it-is," I snap.

"Miriam, we only realised what we had last night." Jamie keeps his voice perfectly level. "There's been no 'goodness knows what'."

"Not what it looked like when I walked in." Her eyes blaze. "The fact that I *could* walk up the hallway and open the door, surprising two people with genetically enhanced hearing, would indicate that something fairly distracting was going on."

"Honestly, Jamie." Barb shakes her head. "How could you be so selfish and irresponsible?"

I know Barb means me as well; she's just too polite to say it. I hate that she thinks her plea meant nothing to me; that I went away and broke my promise without batting an eyelid.

Kitty drops into the armchair like the back of her knees have been taken out. I fix Miriam with a furious look for putting worry in her head. "Kit, don't listen to her, you know it doesn't work like that. It's the signal that matters."

Jamie looks up at Miriam and opens his palms. "Can you at least understand–"

"That you have a *girlfriend*?" Miriam says. "What's her name?"

Jamie exhales through his nose. "Evangeline."

I catch my breath.

"The *other* one," she says.

"Helena," Barb says. Her gaze travels from her son to me before dropping to her lap like it pains her to look at us.

"I know about Helena," I say.

Miriam snorts and clamps her hips. "You *think* you know about Helena."

"If he says there's nothing going on–" Kitty jumps in.

"It's an Affinity thing. They're not–" my throat closes over.

"Miriam, it's not what you think," Jamie begins.

"Sorry, kid, but that's bullshit," Miriam says. "You're over-simplifying and you know what *they* will say."

I'm sick to death of the Affinity Project and out of patience with my aunt. I dig my nails deeper into the cushion seams.

"Evangeline," Leonard says gently. "Mind the leather, dear."

I ball my fists against the sting of encroaching tears. *No. No crying!* Jamie covers my hand with his, releasing my fingers. The unapologetic tenderness of his touch, in the face of my Gestapo aunt, overrides my PDA aversion and makes me want to cry even more.

Barb stares at our clasped hands, and Leonard rolls his eyes to the ceiling. Miriam scowls. "Trust me, Evie. If *they* put them together, he'll choose her."

She may as well have slapped me. Jamie shakes his head.

"That's not fair!" Kitty says. "Jamie would never hurt Evie. They're Synergists!"

Miriam looks even angrier. "So we've heard."

"I'm still not clear what that means," Leonard says.

Jamie explains the phenomenon as briefly and as delicately as he can under Miriam's thunderous glower. Barb's eyes widen while Leonard's narrow, a cautious optimism parting his lips. "It's a major advantage for us," Jamie finishes.

"Right," Miriam says. "I'm sure there's nothing but altruistic motives involved for you."

"Miriam." Jamie sits forwards, his gaze unflinching. "I'm not going to apologise for my feelings for your niece. You know the stats on Synergist coding. Genetically speaking, Everton and I were made for each other."

Made for each other. Wow.

Barb's mouth pops open and Leonard sits up straighter.

"Genetically speaking!" Miriam draws herself to her full height. "Precisely, Jamie. What you're experiencing is a chemical reaction. A Petri dish experiment. Not a relationship!"

I jolt in my seat, freeing my hand from Jamie's. "It's a good thing!"

"No, it's not!" She thumps her fist on the gleaming top of Leonard's desk, rattling photo frames and pens.

"Isn't it?" Kitty asks quietly.

Miriam glances pink-faced at Leonard. "Synergist coding is a very rare and extreme frequency maturation process. There are long-term implications."

I fold my arms, chain-link tight. "Surely-anything-that-makes-me-stronger-and-faster-is-good-for-Kitty!"

"It's not just all about Kitty!" Miriam flushes redder and ducks her head at a pale Kitty and her pale parents. "No offence."

"And there it is!" I rise to my feet, righteous anger burning me up, my arm extended with the finger of judgement, pointing out the unbeliever. "*That's* what it comes down to! You've never really been in the game, have you, Miriam? For all your promises, you've never really had Kitty's best interests at heart."

She rolls her eyes and throws her hands up. "Obviously there are benefits in regard to the short term. Long term, the repercussions aren't good. Your accelerated development is bad enough, let alone Synergist coding on top of that!"

"Why?" I near full volume. "You want me to end up

like you? Bitter and alone?" A light bulb flickers in the ornate fixture above my head. Everyone looks up, then at me. My whole body shakes.

"Easy," Jamie murmurs.

I know I've said something terrible; the silence outside my body tells me so but inside chaos reigns.

Miriam grows quiet. "Aside from what *Affinity* will say about it, it means that you are more susceptible to *Sparking* in the future," her mouth shapes the silent words, making them somehow more fierce. "It makes Jamie more susceptible too."

Barb reaches for Leonard's hand.

I shiver and look at Jamie. "Did you know that?"

"Of course he did." Miriam scuffs her shoe on the rug.

Jamie nods, undaunted. "It's worth it."

"You have to tell yourself that," she says, "in order to justify jeopardising your own future wellbeing as well as Evie's. Synergist coding isn't a game, it alters your body and your brain chemistry." She drops her voice to a mutter. "Like teenage hormones aren't enough – try that to the power of ten."

"For crying out loud, Miriam!" I gape at her, red to the roots of my hair.

"It's the reality, kid. You've got no idea what kind of amusement park your body is now. If he sneezes on you, you'll get pregnant."

"Whoa." Kitty cringes.

Barb baulks.

Leonard clears his throat. "*My* son understands the values of this household and I can assure you …"

Leonard's words are little more than distant white noise in my head. In the split second of Miriam's mortifying warning, my head spins, the collective power of my anger and humiliation rising to a crescendo, like an internal tsunami forcing me to the brink of reason and self-control. I feel in that moment as though one more push could detach me from my body, like a snapped cord, freeing me to inhabit the incorporeal creature of my rage.

"Miriam, you're overreacting," Jamie says.

"It would sound that way to an eighteen-year-old boy who's spent his whole life getting whatever the hell he wants," she says.

The cord stretches. Jamie flinches. Barb jerks in her seat. "Excuse me?"

"Miriam!" Leonard says. "You're out of line."

Her head swivels towards them. "Someone has to tell this boy 'no' for once!"

The cord snaps.

"Not you!" Stars burst before my eyes. "You don't get a say! You're not Jamie's mother and you're sure as hell not mine!" Miriam flinches and colour leeches from her face. High-pitched ringing fills my ears and I stab my chest.

"I'm the one who gets to say 'no'. Me! But I won't, because I want to be with Jamie and it's not just because of some damn science experiment! I felt like this when my DNA was my own and not the property of some bullshit secret organisation!" A tinkling sound precedes an explosion of glass – a vase, lamp and decanter shatter, as well as the four bulbs in the light fixture that hangs above my head. Miriam jumps back and the Gallaghers lean away in their seats. Jamie bolts up from the couch, taking my arms, murmuring my name like he's persuading me back into my body. Tiny sparkling shards rain onto our hair and shoulders, covering the rug at our feet.

I draw air in ragged gulps, staring at the broken glass. I stumble away from Jamie, recoiling from his eyes, their eyes. I cover my face, unable to fight tears. "Oh, Mr Gallagher. Your things. I'm sorry, I'm so sorry. I didn't mean to."

I turn and run to the doors, Leonard and Jamie calling my name. I grab for a handle but it comes off, crushed in my fingers. Waves of humiliation flood through me and my eyes pour.

"Evie, wait." Barb comes and rests her hand on my heaving back. Even through my tears I can see her blue eyes have welled up. "We're trying to understand. We want to understand."

I blurt in a soft rush, "Mrs Gallagher, I'm sorry about everything. I never intended to break my promise. I tried very hard to do what you asked." I draw a shuddering breath but the tears won't stop. "I want to be with your son for the sake of your daughter and for my own sake. I need Jamie if I'm going to survive this. I need him and I want him."

"Evie, stop–" Miriam says, shock in her voice.

Barb frowns. "My son can be very persuasive."

"It's not like that. Jamie hasn't talked me into anything. I choose him."

"Don't say those words!" Miriam hisses, almost leaving the ground.

Jamie shoots across the room and grips my arm. "Actually, Everton …"

Blindsided, I swallow, wiping my face on the back of my hand.

His expression seems almost illuminated, his grey eyes storm-tossed and yet thrilled as he searches my face.

"Don't say, I–?"

He inhales sharply and puts his fingers over my lips. "Careful."

"They're binding words, Evangeline," Miriam says, white-faced, hollow-eyed. "They're repeated in the binding ceremony for sanctioned affiliations only. Jamie, what have you done? Did you give her those words?"

He shakes his head, lifting his hand from my mouth. "No. We've never talked about any of it."

"I don't understand."

Miriam slumps against the edge of Leonard's desk, her hands against her head. "There are synaptic pathways that determine signal bonds and a process by which permanent bonds are formed between *our kind.* Verbal affirmations and ceremonial actions, among other things, seal those synaptic pathways. Only the *Affinity Project* dictates the sealing of permanent bonds. Not you."

"I wasn't trying–" I say, burning with embarrassment.

"Choice is a fantasy," Miriam says. "*If* the time comes, you will choose whom the *Affinity Project* chooses for you. This little romance with Jamie has a time line and an end point. I'm not trying to ruin your life, Evangeline. I'm trying to save you from a broken heart."

"Miriam, just stop." I'm done, emptied out. I reach for the remaining handle and pause, passing the crushed one to Barb. "Could you?"

Barb opens the door and I escape.

BOUNDARIES

I make my way across the foyer on unsteady legs, grateful for open space after the confinement of Leonard's study. I feel like I've been in a fist fight, and I gasp for unpolluted air, free of accusation, threat or bitterness.

"Let her be," Barb's voice carries from the study.

I hurry through the dining room, my warped reflection trailing me either side in night-panelled windows and gleaming table polish. I push through the swing door into the kitchen. The black and white tiles swim beneath my feet. *Synaptic pathways, he'll choose her, time line and end point.* I lurch to the counter, grip the sink and stare out the window. My own face blocks the view.

I want to climb out of my skin, slip through the pane and hide. Instead, I turn the faucet on and place my hands in the flow, staring at the pale length of my fingers, watching the water pool in the porcelain sink before draining in an endless spiral.

I feel Miriam before I hear her quiet steps or the swing of the kitchen door. I bend and splash a shock of cold water on my swollen eyes, patting the counter for a towel. Miriam presses a cloth into my hand. I keep it to my face and straighten up, water dripping in rivulets behind the collar of my dress. When I finally lower the towel, I see myself reflected twice. The other shorter me stands behind my left shoulder with plaintive eyes. I wish it were Mom. "Please, Miriam." I hang my head. "I'm done."

"Evie–"

"We have Richard's DNA." I say it to shut her up. "His blood on my gym shirt."

"You – you read his signal?"

I grit my teeth. "I reacted to him. I don't know if it was a signal. But it's worth testing, isn't it?"

"Of course," she says. "Yes, of course it is. Why didn't you say?"

"It was a little difficult to get a word in."

"Evie, I–"

A pulse in the bandwidth rocks through me, loud in my ears, painful in my head, blurring my vision. I give a small cry and swing around, grabbing the counter behind me. Miriam buckles forwards, bringing her hand to her head. "No," she whispers.

"What the hell was that?"

"You felt it?" Her lips pale. "The Warden's coming."

"Now? Here?" Terror like a siren fills my head. They're coming for me. It's over. *Kitty!* "I won't go, Miriam. I'll fight. They'll have to drag me out."

"Let me think, damn it!" Miriam's eyes dart from side to side as though she's calculating frenetic equations at high speed.

The kitchen door bursts open. Jamie skids into the room. "The Warden–"

"We felt it," I say, dizzy with the let-down of adrenaline.

"*You* did?" Jamie says. "You couldn't possibly–"

"Shut up!" Miriam grabs her head, turning in a slow circle, muttering.

"You have to go, Everton." Jamie pats his pockets for keys. "Take Kitty, take my car and go now."

"It's too late." Miriam straightens. "They will have registered our signals."

"But they can't track Everton. She hasn't been marked."

"They'd catch her eventually, Jamie. She could only ever stay a day ahead of them at the most. But," she fixes him with a piercing look, "if we could mask her signal she wouldn't have to run and she'd be clear until the next sweep."

"Mask it?" Jamie says, the tangle of his thoughts catching behind his eyes until his frown unknots. "Miriam, we haven't even been together for twenty-four hours."

Leonard, Barb and Kitty come through the door.

"Jamie?" Leonard says, taking in the spectacle of the three of us panicking. "What on earth?"

Miriam ignores him, her eyes on Jamie. "You've been living in the same house for days. Your signals will have started to sync whether you're conscious of it or not. If we hide Evie somewhere close to you, while they're here – if you can stay connected – using KMH, KMT, whatever you can manage – it could blur the reading enough to appear like one signal."

My mind scrambles to keep up with Miriam's plan. "Hide me? I don't understand. How does it work? Will they come in the house?"

"I'm the only registered Shield in the district. They'll expect me and therefore they will expect to come in the house."

"Demerits," Jamie warns.

"Screw demerits," she says. "They're on their way anyway."

"What if they thermal scan?" Jamie says, his expression clouding.

"It's not an extraction," Miriam says. "They'd only call in an extraction team if they identified a newly transitioned Shield. It'll just be the Warden and one other agent. Is your tracker up to date?"

"No." He reaches his hand to the back of his neck. "It's almost dissolved."

Miriam nods. "Good."

"What's happening, Miriam?" Leonard demands.

She looks Leonard up and down, a measuring appraisal. "Barb," she says. "You have to leave."

Barb clings to Leonard's arm with her diamond-dressed fingers to her mouth. "Leave? Why?"

Miriam squares her shoulders. "Because I will be posing as Leonard's girlfriend and it's probably better if his wife isn't still in the house. We'll call you as soon as they've gone."

Barb blinks like she's been poked in the eye and Leonard opens his mouth but nothing comes out.

Another pulse in the bandwidth sweeps in. I groan and sway and Jamie steadies me. Miriam holds her head. "We are running out of time!" She slices her hand through the air. "This is what's going to happen. Kitty, you'll wait in the panic room because Evie won't be able to guard you while they're here. Leonard, you will answer the door. They will ask for me and you'll bring them into the living room and then go and wait in the study. I will present myself as Kitty's Shield."

"They won't believe you've Sparked so soon," I say, seeing holes in everything.

"It can happen. Anyway, there are ways I can increase my signal before they get here."

"Wouldn't it make more sense if Jamie–" I begin.

"Siblings can't Spark each other!" Miriam snaps. "And even if they could, it wouldn't explain my presence in the house. Shields are not permitted to fraternise. So, I'm either Leonard's girlfriend or I'm breaking protocol by hanging out with Jamie."

"They'll buy the idea that you're Leonard's girlfriend? Wouldn't they question …"

Miriam growls in exasperation. "Of course they'll buy it, Evie. Relationship protocol is one of the most common tactics among Shields. We're a whole damn secret society of home wreckers! Trust me."

Barb makes a sound like she's half-choked.

Jamie grimaces. "Miriam's right, Evie. It happens all the time."

"This doesn't make sense!" Barb cries. "Why must Evie hide at all? Won't these people help?"

Jamie, Miriam and I produce matching looks of incredulity. "No," Miriam says. "They will order an extraction team and take her, and Kitty will be left without her protector. Do you understand? We're going to try to buy Evie some time. If we can pull it off, we won't have to worry about Affinity until this is all over."

Barb's eyes move to her daughter, to me and back to Miriam. "Do what you have to." She kisses Leonard on the mouth, grabs keys from the counter and walks out the door.

"Jamie," Miriam says. "Can you fetch me the first-aid kit?"

He nods and bolts into the butler's pantry.

Miriam looks to Kitty, who raises her hands. "I know. Panic room." She throws her arm around my neck, her foam support rubbing against my chin. "I bloody hate the panic room."

"It'll be okay." I clasp her back, infusing my voice with more certainty than I feel. "Miriam knows what she's doing."

Kitty releases me, tears tracking her checks. Leonard squeezes her hand and she crosses to the butler's pantry, stopping to make room for Jamie who comes out carrying a large red box.

"It's going to work." He kisses her cheek and she sniffs, stepping past him to punch the access code to the wine cellar. The door clicks and I have one final glimpse of her anxious face.

Jamie deposits the kit on the bench. Miriam strips her shirt off and stands there in her bra, digging through the medical supplies. Leonard swivels away and Jamie turns his back. I stare at my aunt in disbelief – she is so focused and unflinching, taking command of an impossible situation.

"Jamie," she says. "Come here and take your shirt off."

Jamie swallows but doesn't hesitate, shucking his shirt over his head, revealing a white fitted singlet that amplifies his gold skin. He joins Miriam at the counter and her hand blurs. Jamie grunts and a vivid red slash opens on his bicep just beneath the band of his tattoo.

"Miriam!" I want to lunge at her. Leonard spins around, nearly losing his glasses.

"It's okay." Jamie grits his teeth. "It'll spike my signal and help mask yours."

Miriam presses a cloth to Jamie's wound and hands him a bandage. "Go into the living room, close the curtains to the conservatory, find somewhere in there for Evie to hide."

"I can do that," Leonard says, moving towards the door.

"No, Leonard, I need you and Evie."

Jamie rushes out, holding his bleeding arm. Miriam quickly sets about repeating the procedure. Leonard forgets to turn his back, watching as Miriam opens her bicep with the emergency kit scalpel. She hisses. Leonard and I wince at the welling of blood. She staunches the flow, unwinds a bandage one-handed and binds her arm with quick neat loops, reminding me it isn't the first time she's doctored her own wounds. In less than thirty seconds she's back in her shirt. She rounds on Leonard and grimaces. "Try not to freak out but I need you to kiss me."

"What?" He stares like she's lost her mind and takes a step back.

"If we have any hope of pulling this off, I need to spike

my frequency. Conflict or arousal is the fastest way to do it. So either punch me or kiss me!"

He gapes at her, more flustered than I've ever seen him, clearly as blindsided as I feel.

"I guess you're going with option B." She doesn't hesitate but steps forwards and pulls him down to her lips. He freezes, eyes still open in shock. She tries to force a response from him but poor Leonard doesn't seem to know what to do with his hands. She presses against him, kissing him with desperate fervour. "Come on." She pounds her hand on his chest. "Work with me!"

Then she gets what she wants. His eyes close and his hands come suddenly around her back, almost lifting her from the ground. Miriam clasps one arm around his neck and with the other she grips his bicep, digging her nails in. Leonard grunts, knotting his fingers in her hair and tips her head back, devouring her kiss.

It's a paralysing sight, like watching a distortion of Jamie and me. My insides churn. I can't fathom why Miriam needs me to stay.

"Miriam! They'll be here any minute!"

It seems like a major effort for them to break apart, panting and wide-eyed. Leonard looks completely punch-drunk as he rights his glasses and Miriam's face is flushed, her eyes bright. She almost staggers, turning to me. "Now, hit me."

"What?"

"Not the face. Then go and find Jamie," her expression hardens, clearly hating to have to say it, "and repeat what you've seen here."

I'm too flabbergasted to move.

"Hit me, damn it!"

A terrible rush of adrenaline surges through me and I drive my fist into her stomach, lifting her from her feet, shunting her backwards. She folds, wheezing. Leonard catches her. "Good," she says, a barely audible rasp, her face beet red. "Now, go."

WARDEN

"Jamie?" I slip between the heavy curtains, from the living room into the conservatory. The French doors hang open and the cool damp smell of earth and orchid mingle with pungent fertiliser and the split wood scent of sap. Dark leafy shadows loom like malformed hands, reaching high over the mosaic floor, a spangled night above.

Jamie stands at a utility closet, yanking out shelves like he's snapping twigs; nails whine then pop and the whole structure shakes. He's hung his shirt on a potted rose and dust mottles the white cotton of his singlet, his chest and bandage glowing in the moonlight. He tosses the last shelf behind him and straightens up, brushing dirt from his hands. "There. It'll be a squeeze, but you should fit."

"Miriam says we should kiss," I say, like I'm bringing a note from the teacher.

Jamie exhales, a sharp amused gust, regarding me with

his hands on his hips. "I agree." Then he comes for me, cups my head, tips my mouth, bringing his intoxicating scent of winter forest and warm skin, like he's just come in from the cold, sat before a blazing fire, drunk eggnog and eaten cinnamon cookies right before kissing me.

My whole body hums, a bone-deep, homecoming hum.

Soon dizziness sweeps in, but I don't pull back. *Time line, end point, he'll choose her.* Jealousy, it rears in me, a red-hot blaze, vaporising my inhibition and inadequacy, and I dig my fingers in Jamie's singlet, melding my hips to his, as though I'm bold and sexy and have a clue what I'm doing. He catches his breath and I relish the sound. I touch the ridges of his stomach, outline the hard muscle-wrapped cage of his ribs and trace the broad plains of his chest, mapping territory in a heedless rush to stake my claim before I pass out.

The foreign signal pulses, probing for me in the bandwidth. I wince and Jamie groans, squeezing his forehead.

"I'm sorry," I blurt, not looking at him. "All that stuff I said. I know it's only been a day. Obviously, I don't expect – it's not like I think we – what I'm trying to say is, I didn't mean it to sound so creepy and intense. It's Miriam, she does my head in. She wouldn't shut up, and I swear, I didn't know anything about, you know, the binding words, or whatever."

He lifts my chin. "Wouldn't hurt to let me believe you meant it, yeah?"

I don't know how to respond, there's no time. "Listen, if this doesn't work and they take me–"

"It'll work."

"Fine, but we have Richard's blood, if it's him and I'm not here–"

He squeezes my waist. "I'll take care of it."

"Thank you." I pull away and cringe. "I forgot. I'm supposed to give you this." I draw my arm back and ram my fist into his stomach.

* * *

Inside the utility closet, my back pressed against cold wood, shoulders hunched, head ducked, I shiver, not because of the temperature but the bat-shit crazy fear of my fight or flight instinct. I hate picturing Kitty, terrified in the panic room, waiting for fate, or filling the pages of her journal with abject horror. I wonder what time it is, whether I'll get to kiss Jamie again, when I last ate, when my nightmare period will hit, what will happen if they try to take me or if I fight. *Kitty, Kitty, Kitty.*

"They're coming," Miriam says from the living room. She doesn't have to raise her voice. I'm concentrating so hard it's a wonder I haven't burst a blood vessel. "Stay connected," she says. Something about the direction of her voice makes me picture her standing by the double doors to the foyer.

"Everton." Jamie. Close. Just through the wall.

"I'm ready." *They won't take me. They won't.*

I close my eyes, visualise Jamie (as he was before I punched him and he collapsed on his knees, gasping for air), his lips pouty from kissing the life out of me, his eyes all smouldering. I reach into the slipstream of static, looking for his signal. "Ha." He's waiting for me. The familiar vibration, the resonant hum.

Images flicker in my mind, sensation charges my skin, a strange blending of Transfer and Harvest between us, the give and take of physical memory. Then a sound from outside reaches me, tyres crunch on gravel. My eyes pop open and through the closet slats headlights light up the conservatory. I hear wheels turning, slowing, braking then the car engine dies. *Kitty!* Blind panic takes me, that lost-in-the-dark terror of childhood, like waking from a nightmare caught beneath suffocating sheets. My arms fly out, banging the wooden boards that seem suddenly coffin-like in constriction. I heave for air.

"Everton," Jamie whispers.

"No," Miriam hisses. "Pull it together."

I bite hard on the inside of my cheek. I've lost Jamie's signal. I stop breathing as an image blooms brightly in my mind. Jamie's KMT.

Long dark hair fanned across a pillow, a warm wet cloth mopping blood from milk-white skin …

The doorbell. Steps in the foyer. Leonard's voice.

Things become murky. Cerebral images clash with voices from the other room, disorienting me, like trying to watch a television while listening to a radio at the same time.

A man, not Leonard, brief low words.

A woman, an octave higher.

Miriam, formal, welcoming.

Jamie … silent.

Footsteps. The doors to Leonard's study closing. I picture him pacing as he waits.

Movement in the living room, bodies sitting and then finally the voice of the Affinity Project.

The woman: "Is this a secure arrangement?"

Miriam: "Of course. I'm experienced with Relationship Protocol. Irregular work hours are part of my cover. Leonard believes you are here to examine proofs for an installation."

The woman: "I'm not concerned about the Ticket. Your profile is exemplary."

Ticket?

Jamie's jaw, his mouth, his breath …

Silence. Movement.

The woman: "The Gallagher girl is a Spark? Eighteen is late."

Miriam: "Police filed her attack."

The woman: "I see that here … Governor's Ball. Unfortunately high profile … Attempted mugging? Optimistic."

A pause.

The woman: "However, two Spark events so close together, Ms Everton?"

Miriam: "It is unusual."

The woman: "Supply protection is always preferable, but I suppose in these cases, we should be grateful it is at least someone of your experience. The mess some make …"

Miriam: "Mmm."

A feather-light touch, tracing an angel's scars …

The woman: "Your Watcher. Carolyn, is it? We'll have her contact you. Perhaps a full course of Fretizine would be best when you're done here."

Miriam: "I was thinking the same."

The woman: "And I will arrange a Reprieve."

Miriam: "Thank you, that – that would be wonderful."

The woman: "Asset preservation is paramount."

Silence.

An explosion of glass, Jamie murmuring my name …

The woman: "Your presence here is a concern, Mr Gallagher. Only Ms Everton's spike in demerits in the last half hour indicated she might be entertaining a fellow agent."

Jamie: "I haven't interfered. Miriam will tell you."

The woman: "I have met few active family members who don't."

Jamie: "Interference leads to mistakes. I would rather my sister live. I have full confidence in Miriam and no interest in getting in her way."

The woman: "However, your presence infringes protocol."

Miriam: "I'm old enough to be Jamie's mother."

Whoa.

A scalpel flashes, opening a fissure in golden skin beneath a line of black ink …

The woman: "Hardly a deterrent, but I'm referring to Mr Gallagher's current status. It says here you have entered the Deactivation Program with–"

Jamie: "Only the Pre-lim."

Miriam: "Deactivation?"

Deactivation?

The woman: "You have not disclosed your status, Mr Gallagher?"

Jamie: "It didn't seem important."

Deactivation?

The woman: "The state of your signal is very important. Tesla takes his program seriously and–"

Miriam: "Tesla? Ethan Tesla?"

Jamie: "Ethan knows I'm here."

Deactivation?

The woman: "I will have to verify this with Tesla, Mr Gallagher."

Jamie: "Certainly."

Silence.

Jamie? I can't find your signal.

The woman: "It is a concern to me that we could not identify you at all until we cross-referenced the address. How is it that your Marker has been allowed to degrade?"

Jamie: "My Watcher is Kaleb Kent."

The woman: "Is he aware of your return from Berlin?"

Jamie: "No."

The woman: "Would you like me to file a negligence report about Mr Kent?"

Jamie: "Yes, I would."

Silence.

The woman: "There's a niece on your file, Ms Everton. Carolyn has made note of her relocation."

I hold my breath, the siren in my head.

The woman: "And her mother has died. Trauma is often a precursor to Priming, and with exposure to your signal–"

Miriam: "No. There's been nothing."

The woman: "Still, you should be alert."

Miriam: "Of course."

Silence. Movement.

The woman: "Do either of you require any other assistance at this juncture?"

Miriam/Jamie: "No."

The woman: "Before we go, Mr Gallagher. It is my opinion that it would be better for you to remove yourself from the premises until Ms Everton has completed the assignment. The blurring in your signal is quite severe, as though it has divided or multiplied in some way. Even with Tesla's permission for leave, I doubt he would be pleased with your current reading."

CONSEQUENCES

I ache. Shoulders, back, thighs, calves, my bones generally. I trail Kitty through the double doors to the Senior Common Room. Dark-panelled walls, casement windows, roll armed sofas gathered in huddles around fading Axminster. I yawn and rub my eyes. Thankfully, I'm back in stretchy denim and Chuck Taylors; no more of Kitty's restricting designer get-ups for me.

I scan the room, partly for Kitty's sake but mostly for my own. Only a handful of people. No sign of Richard, but we're early.

"Relax, he's probably off having plastic surgery." Kitty pokes me with her elbow, towards a clutch of sofas. "You've successfully duped an international underground organisation, doesn't that make you happy?"

"Delaying the inevitable doesn't make me happy. Thinking about what will happen to Miriam and Jamie doesn't make me happy." I bite my lip. Kitty has enough on her plate (target of the genetically deranged). I struggle to smile. "Staying with you makes me happy."

She isn't convinced. "They'll be in trouble?"

I had lain awake half the night, between nightmares, worrying about what Affinity Project discipline looked like, among countless other things, like how long would it take Doctor Sullivan to compare samples, and what the hell was a deactivation program? A cure? Wouldn't Jamie just say? He was so cagey about it. If Miriam hadn't taken off straight after the Warden left, I might have asked her.

I don't answer Kitty, lowering myself onto the couch, wincing at the collective cry of my musculature. I needed several hours in the gym, post-Warden, to calm down enough to sleep. Not that the sleep I'd had was any comfort, dream-stalking Kitty with sick, twisting hate. In the end, I fought my way back to consciousness at four, sobbing uncontrollably. I'm starting to think I need an exorcism. I try to focus on the positives. Leonard will have delivered my shirt to Doctor Sullivan by now. Who knows, he might already have Richard pinned under a microscope.

"I hate it." Kitty slumps next to me, frowning at her hands. "Everyone's lives screwed over because of me."

"*No.*" I grit my teeth. "There is not a single shit thing about this whole DNA fiasco that isn't the fault of the megalomaniac sons of bitches who conjured it up in a lab."

"Too many double negatives for me to follow, Evs."

"It means, I forbid you to blame yourself. It's ridiculous, like apologising for being short."

"I'm sorry about that too."

"Ugh."

Gil shoulders his way into the common room, brandishing an alarming bouquet of orange flowers. He props the door open and the rest of the guys follow, looking damp from the rain after their meeting down at the boatsheds. Jamie brings up the rear, an amused, long-suffering curve to his lips.

People turn to stare at Gil. He puffs his chest, drawing chuckles and comments. I snort and shake my head until Gil's eyes land on me and his expression becomes ominously gleeful. "There she is!"

I sink into the couch. "Oh no. He's not?"

Kitty quakes beside me, bumping my shoulder as she laughs. "Oh, but he is."

Gil hurdles a sofa, landing on a sunken seat opposite me, laying the flowers on the coffee table, the perfumed waft as eye-watering as the colour. "On behalf of Gainsborough Collegiate, thank you for the best first day of school *ever.*"

"You said that yesterday." I let my hair swing out beside my face to block the rubberneckers watching from the couches next to ours. "And what am I supposed to do with these all day?"

Abe and Pete land either side of Gil, grinning with

the same evil glee. Pete settles in for some prolonged eye contact with Kitty. Jamie sits beside me on the armrest. "Endure?" Jamie says. "As I do, when my best friend gives my girlfriend flowers."

"About that," Gil leans forwards, bringing his fingertips together in a dramatic flourish beneath his chin. "In light of recent nose-breaking events, I would be willing to forgo said friendship. I propose a transferring of affection from your current boyfriend to someone who might on first appearance seem an unlikely candidate but who, given time, may be found to have many endearing qualities."

Jamie sighs.

Gil raises his palm for silence. "I may not have much to recommend me–"

"True," Abe says.

"Not a single scar or tattoo."

"I could give you a scar," Jamie says brightly.

"I am but a humble man, of humble means–"

"In that his father owns the largest sawmill in the Northwest," Pete says.

"With little grace, polish or sophistication–"

"Also true." Abe nods.

"However." Gil lifts his chin. "What I can offer is a lifetime of unwavering devotion."

Jamie groans.

"For breaking one nose?" If I play along, it might be

over sooner. "I'll think about it."

Gil clasps his hands and closes his eyes.

Lila and Imogen appear in the growing crowd, Kaylee behind them. I dig my nails into my legs. I haven't seen Kaylee since yesterday's creeptastic encounter in the corridor where Richard pawed her hair. Given I'd burned my bridges with Kaylee in chemistry, I'm not sure I can take more drama. She doesn't say anything but slides neatly onto the last couch with Imogen.

Lila leans beside Abe. "What's going on?"

"The Bishop is campaigning to displace the Skipper," Abe says.

Lila laughs. "And how's it going?"

"She's wavering," Jamie says.

Lila shrugs. "I'd waver."

Gil's head whips towards her, his face lighting up.

"Hmph," Jamie says.

Lila pouts and nods at me. "Like I could compete with that."

I pretend not to hear and mutter, "Unwavering devotion has a short attention span."

Behind the boys, on the other side of the room, a group has gathered around a large cardboard box. I recognise Angelo, grinning behind his blond hair as he flips the lid and pulls out a neatly folded blue T-shirt with a flash of yellow printed on the front, inspiring immediate laughter.

Several of the group look over and smile at me. Some even give me the thumbs up.

What the hell?

I try to tune in but there are too many voices talking over each other for me to hear anything distinct. The crowd around Angelo grows, the laughs and looks multiply, boys and girls dig in their pockets and packs, fisting out cash.

I rise to my feet and brush past Jamie, making my way slowly towards Angelo's customers. A boy turns with the T-shirt fitted over his button-down shirt. Emblazoned across his chest are the hastily screen-printed words, *Not without a mint*, a volleyball arcing above it. "Wanna sign it?"

My jaw clicks. "No."

"Straight off the press." Angelo squeezes through the group, green eyes sparkling. "It was a late night, but worth it. This is my second box. Should have seen them go in the parking lot – selling like hotcakes."

"Angelo, are you trying to ruin me?"

He claps me on the shoulder, making my spine zap. "Trust me, it's already urban legend."

Jamie appears beside me. "The governor will love them."

Angelo retrieves his hand. "Until 'The Man' shuts me down, it's all supply and demand." His eyes linger on me. "And demand is hot. See you in gym, Evie."

Numbly horrified, I watch him push back through the crowd.

"Bloody hell," Jamie says darkly. "He's keen."

"This is bad."

"I'll take one, if you have it in extra small." Kaylee steps past me, slipping a twenty-dollar bill from her purse. Her eyes met mine and she gives me a small reluctant smile.

* * *

I squint at the whiteboard, stifle my hundredth yawn and arch my back, grateful at least for the ease in my muscles after the stiffness of the morning (score for rapid regeneration). Mr Fenton's diagram has taken on the indecipherable quality of hieroglyphics. I lean over to look at Kitty's work, but she copied it exactly right. Why doesn't mine look the same?

The sound of light feet approaches in the corridor and I look to the door. A frightened freshman runner enters with a note. Mr Fenton opens it and looks at me.

My stomach plummets.

"Principal Hawker wishes to see you in her office."

"Can't I go after class?" I hate the thought of so many corridors between me and Kitty.

Mr Fenton peers over his glasses with a bewildered frown. "Your dedication to economics is duly noted, Miss Everton, but if the principal is asking for you now, then now you shall go." He turns back to the whiteboard.

Murmurs of speculation rise around the room. I'm not the only one who expects me to fry for yesterday's incident.

Kitty taps her watch under the desk, like high-tech gadgets are a comfort.

"Fine." I snap my folder closed, scrape my chair and stalk out the door, sniggers rippling behind me. My pulse pounds in my ears. The immense stupidity of allowing myself to be dragged away from Kitty!

The tether stretches until it evaporates at the turn in the last corridor. I ball my fists and replay breaking Richard's nose to comfort myself. The crunch. The satisfaction.

The principal's welcome is austere. "It is a very great shame, Miss Everton, to see you so soon in the semester and for such an unpleasant matter."

Stay calm. Look repentant. Getting back to Kitty is all that matters.

But it's a lengthy speech about the Deans' "important relationship" with the school. Finally, she lays it out. "You are required to visit the governor's office, at the end of the week, to make a formal apology to Richard in the presence of his father."

I am too slow adjusting my face.

Ms Hawker leans forwards, pressing her elbows on her gleaming desk. "You will make your apology, Miss Everton, and you will be grateful that you are not suspended between now and then. The governor has made it quite clear that your failure to comply will result in legal action."

"It was an accident."

"There are witnesses who say otherwise." She sits back with a sigh. "The best advice I can give you is to swallow your pride and be done with it. The governor does not make idle threats." She slides a small white business card across the desk, and I pick it up with numb fingers. She nods me out of her office.

I close the door and walk head-down into someone's chest.

The bandwidth blanks, like dead air, then bursts back to life as I step away. "Sorry." So much for lightning reflexes.

It's Aiden. "That look doesn't bode well."

I hold up the governor's card.

He grimaces. "Busted, huh?"

"It was too much to hope it wouldn't come back to bite me."

"Is Chuck in there?"

"Chuck?"

"My nickname for the governor. Not a very respectful attitude, is it, given the man's responsible for my current good fortune?"

"I could think of worse names."

"Helps defuse resentment."

"What do you call Richard?"

He grins and we both say, "Dick."

"Governor's not in there," I say. "Just the card."

"Hard labour in the salt mines for you then?"

I explain about the apology.

His expression sobers. "And what if you don't?"

"They'll press charges." I shake my head and Aiden surprises me by putting his hand on my shoulder, muting the bandwidth. It's the strangest sensation – like coming up against a wall – but I can't think past the frustration and anger burning in my chest. "I've got no one to blame but myself."

Aiden frowns and withdraws his hand, digging it in his pocket.

My ears pop and the bandwidth crackles back to life.

"The governor enjoys his power. He'll want to see you eat some humble pie."

I heave a sigh. "You got an appointment with Hawker?"

"Needed my boarding fees signed off." He sounds distracted. "The principal's secretary's photocopying my form." On cue, the secretary returns and hands Aiden the slip of paper like it's an unseemly transaction. "Thanks." He folds the form twice, tucking it in his back pocket. We both turn towards the door and Aiden automatically opens it for me.

"I guess the scholarship came with a few strings?"

"What? Oh, right. Yeah. You could say the governor's

favour comes on hard terms, for sure." He falls back into his thoughts as we make our way out into the gilded corridor. "He likes gratitude," he says, finally. "Don't get me wrong. I'm grateful. But it's a drag having to show it all the time."

As we near the end of the hall, my anxiety spikes and I look at my watch. How long have I been away from Kitty? I picture her sitting safely in economics, but conjuring her face only increases my anxiety and I quicken my stride. Aiden keeps pace with me and there's an awkward pause. I can't concentrate enough to come up with conversation.

When we round the next corridor and the tether snaps to life, I expect to feel relieved but instead I feel an alarming rise in fear. Aiden stops beside me, staring at the floor like he's dropped something. I skitter a few steps ahead.

"Actually … I forgot." He pats his pocket where he has tucked the fees printout. "I needed to ask the principal something."

I wave him goodbye and actually jog the remaining distance to the door.

Aiden makes a fast track back down the corridor.

I hit the handle too heavily, the door springs open and every head turns towards me. I zero in on Kitty like I'm looking down a long tunnel. Someone is in my seat. Someone leaning close to her.

I freeze, scanning for the threat but can't lock on anything. White noise buzzes in my head.

"Don't just stand there, Evangeline," Mr Fenton says from the whiteboard.

Kitty pales, reading the tension in my posture.

I glare at the boy sitting next to her.

"Thanks for your help," he mumbles to Kitty, picking up his textbook, not meeting my eye.

It's an effort to bend my joints to sit. Kitty puts a clammy hand on my arm and the fear in her eyes pierces me. "Can you feel something?"

"It's okay." I stare down at the blurred page of notes. "I was just freaking out."

I force myself to focus. I picture Aiden, his face, his hands as he talked. I focus on the electric tension that rose in me, now ebbing away. *What if I'm overreacting? Worse still, what if I'm not?*

MIRIAM

"This is cool!" Kitty lifts her voice above the wall of music, bumping down the metal stairs behind me. "Miriam has a lair!"

The combination of two days at school without being murdered and last night's victory over the Affinity Project seems to have given Kitty a bolstered sense of morale. Either that, or Pete flirting with her by her locker at the end of the day has worked wonders.

We clear the ceiling and look down on Miriam hammering the sparring dummy. Her arms and legs blur as she strikes the wooden limbs. *Thwack, thwack-thwack!* My bones ache in sympathy. Violent Femmes grind from the speakers and I brace against the volume and the sense memory: the song is one of Mom's old favourites. Miriam's upset.

I turn Jamie's keys in my hand and wonder if it would have been better to stay at school and wait while the boys practised for time trials. But the day, the drama, the attention for being the angsty girl dating the hot guy with the scars and ink had wiped me out. With so many things on my chest that need unloading, I jumped at the offer to drive Kitty home and take a detour to see Miriam without Jamie. I wait by the stairs, not wanting to get in Miriam's way. Kitty wanders over to the display of knives and martial arts paraphernalia.

Miriam finishes her workout with a series of somersaults, landing before me, sweaty and flushed, her eyes wary. "What's going on?"

It's hard to look right at her. "I wanted to talk to you and I wasn't sure if you were coming to the Gallaghers' tonight."

She glances at Kitty, who's now on the treadmill.

"She knows about the kiss."

Miriam cringes then turns away, jogging across the room to kill the music. The quiet seems loud in contrast.

Kitty hops off the treadmill and comes out onto the mat. "You're not worried about snogging Dad, are you?"

Miriam picks up a towel and mops sweat from her brow, though it looks more like hiding to me.

"Barb's okay," I say, with more assurance than I feel. Things were fairly stilted at breakfast this morning.

Miriam looks up. "He told her?"

"Of course he did," Kitty says.

She groans.

"Don't worry." Kitty pats her arm. "Jamie explained it was necessary. Barb's not unreasonable."

"That's optimistic, kid."

What Kitty and Barb don't know about is the intensity of the kiss, its force and – I hate to think the word – passion. I know that's what Miriam feels bad about and I feel bad for her. A civilian would struggle to resist the advances of a Shield. The chemical potency, or "mutant hotness" as Kitty likes to call it, that makes the genetically engineered so desirable wouldn't only have blitzed poor Leonard's restraint but compelled from him an equally potent response.

"You can't hide here forever," Kitty says.

Miriam gives her a droll look. "I live here."

"I'm just saying, you know, don't be a girl's blouse." Kitty throws her hands up. "Now, I'm famished."

Miriam cracks an insubstantial smile. "The cupboard's pretty bare. I could make some cookies?"

"Let me," Kitty says. "Besides, Evie wants a private word to apologise for being so horrible for the last couple of weeks, and to thank you on behalf of all of us for so epically taking charge last night and ostensibly saving my life."

I shoot her a dirty look, my ears growing hot. "Thanks very much."

"You'll be able to ..." Kitty puts her fingers to her

temples and makes a strained expression like she's constipated.

I roll my eyes. "Yes, I'll sense you from here."

She cocks her head, a foam-support hampered gesture of the blithely unruffled and crosses back to the stairs.

Miriam looks like she's bracing for a blow.

"Um ..." *Eye contact.* Pressure builds in my chest. From the moment the Warden left, I knew something had shifted inside me, but I didn't want to bank on it until I could stand in Miriam's presence and test my reaction. Now I'm here, looking into her brown eyes, I know for sure. The block in my mind, the sense of violation against the Fixation Effect, has gone. With the wall down, a flood of suppressed emotion rushes in.

Cutting Miriam off had robbed me of my one true ally in grief, the one person who felt the loss of Mom as much as I did. I let my tears fall and I let her see them fall. "I'm sorry." I barely squeeze the words out before my sob cuts them off.

Her arms surround me and I cry even harder, clinging to her, swamping her with my need, my mother-ache, my relief, regret and loss.

"Oh, honey," she murmurs.

"Kitty's right. I've been so horrible to you and you didn't deserve it but I couldn't stop myself."

"Sweetie, it's okay. I understand. You don't need–"

"I do!" I pull back, wiping tears onto the back of my hands, sniffing hard. "I do need to apologise, and then you were so incredible last night," my voice flies high, "so brilliant and fearless while we were all freaking out and you pulled us together and did this incredible thing, even though you could get in so much trouble and–"

"None of that matters." Miriam pulls me into her arms again and I cling to her sweaty back and sob. Then a vivid image fills my mind. I'm Miriam, hugging Mom, tears flowing, arms around her neck, a hard moving lump pressing against my belly.

I gasp. The image vanishes. Miriam and I break apart. "Did I harvest that?"

"I – I don't know. What did you feel?"

My mouth splits with a smile. "Mom, when she was pregnant with me." I press my hand to my belly. "I could feel me moving. Ha! That is so completely weird and awesome."

Pain and joy contort Miriam's face. "It is."

"I miss her so much it hurts … but, I'm so glad she never had to know what I really am, that I didn't have to hide this from her."

"She loved you so much, Evie. She was so proud of you." She strokes my hair. "I owe you an apology too. I should never have said those things to you in front of everyone."

I am determined not to get defensive.

"Don't get me wrong, I still don't like it but I should never have humiliated you."

"It's not our fault we're Synergists," I say carefully.

"I know that." She sighs.

"How could I not choose Jamie?"

"It's not your choice."

"But, how could I ever want anyone else?" The enormity of saying it aloud terrifies me. I know it must sound ridiculous, the naive stupidity of a teenage girl. "It's like … it's so …"

Her focus grows distant, her eyes weary. "I get it."

Realisation steals over me. "Have you – I mean, were you with someone like that before?"

She drops her gaze and frowns. "Ages ago."

"What happened?"

"Jamie hasn't been honest with you, Evie."

I stall. "What?"

She looks up. "If he's in the deactivation program it means he's been paired with a Cooler."

I shake my head. "I don't know what that means."

"A Cooler is the opposite of a Synergist and almost as rare. It's a person whose signal counteracts and defuses our own. Prolonged exposure to that person under the conditions of the program could make it possible for Jamie to deactivate."

Helena.

My mind races. "Jamie could be cured? I mean, made normal? No Sparks?"

"Yes."

"That's ..." I hate the idea that Helena can give Jamie something I can't. "Wonderful."

"It means Jamie would have to be with his Cooler."

"Yeah, I get it." My ears ring. "How long is the program? Weeks, months?"

"No, Evie, it would be permanent."

My hearing takes on that noise-in-a-tunnel effect where the sound of your own pulse fills your head. I can see her waiting for me to burst into tears. Instead, I shrug my jacket off and turn to the sparring dummy. "Miriam," my voice gets rough. "Would you mind stepping back?"

RIFT

"Please say something." Kitty trots beside my quick-step march from the car to the courtyard entrance of the house, her cookies rattling in the tin she's borrowed from Miriam, her journal balanced on top. "You're freaking me out."

"Everything is fine." Two hours with Miriam's sparing dummy hasn't calmed me down. "I just need to talk to your brother."

"Everything is not fine. You look like you might start blowing things up." She stumbles at the doorstep. She manages to right herself but her journal slips, bouncing on its spine, springing open. Envelopes spill across the mat, six of them, names written in Kitty's neat hand: Kaylee, Lila, Imogen, Miriam, Jamie, one for her parents.

"What's this?"

Her eyes widen. "Nothing."

"Bullshit." I know what these letters are. I know it

immediately. *She doesn't believe I can save her.* Suddenly furious, I bend to snatch them up, but she shoves me before I can get hold of them.

"Don't you dare!" she shouts.

"Move or I will move you."

"Don't you bloody well tell me what to do, Evangeline Everton." Livid patches develop on her cheeks. "It's none of your business."

She shrieks when I take her by the arms and lift her from the ground, putting her down behind me. She drops her tin and kicks and bellows, raising her hand to strike me. I catch her wrist. "Try it." I turn my back on her cries and grab the envelopes.

"Stop it!"

"Letters?" I fan them with trembling fingers.

"Give them to me." Eyes streaming, she swipes them back, creasing the envelopes, whimpering at the damage then smoothing them between her hands. "It's nothing."

"Writing your goodbyes, Kit?" My voice cracks. "Where's mine?"

She lunges for the journal but I'm too fast for her, whipping it off the ground.

Kitty slaps at my wrist. "I haven't … It's not–"

I flip the book open. There are blank loose leaves. Torn pages. My name and a paragraph. She's crossed things out, underlined phrases and written amendments.

I don't read it. I tear the page and screw it up.

"Evie, please."

"Don't-write-me-any-letters." Dizzy with grief, I shove the journal into her hands and stalk inside, down the back hall. I ram the kitchen door and stop short. Leonard stands behind Barb at the stove, his hands on her shoulders, head bent as though he's been whispering in her ear. They both look up, startled.

"You're back. Is Miriam joining us for dinner?" Barb's tremulous voice and smile crumble. "What's wrong?"

"Um, Miriam, she's … no. Not for dinner, she'll come later." I fist my knuckles to hide my shaking. "Where's Jamie?"

"Upstairs," Barb says. "He went to take a shower after Abe dropped him off."

I swivel around just as Kitty walks in with her tear-stained eyes. "Evie."

"What's going on?" Leonard says.

I push past Kitty into the hall and stumble up the backstairs, barely able to see straight with my rage and my hurt and my punctured hope. Leaving school that afternoon, my biggest concerns were Aiden and Miriam, but the worry of the first and the relief of the latter were obliterated by Jamie's lies and now Kitty's letters.

I stall outside Jamie's room, staring at the doors. Music blares.

Stay calm. Don't cry.

I knock and let myself in, bracing against the sensory impact of his scent. I can't hear the shower. "Jamie?" I lift my voice, not wanting to surprise him if he plans to walk out naked.

"Hang on," he calls.

I lean against the double doors, fighting my trembling.

Jamie keeps his apartment-sized room tidy. Shades of white, grey and a deeper charcoal in the soft furnishings. Weathered oars hang mounted above his wide low bed. His navy crew jersey lies slung over a wooden chair, "Skipper" monogrammed in gold. In the corner, looking out on the estate lawn, a drafting table, covered in a series of hull designs.

Oh, that's right. Yachts.

I don't want to look at them or anything, or be moved by the evidence of Jamie's essential … Jamieness. I look at the floor and focus on the screaming chaos in my head.

The door to the bathroom opens and Jamie appears barefoot in his black jeans, a towel obscuring his face as he dries his hair. Water beads his chest and it's impossible not to look when he turns his back to reach for a remote, killing the music. I hold my breath for the angel, knowing I'll never trace its details again. He drops his towel and faces me, caution in his eyes. "Is your phone off? I tried calling you."

I force myself to hold his gaze. "This is extracurricular."

His lips part, his chest expanding slowly as he processes my words, but his expression remains unflinching. "No. It's not."

"Yeah. It is."

"Miriam doesn't understand."

"Yeah. She does."

"Listen–"

"You listen!" I stab my finger at him. "For Kitty's sake, we will remain training partners but there will be no more extracurricular activity. It's over."

His brow knots tight. "You're not being fair."

"Fair!" Roaring fills my ears. "You let me believe – you told me …" But what could I accuse him of? He had made me no promises. "You started something you had no right to start and I was an easy target. That's what's so pathetic, isn't it? I'm just a stupid, predictable girl."

Jamie welds his hands to his hips. "It's not like that!"

"It's exactly like that!" A high-pitched ringing builds in my head.

Calm down.

"You have a chance at a normal life with Helena. A normal life!"

"It's not decided!" His face reddens. "She doesn't know if she wants to deactivate. She has a boyfriend!"

"She'll choose you!" The light bulb flickers above us.

"What if I don't want her to?"

We stare at each other.

"You'd give up a normal life for me, Jamie?" I force a bitter laugh, wanting to hurt him. "You heard Miriam last night, choice is an illusion. Affinity already decided for you."

"I'm not in love with *Helena*!"

My mouth pops open for a cutting retort but there's no air, no words; my mind blanks. The high-pitched hum disappears, Jamie's undeclaration blinding me like an eclipse, pressing down on me with its weight. I feel like I'm slipping, scrabbling on loose ground, unable to find purchase for my feet, careening towards a precipice. If I don't push him away now, with him looking at me like that, saying things like that …

"Do you know what I dream about?" I land on the worst thing I can tell him. "Every night, since I moved in?"

He frowns at the sudden shift.

"I dream I'm him. I dream I'm stalking Kitty in the dark, with sick, twisting hate boiling inside me, poisoning me, killing me, driving me. And in the nightmare, I feel it in my stomach, feel it in my skin, in my head that I won't ever be free until she's dead."

Jamie recoils.

"Do you know how many times I've woken, drenched in sweat and sick to my stomach with the feeling of Kitty's neck snapping beneath my hands?" I shake my head.

"That's what Sparking has done to me, Jamie. If I were you, I'd stick with Helena."

I turn and open the door. Kitty backs against the wall, her face white, her eyes full. "No." I reach for her, but she tears away.

"Shit," Jamie mutters and pushes past me, running after her. I watch him go, the angel and the scars.

* * *

I throw my jacket in the corner and curl up on the bed. I stare at the shadows on the wall, wishing I could escape into sleep but it's early and there's no sleep in me, just a blank, wakeful void.

At some point I hear Barb and Leonard in the hall and know they will be checking on Kitty. I hate imagining their faces when they find out about the awful things I said. I press the tender marks on my arms where I blocked the sparring dummy, imagining the bruises blue on my white bones. I want to think about that warm moving lump I'd felt in Miriam's memory, but I know it'll make me cry. I want to stew about Aiden but have no energy to trawl back over the details. Instead, I scan the bandwidth and think about nothing, concentrate on breathing. It seems like an accomplishment.

When I hear Miriam's car, a juvenile relief fills me, like

here's my grown-up who'll take care of the mess and love me despite my mistakes.

She doesn't come straight up. I know one of the Gallaghers will fill her in. Probably Jamie, what with the awkwardness about Leonard and Barb. I imagine the effort it'll take for him to hide his disgust. Eventually, there are soft steps in the hall. She knocks and opens the door, but I don't roll over. The bed dips as she sits and puts her hand on my arm.

"Kitty's afraid of me."

She sighs, a gentle sound I don't deserve. "No, she's not."

"You didn't see her face."

"She blames herself."

"What?" I jerk on my side to look at her.

This is what Sparking has done to me.

I groan, remembering our conversation from the morning and how I scolded Kitty for blaming herself. In the space of one afternoon, I've ruined everything. I press my hand to my eyes. "You know she's been writing her goodbyes?"

"Maybe she's ... processing."

"She doesn't believe I can save her."

"She's afraid." Miriam strokes my hair. "Jamie said you've been having nightmares."

I tell her everything. "It's not normal, is it? You've never dreamed like that."

Miriam doesn't say anything.

I know I've shocked her and I feel truly worse. "What if–" I squeeze my eyes shut and choke it out, "What if I'm not good?"

She rolls me back against her. "How can you say that? Of course you're good."

"But what if there's something wrong with me? What if it's bad wiring?"

She holds my face and even in the dark her stare is fierce. "You are good. Do you hear me? It's just a dream. You can't fight DNA."

* * *

I make my way up to Kitty's room, carrying a breakfast tray, knock on the door and let myself in. The shower is running in the bathroom. I wasn't prepared for a delay. I had worked myself up to give a speech the moment I came in. I cross to her desk and place the tray on top then sink onto the corner of her bed, tearing a doughy hunk of muffin, stuffing it in my mouth.

A wad of paper catches my eye, balled up by the leg of Kitty's desk. With only the smallest hesitation, I kneel, grab the screwed up paper and unfold it. The sense of breaking taboo churns my stomach. It's a list.

Before the end: To do list:

1. Perfect crème brûlée
2. Fall in love
3. ~~2 kids~~ 3 kids
4. Live in London
5. Editor of my own food magazine
6. ~~Event manage~~

I stare at the paper so long my eyes sting. I picture her sitting at her desk compiling the list. Did she screw it up after overhearing my rant? If her hope is gone, I have no one to blame but myself.

The shower stops.

I stuff the list in my pocket and wait.

Kitty comes from the bathroom wrapped in her towel, frowning. "What are you doing?"

"Breakfast." I nod at the tray, folding my trembling hands under my arms. "And an apology."

She tucks a wet strand of hair behind her ear. "You don't need to. I know you wouldn't hurt me."

"I was angry with Jamie. I should never have said those things."

She nods at the floor. "I better get dressed or we'll be late."

I want to touch her, hug her, force her to be okay. Instead, I turn to the door. "I'll see you downstairs."

BRUISES

"Are you allowed to do that?" Lila straightens up, one trainer tied.

I stop digging in my bag, following her gaze to Kitty. I shoot to my feet. "What are you doing?"

She stands there in her gym gear, bare-necked, the foam support in her hands. "I've had enough." She stuffs the brace in her locker and closes the door, a metallic clap.

I shake my head. "You're putting that back on."

"No, I'm not."

I can't stop staring at her neck, naked and unprotected. "You're being ridiculous. Put the damn brace on."

Her grey eyes aren't as dark as her brother's but there's steel in them now. "No."

A quiet gust of outrage parts my lips, but what can I do, wrestle her to the ground? Her eyebrow arches; she knows I won't do anything in front of the others. "Gym?"

I snap. "Really? That's the best option for going without your brace?"

"What if someone bumps you?" Imogen says, putting her shirt on.

"Exactly!" I nod at Imogen and round on Kitty. "What then?"

"I'm fine." Kitty bends to tie her laces. Her hair brushes forwards. I see the chaffing on the vulnerable curve of her neck, where the brace has rubbed her skin.

I glare, but she keeps her head down.

Imogen and Lila exchange looks.

I clench my teeth so tightly a bone clicks in my jaw. I yank my T-shirt off and throw it in the locker.

"Jeez, Evie. What have you done?" Lila touches my wrist and my pins and needles zip-zap. I had forgotten about the state of my arms, dark blooms from wrists to elbows. My mind blanks and my mouth opens and closes. I can feel the other girls turning towards me. I pull my gym shirt on to stall.

"She slipped on the stairs," Kitty says, briefly meeting my eyes. "Carrying a bloody great box of books and landed on her arms."

"Um, yeah," I say. "Hurt like hell."

Lila grimaces. "Looks like."

"That's what you get when you think you have to do everything yourself," Kitty mutters.

Out in the gym, Mrs Jenner blows her whistle.

I step onto the courts, aggravated at feeling nervous. Will Richard be there? He arrived in the foyer that morning with his nose taped, a black-eyed scowl, and surrounded by sympathisers. I'd caught sight of him from a distance and braced for a day of smart-assed remarks.

Thankfully, he doesn't appear from the locker room, though his friends glower, a campaign of intimidation. One of them hisses through his teeth, "You wait."

"Piss off," Angelo steps in front of me, as well as another couple of kids wearing the blue screen-printed T-shirts. Richard's friends sneer and turn away, not so much backing down as biding their time.

"You okay?" Angelo slings his arm around my shoulders, a casual squeeze, just as Jamie emerges from the boys' locker room. Jamie stares. Angelo doesn't see him and reaches for my wrist. "What happened to your arms?"

I repeat Kitty's excuse and pull away. "I'm fine." I look up but Jamie has moved away and my stomach swoops.

After Mrs Jenner takes the roll, we begin jogging laps. Angelo and a few of the blue T-shirt crew keep pace behind Kitty and I, a buffer against Richard's cronies. It feels weird having people I don't even know defending me. I wish they wouldn't – I hate the attention. I glance at Kitty, jogging glum-faced on my right. I imagine every step jarring up through her spine.

"Is this my punishment?" I keep my voice low, eyes forward. "You endangering your life?"

She sighs, huffy with impatience. "Yes. It's all about you, Evie."

"Point made. I suck. Now put your brace back on."

"I'm self-actualising," she says. "Taking charge of one small portion of my life. I realise it's probably not something you can comprehend, being essentially an indestructible cyborg and all, but having your life dictated to you rather grates on the nerves."

My face grows hot and I fight to keep my voice down. "That – that doesn't make any sense."

"It's *my* neck."

We keep jogging.

I keep fuming. "You think I'm self-actualising? You think I'm the boss of *my* life?"

"Well, you've decided who Jamie's allowed to love and what I'm allowed to write, and Miriam had to pull a rabbit out of her arse before you'd forgive her and clearly you think you know better than I do what's good for me. So, I'd say, yeah, sounds pretty take charge to me."

I stop in my tracks, but Kitty keeps jogging, Angelo and the blue shirts dodging around me. "You okay?" Angelo calls, jogging backwards.

I wave him on. "I'm fine."

Jamie jogs past, his eyes brushing over me, taking in

the bruises on my arms. He doesn't stop. Gil, a few steps behind, frowns and looks at me questioningly. I try to produce a smile and shrug like nothing's wrong but I can tell he doesn't buy it. Neither do I.

***

I drop my satchel on the floor and lean against the locker, closing my eyes. Two classes down and my endurance has waned. I wish I could wall out the noise of students congesting the corridor and wonder if I can persuade Kitty to ditch calculus.

Kitty closes her locker. "Permission to use the restroom?"

I bite back a retort and crack an eye open. "Looks like a queue." Girls are crowding in there. She doesn't reply but walks away. I close my eye and mutter, "I'll be right here." I concentrate on the pulse of the tether, one ear on the bandwidth. Someone stops by me. I keep my eyes closed hoping they'll get the hint.

"My dove?"

I open my eyes and Gil leans his wide frame, one shouldered, against the locker beside me. "*My dove?*" I say.

His eyes glint. "I'm trying it out."

I shake my head. "Nooo."

He shrugs, turning his body to assume the same

posture as mine. "Lot on your mind?"

Quietly hysterical laughter shakes my shoulders. "A bit, yeah."

"Skip seems rather … preoccupied himself."

You've decided who Jamie's allowed to love. "It's complicated."

He nods a slow, contemplative nod. "I'm loath to undermine my own campaign, but you know you've kind of been Jamie's dream girl since he was eleven, right?"

I brace my hands against the locker, a lump forming in my throat. "Seems unlikely given we argued most of the time we were kids."

"You know what they say about that." He lowers his voice. "I won't break tree house confidentiality, but you do remember that he dragged you from the river?"

"He knocked me in."

"I'll admit the details are a little sketchy but, trust me, an experience like that works its way deep into a young man's psyche." He presses his lips together and pushes himself upright. "Just saying. See you later, Sweet Pea."

"Gah."

He shrugs. "I'll work on it."

My insides ache. If Gil has picked up on the weirdness between me and Jamie, how long before the rest of them do too?

The bandwidth crackles.

I freeze and scan the crowd.

Down at the other end of the corridor, Aiden turns the corner. Even from here he looks pale and exhausted. I straighten up, my pulse hammering. I reach into the static. It grows loud, but that always happens when I get worked up. I know I'm supposed to be keeping an open mind, but I remember my spike in fear when we walked from the principal's office. My spine zip-zaps.

DNA.

Get his DNA.

But what should I do? Stab him with a pencil? Scratch him with my nails? My mind turns chaotic flips. He might have hair on his collar.

You're over-thinking. Read the bandwidth.

But I'm so unreliable.

It's the perfect opportunity.

With Kitty only yards away and out of sight – if I could stall him, talk to him, test the bandwidth at this proximity, maybe I could ... An idea seizes me. KMH. Miriam's warned me it doesn't work on civilians, so if I can harvest something, anything from him, won't that be proof?

Oh crap, oh crap.

I remember his hand on my shoulder, that casual touch. I could do that, couldn't I?

He doesn't look up as he trudges towards me, shadows under his eyes, frowning like he has a headache. Is it a reaction to Kitty's nearness? I act before I have a chance to chicken out, stepping right in front of him. I grip his arm, a split second of heart-stopping contact. I reach into the bandwidth and slip into a black hole. I see nothing, hear nothing, not even the white noise I've become accustomed to when scanning for signals. I grope in the emptiness, blind and deaf.

Aiden pulls away.

"Sorry." I shake off the disorientation and try for a breezy laugh. "You're just the person I was hoping to see. How's it going?"

He shoves his hands in his pockets. "I've been conscripted to PA for Dick, since he's been 'incapacitated'."

The mention of Richard coincides with an immediate spike in my pins and needles. Hostility grips me and I struggle to process my body's fight instinct. "But I saw him this morning."

"Apparently, he needs 'support' till he's fully recovered."

"That's ridiculous," I say, reddening. "They can't make you do that."

"I pretty much don't have a choice unless I want to 'undermine my contractual obligations'. Not that I don't like your work, but the nose job hasn't improved his personality." Aiden shrugs and shifts from foot to foot. "I've got history."

"Wait a second." At that moment, Richard appears

at the bend in the corridor, stopping to talk to two other boys. We both stare at him and frustration burns me up. How can I read the bandwidth now? I won't know who I'm reacting to. I clear my throat and rush on. "You helped Kaylee that night at the ball, right?"

He tenses. "I'm not supposed to talk about it."

"I'm sorry."

He rubs the back of his neck, blinking rapidly, then jams his fist back in his pocket. "I'm not trying to protect *him*. He could make life very difficult for Kaylee."

"I get it. I'm glad you were there for her."

His eyes flick from wall to ceiling to floor. "I'm not a stalker."

"I wasn't suggesting–"

"I only followed them because she could barely walk and I know what he's like."

Did Aiden stop to assault Kitty on his way to check on Kaylee? The idea seems ludicrous. I study his face, my chest tight with uncertainty. I can't tell if the subject or his proximity to Kitty agitates him. "Must have been scary."

"She was crying. I didn't really think, I just dragged him off her. He ran for it."

Richard ran for it. Where to?

Did he unleash his frustration on Kitty as she passed the side of the house? The scene paints itself too easily. I watch him at the end of the corridor, managing to look cocky even with his black eyes and taped nose. "But you didn't tell the cops?"

"She begged me not to." He grinds his teeth and small beads of sweat appear above his lip. "Maybe I shouldn't have listened."

We both sigh in the same way at the same time and look at each other.

"And I have to apologise to him."

"Dignity's not everything." Aiden gives a grim nod. "I'm going before Dick makes me carry his books."

Richard walks towards us. Aiden slopes away, looking more depressed than when I stopped him. I would have felt guilty if I could have felt anything clearly. Kitty appears from the restroom and the leap of adrenaline contracts the muscles in my arms and legs.

She frowns. "What's up?"

"Nothing."

Richard seems to walk in slow motion, the bruising around his eyes pronounced. He swings his pack to one shoulder and pauses to eyeball me. "See you Friday."

***

Miriam's strike flashes in my mind but my defence comes too slow. She wrenches my arm, flinging me over her head. I land on my back with a terrific *oof*, winded, gasping. At least heat and exertion mask my embarrassment – Jamie stands at the edge of the blue mat.

"You're not concentrating." Miriam bends over me, grabs my hand and hauls me up.

"Kung fu is hard," I moan.

"Kung fu is a tool."

"I'm a beginner."

"You're a genetically engineered weapon," Miriam says. "You've already learned more in two days than a civ could manage in months of daily training. Quit your bellyaching and tune in."

Kitty sniggers on the swivel chair, glancing up from Miriam's desk where she fiddles with her phone. I'm glad she acknowledges me, even if it's to laugh. I screw my nose up at her to keep it light.

"It's purely psychological," Miriam says. "You've been blocking like a pro for weeks. Your speed is outstanding, your somersaults are almost as good as mine. You beat the crap out of the sparring dummy and throw knives like a damn sniper. There's no reason you can't master this. Now, you registered my intent in the bandwidth before it came."

"Yeah." I lean, hands on thighs, trying to get more air. "But I'm too slow."

"You're thinking about defence instead of attack," Jamie says.

I glance up, surprised he spoke; I thought stony silence was his bag now.

"Exactly." Miriam smiles, an encouraging, let's smooth things out smile. I can't tell if she's being generous or smug, given she must be thrilled we've broken up. "When you look to strike rather than ward, precognition not only allows you to access your opponent's intent but it releases your attack impulse. Forget about avoiding pain. You don't care if you get hurt. You care about overpowering your opponent."

I jerk upright. "I'm not afraid of getting hurt."

Miriam narrows her eyes. "Then you're afraid of hurting me."

I open my mouth to argue and then close it.

"Fight Jamie." She shrugs. "He's a tank."

I turn my back so Jamie won't see my face, giving Miriam a baleful glare.

"You two can put aside your differences for training."

"I'm not ... *I* don't care." I blush. "Fine."

Jamie steps onto the mat. I try to concentrate on loosening my knees and assuming the relaxed stance Miriam taught me, but I'm distracted, anticipating Jamie's scent, his strong arms, the way his muscles move beneath his skin. All the things I'd deprived myself of over the last two days. My hands tremble, like low blood sugar tremors, which is ridiculous. Jamie's not a drug; I don't need a fix.

Stop staring at his mouth, you pervert.

"Ready?" Jamie asks.

The bow of his top lip, the full curve of the lower.

I swallow and nod.

Jamie's body blurs and the bandwidth opens up. I see the strike of his arm before it comes and my block is ready; sense the sweep of his leg before he turns and I leap; read the swing of his elbow and arch my back bringing my leg up and over in a roundhouse kick, catching him in the shoulder blade. Our eyes connect in that moment, and something flares in my chest. We separate and I turn to Miriam. "He's letting me win!"

His mouth twitches. Almost a smile.

Condescending bastard!

I don't wait.

I lunge.

Miriam's right, as soon as I take the initiative it's all there. Jamie's intent arriving with my supplied strategy like the prongs of a zip knitting together, question and answer, strike and defence. We move back and forth across the mat, sometimes tumbling, sometimes leaving the ground, the sound of skin and bone, thudding, slapping, jarring, thumping. I'm sloppy, but my advantage lies in lightness and flexibility – soaring, diving, spinning and then striking.

Jamie flips backwards, twisting in the air. I picture how he hopes to land and roll away. I spring, bringing my knees high in the upward trajectory, dropping squarely onto his back, driving him into the mat with a crunching thud.

I smile, seeing that Kitty has turned to watch, but then she flips upside down and I lose all my oxygen again.

Jamie pins me, both arms above my head, his weight grinding my hips into the floor, his eyes boring into mine.

"All right, all right," Miriam says. "We get the point."

G-DAY

"G-Day". That's what the Bishop has taken to calling my appointment with the governor. After school we have an entourage of supporters on our way to Jamie's car. Gil squeezes into a *Not without a mint* T-shirt, several sizes too small. I still have no clue what my approach will be, but people keep insisting on giving me advice.

"Don't be intimidated, Van." Gil walks beside me, his meaty arm strapped round my shoulders. "Look the son of a bitch in the eye, say 'Sorry' and leave it at that."

Pete nods. "Don't grovel."

"Sweet Cherry Pie doesn't grovel," Gil says.

"Seriously?" I mutter, "I prefer Van."

"Let us know how it goes, okay?" Lila pats my arm. Imogen smiles. I'm a little overwhelmed to see how they've all taken me under their wing.

I barely register the thirty-minute drive to Concord. Next thing, we've pulled up in the parking lot of a diner.

We kill time over burgers and fries, conversation stilted, none of us in the mood to really talk, with things awkward between me and Kitty, and worse between me and Jamie. I spend most of the time hyper-aware of my knees, only inches from his beneath the table. By the time we have to meet Miriam and Leonard, the sun is beginning to set.

Then I find myself outside the car, behind the security gate in the governor's office parking lot. Miriam, already beside me, fidgets with her purse; no doubt riding with Leonard was uncomfortable. He sets a wide warm hand on my shoulder, filling the vacant dad space inside me with an achy sort of yearning. "Evangeline, you look beautiful – and tall. Very situation-appropriate."

I'm not sure my lips will work to form sentences, but at least I've dressed carefully, changing my high-tops in the car for black stilettos. A risk if it means pursuing Kitty's Stray, but I'm banking on being in a well-guarded place with witnesses to discourage that possibility.

"Just remember," Leonard says, "Charles doesn't want to press charges. He wants to intimidate you and make his point. Getting us to drive out here to his office instead of coming in to meet at school, making the appointment at a ridiculous hour – it's all to remind you that everything is at his convenience. But you, my girl, need not be intimidated. You're not here to see a governor. You're here to see an unpleasant boy's father who's upset about losing face."

"That bit still sounds scary."

Leonard grins and brings me into his arms, like a dad would. It feels weird and kind of wonderful. "I'm here for you, Evie. We all are." I catch Jamie's eye over Leonard's shoulder. He averts his gaze, frowning instead towards the office.

"You'll be fine," Kitty chimes in, making a play at cheerfulness for my sake. "Just think, if the governor pushes you too far, you can always break his nose." It isn't well received by the others. "Joking." She hunches her shoulders. "Obviously."

We follow Leonard to the entrance. Jamie walks by his dad, and I have a moment of weakness, wishing he was beside me. We enter the foyer, dark, conservative and plush. Leonard announces my arrival to the receptionist. She pushes buttons on her keyboard and nods us towards the elevator. "He's expecting you." Her eyes sparkle at Leonard and widen when she sees Jamie. Neither father nor son notice.

None of us speak in the elevator and when the door chimes it seems to open with dreamlike slowness. Jamie holds the door, letting us file out. As I pass, he presses his lips together, not quite a smile.

The moment I step into the reception hall, my senses ignite. An unpleasant chemical odour reminds me of the Stray and Richard's bad breath. Adrenaline charges and my muscles cramp. Unthinking, I grip Jamie's arm and turn to find his frown.

"You feel something?" he whispers.

I let him go. "I can't tell."

Now is not the time for an episode.

I can't feel my legs as we make our way up the wide hall.

I focus on the tether.

She's safe. You're with her. It's okay.

I try to feel for danger, alert for any shadow in my mind, but I can't tell if I'm reacting to my own stress or signals in the bandwidth. I note exits and windows with latches, and objects that could be used as defensive weapons: a heavy lamp stand, an expensive-looking vase. I scan for potential assailants. I recognise Aiden, standing behind a desk. Another young man leans towards him, flapping his hands at Aiden's legs. A guard stands by the large double doors that must be the governor's office.

He'll have a gun. I could get that gun.

Rein it in.

We stop at the desk. Aiden turns, his face strained.

"Sorry, Aiden," the hand-flapping aide says and straightens up. "I'll get you a cloth." He makes to go but stops and stares at me, his lips parting, eyes gormlessly blank.

Aiden clears his throat. "David? I'd appreciate that

cloth." I can smell the spilled coffee and see where it has drenched the hem of Aiden's blazer and soaked through the thigh of his pants.

"Of course, sorry. I'm on it." David gives us a sheepish smile and darts away.

"Mr Gallagher." Red-faced, Aiden comes out from the desk to greet Leonard with his coffee wet hands still dripping. "Please excuse the state of me. Third degree burns. I promise it's not a habit."

Leonard nods, his laugh generous. "Aiden, good to see you."

Obviously, they share some sort of private joke, but now that I have Kitty beside me and Aiden before me, I have both ears on the bandwidth. The static rings loud and my anxiety stays sky-high. He looks handsome and aside from the stain, well put together in his suit. But he also looks agitated, pulling a handkerchief from his pocket to mop his hands.

Kitty's smile reminds me of the receptionist downstairs. She views him as a hero after what he did for Kaylee. It spins me out to imagine what she would say if she knew Aiden rode high on my list.

Miriam's voice cuts in. "I – I think I need to use the bathroom."

"It's just back beside the elevator." Aiden points down the hall.

"Are you all right, Miriam?" Kitty asks.

"I'm fine." She doesn't look fine. She squeezes my hand. "Sorry, kid. I'll be back in a minute." Shoulders stiff, she walks away.

Aiden says something I miss.

"... but you'll be fine," he says. I hear effort behind his casual tone, feel his awkward pause, note his rapid blinking. He lands on a thought. "Angelo's T-shirts. Got one today. That's about as much subversion as I can get away with."

I can't speak.

Kitty fills the void. "Fight the power." She smiles, tilting her head on her vulnerable neck. Is she flirting?

He nods at his shoes.

Jamie stares, his face inscrutable.

Aiden gestures to the sitting area. "I'll let the governor know you've arrived then I better go clean up." David returns and waits behind the desk with some handtowels. Aiden rolls his eyes.

My thrashing pulse makes it hard to breathe and my joints feel stiff. Kitty leads me to a couch and makes me sit. Leonard and Jamie take the single chairs.

"What T-shirts?" Leonard asks. Kitty explains the *Not without a mint* phenomenon. Leonard's eyebrows rise. "Charles will love that."

I don't think it will be long before the shirts are

outlawed, especially now Richard is back at school. He'll probably have Angelo sued.

Jamie watches me, questions in his eyes, but I can't read the bandwidth through the panic storm. Nothing comes into focus. I don't feel good. I watch Kitty watching Aiden as he takes off his blazer. She plays with her hair, leg crossed, foot bobbing until Aiden disappears into an adjoining room, probably to change his clothes, and she sighs. I cover my watch.

"Do you think Miriam's okay?" Leonard peers down the corridor.

"I can go check?" Kitty says.

"No." I stand up. "You stay here." I flick a look at Jamie to keep an eye out and manage to coordinate my legs to the restroom. I hate not being able to trust my senses with everything fuzzed by white noise. When I push the door open, I find Miriam leaning over a porcelain sink, her reflection in the mirror red-eyed. I let the door swing closed behind me. "What's wrong?"

She sniffs and shakes her head. "Nothing's wrong. I'm an idiot. I don't know what's gotten into me."

"You're freaking me out."

She dries her trembling hands on a paper towel, taking her time and not looking at me. "I've made a mess of everything."

"What are you talking about?"

"You wouldn't be in this position if I had taken better care of you."

"What?" I gawp at her. "That-is-completely-not-true."

She screws the paper towel up and throws it in the bin. "I'm getting it all wrong. If your mom were here …"

"What? If Mom were here, I wouldn't have broken Richard's nose?" I need to reel things in and try to sound brisk and matter of fact. "That's ridiculous. If Mom were still alive … for crying out loud, can you even imagine how hideous it would've been for me to transition in Pennsylvania without you to guide me through it? Miriam, I'd have lost it by now if it weren't for you."

Miriam softens her mouth but something behind her eyes tells me I can't talk her out of it. Exasperated, I wrap my arms around her. "Trust me, in the parenting stakes you're doing all right given what you're stuck with."

We make our way back to the others, Miriam pale and drawn, me irritated and confused. The last thing I need is her falling apart.

By the doors to the governor's office, David waits to let us in. Unlike Aiden, his suit makes him look like a boy playing dress-ups. "Just through here," he says. I can't return his smile, my mind on Kitty where she waits with Jamie and on the unknown across the threshold.

We step into a large room. If Leonard's take on the governor's motives are right, then Charles Dean has gotten his way – I am officially intimidated. The room is grand and almost aggressively masculine. A stag head looms above an ornate fireplace, its antlers thrusting wide and high; a musket gleams beneath it on the mantelpiece. An antique map eclipses one wall: New Hampshire's borders, mountains, rivers, lakes. The state flag covers the other. There are plaques, photographs and bookcases stacked with leatherbound tomes and heavy velvet drapes cover ceiling-height windows.

Richard stands with his back to us, looking out to the street through a gap in the curtains. He turns, providing a profile of his plastered nose. The governor writes at his desk, his shirtsleeves rolled part way up, a vivid blue tie loosened at the neck, all giving the impression that it has been a long day at the office, with a governor's work never done and so on. He signs off with an impatient flick of his wrist, dropping the pen on his jotter, and leans back in his throne-sized chair. "Ah, the volleyball girl." Then he frowns. "Leonard?"

He rises, eyes narrowed, and crosses around his desk to shake Leonard's hand. "You're here with the girl?" Leonard nods and the governor turns to Miriam. "Miriam Everton?" He shakes her hand. "I thought you were the girl's guardian?"

"I'm out of town a lot for work." Miriam coughs to clear the constriction from her voice. "It's easier for

Evangeline to stay with the Gallaghers on weekdays."

"I see." He turns sharp eyes on me and extends his hand. "Evangeline, I'm Governor Charles Dean."

The roar of adrenaline makes it difficult to engage. I take too long to reach for his hand, grasp too tight when I do and release too suddenly when I realise. I stare at the empty space our hands left behind. He frowns, flexes his fingers and gestures to the polished couches. Leonard takes me by the elbow to get me moving.

"Richard." The governor clicks his fingers. Richard scowls, but comes and sits beside his father, resetting his expression so his advantage as the complainant shows in the set of his mouth.

"Any progress with your daughter's case?" the governor asks.

"There seems to be a hold-up on the DNA results."

"Would you like me to see if I can hurry them along? Apply a little pressure from above?"

"Don't trouble yourself, Charles," Leonard says. "The results will come. As will an arrest." His restraint impresses me. I've heard his tirades about Charles Dean's interference.

The governor nods, his expression complacent, then he turns his eyes to me.

I stare back at him, lost in the static in my head.

Leonard clears his throat.

"Right," I croak.

"Just tell them what's on your mind." Leonard touches my arm, and I nearly jerk in my seat.

"Okay, then."

Say sorry.

"Um. Richard." Saying his name requires looking at him. I hold his gaze. "Sorry I broke your nose."

Richard turns to his father. "That's it?"

The governor steeples his fingers, then fans them towards me. "You must have more to say for yourself."

"I'm … *very* sorry?"

His smile only makes his face harder. "Try again."

Leonard shifts next to me. "What more would you like, Charles?"

"An explanation. Some remorse?" He relaxes back into his seat. "It doesn't seem much to ask given the pain and humiliation inflicted on my son." He reaches for a paper folded next to him and flips it over. It's this week's edition of the school's newspaper, *The Collegiate Times*. A comic strip called "Angel Avenger" heads the page. She wears short shorts and a skin-tight shirt, her dark hair flying behind her, a volleyball under one arm. Her nemesis, an old-school moustache-twirling villain called DD. The governor traces the print and lets the weight of offence settle. "I understand there are T-shirts as well."

My stomach ties in double knots. "I've never seen that."

"Evangeline is not responsible for the actions of her

classmates," Leonard says. "She had nothing to do with either the newspaper or the T-shirts. It was an accident in gym class, Charles. These things happen."

"It was an assault," the governor says, cool and categorical. "There are witnesses to corroborate that she was antagonising my son and deliberately spiked the ball in his face." He opens his hands. "I want to understand. Is it a medication issue?"

Miriam breaks from her trance. "What?"

Leonard's control is as impressive as the governor's. "I beg your pardon?"

The governor raises his palms. "I'm not unsympathetic, given the circumstances. Her mother recently passed, relocating to a new town, difficult times for any family, but no excuse for lashing out."

I sit paralysed. He knows about my mother and he thinks I'm medicated.

The governor exchanges a look with his son. "I understand Evangeline's behaviour at school is quite erratic. Trauma often results in chemical inbalances."

"How dare you?" Miriam's voice trembles. "You have no idea."

"I think I have enough of an idea to realise that things are not what they should be," he says. "Who has control of this girl? You, Ms Everton, or her *boyfriend's* father? This living situation is very unorthodox. It goes some way to clarifying things but an explanation from the girl is required."

My tongue thickens and dries in my mouth.

"Charles Dean." Leonard sits forwards and cocks his head. "Are you being deliberately offensive, or have you lost all sense?"

The governor's face hardens. "She's in your care Leonard? I'm beginning to question if you have a handle on things. I would have thought the kind of rumours circulating about your son and this girl would be a matter of concern, given she's living under your roof."

"What are you talking about?" Miriam's voice cracks like a whip and I officially leave my body. Richard seems to enter a state of rapture.

"Apparently they're both covered in bruises."

Score for the locker room grapevine.

"I would have thought," Leonard cuts in before Miriam explodes, "that a man who's invested so much money and energy squashing rumours about his own son's behaviour would know the danger of baseless allegations."

Silence opens like a chasm.

The governor grows rigid.

Richard scowls behind his medical tape.

I throw myself into the unbearable gap.

"You're right. I let my – my frustration get the better of me. Things have been ..." I look at the carpet, heat flooding my face, "… stressful, lately. The details, you seem to be–" I press my fingernails into the couch. "New home, new school. That sort of thing." I glance up briefly, catching the governor's narrow look. "I realise I was oversensitive and took some of the things Richard said the wrong way. I lost my cool and flipped out. I was wrong." I get to my feet. "I'm very sorry." Looking Richard dead on, I extend my hand. "I am sorry, Richard."

I see the conflict in his eyes, the tension in his throat as he stands and takes my hand. I go deep, locking his bright blue gaze, reaching into the bandwidth. The Kinetic Memory Harvest is immediate, vivid and unmistakable. The struggle of flesh, shadows shifting over trees and shrubs. Damp grass soaks through the knees of my trousers, black satin bunches in my hand – Richard's hand. Her brown eyes roll back. Her long dark hair, tousled in my fist. I clamp her red mouth and feel the thrill in my skin.

The sun has gone by the time we step out into the night air. I give silent thanks for shadows to hide my face.

"Well?" Kitty finally bursts out, sick of biting her tongue. "What did he say?"

"It doesn't bear repeating, but he's got a bloody nerve." Leonard curls and uncurls his fists.

Jamie bends close. "Were you picking up signals in there or what?"

"I–"

"Evie." Miriam catches my hand. She looks worse than me. "Sweetheart, I'm so sorry. I should have marched you out of there. He's a–" She shakes her head, lacking the words.

"What did that bastard say to you?" Jamie says.

What can I tell him in front of Kitty? I don't want to frighten her. I hold his gaze and push the borrowed memory into the bandwidth, willing him to see what I harvested from Richard.

Jamie's eyes glaze then clear. He swallows, looks at Kitty, me then back at the building. I'm suddenly afraid he might storm the governor's office and break Richard's neck. Resolve hardens in his eyes and he takes me off guard, scooping my hand into his, sending a tingling current up my arm. "Kit, you mind riding with Dad? I need a little time alone with Evie."

The others look at us in varying degrees of surprise.

"We'll stay right behind you," he says.

"Um … sure," she says, her eyes round.

"Miriam can you stay with her?" Jamie turns me towards his car and opens the door. I stall, torn between addressing Richard as a current threat and the possible danger in leaving Kitty's side.

"Dad'll keep me on the road, Evs." Kitty's mouth curls in the corner. "Try to be nice. Genetically speaking, he was made for you."

Leonard purses his lips and opens the passenger door of the Mercedes. Kitty looks at Jamie like she wishes him luck and slides into her seat. But I can't let go until Miriam gives the nod, her eyes so tortured they hollow me out.

I sit forwards in Jamie's car, pressure in my chest, chaos in my head.

Jamie drops into the driver's seat. "That was Kaylee, right? Richard's memory? Tell me that was Kaylee."

"It was Kaylee."

"What does it mean?"

"I don't know!" I grab my head. "It doesn't make sense. It's not supposed to work on civs. I just thought, if I tried and got anything then it would be some kind of proof that he was, you know, like us. But is it proof? What the hell am I supposed to do, go back and confront him?"

"No." Jamie shakes his head. "Not like that, not here. We need a plan."

Leonard backs out and drives up to the security gate, waving his pass at the sensor. The gate rolls slowly aside. Jamie starts the engine and slings his arm across the back of my seat to reverse. I tense with awareness, conscious of his scent. Leonard pulls out and the gate rolls closed. Jamie digs for the pass the secretary gave him at reception and draws up to the sensor. I watch through the bars, jolting when the Mercedes joins the flow of traffic. "He didn't wait!"

Jamie's window slides down and he waves the card.

The light doesn't come on.

Nothing happens.

The tether stretches.

"Jamie!"

"It's not working." He waves the pass, bangs his fist on the console and still nothing happens.

Anxiety grips me. "Jamie, something's not right."

His head snaps towards me.

Static explodes in my head. "Open the gate."

Tires squeal on the road, an engine roars, cars skid.

A grey sedan tears past.

My panic comes in quick. "Open the gate!"

"The sedan?"

"Now!"

Jamie flings the door open, moving so fast his body blurs. He comes into clear outline, grabs the bars and wrenches the gate aside in one sweep, driving it back into the recess, causing a terrific grinding of metallic gears. Sparks erupt from a box on the wall. He lands behind the steering wheel, slams the door, guns the engine and I'm thrown back into my seat as we shoot out through a gap in traffic, skidding wildly.

The tether has almost completely faded. "I'm losing her!"

"It's *him*?" Jamie's knuckles whiten on the steering wheel. "Richard?"

"I don't know, it's not right."

"Read-the-signal!"

"I'm trying!" But Kitty's signal has faded so quickly that I have nothing to anchor my search. "I can't feel her. They're too far away. Hurry, can you see them?"

I kick my heels off, scrabbling in the backseat for my high-tops. I jam my feet in one then the other, struggling to tighten the laces. Jamie drives so fast the speedo hits the red line. We're all over the road, careening through traffic. Cars swerve and honk. I draw the band off my wrist, fumbling, numb fingers trying to pull my hair into a ponytail. My ears crackle and with all my might I reach to feel the threat.

I can't see Leonard's car or the grey sedan that streaked past, tyres squealing so threateningly. I grip my watch, dreading any transmission that might confirm my fears. "I thought it was Aiden," I say. "I really did, until yesterday. None of it makes any sense."

"Aiden? You said Richard!"

"I tried KMH on them both! Okay?"

"Why the hell didn't you tell me?"

"We weren't exactly talking!"

He swears, pulling out to overtake a truck. "Well, what happened?"

"That's what I'm uncertain about," the words tumble together. "I normally feel something when I touch people, static, you know? But when I touched Aiden it was like going deaf and blind. I couldn't hear or see anything in the bandwidth."

"What the hell does that mean?"

"I don't know!"

"But ... but the memory you showed me was Richard's, right?" Jamie demands. "Then it's him! It has to be him!"

Our wrists light up simultaneously, a three-bell chime

that drains blood from my body and air from my lungs. I hit the response tab so she knows, *I'm coming*.

Jamie lifts his wrist to check the GPS. "They're still on the road."

"They're heading home."

"Dad's going for the panic room."

"You think the sedan's trying to run them off the road?"

"If Kitty's signalling us, he's tried something!"

Terror and rage consume me and then I'm screaming. "Damn it, Jamie! This is your fault! I should never have listened to you!"

He flinches but keeps his eyes on the road.

Then crushing guilt outweighs my anger and I groan like a woman in labour. "Why did I leave her? I should never have left her. Please, Jamie, hurry."

A trip that should have taken twenty minutes becomes ten, according to the readout on the dash. In terms of living through it, it feels more like some kind of time purgatory, endless and agonising.

Before we even reach the estate, the tether snaps to life and I gasp. "She's alive." Jamie looks at me once then back at the road, his mouth set in a grim line. I would have cried with relief as we sped up to the familiar boundary wall but the scene is all wrong.

"The gates are closed," Jamie says.

"They're here! I can feel her!"

Jamie scrabbles for the remote but I can't bear to wait. I growl, throw the door open and, leveraging off the bonnet of Jamie's car, I jump, landing messily, high up on the boundary wall, skidding on dewy concrete before leaping again. I hit the ground running, power in my legs, senses sharpened. As though Kitty reels me in, I follow the pulse of the tether up the sloping lawn, the house rising before me, brightly lit, bodies moving within. I hit the side door, springing the handle and bringing it with me as I skid into the kitchen where Miriam stands, her gun trained at my head.

"Evie!" Her arms collapse. "Thank God."

"Where is she?" I cry, dropping the handle and pushing past Miriam to the butler's pantry, answering my own question as I follow the tether. I beat the access code into the keypad. Leonard crashes into the kitchen behind us.

"It's Evie," Miriam says.

"Wait!" Leonard calls as the door unlocks, but I push through it, not bothering with the stairs to the wine cellar, leaping the rail to land softly on the floor. "Is it safe?" Leonard's voice echoes off the ceiling. I skid to a halt at the concrete slider, thump my hand on the security panel, red light licking my palm. The door slides back and screams echo inside the cell. A gunshot cracks the air.

WOUNDS

"I don't have any anaesthetic," Miriam mutters, pawing through her leather case, scattering sutures, cotton swabs, medical tape. "How far is the doctor?"

"Sullivan's not answering." Leonard paces the kitchen, hitting redial again.

"It's not that bad." I struggle to sit up, igniting fire in my bicep, but collapse back on the counter, my head thunking on a rolled towel, rattling my skull. I wince against the light, my pupils still dilated from adrenaline. "Okay," I pant, "maybe it's a little bad."

"Jamie's not answering either." Kitty huddles on a stool beside me, her hands shaking so much I think she might drop her phone. "Just keeps going to voicemail."

"Where is he?" Barb says, her shoulders shaking with renewed tears. "Why won't he call?"

Poor Barb, she can't bear to look at me, though I've told her over and over she has nothing to be sorry for.

I couldn't be happier she'd had the guts to pull the trigger, despite the lapse in reason. I'd been fast enough to bat her hand aside to avoid any major damage. At the time I felt nothing, saw nothing, heard nothing but Kitty where she stood backed against the panic room wall, a scream dying on her lips. I feel the bullet wound now though, white-hot pain.

It's been a half hour since we returned. We all guess Jamie has gone after the sedan. But that means he'll be looking for Richard and what if I've got it wrong?

"Did you see the driver, Mr Gallagher?"

Leonard shakes his head. "It was too dark. He drove without lights. The car had no plates."

"No plates?" My head swims.

"Shit," Miriam mutters, bending over the bandage.

Trying to peer down my arm makes me cross-eyed.

A lot of red.

"This is saturated," she says.

"Can you get the bullet out, Miriam?" Leonard stands beside his daughter.

"It's a lot of blood but the bullet is probably what's keeping more in her body than out at the moment. Besides which, I only have Fretizine. It's not a real anaesthetic."

"I'm calling an ambulance," Leonard says.

"No!" Miriam and I shout in unison; the effort nearly wipes me out.

She squeezes her temple between thumb and forefinger. "We need Jamie."

"I don'eed Jamie." Closing my eyes only makes the dizziness worse. "Jus'take it out, Miriam. Gimme the damn Fretizine."

"You'll heal faster if Jamie's here." She purses her lips, somehow managing to look both worried and grudging. "Skin to skin contact with your Synergist would quadruple the rate of recovery and ease the pain."

Kitty fumbles her phone, trying for him again. It clicks to voicemail. "Turn your bloody phone on! Evie needs you! Barb shot her!"

Barb's sobbing becomes shrill. Leonard gives his daughter an exasperated look before crossing to his wife, wrapping his arms around her.

Kitty cringes. "Sorry."

"Mrs Gallagher – Barb," my lips move numbly, my tongue loose in my head. "Please don'be upset. It wasn'your – I shoulda warn ... totally di'the right thing. Protecting Kitty – only thing that matters."

"You matter too." Barb turns in Leonard's arms. She comes to the counter, her face grief-stricken. "Not just because of what you can do for Kitty."

Fog pearls at the periphery of my vision and Barb's shuddering speech dims in my ears ...

Agony pierces my arm and I jerk back to consciousness,

a cry ripping from my throat. Miriam leans over me, her eyes drilling mine. "No fainting."

"Okay, damn it." I shiver and then can't stop shivering. "Just get it out."

Miriam swallows. "Try to reach Jamie."

"What?"

"Like you did when the Warden came, the same way you Harvest or Transfer."

"That was through a wall," I groan. "I have no idea where Jamie is … He could be miles away."

"Try." She grabs supplies from her kit. "I'm going to give you some Fretizine. Kitty, if you think she's about to faint, I want you to pinch her – hard."

Kitty's hand slips coldly under mine, her grey eyes round with fear, her trembling blending with my own. "Evs, you hear Miriam? I'll pinch you."

"I heard."

"Leonard, can you …?" Miriam nods at Barb then the door.

He nods and leads his wife out through the dining room.

I close my eyes, trying to think past the pain in my body, reaching into – "Ouch!"

"Sorry." Kitty's shoulders pop up by her ears. "I thought you were fainting."

I grit my teeth. "I'm *trying* to tap the psychic hotline."

"I said, sorry."

Still frowning, I close my eyes again and take a wild leap into the bandwidth, a cliff-jump-arms-flailing leap into a sea of static. I draw Jamie to the foreground, demanding from my sense-memory the most potent details I have stored there, two days worth of electric touch. I imagine my signal like a magnet extended into the ether, to which only the right frequency will respond, and I pour myself into it. *Jamie … Jamie … Where are you? I need* – it grates me to think it – *help. Jamie, please. I'm hurt. I need* – damn it – *you.* Something spikes, making my ears crackle and roar. For a split second I find him, a lightning strike of recognition and my chest fills, arching my back above the counter, then the fog rolls in and I collapse again.

Distantly, I feel pressure in my arm, the prick of a needle, the pinch of skin on the back of my hand. I hear a cry and a cell phone ringing, Kitty's desperate voice, then I slip beneath the film of a dream.

I rush the stairs two at a time, not feeling the slap of my shoes or the jarring in my knees. Pain, static, rage roars in my head, consuming everything. I give myself to it, heedlessly, abandoning hope, letting the darkness take me. There's no fighting it, not any more. I ram the security door, blundering into darkness. Three cars. The left. I skid to the ground, hooking my fingers around the licence plate, the corner bolts popping …

I twist the steering wheel, braking hard, bracing my arms to keep my body from slamming forwards, then the whiplash back, my head on the upholstered rest, headlights flash, brake lights red as blood. The Mercedes pulls ahead, swerving over the centre line. The sickening pulse throbs back to me, and I grind the ball of my foot into the accelerator, gunning the engine. My black eyes flash in the rearview, then another jolt, the shriek of metal, as I ram the tail guard …

"I don't want to take my shoes off." I would fold my arms but my bicep burns too much and I need them out for balance. The Fretizine and painkillers love gravity and my body keeps trying to give in.

"When was the last time you slept under covers?" Miriam lowers me by the elbows onto the edge of Kitty's bed. I can hear Kitty in the bathroom, brushing her teeth, an act so outrageously normal against the unreality of the night.

"I want to be ready."

Miriam fixes me with troubled eyes; I've never seen her so completely drained. She looks older. "If you want to be ready, you need to heal, which means you need sleep … and Jamie."

Due to Fretizine and blacking out, I have no memory of Jamie returning or of his hands holding me down while Miriam dug in my muscle. Only when she completed the last stitch did I lurch my way back to consciousness. Jamie held me still and said my name, terrifying me with his pallor, his undisguised fear. Something in that moment, in the raw nakedness of his expression, unlatched the clamped box in my heart. I wept, horribly, and let him think it was the pain instead of the futility of wanting him.

Miriam slips my shoes off, helps me to stand, unzips the skirt from my hips, leaving me in my underwear and tank top. She pulls back the covers and helps me lie down, turning me on my right side, propping pillows beneath my damaged arm. I groan, partly for the pain and partly for the bliss of unbound feet beneath crisp laundered sheets.

I want to talk to her, tell her something of the confusion in my head, but Kitty comes shuffling out of the bathroom in flannelette pyjamas, looking thirteen and making me ache with her smallness, her vulnerability. She doesn't say anything, just turns down the quilt and slips like a stone under the covers, sighing like she can't bear her own weight any longer. She reaches for my good hand, her fingers icy, keeping no heat from the shower.

"*Ow.*"

"Sorry." Miriam withdraws the needle from my shoulder. "Last dose of Fretizine. Hopefully, Dr Sullivan can provide us with more pain relief in the morning."

"Thanks," I grumble.

"Jamie will be in shortly." She nods at the over-stuffed

reading chair Kitty keeps by the window.

How will I sleep with him sitting there?

"Love you, kiddo." She kisses my forehead. "Kitty, your father and I will be keeping watch tonight. You're safe."

Kitty nods and Miriam slips away, the door clicking behind her.

Kitty squeezes my good hand. "Barb gave me sleeping pills."

"Good."

She stares at me, glassy eyed, heavy lids sweeping low. "Is it Richard or Aiden?"

My mouth dries, my mind too slow in a Fretizine swamp to handle denial and reassurance but my face has already given me away. "I'm sorry ... I don't know."

Her lips quiver. "I hope it's not Aiden."

My throat aches.

"I liked Aiden ..." Her tears spill.

"I'm so sorry."

"What's going to happen?"

I wish I knew.

"Jamie and I will come up with a plan. Miriam will help us. We'll stop him, Kit. There's three of us, only one of him. You'll be safe."

Her whisper thins. "I don't want to die."

"You're not going to die." I knit my fingers through hers and she slowly unravels. I shape my lips to soothe, praying my promises won't be empty ones. "Shhh. You're safe, I'm here and you're safe."

We stay like that, hands linked. Soon her breaths lengthen and I know she's asleep. I hold on for as long as I can but Fretizine and fatigue push me down and I fall into sleep darkly.

My dreams are formless but menacing and at some point I must have rolled onto my back, the white-hot pain knifing me awake. Kitty snores softly on her pillow and though the drug-haze still fogs my brain, I can sense Jamie in the room. I open my eyes on darkness; he must have turned the lamp off when he came in. He sits in his sister's reading chair, the curtain open so he can look out at the night in silent vigil. A gleam of light on metal rests on his thigh; one of Leonard's guns, Jamie's hand loose around it.

He turns, his eyes meeting mine, moonlight and shadow dividing his face. If I could crack open his thoughts and dip my head in …

I rise on my good arm, heavy in my bones. Far off, in the back of my head, a whisper of warning, *don't be a fool … stay where you are*, but I disable the alarm simply by folding back the quilt and lowering my feet to the floor. I wonder if I have strength to get up and then, somehow, I stand. Almost trancelike, I move through a black-and-white dream, my blissfully naked feet padding from rug to polished boards, instinct, need, inevitability automating my limbs.

Jamie straightens in the chair, his dark eyes wary.

I stop before him, cradling my injured arm. "It hurts," my voice muffles. "Miriam said ..."

He places the gun on the floor then pulls his shirt off over his head, mussing his hair. He bunches the fabric in his hands, looking up at me beneath a knotted brow, waiting.

I swallow thickly then brush my knuckles over his cheek, letting it mean what I can't say. One stroke dismantling a blockade, releasing my slow hot tears. He closes his eyes, exhaling like he's been holding his breath, tension lifting from his shoulders. The shirt falls at my feet and he slides his hands around my waist, leaning to press his forehead against my stomach.

One armed, I dig my fingers through his hair and curl forwards to follow the broad slope of his back, tracing the angel, mapping his scars. We both sigh, moving like we're under water, his hands gliding over the swell of my hips, my fingers relearning the curvature of his shoulders.

When I begin to sway, Jamie steadies me. I brace my hand on the back of the chair, easing myself against him. He shifts to make room, reclining the seat, releasing the footrest so our bodies fold together. I lie on his chest, my face pressed against his throat, salting his skin with my tears, savouring his scent and the current humming between us.

Jamie reaches for the comforter on the end of Kitty's bed. He shakes it out and draws it over us, careful with my injured arm, bringing my hand to his heart and covering it with his wide warm palm. He holds me and kisses my hair. I close my eyes and fall deeply.

UNCERTAINTY

Thirst brings me quickly to the surface. I wake to the sound of rain pouring outside and stiffen, fully aware of where I lie, my body hotly corrugated to Jamie's. His arms tense around me and then relax. I know by the change in his breathing that my waking has woken him.

Indecision paralyses me. My arm aches and I need water, desperately, but how will I explain throwing myself at him in the night? And what does it mean? And should it mean anything? And what time is it? And what will Kitty think if she wakes and finds us entwined?

"Are you thirsty?" Jamie's very naked chest vibrates under me.

I crack my lips to speak, "I'm dying."

"Here." He moves and I lift my head. "Barb brought it in." He picks up a glass of water from a tray on the side table, also heaped with untouched food. I blush at the thought of his mother. I dart a look at the bed. No Kitty.

"What time is it?" I croak.

Jamie brings the water to my lips, tipping carefully. I drink, quick demanding gulps, bumping his hand, spilling water on my chin. It slides down my neck and pools on his chest, wetting my fingers, but I don't stop until I've drained it, panting when I finish.

He returns the glass to the tray then wipes the water from my chin with his thumb. "Around three, I think."

"In the afternoon?" I try to brush the water from his skin but each stroke makes my blood pound so I stop, unable to meet his gaze. Beneath the comforter his fingers fan over my lower back and he traces exquisite spirals at the base of my spine.

"Help me get up," I say, flustered and tingling.

"You don't have to. Go back to sleep. Sleep heals."

I finally bring my eyes up. "Miriam–"

"Has been in."

I cringe. "She has?"

"So has Dad. Kitty's been in and out."

"Oh."

A rueful smirk curves his mouth. "They all know about the skin to skin benefits for rapid regeneration; nobody thinks we're up here making wild monkey love."

I fight off an uneasy desire to laugh.

"Though," he says, "the traffic may have been to discourage it."

I close my eyes, brow tightening.

"Listen," he says. "You have to know that I–"

"Don't."

"But, if you could just understand that–"

"Please," I come to my conclusion in a snap. "Let's not make speeches."

"But it's a very good speech and I've been working on it all night."

"Jamie," I groan. "You make it so hard to …" His eyes shift to my mouth and he teases his lower lip through his teeth. I trail off, losing my thread. "You make everything …" I try again but he leans down, slowly, nudging my nose with his, our breath mingling, scrambling my brain. "I mean …" His lips brush mine, a test, a question, then a petition, building in frequency and depth. I forget my point altogether and I'm in it as much as him.

The tether pulls and I break away. "Kitty."

He kisses me again. "Pretend to be asleep."

I shove his chest and he chuckles, tipping the chair up, lifting me wrapped in the comforter and depositing me on the end of the bed. Before Kitty reaches the door, Jamie manages to pull his shirt on, throw me a bagel and nab one for himself, his eyes playful.

The door clicks open. Kitty steps in. "About time." She crosses to sit next to me. "How's the arm?"

"Better." It still burns but nothing like the night before

and my body no longer feels out of kilter. "Definitely better."

"You're welcome," Jamie says.

Kitty gags.

I don't look at him. "How's your mom?"

"Oh, you know." Kitty tries for a smile but can't sustain it. "Bit worried about signing my death warrant after taking out my bodyguard."

"I'm not dead yet. You survived the night and apparently most of the day. I'd say things are looking up."

"Now we know it's either Richard or Aiden."

Jamie sits bolt upright. "You told her?"

Kitty clicks her tongue. "I'm not a complete idiot. It's not like I haven't wondered about both of them since the ball. We've been debating downstairs, leaning towards Richard. Aiden gets the sympathy vote on account of being nice and poor and a protector of girls from date rapists."

"Nice and poor doesn't save you from mutant genes," I mutter.

"What does Miriam say?" Jamie asks, reaching for more food.

"She left a few hours ago. We're supposed to call her when Evie wakes."

I frown. "Where did she go?"

"She didn't say. She was in her running gear and didn't take her car. She's been odd all morning. Barb said she disappeared for a few hours last night as well."

"You don't think she's after Richard?"

"I wondered that," Kitty says. "If Richard were dead, you'd know, wouldn't you?"

"She would," Jamie says.

I get to my feet, the comforter falling away. I start pacing. "I need to think. I need a shower and I need to think."

"I'll get something to cover your bandage." Kitty crosses to the door pursing her lips. "Can I remind you both that this is my bedroom? I'd rather not have to get it decontaminated."

"What?"

Jamie grins, rising with the comforter and wraps it around me. "Best keep this on, love, or she'll need a hazmat team."

Kitty scowls.

"Wait," I say. "Has Doctor Sullivan been? Has he called?"

"No," she bites her lip. "He's not answering."

Jamie touches my shoulder. "He's not likely to have processed Richard's sample in three days, yeah?"

"It's taking too long," I mutter.

Kitty exchanges a look with her brother and slips out the door.

"Tell me what happened last night."

Jamie lowers his head. "I drove around for a while, looking for the sedan. In the end, I went to Richard's house. There were a couple of grey cars in the back."

"One without plates?"

"Dad mentioned that when I got home, but I didn't notice." He frowns. "I saw Richard with his father in the library."

"How was he acting? Did he seem wound up?"

"Like someone who'd just been driving like a lunatic, trying to run a car off the road?" Jamie arches his eyebrow. "Extremely wound up. They were arguing. Richard was screaming."

"Screaming?"

"He hates his father for ruining his life and being a compassionless bastard who understands nothing and he hopes he burns in hell."

I stare at Jamie and swallow, thirsty again, post-Fretizine.

"I was waiting for him to go upstairs and then …" he taps his temple.

I feel weak and faint. "You would have broken in and … if I hadn't reached you?"

He cups my face, his eyes hardening. "Yes."

The unimaginable truth. Life snuffed from an actual person, even a completely revolting person with almost no redeeming qualities. It seems inconceivable, the ceasing to exist and the aftershock of such an end, rippling through a family, a community. Even with all my paranoia, the act of killing is something I've envisioned only in the heat of the Fixation Effect: that blind, primal instinct responding to a present threat, the culmination of adrenaline and electricity and genetically fueled rage, where you became something entirely other, controlled by stimuli and synaptic response. But to come at it this way, coldly, by an act of will?

"This is so messed up," I groan and lean my forehead on his chest. "I still can't be sure."

"You may be advanced, Everton, but you can't Harvest from civilians."

How can he be so adamant? "What about Aiden, the blank wall of nothing? That's not normal either."

"You want it to be Aiden?"

"No!" I say. "Of course not."

Jamie tips my chin up. "You don't want to be responsible for someone's death."

"For the *wrong* person's death."

"Then we'll test it. Try it on Barb or Dad, but we need to act. For him to attack like that, out in the open, it means he's getting desperate. He'll try again and it will be soon."

"Call Miriam. I want her here. I need to know what she's thinking."

TESTS

"Do I need to do anything?" Leonard sits on the edge of the sofa, his fingers curling into fists on his knees. "Should I try to visualise something?"

"No, Dad, relax." Jamie rubs his father's shoulder.

I stand at the window, looking out on the grey afternoon. The rain hasn't stopped, the doctor hasn't called, and still no sign of Miriam. I cross to the sofa, taking a seat beside Leonard, feeling horribly self-conscious with everyone looking at me.

"Mr Gallagher, I'll need to hold your hand. The rain makes it hard for me …"

He opens his palms, wide and warm like Jamie's, and cocoons my hand in both of his, giving me an encouraging squeeze. Immediately, the static increases.

It always feels like this with civs, it doesn't mean anything.

"Maybe close your eyes …"

He does and I do too.

My dip into the bandwidth is as timid as last night's reach for Jamie was bold. I look, not wanting to see; reach, not wanting to connect. I can feel Jamie's expectation – or non-expectation – rolling at me, his certainty about Richard's guilt. I open my eyes. "That's not actually helpful."

Leonard opens his eyes and everyone looks between Jamie and me.

"You can read each other's minds?" Leonard says.

I blush. "No. It's not like–"

"I thought rain interfered?" Kitty says.

"Not between us," Jamie says. "Not at this proximity."

His family look at him, bewildered.

"Synergist perk," he says. "Sorry, Everton, I'm not trying to–"

"Can you move away?" I say, irritated by my own embarrassment. I hate feeling like a sideshow freak. "You're distracting me."

He pushes up from the couch, taking up my sentry post at the window. He lifts his hand. "I'll be good."

"This is creepy." Kitty shivers. "Like being at a seance."

Barb's eyes widen. "It really is."

"Sorry," I say to Leonard. "Can we try again?"

He draws a deep breath, as though about to plunge under water, and closes his eyes. This time colour bursts in my mind and sensation sweeps over me, shocking in detail and intensity. His hands, my hands on Miriam. The heat of

her mouth. I have to fight my way out of it, almost falling off the couch.

My cheeks flame.

I scramble to my feet.

Leonard jerks back. "You … you saw something?"

"You didn't?" I pant, my hand pressed to my chest, pain stabbing my arm.

"No," Leonard says. "Nothing."

I see truth in his eyes, but the impact of the KMH has me reeling. I look to Jamie who stands frozen, colour draining from his face. "You can Harvest from a civ." He turns his back, bracing his hands on the window frame, lowering his head. "That's twice I nearly killed the wrong person."

Leonard goes to him.

Kitty covers her face. "Oh, shit … then it's Aiden."

I fumble for my phone, texting rapid fire to Miriam that things have changed and it might not be Richard and hit send. *Please check your phone.*

I grind my fingers into my temple then go to Kitty. I kneel in front of her seat. "Kit, listen." I detach her hand from her face, bringing it down between mine. "It still might be Richard. Jamie says he was strung-out and acting crazy when he tracked him home. I'm just not a hundred per cent."

She shakes her head, tears streaming.

"Maybe someone else was waiting for us to leave the governor's office?" But I feel the emptiness of my words and grit my teeth.

Miriam, please, I need you.

"Listen to me, Kitty." I try to sound as brisk and authoritative as my aunt does under pressure. "It was always going to be someone, a person, not some shadow monster. And let's face it, it was likely to be someone you knew. I hope it's not Aiden. Really, with all that's in me, I hope it's not, but you're right, the evidence against him for timing and location … it's not good."

She doesn't stop crying.

I stand there, feeling totally useless. "I'm going to try Miriam again."

I walk out into the foyer, away from the sound of Barb murmuring to her daughter and Leonard speaking softly to his son, a father's comfort. I sit on the bottom step of the staircase and look up at the chandelier and try to imagine my mother sitting beside me, her arms around me, promising things will work out in the end. The image barely forms, an insubstantial mist that leaves me cold. Someone will die. I shake my head, dig my phone from my pocket and hit redial. It goes straight to Miriam's voicemail. "Where are you?" I lean, elbows on knees, hand in my hair. "Come home. I need you."

Thunder rumbles over the house, a deep rolling growl.

The front door clicks and Miriam slips in, hair plastered to her face, jogging gear slicked to her body. Relief and anxiety make my legs shaky as I rise to meet her. Miriam leans against the door, drawing ragged breaths, desolate eyes, sheet-white face. "It's not Richard."

I stop on the rug, uncertain whether to touch her. "So, you got my message? Where have you been? I Harvested from Leonard."

The last part breaks her trance. "That's not possible."

"Yeah, it is," I say, confused. "You didn't get my message?"

She covers her mouth then slides her hand up to her eyes, water dripping from her hair down her forehead.

"What's going on?" Jamie and the rest of the Gallaghers gather in the entrance to the living room.

"Where have you been?" Barb says.

"I needed to think." Miriam pushes past me towards the stairs. "I couldn't think clearly. I needed to check … with Sullivan."

"You've spoken to the doctor?" Jamie joins me beneath the chandelier. "Where the hell is he?"

Miriam leans on the end of the banister. "I need to talk to Evie."

"Wait. You know who it is?" Kitty breaks away from her mother to stand beside us. "It's Aiden, isn't it? Doctor Sullivan told you."

"I told him."

"What?" We all seem to say it together.

Miriam sinks on the step. "I need to talk to Evie. Alone."

I can feel myself recoiling. "You're not making sense, Miriam. Just spit it out."

"Doctor Sullivan said he'd meet me here."

"But it *is* Aiden?" Impatience and frustration burn in my chest. "You're telling me that Doctor Sullivan has evidence that *proves* it's him?"

"Yes."

"See!" Kitty's voice is high, but the sound seems to reach me from a distance, my own seismic response consuming everything.

Miriam's "yes" triggers a shadow in my mind, and my breathing becomes short, sharp and shallow. I rub my face, squeeze my eyes and focus on the pull of the tether. Kitty alive beside me. Even through the internal storm, I know there's no immediate threat; it's simply a physiological reaction to the news.

Aiden.

I try to think straight for a minute.

Aiden.

I fight my way to the niggling feeling in the back.

Aiden.

It shocks me to find I can feel anything beyond the

feral burn of my instinct, but it's in there – the small piece of rational me not quite swallowed by the Fixation Effect. The sense of regret.

"Damn it."

In a flashflood of memory, I see all my suspicions confirmed: Aiden's tension, the white knuckles, the agitation, the shadowed eyes. It makes me ashamed, how willing I was to cast Richard as the villain – not for Richard's sake but for the lapse in my duty to Kitty. Am I so unreliable? Is my frequency so weak that I can't even discern friend from foe? My failings crash in on me and I ball my fists, appalled at myself. He's come so close, time and again.

Kitty whimpers. "He saved Kaylee."

"He's a killer," Jamie says, a compassionless monotone. "You can't fight DNA."

"You told Sullivan?" I say to Miriam. "How did you know?"

"I guessed at the governor's office."

"That's why you freaked out?" I gape at her. "Why didn't you say? You know what nearly happened?"

"I didn't know Jamie would go after Richard. I wasn't completely sure ..."

"You sensed something?" Jamie says.

"I recognised him," she says. "Look, Evie–"

"How?" My ears pop and roar. "You *know* him?"

Miriam unzips her windbreaker and digs inside,

pulling out a rolled-up sheaf of paper, dog-eared and faded to yellow. Her hands shake as she flattens it out. I try to see what's written on the top sheet. It looks like an official document: heavy paper, a governmental stamp and date marks. "He's my son."

The high-pitched hum builds in my head, making me nauseated. I stare blankly at the paper. "What?"

"I have birth certificates." She holds them out.

"A child?" Barb, her voice weak as a wisp.

"Twins." Miriam looks up at me. "I adopted the boy out and April took you."

Lights flicker above me and I stare at her hollow eyes. "Is this a joke?"

Miriam says nothing.

My head swims. "It is a joke."

A tinkling sound sings above our heads.

Miriam looks up at the chandelier.

"Jamie." Barb's anxious voice.

"It's not true," I say.

A light bulb flickers out, then a second and third.

"Jamie!" Leonard, that time.

"Easy, love." Jamie looms in front of me, his hands either side of my face, but the hum rises and the droplets dance, the whole foyer shimmering with moving light. "Listen to me." Jamie crushes me to him then lifts me from the ground. The foyer blurs and he carries me, shoulder

barging the doors to his father's office. "Everton, listen to me. Hey, hey, come on." He kisses my face, presses his forehead to mine. "Easy, love. Stay with me."

"Jamie, she's lying. Why would she lie?"

The door swings slowly back and Kitty stands at the threshold. "Doctor Sullivan's pulled up." She holds Miriam's papers in her hand. "Evs, you need to look at these."

BLOOD

"I am legally obligated to turn this evidence over to the police." Doctor Sullivan wipes raindrops from his spectacles before adjusting them on his nose. "I can hold it overnight, perhaps give you a head start, but the authorities will have to be informed by morning or I'll be in breach of my oath."

"Give us the bullet points." I sound brittle. I feel brittle. Kitty sits next to me at the dining table, stroking my arm. Jamie's on my left, his body so tense I imagine if I tapped him with a tuning fork, his skin would ring. Grey-faced, Miriam sits opposite me, Leonard and Barb either side of her. I can tell Barb is holding Miriam's hand beneath the table, like moms have to stick together.

It took me a good hour to calm down, look at Miriam's papers and agree to hear what the doctor said, and now I regret the waste of those minutes. We might only have the night to act.

"I took your blood samples as a reference point to help me map the markers of the original sample from Kitty's attack. Extremely useful exercise. The synthetic gene is wonderfully complex, overlaying the unmodified genome in a marvellous ..." he looks up from his folder at our cold faces and clears his throat. "However, due to the complexity of the markers, it took me much longer to map than regular DNA. I had Jamie's two weeks before yours and Miriam's, and had a fair idea of the patterns I should expect. But the Stray anomaly maps differently. I was eager to see how your two samples compared with Jamie's and the original sample, to see how the patterns played out."

My eyes dry from staring at the sheen on Sullivan's nose. "And Richard's?"

"I didn't get very far with it, my dear, but my initial findings would indicate he has unmodified DNA."

"But you're not certain." I can feel what everyone's thinking: I'm grasping at straws.

"In light of these results, it's unnecessary to investigate Mr Dean's sample any further." He pauses to let it sink in then presses on. "It was only in the last two days that I started to suspect the familial links. When Miriam came to me last night with her suspicions about the original sample belonging to her son, I adjusted my analysis to map for twin markers. It took most of the night and day but this is what I found."

He picks up two transparencies covered in lines of code. "This is the original sample from the skin I took from under Kitty's nails." He lays it on the white cover of his folder. "This is your sample." He lays the second sheet over the top, aligning the edges, revealing the matches. "This is Miriam's." He places a third transparency on top. "There are slight differences in the maternal code but the key markers remain the same."

I can feel everybody looking at me. I stare at the official papers spread across the table: Miriam's faded certificates, an adoption file, a xeroxed black-and-white photo from a school yearbook; Aiden looks about five. His startling eyes stand out and the spray of freckles across his nose. A newspaper cutout details the death of Aiden's parents, Bailey and Kendy Templar, in a home invasion. Aiden was seven. He escaped through his bedroom window.

Each proof winds me: same birth date, same blood type, same DNA.

"If you would like, I could talk you through the twin markers and how they–"

"No, thank you. I don't need to see anything else." I sense the quiet exhale of relief from everyone. I've given in.

Doctor Sullivan squints at me through his glasses. "I could check your arm?"

I shake my head, even though the wound aches. "I'm fine and we don't have a lot of time."

Leonard gets up. "Thank you, Doctor Sullivan, your help has been …"

I don't hear the rest.

The doctor gets to his feet, speaking rapidly, waving his hand at the documents. They go out into the foyer and I hear the front door open and close.

I stare at Miriam as though I don't recognise her. The angles of her face, the shape of her mouth, the curve of her cheekbones, the ghost of my mom, of April. It's like the parts don't add up.

"Um, could Miriam and I …"

"Of course." Kitty rises quickly to her feet, gesturing for her brother and mother to follow. Barb rises up, her hand on Miriam's shoulder, a gentle squeeze before she steps away. Jamie waits for the others to exit and turns to look at me before closing the doors.

"You never needed to hear this," Miriam's voice crackles. "I'm so sorry."

"We better be quick."

She lowers her eyes. "I met your father when *they* took me in for orientation."

Your father.

Two words put together becoming a foreign, inconceivable thing.

April had told me he was a boy she met at a college party, she didn't even know his name … too much drink.

She pitched it as the best-worst night of her life because I was the greatest gift she had ever been given. Of course, that last part now seems like a bit of a hint.

"Your Synergist."

She nods.

"What's his name?"

"I can't tell you." She brings her hands up on the table and clasps them together. "It wouldn't be safe."

"What?"

"An unsanctioned affiliation between Synergists producing unsanctioned offspring?" She presses her lips together.

I read horrible things into the silence.

"They're much stricter now," she says, "keeping male and female operatives apart."

"How did you keep it from them at all?"

"Your father got me an assignment that allowed me to go off-radar. I went to the UK, April came with me. She returned home with you and the boy went to the Templars."

"Mom knew what you were?"

"I told her everything."

"That I might be like you?"

"She wanted you very much, Evie. She wanted you like I wanted you."

The questions back up; the confronting sense memory of the moving lump I had Harvested from Miriam, misinterpreting it as Mom's, as April's. "Was she even a gene carrier?"

"She was. She had a fifty-fifty chance of producing offspring with AFS. Your mother was far more sensible and careful than me. Once I told her about everything, she would never have gotten herself – she knew she would never have children of her own, so she took you without a second thought."

"Why not keep Aiden?"

"Boys are more likely to be *Strays*." Miriam whispers the illegal term and lowers her head. "Exposure to active frequencies can activate *Priming*. It would have been too dangerous for Aiden to be near me at all."

"Giving him up didn't do him any favours."

She winces. "I took Fretizine throughout the whole pregnancy. We hoped it would neutralise the synthetic gene, that you would simply be carriers."

"Why bother? You could have had an abortion."

"No, no, I could never ..." She closes her eyes. "I couldn't live with myself."

"You can live with this?"

She covers her face. "I loved you the moment I knew you existed–"

I slam my hands on the table and shove my chair back. "That doesn't help me! It sure as hell doesn't help your son!" Black fog swirls, and I grip the table.

All her safeguards. The sacrifices. For nothing.

A tap on the door and Jamie's head appears. "We need to move." His eyes dart between us, and I rise to my feet, feeling weak and giddy.

"Jamie, hang on. I need to get my head around this."

He closes the door behind him, approaching with caution in his eyes. "Nothing has changed. It was too late for Aiden the moment he touched Kitty."

The nightmares flicker in my head. The feeling of being lost in my own mind, eaten up on the inside by terrible thoughts. If they're more than dreams, if they're some kind of sick, psychic, twin-related KMH then I can't deny it. Aiden is lost.

My brother.

Jamie squeezes my shoulder. "Nobody expects you to raise a hand against your brother. You stay here with Kitty. Miriam, obviously we don't expect you to be involved in this, but I have to move now. If he gets wind he's been identified, he'll disappear and we'll be back to square one, waiting for his next attack. If I go now, I can deactivate him."

Deactivate.

A bland euphemism.

I can't articulate the clash of feeling inside me. "Why not let the police …"

A gently incredulous look fills his eyes. "You think he'd let them take him?"

I open my mouth and close it again.

"Three times he's come after her," Jamie says.

"I know, I know. You're right. It's just–" I turn to Miriam, hoping for what?

She shakes her head, tears streaming. "There's nothing we can do to save him. It's all my fault."

"I called the boarding house," Jamie says. "The dean said he's in his room … I need to go now."

I grip Jamie's arm. "It's early. There'll be kids around."

"No one will know I'm there."

Chilled by his certainty, I release him.

Jamie turns to my aunt. "You should probably go."

"I'll stay."

He looks for a moment like he'll press his point but then he concedes with a nod. "I want Kitty in the panic room while I'm gone and everyone on alert. Keep her there until I can give you confirmation."

Code for, I'll let you know when your brother is dead.

Miriam looks up from the table, her face desolate. "Don't let him suffer."

I can't feel my legs as I follow Jamie out into the foyer. I can't swallow for the lump in my throat. It's all moving too fast. He zips up a black backpack waiting at the foot of the stairs; I don't want to know what's in it.

Kitty stands with her parents at the entrance to the living room, her dove eyes huge and glistening with tears.

She looks terrified. Leonard, as pale as I have ever seen him, stares at his son with unreadable eyes. Barb sobs quietly in her husband's arms.

After all these weeks of preparation, to be doing nothing, to think of sitting and waiting while Jamie goes out to take care of things. The roar of adrenaline almost deafens me and, impossibly, I feel an irrational urge to warn Aiden, but to wish him safe is to wish Kitty dead. Synaptic treason.

I could never wish that.

I never will.

"No. No. This isn't right. I should go too."

Jamie slings his backpack over his shoulder and goes to his sister. His lips move and he rubs her arms then he takes her by the hand and they come towards me in slow motion. He deposits Kitty beside me, cups my cheek, his eyes tight with regret and determination.

"I should do it," I say. "This is my responsibility."

"And what would it do to Miriam if you did?" he says. "What would it do to you once the Fixation Effect is gone?"

"I could live with it."

"You shouldn't have to. No one should." He lets his hand fall. "Keep her safe."

The sound of the door closing echoes in my hollow chest.

STATIC

"If Aiden had never met me, he'd be normal," Kitty says. "I'm like an infection, destroying people's lives."

"Kitty." Barb turns in Leonard's arms.

"That's bullshit," I say. "How many times do I have to tell you it's not your fault? Now, go to the bathroom." It seems like sensible advice. "You've got five minutes then you're in lockdown."

She shudders and turns to the stairs like her feet are cast in lead. I watch her all the way up to the landing, wishing there was something I could say that would make a difference. The bandwidth has emptied, adrenaline drains away. I feel bloodless, lifeless with the drop in energy. "Mr and Mrs Gallagher, Jamie wants us to be on alert while he's away."

"I'll watch the gate," Leonard says. "Barb'll stay with Kitty."

Barb reaches for my hand, looking tortured. "I'm so

sorry … your brother … I wish there was something …"

"I'm going to go get changed." I withdraw my hand gently and jog upstairs, fleeing sympathy, ignoring the pain in my bicep.

It's a forty-minute drive to Gainsborough. I have no idea how long it will take for Jamie to locate Aiden. I wonder if he will extract him from the boarding house. I doubt he'll want to take care of things in a building full of kids.

Take care of things.

Aiden's going to die.

I shake myself. I need to feel ready, even if I just sit here all night and Jamie returns without complication. I need pockets and none of my pants are up to the job. I run back along the landing to Jamie's room.

It would have been funny in different circumstances, rummaging the shelves in his dressing room for cargo pants. I pull an old pair out and something flutters to the ground. The photo falls face up. Jamie and Helena – the picture Barb showed me. Did she take it from his room without him knowing? Put it back here? Is he hiding it? Looking closely at it now, Helena looks older than me, grinning in her snow gear, cheek pressed to his, the mountains behind them. Such blue eyes. I think of Jamie's parting words in the foyer, that no one should have to go through this. And here she is, his ticket out. Feeling heavy in my chest, I return it to the shelf and go back to my room.

The pants are loose in the waist and too long, but I slide one of my belts through the loops and roll the hems. I change my bulky sweatshirt for a fitted black turtleneck, burning my bicep with the movement. To complete the sense of ritual, I secure my hair in a ponytail. I don't look in the mirror. I can't bear to see my face.

Back in the hall, I meet Kitty coming from her room. She is pale, journal tucked under her arm, iPod clutched in her hand. She gives a tremulous smile, lifting her eyebrows at my pants. "You make those look good. Very Lara Croft." Her voice falters as she sees me glaring at her journal. "No letters. I promise."

I fumble in my back pocket for the piece of paper I've brought from my room. I hand it to her. "Write more of these."

She unfolds it, biting her lips, and stares at her crumpled To Do list. Her eyes well up. "This is kind of embarrassing."

"It's a good list."

We stand there staring at the piece of paper.

"Evie." Leonard appears at the bottom of the stairs, wearing a thick parka. "Can I have a word?"

Kitty and I make our way downstairs. Barb comes from the living room. "I'm with you, sweetie." She circles her daughter's shoulders, her smile tight and thin. "You know where to find us." Kitty squeezes my wrist and goes with her mother. Leonard nods me towards his office and I follow.

He drops into his chair, his parka shushing as he sits. On his laptop screen, six security footage windows show images of the grounds: shrubs shake in the wind, trees flail wild limbs, rain falls in torrents. "I'll be here." He points to the bottom corner, which shows the front gate. "But I'll patrol along the east border to here." He points at the window above.

"The weather's miserable." I cringe. "You don't have to. I'm sure Jamie won't be long."

"I want to feel useful, Evangeline. Just this once." Leonard adjusts his glasses and looks up at me with his son's grey eyes. "Let me see your watch."

I lift my wrist and he taps the screen and turns the face, then does the same with his. "We'll be able to stay in audio contact."

I swallow.

"You'll want a gun?" he says.

"I was going to ask."

He turns to the safe beneath his desk. He taps an access code and the hydraulic release pops the door. He pulls out two silver handguns and extra clips of ammunition, lays them on his blotter and holds one up for me. He shows me the gun is loaded and how to work the safety latch. "It's basic point and shoot."

I take it from him; the cool weight of it makes me shiver. I slip the spare clip in a pocket on my left thigh. "Will I blow my leg off if I keep it in here?" I unzip the big pocket on my right thigh.

"Not if the safety's on."

I walk with him to the foyer. He tucks the other gun in the back of his belt, pulling the long parka down over it. The rain sounds terrible. It makes me nervous, the way it muddies the bandwidth, interfering with the pulse of the tether.

Leonard pulls me into his arms, a quick crushing hug, planting a kiss on the top of my head. He goes out the door, misty-eyed behind his glasses.

I turn to the dining room, bracing inwardly to face Miriam, but she isn't in there. I check my watch. Jamie has only been gone a quarter of an hour. My pins and needles crackle and I curse the rain. I push through the swing door, the smell of another forgotten meal grown cold on the stovetop.

My stomach growls.

Miriam leans on the sink.

A gun lies on the counter beside her.

"You should eat," she says.

I don't argue. Crossing to the oven I nab a cold potato and stuff it in my mouth. My body needs fuel and I stay there, working my way through the roast vegetables, pretending not to feel Miriam behind me, trying not to hear the swelling silence.

"Where do you want me?" Miriam finally says.

I cross to check the butler's pantry, to keep from facing her. The cellar door is locked. "They're in?"

She nods.

I swallow my last bite and turn to the sink, still not looking directly at her. "Excuse me."

Miriam moves aside.

I open the faucet, bend and drink. When I straighten up, Miriam offers me a towel, but I wipe my chin on the back of my hand instead. Stupid and petty. I can feel her waiting for me to say something, but what does she expect, *It's okay, Mom*?

"Leonard's on the gate. I've got him on audio, so maybe you want to set your watch, so we're all on the same page. I'm going to lock down the house. You could stay here till I get back. Whatever."

"Okay." She takes her gun in hand and checks the cartridge.

I turn to the back hall, willing myself not to bolt, willing her not to speak and just let me go.

"Evie."

I stop but can't face her.

"Forgive me."

"For what? For having me?" I push through the door.

STORM

I focus on the simple demands of moving my body and completing small tasks, locking doors and windows downstairs. It feels good to do something. In Leonard's study, I check the security feed. Leonard is at the gate. The other squares of the grid show the same shrubs and trees and rain. My brain tries to morph the shadows into an assailant.

No, there will be no assailant. Jamie will see to it. Jamie, who I love. *There, I admit it.* Jamie will kill my brother. *My brother.* I struggle to imagine a life where that exists. A pair. Twins. Evie *and* Aiden.

I call his face to memory, our last meeting at the governor's office, the way he moved, the way he spoke. The way I responded to his proximity at school and how I always second-guessed myself. Did he feel my presence the way I felt his, without comprehending what it meant?

Is he terrified? Does he sleep? Does he run? Does he know what's happening to his body?

With Aiden haunting me, I make a quick pass along the second floor to Kitty's room. I try not to picture her in the cellar, it makes me cold. *Jamie's doing the right thing.* I have to tell myself over and over.

A loud crackle from my watch nearly has me on the ceiling. I tap the screen, my hands shake. "Yeah?"

Nothing but a faint hiss.

"Mr Gallagher?"

Nothing.

"Mr Gallagher?"

I cross to the window and pull back the curtain. It's fully dark now. I can see the gate in the distance but with the rain I can't judge what's out there.

I jog back down to Leonard's study, jelly legs and jangling nerves. I flick through the security feed but can't see him. Anxiety fizzes beneath the surface of my skin. I tap my watch, lifting my wrist close to my mouth. "Are you there, Mr Gallagher?"

Nothing.

I stare blankly at the screen in momentary paralysis then lurch to my feet, bruising my thigh on the corner of the desk as I hurry from the study out into the foyer. A clap of sound from my watch stops my heart and I skid to a standstill. An echo comes from outside, the report of a gunshot.

"No!" Fire erupts in my spine, a sickening note pierces

my eardrums and glass explodes above my head. Darkness. Crystal from the chandelier rains down.

Miriam bursts from the kitchen. "Leonard!"

"Stay here!" I almost wrench the front door from its hinges. My feet don't touch the porch. I land on gravel. Shadows storm my mind.

Maybe it's a mistake.

Maybe Leonard got spooked.

Maybe his watch shorted.

Torrential rain slicks my hair, my clothes, driving splinters from the chandelier beneath my collar as I tear down the long drive, cursing the sky. The storm's roar blurs with the static shrilling in my head, making me feel blind and afraid.

He isn't at the gate.

I cut along the eastern boundary, slipping in the wet when I see him, his legs spread-eagled in mud and grass, his body obscured by shrubs. I hammer my watch, bringing it to my mouth as I run, screaming incoherently, not hearing Miriam's crackling response. I punch the screen to send out the alert and land on my knees, panting, hysterical, smelling blood.

He lies face-down, his glasses in pieces. He twitches and gurgles when I touch his shoulder. "Mr Gallagher, it's me." I drip water and crystal as I turn him, like my arm isn't agonised and he's not a full-grown man twice my weight, lowering his head on the grass. He bleeds from the neck where his shoulder slopes up, an oozing gash that bubbles and shines, wet with the ebb of life.

Miriam, don't let Aiden in the house.

"You're okay. It's okay." I rip the fabric of Leonard's torn pant leg into two long strips, moving quickly, my hands trembling.

Oh God.

I wad the first strip, pressing it against the flooding wound. The other I feed under his neck to tie the compress. My watch chimes, Jamie acknowledging the alert. "He's coming, Mr Gallagher. Jamie's coming." I fumble for my phone and dial, fingers wet with blood and water. I rest my hand on Leonard's chest as he blinks at the rain. I give the emergency services operator clipped mechanical details and don't wait for her questions. I leave the phone on by Leonard's head. "You're going to be okay."

Leonard forces air through his lips, a bubbling rasp, "Go."

I stagger to my feet, eyes on the house, my legs numb beneath me as I sprint up the soaking lawn. I force the image of Leonard to the back of my mind; I can't let it undo me. The light is still on in the kitchen, but I can't see Miriam. I try to feel the tether in the chaos – a pulse, distorted, faint, but there.

She's alive.

I speed up the side of the house, bee-lining for the kitchen when a foreign signal cuts through the static – a shadow so black in my mind it almost blinds me. My spine shoots with fire and instinct takes over, quickening the chemical taste on my tongue. My hands know what to do. I slip the gun from my pocket and release the safety.

I crash into the kitchen, brightness stabbing my eyes, but he's already down there. I can sense it and rage sweeps through me, hot, black, disorientating. Where the hell is Miriam? The surge of adrenaline carries me silently through the butler's pantry. The door has been ripped open and the security console is bloody. He has Miriam in the cellar with him. I shiver, grip my gun, slip inside and hurdle the rail.

I hit the cellar floor.

Aiden crowds the still-closed panic room door, a red gouge on his cheek. Miriam, on her knees beside him, her arm hanging at an odd angle. Broken bottles. Spilled wine, sweet and cloying.

I hesitate for one second, waiting for my finger to squeeze, for the trigger to give, expecting a shock of sound that will make my eardrums flinch. Surely his skull is about to jolt, splatter on the metal door. Nothing happens.

The second passes.

Miriam groans.

Aiden pushes her hard against the wall, forcing her hand onto the security panel.

Why is he still moving?

Why isn't he dead?

Why haven't I pulled the trigger?

"Stop." Thick air swallows my voice, makes it small.

His shoulders square, the infrared scanner flickers and Miriam crumples senseless to the floor.

"If you don't stop, I'll blow your brains out."

The door slides back.

Emergency light cuts the room.

He lifts a gun.

I fire.

Screams ring from the panic room.

Blood bursts from his hand.

His gun ricochets off the wall.

He screams.

I launch myself across the cellar floor, slamming Aiden into the wall. His skull hits concrete, a muted thwack, his body jerking powerfully against me. A cry rips from my throat, rising above the clamour. "Run, Kitty! Go!"

She and Barb scramble behind me.

I struggle with Aiden, his body lean, hard-muscled, his good arm wrecking havoc on my kidneys, fierce blows as he bucks. I hear Kitty and her mother scrabbling up the stairs and I will them away. Aiden writhes and I grasp his injured hand and squeeze. He shakes and screams. I force my elbow under his chin and ram his head back, once, twice and he goes limp. I hold him up by the neck, bringing my gun to his head. His black eyes roll back.

Do it.

My muscles contract to pull the trigger, but there's something else in that moment, the same thing that shifted my aim in the first shot. I growl and shudder.

Pull the trigger.

I step back, let him slump to the floor and stand over him, shaking, bracing my arms, cradling the gun with both hands, pressure building in my head.

Kill him.

"I will!" I burst out, panting, startled by my own voice, the stinging wetness in my eyes. "Now! I'm going to do it!"

BANG.

I shoot wide, the bullet smokes in the concrete. An animalistic groan shudders out of me, seismic strain threatening internal combustion.

Do it now.

His eyes move beneath milky translucent lids, long lashes brushing beneath. I stare at his face, paralysed by the details: the slope from brow to nose, the high arch of cheekbone, pale skin, freckles dusting his nose, the strong jaw, lips budding and innocent in sleep. I stay like that, staring and not killing, until my eyes dry and sting.

Seconds string out, becoming minutes …

How long? I grip the gun tighter, staring and not

killing. The handle grinds against the bones in my thumb, sweat beads on my lip, my arms ache from the tension.

His eyes open.

I jolt back, clutching panicked breaths.

His pupils have shrunk, his focus goes in and out and he groans, his face stricken, tears spilling. "Don't let me hurt her." His voice catches. "Don't let me – oh God, Evie?" His body arches, muscles spasming, mouth contorting. "Help me. It's coming, please, I can't."

Distant noises echo above us and I look up at the door. Pain strikes me in the chest, driving air from my lungs – Aiden's foot, ramming me backwards. I have one brief glimpse of him, black-eyed and springing upright before my head hits the wooden shelf with a blinding thwack, my gun clattering into the shadows. My skull feels split in two, and he flies up the stairs.

STRAY

I yank a knife from the block by the stove and stagger out the kitchen door. The rain has stopped but the wet night air hits me like a cold slap. My vision blurs from the blunt-force trauma and the sweet reek of wine fumes up from my shoes. I can't think about Miriam, still lying on the floor of the cellar. I close my eyes to feel for Aiden's retreat. A frenetic note spikes in the interference and behind it, thinly, the pulse of the tether. I veer right, working hard to straighten my body from its defensive hunch, pain pressing like a cinder block on the back of my head.

Rainclouds obscure the moon and I struggle to bring the landscape into focus. I can hear sirens and the lights of emergency vehicles flicker across the grass as I run past the pool house.

Please, let them reach Leonard in time.

A dark blur at the far corner triggers a charge in my system, sharpening my vision. I race after Aiden, into the stable yard and come to a sliding standstill. He has stopped beside the utility shed and he stares towards the forest as if he's listening – his head rocks back and his chin juts forwards. The faint pull of the tether dies and my heart stops beating.

He feels it too.

Kitty has crossed the river.

Fear flashes through me. I draw my arm back and hurl the knife, picturing where it will cut through his temple, but he shoots away and the blade buries itself in the shed wall, right where his head had been. I fly after him, wrenching the knife from its hold. Racing down the sodden lawn, I just glimpse him as he disappears through the trees.

"Aiden!" I scream. I swipe snot and tears from my face as I run, surprised to find myself crying. Finally, I reach the dark wall of the forest and whip between the grey trunks where the night sounds close in. Branches slap at my face, brambles scratch my arms, tear at my waterlogged clothes and my terror for Kitty throbs in each footfall.

I follow the sound of him, the feel of him ahead of me, instinct and desperation driving me like a machine. The air grows frigid as we near the river, as cold as my panic at the sound of water on stones. Almost immediately there's a break in Aiden's stride and my senses blind as he crosses over.

"Aiden!"

I clatter down the stony bank, see the leap I will make and launch in a hurdler's stride. The black gleam of the river ripples beneath me then his signal bursts back to life and the tether snaps strong and clear. I land running. He has turned to the left, following the bank towards his goal.

I gain enough ground that I can make out Aiden as he darts through the trees. "Aiden!" I scream again.

The sound of Kitty's terror echoes back to me; she's heard my warning. Her cry goes up, it swells and dies and swells again. She's so close – so close and now she knows he's coming.

Aiden skids and veers right.

I glimpse the pale flick of Kitty's hair, Barb beside her, sobbing as she pulls her daughter by the arm. She shouts as we close in, pushes Kitty on and turns, hands out. Aiden mows through Barb like she's nothing and sends her slamming into the mud-packed ground, knocking her head hard.

Kitty screams.

Aiden launches at her, his good arm collecting her across the face, a thwack of bone on bone. I roar, terrified the blow has broken her neck, and throw my knife again but he lunges and the blade impales the slope of his shoulder. He grunts, tearing the dagger loose just as I slam into him, our joint momentum driving Kitty into the ground.

She cries out.

She's alive.

I hold Aiden tight around the neck and chest, breathing sweat, earth, pine and that stink of ammonia as we roll off Kitty. I'm barely conscious of his weight as I hit the dirt under him.

"Kitty, run!" I fight to keep hold of him.

She struggles to stand, listing to the side, holding her arm.

Aiden drives his elbow into my chest, winding me as he thrashes upwards. I scramble to my feet, gasping. He looks at Kitty then whirls towards me, teeth bared, eyes black and wild with hate. The knife is gone but there's no time for it anyway. He comes at me, berserk. No form to his attack, terrifying force in each strike. I struggle to block his fists, shocked by his strength, my bicep screaming as I slip on the mud, my knee ramming the rocky ground.

Kitty moans.

Something in the hopeless terror of that sound …

My instinct flicks from defence to attack and instantly precognition gears to life. I push him back, driving up to my feet. I see his moves before they come, counter deliberately, make room for my retaliation, forcing him on the defensive. Speed, lightness, flexibility, allowing me to dive, spin and strike.

Snap his neck his spine cave his skull gouge his eyes rip his throat out – anything – anything – just do it now take him end it save her save her save her save her!

But I stall. Why am I stalling?

"Go!" I shout. "Kitty, get out of here!"

"Run!" A voice booms in the dark. "Kitty, go!" Jamie bursts from the wall of trees twenty feet away on my left. Above us, a cleft in the clouds releases moonlight, and Jamie's arm unfurls with the gleam of his gun.

I ram my foot into Aiden's stomach. He buckles and I spin towards Jamie, shifting to place myself between them, not ready, not yet, for the end.

"Get down!" He stalks towards us, gun trained.

Let him do it.

I don't move.

The bandwidth shouts Jamie's intent.

I picture him firing and Aiden crumpling.

My instinct roars agreement, but something in me resists, tearing me in two.

"Evie, move!"

Let him do it.

Jamie's eyes flick left.

I know Aiden has recovered and stepped out from behind me.

I don't feel my lips move. No.

White powder explodes from the barrel before I hear the shot but it's too late, I've already leaped. The bullet tears through my shoulder, a red-hot shock beneath my collarbone and bursting from my back. Aiden's cry, behind me, a sound without volume or power, the dull cry of someone surprised by pain. I fall for the longest time – a life's journey in falling.

Jamie's there, his face creased in fear, his mouth moving in the endless repetition of my name. The curve of his lips … I could stare at him forever and not grow tired of looking. Adrenaline has dilated his pupils, but even with his irises black for the fight, he is still beautiful.

I try to move but fire licks the hollow of my shoulder and I groan.

Jamie's hands are under me, lifting me, gathering me into his lap.

The movement makes me cry in pain.

I struggle to work my lungs.

Kitty sobs.

The tug of the tether startles me.

Kitty!

Why isn't she running?

Jamie supports my back. "It's okay. Kitty's okay."

Somewhere behind me comes a low moan, a bubbling sound, life pulsing from a body. I turn. Aiden lies just feet away, eyes wide in the gloom, a scarlet ribbon threading from the corner of his mouth and down across the white stretch of his throat.

"Aiden." I push up, grunting, agonised.

"Evie," Jamie says. "Leave him."

I twist away and crawl one-handed to Aiden's side. His eyes glaze in and out of focus, pupils retracting. "Aiden?" Blood pools on the ground where I cut his shoulder. A dark patch spreads on his stomach. I cover the stain and wonder at the trajectory of the bullet through my body into his.

"What are you doing?" Jamie says.

"I – I don't know." I don't.

Kitty sobs and hugs herself.

"I need to finish this," Jamie says.

Chaos churns inside me. "He had no choice."

"Evie–"

"It's not his fault. He didn't want to hurt her. He told me."

Jamie lifts his gun.

I grip my head. The sound of Kitty's weeping, the pull of the tether, Aiden bleeding on the cold ground. My vision blurs. I cry out with the pressure that's tearing me apart. "Don't kill him, Jamie." I cough and taste blood. "I don't want you to kill him–"

"Evie!" Jamie pulls me up. I didn't know I fell. The pain in my shoulder blinds me and I cry out. My lungs struggle to fill and all I can taste is blood. There's nothing but the tether and I cling to the pulse until it too disappears and I'm gone.

BONDS

I cough and choke, clamping my teeth on a hard plastic tube, gagging against the foreign feel of it lodged in the back of my throat. I grasp the line with numb fingers, desperate to pull it out, squinting through white fog. There is a dull ache in my shoulder.

"Hold on! Don't pull it. Shit." Hands grab for mine, too late.

I buck and retch as the tube comes up out my mouth, a hot surge of blood and vomit splattering my chin. I gasp and shake in the aftermath.

"Damn! She's strong."

"Hold her!"

"No!" My throat burns. "I can breathe on my own." I can't see through the bright light and I turn my head side to side, my eyes running.

Shapes emerge in the haze, colours. White and pale green. The backs of my hands bump against cold, metal rails, a hospital bed. Tubes tunnel in my arms and machines beep by my head. Something tugs behind my bellybutton and I move to cover it with my hand. There's a sting and pop as a needle tears from my wrist.

"Kitty! Where is she? Is she okay?"

"I said hold her! She's torn her line!"

A man in blue scrubs leans over the bed and his ebony skin almost glows in the white light. "Sweetheart, your friends are fine but you have to stop moving. We're trying to help you." He presses a stethoscope to my chest near the wound, frowning as his lips part. "Shhh!" The others in the room grow still. "Unbelievable." He straightens up and shakes his head. "Lungs are clear."

"What about Aiden?" I pant. "He was shot in the stomach."

"She means the kid in oh-three."

"It's a mess."

"He's bleeding out."

Aiden is still alive? Jamie didn't kill him. The tether's strong. Kitty's safe.

He's bleeding out.

"He's my twin," I blurt, unthinking. I needed to say it.

The room goes quiet, except for the beeping monitors. I can count them now, the bodies moving around my bed. Five people looking at me then at each other. Then the room comes alive in noise and motion.

"Move, move, move!"

In moments my bed is being pushed down a corridor. My head bounces on the hard mattress and fluorescent lights, set in pockmarked ceiling panels, run above me. Four different hands hold me down and the ebony-skinned doctor squeezes my shoulder. "Let's go, let's go."

"Evie!"

"Jamie?" I try to sit up and the four hands push me down.

"What's happening? Is she okay?" He comes into my line of sight, his face etched in dismay.

"Out of the way, kid! Move!"

A nurse pushes him back and they wheel me into a theatre. Aiden lies grey and unmoving on a metal gurney, stripped to the waist, a blood-soaked sheet over his hips. Blood is on the floor, on scrubs and rubber-gloved hands, blood everywhere. The metallic tang of it competes with the reek of disinfectant. His stomach and chest are smeared red and a nurse stands with her hands pressed hard over his wound. I can't hear his pulse above the urgent voices but it's there on the monitor, a faint erratic stab cutting the horizontal line.

Doctors and nurses bark terse instructions back and forth across the room. They park my bed beside Aiden's. A woman turns my arm, a stinging prick and she digs a needle deep in the crook of my elbow. I watch my blood pulse through a smoky white tube, inching along the track in time with my pulse. With quick, sure hands she attaches the line to a stubby nozzle in Aiden's arm. She opens a valve then tapes the join and the top of the tube to his skin. The swarm of blue and green scrubs grows still, watching with me as the blood reaches my brother.

"Hold him."

"Wait."

I hold my breath, as if I know what they wait for. Do I expect him to open his eyes, or gasp for air? Nothing happens. A collective sigh rises around the room and people begin to move again.

"Is it working?" I ask.

"We'll see," the doctor leans in again. "The last three transfusions produced instant seizures. So far so good. Watch his skin. It should get some colour."

Aiden's arm changes from grey to white and gradually a pink tinge appears. I exhale.

"Slowly now, folks. Don't drain her dry."

The nurse adjusts the valve on the tube. The doctor begins a running commentary. They're stabilising Aiden to remove the bullet. It's lodged in his spine. He should have died. I should have died but my bullet wound has already closed. Internal bleeding stopped. Lungs clear. Vitals strong. Rate of recovery, unheard of. I can't concentrate to really listen; I just lie there, feeling too many things at the same time, watching Aiden change colour.

Jamie let him live. He let Aiden live when it went against everything that was in him as a Shield, as a brother, as a son. What had it cost him? Kitty is in the hospital somewhere; the tether is strong but there's no anxiety. I can feel Aiden's signal in the bandwidth but the shadow is like a distant cloud, a storm that's retreated. I wait as my blood courses into him, to see if the shadow will threaten again.

They bring in a curtained metal stand and slide it between the beds so all I can see is Aiden's head and shoulders. Something brushes against the curtain and then I see Aiden's shoulder move and his pale arm hangs down off the bed. I can't explain what compels me but, carefully so as not to pop any more wires or tubes, I slip my hand inside his. The bandwidth goes blank, a black hole without sight or sound. It disorientates me but I don't let go. I stay in the void, wanting a miracle.

I wish I could reach through time and undo everything, make it so Aiden and Kitty never met. But I know it wouldn't be enough. Aiden would have transitioned sometime with someone else.

I wonder when it happened and what it looked like when Aiden touched Kitty and the transition began. It's in here somewhere, the moment of impact. There has to be a way past the wall that keeps me out, all those nightmares I've seen through his eyes. Maybe that's the key, his unconscious state – his guard down? I lean into the bandwidth, pressing against an invisible film of resistance. I summon Kitty to the forefront of my mind and push again. Something gives, and it's like falling through a split seam. Vivid colours burst before my eyes.

I'm crouched in the service entrance of the governor's mansion, almost groaning with the sick twist of the invisible umbilical cord. Poison pulses to me from the girl in blue, diamonds glittering on her neck. Certainty fills me. It's her. She's the virus, eating me alive. Everything about her is a lie. The soft fragile body, the small mouth, the pretty eyes. Static screams in my ears and I lurch up from the wall and run at her.

I gasp and release Aiden's hand, almost blinded by the lights above the bed. A nurse leans over me. "Are you in pain?"

"No." I want a clear head to try KMH again. "It doesn't hurt."

She pats my arm. "You tell me if it hurts. Don't be brave."

She turns back to the readout and I don't hesitate, grabbing Aiden's hand, closing my eyes. Again, the blank resistance, but I throw myself against it like pushing through a seam in a thick plastic wall. The roar fills my head. I search for Kitty and the images come quickly, layers of moments:

her face over and over, and with each image, fear, sickness and rage. I lean harder until the roar reaches a peak, then my ears pop and clear. My mind fills with light and colour.

It's hot. There are too many people. My suit is tight through the shoulders and the collar of my shirt constricts my neck. There's a sharp zap in my spine, and I bite hard on the inside of my lip. Damn it. I curl my toes and clench my fists, willing the pins and needles to pass. It's getting ridiculous. I haven't slept more than two hours together for the last few nights. My body is falling apart, stretching, thinning, buzzing with static.

I straighten up at the sight of the governor making his way through the crowd towards me. That's Leonard Gallagher beside him. I recognise him from Forbes *magazine. He's tall, square-shouldered, polished-looking. The governor says he's a difficult man, which about sums up anyone whose opinion differs from his.*

"Look." A coiffed women nudges her friend. "I told you Leonard Gallagher was gorgeous."

"Shhh," the other woman says, "they're coming over here."

I make to step away, but Richard appears from the library with his stumbling girlfriend and I stop where I am, tingling and hyper-aware. Richard pushes a glass of champagne into her hands, smirking and raising his eyebrows at me. I glare. The girl leans heavily on Richard's arm, tips her head back and drinks. Richard runs his fingers over her throat, along her collarbone and down over the swell of her breast. Anger and revulsion kindles inside me – I know that son of a bitch and his MO.

I lose my chance to slip away. The governor arrives in front of me with Gallagher. We shake hands. I try to tune in but an uncomfortable electric stabbing ignites in my spine.

A girl comes up beside Gallagher and touches his arm. His daughter. Kitty. I remember her from school. A petite blonde with dark eyes and a soft pink mouth that curves with a laughing smile. She presses up on her toes to whisper something in his ear and his lips purse like he's trying to hide his amusement. The governor kisses her cheek in greeting. Her father turns to introduce me.

I squint as though I'm looking down a long tunnel.

"I know Aiden," Kitty laughs. "We had bio together last year."

I don't laugh. I can't take my eyes off her. My heart begins to pound. What the hell is wrong with me? She's pretty but there are plenty of pretty girls at the party. Why am I staring at Kitty like I've never seen her before? I wipe my free hand on the leg of my pants. Am I really sweating? I reach for a glass of water from the table. My hand shakes and pins and needles zip-zap.

A waitress passes, bumping me with her arm and water slops over my fist. Kitty exclaims as it splashes her dress and she stumbles back. "I'm so sorry." Without thinking, I reach to steady her. The moment I touch her, my ears pop and roar.

Everything amplifies: the hammer in my chest, the static in my head, the electric stabbing in my spine.

"Oh dear." She laughs again.

"Don't just stand there, boy," the governor says. "Get the girl a towel."

"Of course. I'm so sorry–" I almost topple sideways as my head swims. I barely make it to the bathroom before my stomach heaves and the tiled cubicle spins to black.

I come out of the vision into the cool white light of the hospital. My hand is so tight around Aiden's, I can feel his bones grinding together. I force myself to relax my grip and lie there, trembling.

I don't know how much time there is left for Aiden. Somehow, I have stopped myself from killing him when everything inside me required him dead. Even now the dark cloud of his signal sits in the bandwidth, without strength or menace but still there. If it grows strong again, will I act? And what about Jamie? How far can his mercy stretch?

An irrational idea takes hold of me. What if I can give Aiden a new memory? What if his body could experience a Shield's potent reaction to Sparking? What if that memory could replace, reprogram, recalibrate the twisted code of his instinct, to love, protect and save? It's a ridiculous idea … Didn't I just experience his transition? It didn't change me. But desperation makes me reach into the bandwidth anyway, pushing my memory before me.

Effortless Kinetic Memory Transfer. I let it fill out till the hospital disappears and I'm back at the governor's mansion, leaning on Jamie, holding my cut hand, Kitty coming towards us in baby blue chiffon and diamonds, laughing at our matching stains. My panic, my thrashing pulse, my electricity, Kitty's arms around me and the end of the world.

As I fall in the memory, the storm erupts in my body, an explosion of static seizing my joints. Voices rise around me as I arch on the hospital bed. Bodies rush, arms reach, hands press me down. I still hold Aiden, crushing his fingers in an iron grip. I can feel a violent tug and pull on my arm. I manage to turn my head to see his pale, blood-stained chest arch high on the gurney as he convulses beneath the desperate grasp of doctors and nurses.

My head swims and the room becomes dark. Static in my ears grows dim. The tether pulses once, twice … the hook releases behind my bellybutton and I'm falling again, falling, falling and never finding the ground.

HOPE

I leave the hospital-issue gown, with its unreliable ties and unpredictable gape, on the bed. It feels good to be dressed, rediscovering my land legs after lying down for so many days – more days than I needed, but the medical staff were insistent. More noticeable than the stiff ache of my shoulder is the sense of feeling so different. I pause at the end of the corridor, testing again, spreading my hand over my stomach where the tether used to be. No pull, no static, just a faint hum in my bones. I doubt I will ever get used to the quiet.

The sling is for show. I resettle my arm before turning the corner, steeling myself. The guard on morning shift looks up from outside Aiden's room. I stare past him, through the window, wishing I could cap the hope that rises in me and brace for disappointment. Instead, I cross to the window and chew the inside of my cheek.

Aiden looks only a shade less white than the sheets

he lies on. His face bears only traces of fading purple and yellow, the gouge on his cheek has almost completely healed. His survival and rapid recovery after they removed the bullet isn't the miracle. The miracle is the absence of fear, a bandwidth without shadow. No pulsing tether. I know he has deactivated. Either by blood or KMT, something has happened in the operating room that changes everything. Kitty's safe.

Whatever the case, it will make no difference for Aiden. The Affinity Project will finish him – no matter what my theory is. Jamie has made that clear. I realise his choice not to kill Aiden was a stay of execution for my sake, so it wouldn't stand between us, but to wait at all is a sacrifice for Jamie, a sacrifice for his whole family – a risk. We can't be sure when Affinity will come. In the meantime, Jamie's contingency plan is the private guards, coordinated with the police department – if Aiden tries to run, it will be game over. Jamie has warned Aiden himself.

I sigh, resting my head on the reinforced glass. Though Aiden's eyes are closed, the rapid beat of his heart tells me he's conscious. Steel cuffs gleam at his wrists. He could easily break them. I wonder if he took Jamie's warning to heart. Across his bandaged chest and abdomen are more restraints and I know his legs are strapped in place beneath the sheet. Compared to the frenzy the night he arrived, the scene is peaceful.

"Can I speak to him?"

"You can try." The guard hauls himself up and taps the door. The nurse and a second guard, already crowding the small room, turn to watch me enter. "She has five minutes," he says.

The nurse edges around me. "I can monitor him from the nurse's station."

"Can I speak to him alone?"

"You know that's not going to happen," the first guard says.

I shrug and move around to the far side of the bed. He closes the door. The second guard positions himself in front of it and watches me with bold curiosity. I frown until he looks away.

"Aiden."

His chest rises and falls slowly.

I wait.

He doesn't move.

"I know you're awake. I can hear your heart racing." I can't help glancing at the guard. Sure enough his eyebrows lift. "I'm going home today."

Aiden's eyes flicker open to stare towards the foot of the bed and my own pulse quickens in response.

"What do you want?" His voice cracks from lack of use and the guard straightens up at the door.

I'm surprised too, that I get a reaction. I reach for the

pitcher of water, stalling for time. I make awkward work of it, filling a glass with my left hand, but I manage to bring the straw to Aiden's dry lips.

He frowns, confused by the gesture, but he must be thirsty because he drains the glass. I refill it and Aiden shakes his head, attempting to wave the offer away. At the clank of his cuffs he quickly lowers his hand, staring again at the foot of the bed. "What do you want?"

I'm not sure I really know and I stare at his profile, measuring in my mind the arch of his brow, the slope of his high cheekbone and the edge of his jaw. Are they echoes of mine? "How are you feeling?"

"I don't know," he finally says. "Hard to get things straight in my head. Bad dreams." He swallows, unable to hide the fear in his voice. "Is she all right?"

I nod.

Sweat beads on his forehead and his knuckles whiten with strain. His eyes lock on mine. "I didn't hurt her?"

"We stopped you."

His cuffs rattle on the bed railings as he grips the chains. He falls back on his pillow. "I thought …" Barely audible, he trembles as he speaks. "I saw it so many times. I dreamed it. So many times. I thought … I had …" He swallows again, wincing at the effort. "But she's okay?" He looks directly at me. "She's okay, right?"

I nod. "She is."

He closes his eyes. Tears track down his cheeks, and I stand, staring as hope and despair war inside me.

There is a tap at the door. "That's time."

* * *

There's one more room to visit before running the gauntlet of well-wishers waiting by the nurse's station. I walk slowly to Leonard's room. Bandages wrap his neck and shoulder, cutting across his chest and beneath his arm, but he sits propped up on pillows, awake, talking, smiling at Barb. She rises to greet me, her eyes shimmering, her arms coming around me gently, her lips brushing my cheek. Leonard holds his hand out to me and I take it, feeling choked up with joy and guilt and regret.

"I'm glad you stopped in to see me."

"Of course."

"You're going to stop terrorising the doctors with your mystery blood?"

I snort. "Yes."

He runs his thumb over my knuckles. "Have you talked to Jamie?"

I screw my nose up. "He has avoidance issues."

Barb sighs. "He's slept in that horrible chair in your room every night you've been here."

"I know. I've heard him arguing with Miriam for dibs."

Leonard chuckles. "Gallagher men are notoriously unforgiving … especially of themselves."

"That's not true," I say. "You forgave me."

He squeezes my hand. "There's nothing to forgive. You protected our daughter. You saved your brother's life. I couldn't be prouder of you."

I bite hard inside my lip, not wanting to cry, glancing warily at Barb. She strokes my arm. "We love you, Evie, even though you've cost us a fortune in household repairs."

* * *

My *friends*, and it's weird but nice for me to think of them as mine and not just Kitty's, wait at the end of the corridor. Miriam comes towards me, looking worn out. She suffered a dislocated shoulder and hip, another split lip, cuts to her legs and a concussion. Her face is almost completely healed now. The dark shadows under her eyes are from sleepless nights shared between hospital rooms, watching over me and watching over her son – from his room's viewing window.

Neither Miriam nor I have touched on the big issue between us – her being my mom – keeping that and the matter of my twin brother, and all that means, a secret. For my part, I have no clue what I'm supposed to do about it or if there's anything to be done at all. I sure as hell don't want to talk about it. I know she won't push it. She'll wait for me, but that feels like pressure too.

She touches my arm. "How's Aiden?"

I keep my voice low. "He spoke."

Her eyes widen. "He did? How did he seem?"

"He wanted to know about Kitty." I can see by the narrowing of Jamie's eyes, over Miriam's shoulder, that he's heard me.

Her face creases in concern. "What do you mean?"

"He wanted to know she was okay." I hurried through the explanation. Now isn't the time. "He was relieved."

Hope overshadows her surprise and disbelief. "Okay." She smiles. It's all a bit weird, the pressure of so many things that need to be said. She pats my hand. "I'll come back to see him tonight."

Kitty reaches me first. The bruising on her cheekbone has turned a spectacular purple. She wraps herself around me and hugs me tight.

"Gently," Barb warns.

Kitty steps back, allowing room for Imogen, Lila and even a quietly concerned Kaylee to crowd in for a moment.

"Jeez, Evie," Lila says. "Who looks that good after a gunshot?"

"Van, of course." Gil Bishop smiles across the heads of his friends. Abe and Pete are there as well, grinning at me.

"Shall we go?" Miriam says.

"Where precisely?" Kitty asks.

I stop in my tracks. So does everyone else. I haven't given it a single thought. I no longer need to return to the Gallaghers'. Kitty's safe. I can go home.

"Come back to our place." Barb steps beside me. "Your aunt–" She swallows and those in the know look awkward for a moment. "Miriam won't mind sharing you a little longer."

Miriam nods. What can I say? I don't have it in me to argue, though the idea of smiling my way through dinner is exhausting. I let them lead me up the corridor.

Jamie walks stiffly behind his sister, quiet and introspective. He has come to see me every day but never by himself, always with Kitty. The nights he has spent propped in the vinyl recliner that sat in the corner of the hospital room, leaving before I stirred in the mornings. I hate to see him torturing himself.

The silver lining of this dark cloud is Kitty – to look at her and see her easy smile. There's lighthearted banter as talk swirls towards the Halloween Ball. Habit makes me want to walk beside her. Habit makes me close my eyes, briefly feeling for danger. There's nothing. No tension beyond my own emotional baggage. No alarming zapping in my spine. Nothing.

The oversized hospital elevators allow room for the crush of supporters and Barb hits the button for the basement. "Reporters out the front," she explains. "We can make a discreet exit."

I nod, feeling a little weak at the thought. Barb used her husband's clout to minimise the media fallout. There were no names mentioned, the assailant's identity suppressed and though it made national news, the details were ambiguous.

As the elevator takes us down to the lowest level, the others chat around me. It's bizarre being with schoolfriends. That whole world seems so distant. None of them appear to question the whitewashed version of events Kitty has fed them. The intruder attacked Kitty and shot Leonard and me before Jamie finally overpowered him. It's being described as a home invasion. No mention of the fact it took place out past the estate grounds. No mention of Aiden, though I doubt that can be kept quiet for long.

There has been a lot of debate about the audacity of the attack and whether it was connected to what happened to Kitty at the ball; debate about the intruder's goal. Looking for cash? Jewellery? Priceless artworks? Perhaps someone hoping to get into Leonard's business files? Some kind of personal vendetta?

The musical ding of the elevator's bell has us all turning to the doors. I use the opportunity to position myself next to Jamie. He glances down at me with his permanent frown. I take his hand, weaving my fingers through his. I need to get him alone though I don't like my chances in the crowd. He wants the buffer of our friends between us.

There's some indecision about who will go in which car. I stick by Jamie so that he won't be able to dispatch me with someone else. He resigns himself to the fact and opens the passenger door of his car for me. I wave at Pete, Abe and the others. They crowd into Gil's SUV, winking and grinning. They know Jamie blames himself, though they have no idea why, and I feel a rush of affection for them all for giving me a chance to talk to Jamie alone.

Jamie slides into his seat and starts the engine.

"Take me to the willow tree," I say.

He looks at me, meeting my eyes properly for the first time in days. His confused frown gives way. He knows where I mean.

I smile. "Time for you to right a wrong."

WILLOW

In the late afternoon light, the sky is hazy pink. Leaves fall in splashes of dying colour and the sun, a diffused golden ball, hangs low above the trees. The air is cold and sweet and the river sparkles in the shallows.

I leave my shoes and sling in the car and make my way gingerly to the water's edge, where the smooth round stones give out to freezing gravel. I relish the icy burn when the current pushes the flow up the bank and over my toes. Jamie makes his way higher up onto the boulders, whitewashed relics heaved from the mountain. Hands in his pockets, he navigates the rocks with little concern for the placement of his feet. "We'll be late."

"They won't care," I say. Miriam and Barb both like to feed people, the boys like to eat and Gil will love being the centre of attention with four girls to look after him. I point downstream to a press of willows, anticipation rising in me. "There it is."

I reach the tree first. Looking back over my shoulder, I wait for his hooded eyes to meet mine before I brush through the branches, a fragrant curtain with moving shades of gold, catching my clothes, tugging my hair. It's much darker inside the almost perfectly spherical underside of the tree, but the effect of the late afternoon sun is magical, gleaming behind the long willow fingers.

I remember the fallen branch that forms a makeshift seat. There's new graffiti now and the bark has worn smooth. I remember his warm lips and feeling that something momentous was happening to me. I remember the crowing boys, my burning shame and anger, and my heart swells, not at the memory of an old wound but the deep ache of present longing.

I listen for him, and swivel on the stones to face him, biting my cheek to keep from smiling. Jamie, furrowed brow, pursed lips, digs his hands in his back pockets, stretching his shirt against the broad plains of his chest and stomach, surly, stubborn. I hold my hands behind my back so he won't see the tremor in my fingers. How many days has it been since we last kissed?

You're an addict.

"Okay. Before you right your wrong, I have a speech."

His eyes narrow. "I thought we weren't going to make speeches."

It feels like stepping into empty space. "I'm sorry about

Aiden." It isn't quite right. "Or, I'm not," I say. "I'm not sorry he's not dead." This is complicated. "I mean, I'm sorry that Kitty got hurt. I'm sorry I didn't keep her safe." I spent my hospital nights torturing myself about Kitty's close call. "I'm not sorry that Aiden's alive." I sigh. "But I am sorry about what that means for you." I'm making a crap job of it so I stop.

Jamie stares at his shoes as though he wants to set them on fire. There's a long pause. "I don't begrudge your brother his life. I'm trying not to. But I don't understand. How did you do it?"

"Do what?"

"Not kill him." He looks up. "Was he too strong for you?"

I shake my head, waiting for his disapproval.

"You were about to finish him but you resisted your instinct?"

The conversation isn't going where I expect. "I guess."

"How is that even possible?"

"It was very hard." Like confessing a dirty secret. "I nearly couldn't … not. I wanted to kill him."

"Of course you did!" Jamie throws his hands up. "That's the way it works."

I'm confused now about what I should be feeling bad about – about wanting to kill Aiden or about not killing him? "I'm sorry?"

His mouth hangs loose. "Why are you apologising?"

"I have no idea."

A choked laugh bursts from Jamie's throat.

"Please don't be angry with me. I can't stand it."

Another choked laugh. "Angry?"

"You're not?"

His face softens, a thaw that makes me warm with hope. He rolls his eyes. "I am amazed. I am envious. I am confounded. I am not angry."

"Oh, all right." I want to kiss him, badly, but I know I have to play it cool. "Why envious?"

"You were able to make a choice."

I don't know what to say to this. I'm not sure I did have a choice. "Well. We're here." I make my voice velvet soft. "You may right your wrong."

His face immediately hardens and he lowers his head. "I can't."

My shoulders slump. "Don't be ridiculous, I'm standing right in front of you."

He runs his hand over his eyes and rakes his fingers through his hair. "I can't make it right. It's unforgivable."

"*Pfft.*" I shake my head. "That's a bit dramatic. Even I can accept you were a smug bastard, but breaking my fourteen-year-old heart is hardly guilt for the ages."

He glares, not impressed by my dodge. "I nearly killed you, Evangeline. You could have died. Do you have any idea–"

I flick my wrist. "*Pfft.*"

"Stop-making-that-noise."

"You weren't trying to kill me, Jamie. It was an accident." I fold my arms. "Now, I want my apology."

His brow buckles tight. "You are deliberately being obtuse."

"You are deliberately being an ass. Isn't the offended party the one who decides whether an act is forgivable or not? Being shot, accidentally, has not offended me." I wave my fingers at him. "I release you from your unnecessary burden."

He makes infuriated sounds and clenches his fists.

"You know," I begin quietly, determining not to be embarrassed, "that whole summer, all I thought about was what it would be like to kiss you."

He sighs and squints up into the roof of the tree. "You're changing the subject."

"No. It's the subject I came here to discuss. Every day I was at your house with Kitty, watching your TV or eating cookies in your kitchen or swimming in your pool ... I was imagining what it would be like to kiss you."

His lips twitch. "You always ignored me."

"You were mean."

"You never gave me the time of day unless I was hassling you. You had this whole aloof thing going on. It drove me mental."

"I was fourteen! Of course I had a huge crush on you."

"I didn't know that," he mutters. He shifts his weight, facing me again but keeping his eyes on the ground, his voice heavy and serious. "If it's any consolation, I spent a great deal of time thinking about you swimming in my pool."

Silent laughter shakes me and I can see him trying hard not to smile.

"It exceeded my expectations, that kiss. I don't mean the psychological trauma of being a joke to your friends. I mean the actual kiss, itself, the way your lips felt against mine, the softness, and the taste and some combination of limited oxygen and body proximity and location and, I suppose, the fact that I had never been kissed before."

He looks up, sharply. "Never?"

I shake my head.

"That was your first ever kiss and those bastards …"

I nod.

He widens his eyes. "That's awful."

"It was. I was very upset."

"I am extremely sorry."

I grin. "Thank you."

He lowers his head, his teeth flashing. "You don't know how many nights I spent re-orchestrating that whole thing in my head." He drops his voice and lifts his eyes. "Many nights."

It's hard to look at him, hard to comprehend the echo of my feelings painted so exactly in his face. Fascination, familiarity, the shade of longing and things I can't name. I force myself to hold his gaze, force myself to let him see the mirror of it all in my eyes. My courage grows with his slow smile. "Show me now. Give me back that kiss."

"Do you promise not to faint?"

I laugh. "No."

"Then I will just have to catch you." He looks around the glittering hollow, moves close and shifts me to the right. "Let's see. I think it was like this." Lit from the side, he seems almost luminescent, holding me with his grey eyes. I make the decision in that moment to push aside the clamour of my fears for the future, what Affinity will do when they find me, what will happen to Aiden, how things will be with Miriam, right and wrong, and Helena, all of it. I love Jamie and I only want to think about him right now. He smells so good and I breathe him in and like three years ago, the sense that something momentous is happening swells inside me.

He rests his hands on my waist and draws me against him, his lips opening mine, softly, carefully, a tender exchange. The memory reforms in my mind, I press it into the bandwidth, the taste of sun-warmed skin, the smell of sunscreen, the brush of hesitant hands, my fluttering pulse. He chuckles against me and the KMT fades, blending with the present, then it evolves into something new, urgent and ripe with meaning.

I slip my hand around his neck and dig my fingers up into his hair. My wounded shoulder keeps my right arm lingering at his waist, gripping the hem of his shirt. I begin to sway and he bends down, lifts me to his chest and carries me to the branch seat. It brings us nose to nose. He slides my hips forward. I wrap myself around him. Our kisses grow insistent. He cups the back of my head and fog rolls in. I cling to him, resisting my thrashing pulse, but lights pop behind my eyelids, the sea crashes in my ears, and a sigh lifts in the back of my throat.

"Evie," he murmurs against my lips, whispering as I go under, "I choose you."

ACKNOWLEDGEMENTS

Short of sounding like an R&B singer accepting a Grammy, I'd like to thank my Heavenly Papa for the dream that "sparked" this story, in answer to my prayer, and the grace that has sustained me.

Heartfelt thanks to Audra Given, my first reader and cheerleader, for voraciously wanting "more pages, please" and your tireless encouragement and love. Hayley George, my first "editor", beloved friend, thank you for living this journey with me. Your generosity of heart (in all things), your words of life and hope are a gift to me.

To the Walker Books family, my deepest gratitude. Sarah Foster, thank you for welcoming me to the fold. Nicola Robinson, thank you for cultivating the best in my work. You are wise and cunning as a fox, patient, kind, insightful, a true advocate and I am so glad you are my editor. Amy Daoud, thank you for creating a cover that makes my heart burst with pride. Jaclyn Prescott, thank you for being my tour guide, publicist and ally. Thank you to the marketing team, assistant editors and "Spark" enthusiasts who have been so kind to me at WB.

Chris and Barbara Else, my mentors and agents, thank you for championing my work. Barbara, you are a wonderful role model and inspiration. Chris, you are a generous teacher and guide, you always tell me the truth and expect the best of me. I have greatly benefitted from your wisdom, experience and listening ear.

To the many family members and friends who have endured me banging on about this book for years, Ann Ridden, Tracey George, Michelle Wilson, the gals from the Diamond Mine, Lifegroup and Write Club who have cared, prayed, encouraged and been so supportive, thank you.

Finally to my forbearing husband, Ian, and my beautiful girls, Sophie, Isabelle and Evangeline (yes, darling, Mummy stole your name), thank you. Your love and support makes this possible, makes this worthwhile.

ABOUT THE AUTHOR

RACHAEL CRAW studied Classical Studies and Drama at the University of Canterbury, but became an English teacher after graduation. Working with teenagers has given her a natural bent towards Young Adult fiction and a desire to present a feisty female protagonist in her writing. Rachael was born and raised in Christchurch, New Zealand, and currently lives in Nelson with her family. Visit her online at www.rachaelcraw.com

It all began with a **SPARK**

coming soon

BOOK TWO

STRAY

BOOK THREE

SHIELD